LAST
INSTRUCTIONS

ALSO BY NIR HEZRONI

THREE ENVELOPES

LAST INSTRUCTIONS

NIR HEZRONI

TRANSLATED FROM HEBREW BY STEVEN COHEN

THOMAS DUNNE BOOKS
ST. MARTIN'S PRESS
NEW YORK

To all the people who made this book happen
(yeah, you!). You move mountains and
make the world go round.

LAST INSTRUCTIONS. Copyright © 2018 by Nir Hezroni. Translation copyright © 2018 by Steven Cohen. All rights reserved. Printed in the United States of America. For information, address St. Martin's Press, 175 Fifth Avenue, New York, N.Y. 10010.

www.stmartins.com

Library of Congress Cataloging-in-Publication Data

Names: Hezroni, Nir, 1968– author. | Cohen, Steve, translator.
Title: Last instructions : a thriller / Nir Hezroni ; translated from Hebrew
   by Steve Cohen.
Description: First U.S. Edition. | New York : St. Martin's Press, 2018. |
   Sequel to: Three envelopes.
Identifiers: LCCN 2017060166 | ISBN 9781250097613 (hardcover) | ISBN
   9781250097620 (ebook)
Classification: LCC PJ5055.23.E98 L37 2018 | DDC 813/.6—dc23
LC record available at https://lccn.loc.gov/2017060166

Our books may be purchased in bulk for promotional, educational, or business use. Please contact your local bookseller or the Macmillan Corporate and Premium Sales Department at 1-800-221-7945, extension 5442, or by email at MacmillanSpecialMarkets@macmillan.com.

First published in 2018 in Israel by Keter Books

First U.S. Edition: May 2018

10 9 8 7 6 5 4 3 2 1

ACKNOWLEDGMENTS

I would like to thank Jad Abumrad, Robert Krulwich, and everyone at the RADIOLAB team for their show and podcast where I first learned about the Eye in the Sky.

December 12, 2006

"Why didn't he close his eyes?"

Dr. Weinberg removed fragments of glass from the eyeball of the attempted suicide victim using a pair of tweezers, placing each piece in a small aluminum basin. The blood that clung to the pieces of glass created circular patterns as it came in contact with the sterile substance in the metal bowl. This wasn't the first time that Dr. Weinberg had encountered a road accident in which the victim's glasses had shattered into his eyes, but usually the shards penetrated the eyelids first, which closed instinctively to protect the eyeball. This victim's eyes had remained wide open.

"I've never seen anything like it." The nurse standing beside him handed him an even smaller pair of tweezers. Several doctors were working simultaneously in the operating room on this nameless suicide attempt. He wasn't carrying any documents, and his face had been smashed beyond recognition. The plastic surgeon next to them was busy trying to piece together bits of his shattered cheekbones.

"How did he manage to do this to himself again?"

"Jumped in front of a bus on Ibn Gvirol Street. Lucky for him an ambulance was in the area. Otherwise he'd be downstairs on the slab by now."

"I'm not sure if you can call it luck. He may have been better off dead," said the orthopedic surgeon on the other side of the table. He was cleaning denim thread from two open fractures in the victim's thighs.

"We still have a good few more hours of work on him. We need to bring in a psychologist for when he wakes up. Make a note of that. I don't want him jumping again the moment he wakes up."

"The last thing he's going to be able to do when he wakes up is jump."

"If he wakes up."

Dr. Weinberg made a note in the records and then went back to

1

removing fragments of glass. "We'll keep him under for at least two weeks; there's no point in waking him yet." He started humming the words to the song "Ten Little Fingers" from his young son's favorite CD.

"Are you familiar with the definition of anxiety?" he asked the nurse beside him.

December 5, 2016

An incessant drizzle had been falling on London since early in the morning. The city's residents went about their business. It was a Monday and Oxford Street was packed with umbrella-carrying pedestrians. One of them held a white plastic box with a black handle, crossed the busy road coming from the Marble Arch tube station and turned toward the entrance to Hyde Park. She wore a yellow hoodie and black sneakers, walked at a brisk pace, and glanced occasionally to the side. The park was quiet. Squirrels scampered among the trees, and a small group of giggling girls strolled leisurely along an adjacent walkway. She stopped beside one of the trees and placed the box on the ground and looked around. The park was quiet and peaceful. The weather had left most of the tourists on the streets of London to themselves, with the option of fleeing from one store to the next rather than getting soaked in the city's parks. She lifted the lid off the box and tipped the container over. Dozens of white mice poured out onto the ground.

They froze momentarily in a white pile on the green grass, before scurrying off in all directions, some even hopping with delight. They were free.

Carmit closed the box and walked over to a green garbage can. She placed the box on the ground and left it there.

She then continued walking, breathing in the scent of freshly cut grass. Two people on horseback trotted past and she waved to them. If not for the dreams that plagued her nights, she was almost happy with her husband, Guy, and their children. She'd thought the dreams would disappear once she stopped doing transformations, but they hadn't.

She'd even tried exhausting herself by going for a run every night before bed.

They continued.

Carmit made her way back to the Underground station. She decided to take the Central line to Notting Hill Gate and then switch to the Circle line to Gloucester Road. The Piccadilly line would take her from there to Hammersmith. She'd arranged to meet Elliot at the Starbucks there. Besides her clients, he's the only other person who's aware of her work outside the bookstore. Actually, the bookstore is her only job now. She'd thought that dismantling the laboratory in the back of her store and releasing the mice in Hyde Park, would make her free, just like the mice; but she only felt emptiness. She'd speak to Elliot about her recurring dream.

Maybe he could help.

A hawk hovered above the trees in the park, following the movement of the mice in the grass below.

```
DATE:              12/05/2016 [08:31]
CLASSIFICATION:    BLACK
REFERENCE NO.:     623846635
TO:                INNER CIRCLE
FROM:              OPERATIONS DEPARTMENT HEAD
DISTRIBUTION:      RECRUITMENT DEPARTMENT HEAD
                   PERSONALITY AND PSYCHOPATHOLOGY RESEARCH
                   DEPARTMENT HEAD
SYSTEM:            ORION / BASE: OTR / EXPIRY DATE: 12/13/2016


RE.: REAPPEARANCE OF AGENT 10483
/
I WISH TO SUM UP THE EVENTS OF THE PAST 24 HOURS DURING
WHICH WE HAVE LEARNED THAT AGENT 10483, BELIEVED DEAD,
APPEARS IN FACT TO BE ALIVE AND OPERATING AGAINST US ON
ISRAELI SOIL.
```

BACKGROUND:

IN 2006, IN LIGHT OF INFORMATION RECEIVED FROM MILITARY INTELLIGENCE'S UNIT 8200, WE LEARNED OF EFFORTS BY AN UNKNOWN PARTY, POSSIBLY IRAN, TO GET ITS HANDS ON A RUSSIAN NUCLEAR DEVICE FROM AMONG THE ARSENAL OF 1,400 NUCLEAR WARHEADS RETURNED TO RUSSIA BY KAZAKHSTAN DURING THE LATTER'S VOLUNTARY NUCLEAR DISARMAMENT PROGRAM FROM 1991–1995. (IN ALL LIKELIHOOD, THE DEVICE IN QUESTION IS A 42–KILOTON RDS–3 MODEL, A 62–KILOTON RDS–3I MODEL, OR A MORE MODERN WARHEAD FROM THE EARLY 1960S)

WE KNOW THAT THE INDIVIDUAL WHO SERVED AS THE GO–BETWEEN FOR THE TRANSACTION WAS ONE OF 12 SCIENTISTS WHO PARTICIPATED IN A CLOSED CONFERENCE IN SWITZERLAND DURING WHICH THE DEAL WAS FINALIZED BY MEANS OF AN ENCRYPTED TELEPHONE MESSAGE. SINCE WE WERE UNAWARE OF THE IDENTITY OF THE DEALMAKER FROM AMONG THE GROUP, WE DECIDED TO ELIMINATE ALL 12 OF THEM (PROJECT CODENAMED "BERNOULLI"). ONE OF THE AGENTS (10483) ASSIGNED TO THE MISSION RECEIVED (APPARENTLY ERRONEOUSLY) 3 TARGETS OUT OF THE 12, INSTEAD OF JUST 1. THE COLLATERAL DAMAGE HE CAUSED IN CARRYING OUT THE 3 ASSASSINATIONS WAS EXTENSIVE:

1. 40 INCIDENTAL FATALITIES IN THE FRAMEWORK OF THE ASSASSINATION OF YASMIN LI–ANG IN GENEVA (YASMIN LI–ANG'S 2 DAUGHTERS, PLUS 38 RESIDENTS OF A BUILDING AT 21 RUE DE DELICES THAT COLLAPSED AFTER 10483 SEALED ONE OF THE APARTMENTS ON THE TOP FLOOR AND FILLED IT WITH WATER, THE RESULTING PRESSURE BROUGHT DOWN THE ENTIRE STRUCTURE)

2. 128 INCIDENTAL FATALITIES IN BARILOCHE IN THE
FRAMEWORK OF THE ASSASSINATION OF FEDERICO LOPEZ IN A
PARK NEAR THE INSTITUTO BALSEIRO (FEDERICO LOPEZ'S 3
BODYGUARDS, PLUS 125 INNOCENT BYSTANDERS IN THE PARK,
WHICH 10483 SET ABLAZE USING A GAS TANKER THAT HE
HOOKED UP TO THE PARK'S SPRINKLER SYSTEM)

3. [NEW INFORMATION] SOME 11,000 INCIDENTAL FATALITIES
IN MONTREAL IN THE FRAMEWORK OF THE ASSASSINATION OF
BERNARD STRAUSS (APPROXIMATELY 11,000 PEOPLE—INCLUDING
53 ISRAELI CITIZENS, 3 OF WHOM WERE OUR AGENTS—DIED IN
A STRING OF ROAD ACCIDENTS CAUSED BY THOUSANDS OF
DRIVERS SIMULTANEOUSLY FALLING ASLEEP AT THE WHEEL OF
THEIR VEHICLES AFTER HEARING A HYPNOSIS-INDUCING AUDIO
TRACK BROADCAST OVER A LOCAL RADIO STATION, CBC RADIO
ONE)

FOLLOWING THE ASSASSINATION OF BERNARD STRAUSS IN
MONTREAL, 10483 RETURNED TO ISRAEL. MEMBERS OF A
SURVEILLANCE TEAM ASSIGNED TO HIM FROM THE MOMENT HE
LANDED SUBSEQUENTLY FOUND WHAT THEY THOUGHT TO BE HIS BODY
IN HIS COMPLETELY TORCHED APARTMENT. DENTAL RECORDS SERVED
TO IDENTIFY THE BODY AT THE TIME AND A SUICIDE NOTE WAS
FOUND IN THE REFRIGERATOR.
IN LIGHT OF THE ABOVE, THE CASE WAS CLOSED. THE 12 BERNOULLI
SCIENTISTS WERE ELIMINATED, 10483 PRESUMED DEAD, AND THE
IRANIAN CELLS THAT WERE TRYING TO FIND THE WARHEAD LOST
TRACK OF ITS LOCATION.

NEW INFORMATION:
TWO DAYS AGO (12/03/2016), AMIRAM HADDAD, 10483'S FORMER
HANDLER, RECEIVED A PACKAGE THAT 10483 HAD DEPOSITED WITH

A LAW FIRM WITH INSTRUCTIONS FOR IT TO BE SENT OUT ON THAT SPECIFIC DATE. AFTER READING THE NOTEBOOK HE RECEIVED, AMIRAM WENT TO THE HOME OF AVNER MOYAL, THE HEAD OF THE RECRUITMENT DEPARTMENT, TO DISCUSS THE IMPLICATIONS OF THE MATERIAL IT CONTAINED. THE PACKAGE INCLUDED A LARGE LINED NOTEBOOK ALONG WITH NUMEROUS ADDITIONAL DOCUMENTS—SKETCHES, CALCULATIONS, MATERIAL FROM THE ORGANIZATION, AND MORE. FROM A REVIEW OF THE CONTENTS OF THE NOTEBOOK, THE MAIN FINDINGS ARE AS FOLLOWS:

1. 10483 IS ALIVE. HE STAGED HIS OWN DEATH 10 YEARS AGO USING A BODY HE'D BEEN KEEPING IN HIS BASEMENT ON WHICH HE'D CARRIED OUT THE APPROPRIATE DENTAL WORK TO MATCH HIS OWN (FILLINGS, EXTRACTIONS, ETC.). WHEN HE TORCHED THE APARTMENT, HE KNEW THAT WE WOULD IDENTIFY THE REMAINS BASED ON DENTAL RECORDS BECAUSE HIS DNA IS NOT IN THE SYSTEM (HE MUST HAVE DELETED THIS DATA FROM THE ORGANIZATION'S SYSTEM AT SOME POINT).

2. 10483 IS PERSONALLY RESPONSIBLE FOR KILLING 3 OF OUR AGENTS WHO WERE SENT TO LOCATE HIM DURING THE COURSE OF HIS MISSIONS. ONE IN THE NETHERLANDS (AGENT 6844—PUSHED ONTO THE TRACKS IN FRONT OF A METRO TRAIN) AND 2 IN TEL AVIV (AGENTS 6452 AND 7274) IN THE BASEMENT OF HIS APARTMENT.

3. THE HYPNOSIS INCIDENT IN MONTREAL—BELIEVED UNTIL NOW TO BE A NONNATIONALISTIC ATTACK CARRIED OUT BY A PSYCHOPATH—WAS ORGANIZED BY 10483. THE NOTEBOOK CONTAINS MATERIAL THAT INCRIMINATES BOTH HIM AND US.

4. 10483 ACQUIRED ADMINISTRATOR ACCESS TO ORION. HE KNOWS ABOUT THE BERNOULLI PROJECT AND HIS ROLE IN THE

ASSASSINATIONS. HE SUFFERS FROM PARANOIA AND BELIEVES
THAT THE ORGANIZATION BETRAYED HIM. HE ALSO MANAGED
TO GET ACCEPTED TO THE ORGANIZATION DESPITE THE
VARIOUS PSYCHOLOGICAL DISORDERS HE SUFFERS FROM BY
HACKING INTO OUR SYSTEMS.
5. 10483 HAS EMBARKED ON A REVENGE MISSION AGAINST THE
ORGANIZATION THAT BEGAN 2 NIGHTS AGO.

EVENTS OF THE PAST 24 HOURS:
AVNER SPENT THE NIGHT READING THROUGH THE NOTEBOOK, THEN
BROUGHT GRANDPA UP TO SPEED. GRANDPA CALLED IN ROTEM
ROLNIK, HEAD OF THE PERSONALITY AND PSYCHOPATHOLOGY
RESEARCH DEPARTMENT, WHO ALSO REVIEWED THE MATERIAL.
AT 09:00 THIS MORNING, A TEAM OF OUR AGENTS—ACCOMPANIED BY
POLICE, FIREFIGHTERS, AND A SWAT TEAM—WAS SENT TO THE
BASEMENT TO FIND OUT WHAT WAS THERE AND TO RETRIEVE THE
REMAINS OF THE 2 AGENTS THAT HAD BEEN THERE FOR 10 YEARS.
BECAUSE 10483'S NOTEBOOK DESCRIBES HOW THE BASEMENT WAS
BOOBY-TRAPPED, ALL THE BUILDING'S
RESIDENTS WERE EVACUATED, AND THE STREET WAS CLOSED TO
TRAFFIC.
FOLLOWING A BRIEFING THAT INCLUDED WARNINGS NOT TO TOUCH
ANY LIGHT SWITCHES, THE TEAMS ENTERED THE LOCATION. AT
09:40 THE BASEMENT AND THE BUILDING ABOVE IT WAS BLOWN UP.
EVERYONE IN THE BASEMENT—THE SECURITY AND RESCUE TEAMS AND
OUR AGENTS—WAS KILLED IN THE BLAST, AND THE BUILDING
COLLAPSED. THE AREA HAS BEEN CORDONED OFF AND TEAMS FROM
THE ORGANIZATION, THE FIRE DEPARTMENT, POLICE, AND THE HOME
FRONT COMMAND, ARE CURRENTLY SIFTING THROUGH THE RUBBLE IN
AN EFFORT TO RETRIEVE THE BODIES AND ANY OTHER MATERIAL
THAT 10483 MAY HAVE LEFT IN THE BASEMENT THAT COULD ASSIST
IN HIS CAPTURE.

AT 10:05 THIS MORNING A MESSENGER DELIVERED A PACKAGE TO
EFRAT MOYAL, AVNER'S WIFE. HER DESCRIPTION OF THE MESSENGER
HAS LED US TO SUSPECT THAT IT MAY HAVE BEEN 10483 HIMSELF.
SHE WAS INSTRUCTED NOT TO OPEN THE PACKAGE AND TO GO
IMMEDIATELY TO THEIR NEIGHBORS' HOUSE. AVNER RETURNED HOME
AT 10:39. RESTING ON THE KITCHEN TABLE WAS A PAGE THAT HAD
BEEN TORN OUT OF 10483'S NOTEBOOK. ON THE PAGE, 10483
OUTLINES HOW HE "DEALT WITH" THE TEETH OF THE BODY LEFT IN
HIS TORCHED APARTMENT SOME 10 YEARS AGO; HE ALSO DESCRIBES
HOW HE SPOTTED THE SURVEILLANCE TEAM OUTSIDE THE APARTMENT
AND ASSUMED (MISTAKENLY) THEY WERE A CELL SENT BY THE
ORGANIZATION TO ASSASSINATE HIM, HOW HE SET FIRE TO
THE APARTMENT, AND HOW HE THEN WENT TO THE ORGANIZATION'S
NEAREST BRANCH WHERE HE RETRIEVED INFORMATION ABOUT
THE BERNOULLI PROJECT AND THE MEMBERS OF THE INNER
CIRCLE.
THE PAGE ALSO NOTES THAT HE PLANS TO TAKE ACTION AGAINST
EVERYONE INVOLVED IN HIS RECRUITMENT AND HANDLING, AND
AGAINST THE ORGANIZATION'S MANAGEMENT—THE INNER CIRCLE.
PRESUMABLY, THE BLOWING UP OF HIS BASEMENT AND EFRAT'S
DISAPPEARANCE WERE THE INITIAL STAGES OF HIS PLAN. ATTEMPTS
IN THE PAST FEW HOURS TO CONTACT AMIRAM HAVE COME TO
NAUGHT. IT SEEMS LIKE 10483 HAS GOTTEN HIS HANDS ON
HIM, TOO.
WE CLEARLY MADE A MAJOR MISTAKE AND RECRUITED A PSYCHOPATH
WHO SUFFERS FROM AN ENTIRE RANGE OF MENTAL DISORDERS. HE
MANAGED TO PREPARE HIMSELF VERY WELL FOR ALL OUR TESTS
(INCLUDING A POLYGRAPH) AND WAS ACCEPTED INTO THE
ORGANIZATION. THEREFORE, IN ADDITION TO THE IMMEDIATE
ACTIONS WE NEED TO TAKE IN ORDER TO APPREHEND 10483 AND
LOCATE EFRAT AND AMIRAM, THERE ARE ALSO THINGS WE NEED TO
PUT IN PLACE TO SERVE US IN THE LONG TERM:

- A REVIEW AND ADJUSTMENT OF OUR RECRUITMENT SYSTEM IN ORDER TO PREVENT THE HIRING OF INELIGIBLE CANDIDATES IN THE FUTURE (LESS DEPENDENCE ON FORMAL TESTS AND MORE WEIGHT ON PERSONAL INTERVIEWS, GROUP BEHAVIOR UNDER PRESSURE, AND INTERVIEWS WITH FRIENDS, FAMILY MEMBERS, TEACHERS, AND NEIGHBORS.)
- CLOSER COLLABORATION WITH THE ARMY WHEN IT COMES TO ITS SCREENING PROCESS FOR CANDIDATES FOR SENSITIVE POSITIONS.
- MAINTAINING CONTACT WITH THE DISTRICT HEALTH OFFICES IN ORDER TO GAIN ACCESS TO INFORMATION ON PSYCHOLOGICAL PROFILES / PSYCHIATRIC TREATMENTS CONCERNING FUTURE RECRUITS, ALONG WITH A REVIEW OF OUR ENTIRE NETWORK OF EXISTING AGENTS+RETIREES. (DOCTOR–PATIENT CONFIDENTIALITY DOES NOT APPLY IN THIS REGARD.)
- THE MECHANISMS IN PLACE TO RESTRICT ACCESS TO THE ORGANIZATION'S SYSTEMS ARE SORELY LACKING—WE NEED TO IMPLEMENT INTERNAL ENCRYPTION MECHANISMS AND AUDIT SYSTEMS THAT CAN IDENTIFY SYSTEM ADMINISTRATOR ACCESS. IMPLEMENTATION MUST BE CARRIED OUT EXTERNALLY BY A DATA SECURITY GROUP, WITHOUT THE INVOLVEMENT OF OUR INFORMATION SYSTEMS UNIT.

IN CONSULTATION WITH ROTEM AND AVNER, WE MUST PUT TOGETHER A TEAM CHARGED WITH APPREHENDING 10483. I REQUEST YOUR AUTHORIZATION TO APPROACH THE SHIN BET FOR ASSISTANCE TO THIS END.
SINCERELY,
MOTTI KEIDAR
OPERATIONS DIVISION CHIEF
/

Avner reviewed the document circulated via the Orion system. It looked a lot better than the version he'd written during the night.

After spending part of the morning looking for Efrat, Rotem asked him to return to the Ganei Yehuda Base, where she'd spent the night. Unaware of the device that had been attached to the underside of his car during the night, he drove back to Ganei Yehuda and contacted his connection at the police on the way, asking him to arrange for a forensics team to examine his home in an effort to find something that 10483 may have left behind and could assist in his capture. The man asked Avner if he wanted to blow up another one of his teams because the last one he'd requested was still buried under a building that had been blown to bits. Avner asked him what he would do if a psychopathic killer had abducted his wife.

Even though Avner knew his body needed sleep, his state of mind wouldn't allow it. His head was filled with thoughts of Efrat in the clutches of that psychopath. Where could he have taken her? What had he done to her? He couldn't bear the thought of Efrat in his clutches. The shock she must have felt when he abducted her.

He assumed Grandpa would try to take him off the case. But he wasn't going to let that happen. He had to be there when they close in on him. He had to make sure that they go in carefully so as not to harm her.

Avner listened to the sounds at the satellite base—Rotem speaking to the guard, the rattle of an air-conditioner compressor, soft and muffled music coming from the house upstairs that served as a cover for the activities taking place below, someone flushing a toilet. His weariness was fading. He would find her and rescue her even if it's the last thing he does.

DATE: 12/05/2016 [09:14]
CLASSIFICATION: BLACK
REFERENCE NO.:   623846649
TO: SENIOR DIRECTOR — 9
FROM: PERSONALITY AND PSYCHOPATHOLOGY
                     RESEARCH DEPARTMENT HEAD
DISTRIBUTION:
SYSTEM: ORION / BASE: OTR / EXPIRY DATE: 12/06/2016

RE.: REAPPEARANCE OF AGENT 10483

/

HI GRANDPA!

FURTHER TO MOTTI KEIDAR'S REPORT FROM EARLIER TODAY: THERE
IS NO WAY THAT AGENT 10483 WAS ABLE TO PASS THE ORGAN-
IZATION'S TESTS. IT'S SIMPLY IMPOSSIBLE. REGARDLESS OF HOW
WELL HE MAY HAVE PREPARED HIMSELF, AFTER READING THE
NOTEBOOK, I AM ABSOLUTELY CERTAIN THAT SUCH AN INDIVIDUAL
WOULD NEVER HAVE MADE IT THROUGH A COMBINATION OF
MINNESOTA, MYERS-BRIGGS, DSM-5, AND VARIOUS OTHER SUCH
DELICACIES, AND THEN A POLYGRAPH FOR DESSERT.
SOMEONE WANTED HIM IN THE ORGANIZATION.
THAT SAME SOMEONE WAS ALSO THE ONE WHO MADE SURE HE WAS
GIVEN 3 TARGETS AS PART OF THE BERNOULLI PROJECT, AND NOT
JUST ONE LIKE THE OTHER ASSASSINS.
HIS 3 TARGETS WERE ALL NUCLEAR SCIENTISTS. THAT, TOO, IS NO
COINCIDENCE.
WE NEED TO TALK.

Rotem sent the mail to Grandpa, locked the computer screen, and
went to find the satellite base's security guard, who was reading a
thick book.

"Is there a shower here? I stink like a skunk," she said.

"No, we're all about the bare necessities here," the guard responded. "And the aboveground areas of the building are off limits."

"Okay then, I'm off to the home base. When you see Avner, send him there, too. I'll shower there and take a nap in my office. Tell him to wake me when he arrives. I need to get hold of Grandpa in the morning."

```
DATE:              12/06/2016 [11:30]
CLASSIFICATION:    BLACK
REFERENCE NO.:     623846762
TO:                INNER CIRCLE
FROM:              SENIOR DIRECTOR — 9
DISTRIBUTION:
SYSTEM:            ORION / BASE: OTR / EXPIRY DATE: 12/07/2016


RE.: REAPPEARANCE OF AGENT 10483
/
GOOD MORNING,
FURTHER TO OUR MEETING YESTERDAY, AND IN THE WAKE OF
EFFORTS BY THE HEAD OF THE PERSONALITY AND PSYCHOPATHOLOGY
RESEARCH DEPARTMENT TO GET TO THE BOTTOM OF OUR REASONS
FOR USING 10483, I INTEND TO FILL HER IN TO A CERTAIN
EXTENT IN ORDER TO ALLOW HER TO BEGIN SEARCHING FOR HIM.
FURTHERMORE, AN ADDITIONAL TEAM FROM THE OPERATIONS
DIVISION HAS ALSO BEEN ASSIGNED TO HUNT FOR 10483. ITS
MEMBERS ARE WORKING WITH THE SEARCH AND RESCUE PERSONNEL
AT THE SCENE OF THE EXPLOSION IN TEL AVIV, THEY'RE LOOKING
FOR CLUES FROM THE VIDEO FOOTAGE CAPTURED BY THE TEAM THAT
WAS IN THE BASEMENT AT THE TIME OF THE BLAST. THE CAMERAS
WERE DESTROYED BUT A DATA FORENSICS TEAM IS TRYING TO
RECONSTRUCT THE MATERIAL FROM THE MEMORY CARDS.
```

APPREHENDING 10483 IS A MATTER OF THE UTMOST URGENCY. WE
NEED TO ASSUME THE WORST—THAT HE IS IN POSSESSION OF THE
NUCLEAR DEVICE THAT DISAPPEARED DURING THE COURSE OF HIS
ACTIVITIES SOME 10 YEARS AGO, AND THAT HE INTENDS TO USE
IT. ALL NECESSARY RESOURCES FOR THE PURPOSE OF LOCATING AND
CAPTURING HIM WILL BE AT OUR DISPOSAL. IN DEALINGS WITH
OUTSIDE ENTITIES (THE SHIN BET, IDF, PRIME MINISTER'S
OFFICE), OUR COVER STORY IS THAT THERE'S A TERRORIST /
ISLAMIC STATE CELL. PLEASE INFORM YOUR RESPECTIVE TEAMS.
I BELIEVE THAT THE HEAD OF THE PERSONALITY AND
PSYCHOPATHOLOGY RESEARCH DEPARTMENT CAN OFFER ADDITIONAL
INSIGHTS THAT MAY HELP US TO LOCATE 10483. I PLAN TO TELL
HER IN GENERAL TERMS ABOUT THE TRANSFORMATIONS AND THE
TRANSFORMATION CONTENT (THE FINAL ONE ONLY) THAT 10483
UNDERWENT, INCLUDING THE IMPRINTED EXPIRY DATE, SO AS TO
GIVE HER A LEAD TO WORK ON. I ALSO INTEND TO SHARE THIS
INFORMATION WITH THE HEAD OF THE TEAM THAT IS CURRENTLY AT
THE BLAST SITE.
I WILL ALSO INFORM THE AFOREMENTIONED ABOUT THE SECONDARY
OBJECTIVE (ONLY) OF THE BERNOULLI PROJECT—THE ELIMINATION OF
THE SCIENTISTS. THE PRIMARY OBJECTIVE OF THE BERNOULLI
PROJECT WILL OF COURSE REMAIN CONFIDENTIAL.
YOU SHOULD BE AWARE, TOO, THAT THE SUBCONTRACTOR WHO
CARRIED OUT THE TRANSFORMATIONS ON 10483 DURING THE COURSE
OF HIS BERNOULLI PROJECT ACTIVITIES HAS SEVERED TIES WITH
US AND WE HAVE NO WAY OF LOCATING HER.
I WILL ARRANGE A FOLLOW-UP DISCUSSION ON THE SUBJECT IN
KEEPING WITH THE DEVELOPMENTS IN THE INVESTIGATION.
REGARDS,
GRANDPA
\

The parched orange earth appears to stretch on forever in every direction. Cracks cut through the ground and a fine orange dust rises up with my every step. Fossilized crustaceans are scattered about, red and pinkish hollowed-out crab legs and black and empty sea urchin shells with long spines.

I tread carefully to avoid them.

I don't know which way I'm supposed to go, so I head in the direction of the sun that's casting a bright orange light over everything. A smaller white sun is rising on my right and my shadow is split into 2—1 behind me and 1 to my left. Once every 16 days the 2 suns are aligned and then I have just a single shadow for a few minutes.

I retrieve a somewhat battered metal water flask from my backpack, unscrew the top and take a sip of warm water that tastes like sand. I screw the top back on, return the flask to my backpack, and continue walking.

In the distance, I see a black dot. I walk toward it. My steps kick up orange clouds of dust. That's where I need to go.

As I move closer, I can see that the black dot is a large black rock, like the dome of a mosque buried in the ground with only the very top protruding from the earth. The portion of the rock protruding from the earth looks about 3 meters in diameter and it's dotted with small holes the size of a coin on all sides. Scattered around the rock are the remains of those who got here before me. I refrain from stepping into the kill radius and slowly circle what's left of those who were here before me at a safe distance. Some of them are nothing more than whitened skeletons, while some are still partially covered with bits of clothing, their dried-out skin still stretched over their bones. It's extremely dry. It never rains here. They've probably been here for a very long time. I sense something I haven't felt in years.

Fear.

I wake at 3 in the morning and do a few sets of stomach crunches and push-ups.

6 weeks and 3 days are 45 days since I opened my eyes in the Lowenstein rehabilitation hospital and my body is recovering fast from the 9 years coma. 45 is the sum of all the decimal digits. 0 to 9.

I drink some water from the tap in the basement, get dressed, and wait.

The family above me wakes up and leaves the house. I ascend from the basement into the apartment through the opening in the floor of the closet in the master bedroom that was once my bedroom and wander through the rooms. The 2nd bedroom contains 2 children's beds. Lying on 1 is a stuffed purple dinosaur. I climb through the window into the backyard and shut it behind me. I have several errands to get through today.

1st I throw away the garbage bag I brought up with me from the basement, then I take a cab to the Seven Stars Mall in Herzliya and purchase an HP laptop at the computer store. It's nice to see how far technology has come over the past 9 years. The laptop is superfast and has an SSD drive that allows for close to 9 hours of work time without having to recharge the battery. I also discover that Internet connections are wireless now and available pretty much everywhere. I walk around the mall to give my legs a bit of a workout and then I sit down at a table at Café Greg and order a large green salad and a big bottle of mineral water. I turn on the laptop and attempt to log into my bank account. I enter my password and receive a message that says the account has been locked and that I need to call the bank to reactivate it. I call the bank's customer service line. A call service operator by the name of Yoel picks up. He tells me the account was locked 8 years ago following 12 months of inactivity. I explain to Yoel that I'd been living in an ashram in India for an extended period of time and am now back in Israel again. He asks me for the 1st letter of my maternal grandfather's name and the 4th letter in the name of the elementary school I attended and also my ID number. He lifts the restrictions and grants me online access to my account. "We've emailed you a temporary password," Yoel says. "You'll be prompted to change it when you log into the account for the first time."

I thank Yoel and log in with the temporary password. I replace it with a new 1 and access the account I opened under an assumed identity while still working for the Organization. I open a 2nd tab. I log into my Gmail account and open an old mail with the subject line, "Investments."

The email reads:

> Aug. 2006:
> Canadian Dollars   102,000 * 0.91 = 92,820 USD
> Swiss Francs   30,000 * 1.09 = 32,700 USD
> Argentine Pesos   130,000 * 0.12 = 15,600 USD
> Total = 141,120 USD

$141,120 / $9.6 = 14,700$ Apple shares

I return to the bank account page and access my investment portfolio. The current Apple share price as quoted this past Friday stands at $101.42.

$14,700 * \$101.42 = \$1,490,874$

The 14,700 shares I purchased almost 9 years ago are now worth $1,490,874. I have enough money to carry out my plan. That's good.

I continue browsing the Internet.

I buy and download Russian and Spanish language tutorials.

I check where I can get an international driver's license. There's a branch of the Automobile Association on Raoul Wallenberg Street in Ramat HaHayal.

I pour myself another glass of cold mineral water and drink it slowly. After years of enteral feeding, my throat has yet to grow accustomed again to the passage of food.

The salad is very good. I eat all of it and turn to the right to look at some children playing on an inflatable castle. Their parents are sitting across the way and drinking coffee.

I buy a mobile phone. I learn that the leap in cell phone technology far outstrips the advances made in the field of laptops. The phone, for all intents and purposes, is a minicomputer, with Internet access and a high-resolution screen. It's an Apple device, too. When I lost consciousness 9 years, 1 month, and 13 days ago, cell phones were only good for voice conversations and text messages.

I buy a prepaid SIM card from Cellcom. The representative at the cellular service provider's booth in the mall shows me how to insert it into the phone. He also shows me how to use the phone for browsing the Net via my laptop. That's very good.

I go into the large supermarket at the mall and buy fresh vegetables, some beef, and chicken liver and place all items in my backpack. Nutrition is important.

At an electrical appliances store I buy a small hot plate, a frying pan, and smart-power kit with which allows you to turn on an electric device remotely via the Internet. That's very useful.

I buy a bicycle. You don't need to show your ID or complete any paperwork to buy 1 and it will allow me to work on my fitness while riding from place to place. Besides, it's almost impossible to find parking in Tel Aviv. It was terrible before I jumped in front of the bus and it's even worse now. They've started digging up the city for the Light Rail and entire roads look like open trenches. They say it will take 6 years for the train line and stations to be ready. When they started work on the Jerusalem Light Rail, they said it would take 3 years—it took them 10 instead.

I buy a 2nd mobile phone at a different store, together with an Internet package and webcam that I'll install later in the basement.

I open the laptop and search for an airline ticket to La Paz in Bolivia. There's no direct flight. I'll have to fly to Madrid, then to

Lima, Peru, and to La Paz from there. I buy the ticket at a travel agency and pay in cash that I took from my basement.

I pay for everything in cash so as not to leave a credit card trail.

I leave the mall and ride my bike to the Aharoni-Shamir law firm's offices. I watch a tricolor cat—black, white, and ginger—walk past the entrance to the building. Sitting in the lobby on the ground floor is a security guard whose job it is to screen the people entering the building. I chain the bicycle to a lamppost nearby and go inside.

"Hi," says the guard. "How may I help you?"

"Where will I find the offices of Aharoni-Shamir?"

"Third floor. Who do you need?"

"No one in particular. I just wanted to make sure they're still here in this building."

"Yes, they're here."

I leave the building. The Aharoni-Shamir law firm is still here and the notebook I gave them 9 years, 1 month, and 21 days ago will be released and will make its way to Amiram in 10 months and 10 days. I could break in during the night and remove the notebook but I choose to leave things as they are. I'd rather stick to the plan's original timetable. 10 years would have been an adequate time for planning how to bring down the Organization. Since I spent most of this time unconscious in bed I need to revise the plan to fit into the 10 months and 10 days I got left. The execution date must remain the same.

I get on the bike and begin riding toward my apartment. Soon I'll have to part ways with the basement. On December 4, it will serve as the opening shot in my retribution against the Organization. Well, not actually an opening shot. But more like an opening salvo. A shot is the conversion of the chemical energy of gunpowder into the kinetic energy of a small piece of metal. That doesn't describe what's going to happen in the basement when it's filled with Organization officials looking for clues concerning my whereabouts. Amateurs. The body I removed from the aquarium in the basement and placed on my bed, complete with the thorough dental work I performed on it, kept them away from me for the 9 years in which I, too, was unaware of my existence. The empty aquarium with the layer of cooking oil that remained at the bottom is crying out for a new creation—but I remain focused on the task at hand.

My phone vibrates and I read the text message that informs me that the RAM R-200 device I ordered has arrived and is waiting for me at the post office. I'll collect it on my way home. The device is a sensitive Geiger counter that can detect a wide range of gamma radiation. It runs on a standard 9-volt battery that provides 100 hours of operation and can be easily replaced in Bolivia.

It takes me 20 minutes to ride back to my apartment. I secure the bike to the fence behind the building using 2 strong iron chains and then I dismantle the seat and take it with me.

The parents must be out at work but the children are in the apartment. I can hear them watching TV as I slip down to the basement through the closet in the master bedroom.

I had a few sets of passport photos taken while at the mall. Back in the basement, I replace the photographs in my passports and deal with the official seals using basic forgery equipment. I plug the hot plate into 1 of the electrical sockets and make myself a late lunch. I'll devote some time afterward to my physical conditioning and then do some online research. I plugged the mobile phone into its charger and left it at the top of the ladder leading up into the apartment. It has reception and will allow me to browse the Net with my laptop while I'm in the basement.

I'm sitting in economy class on Iberia Airlines flight IB6651 from Madrid to Lima. Earlier I flew from Tel Aviv to Madrid, and later I will fly from Lima to La Paz, Bolivia. A baby is crying in the row of seats in front of me. He's been crying since takeoff, 46 minutes ago. The number 46 can be divided by 1, by itself, by 2, and by 23 only. The baby's shrieks are piercing and I'm struggling to focus on my Spanish studies. I can see the baby's milk bottle through the gap between the seats in front of me. If he continues to cry, I'm going to get my hands on that bottle and mix a few crushed sleeping pills into the milk. I always have sleeping pills on me. I find they come in handy.

After my Avianca Airlines flight lands in La Paz, I'll have to get ready for my trip to Uyuni, 857 kilometers away. At a speed of 120kph, it should take me about 7 hours and 8 minutes to get there, but according to Google, driving there will take more than twice that. I'll split the trip into 2 days. I'll drive to Oruro on the 1st day, where I'll have dinner and spend the night, then I'll drive from there to Uyuni. I could fly to Oruro but I'd rather hire a car in La Paz and drive. I need to familiarize myself with the route so I can make the return trip to the Bolivian border with the cargo I collect in Uyuni.

The baby in the seat in front of me has fallen asleep without my help, and the cabin crew is serving lunch. A flight attendant asks what I'd like to eat. *"Carne de res y el vino tinto por favor,"* I respond. *"Por su puesto,"* the flight attendant says with a smile.

The parents of the sleeping baby in the row in front of me are arguing. "You shouldn't have spoken to him like that," the woman says. "Screw him if he doesn't like it," the man responds.

I go back to reading on my laptop. Most of the nuclear devices of the type that were in Kazakhstan before they were returned to Russia weigh between 100 kilograms and 3.5 tons. In general, those designed to serve as warheads weigh between 100 and 600 kilograms and have the capacity to create a blast of 100 to 600 kilotons, depending on the quality of the device and its technological specifications. The 1 I'm on my way to collect is pretty old. I'm assuming its yield-to-weight ratio won't be very good—a 300-kilogram bomb with a 50-kiloton blast capacity perhaps.

It's interesting.

I read about the Russian bomb known as the Tsar Bomba, the most powerful nuclear weapon ever detonated in a test. Developed by the Soviet Union, the 3-stage lithium-activated bomb had a yield of 50 megatons, which is equivalent to 50 million tons of TNT, or about 3,333 times more powerful than the Hiroshima blast. It weighed 27 metric tons and the Russians dropped it out of a plane in 1961. The explosion fireball was visible from 1,000 kilometers away and all the buildings, both wooden and brick, in the village of Severny located 55 kilometers from ground zero were destroyed.

Too bad my warhead won't be as impressive.

My eyes are open, but I can't see a thing. Only darkness.

The air I'm breathing is cold and dry.

I'm outside.

I can feel something like soft grass under my feet.

I'm startled by the sudden voice of a young girl on my right. "I'll help you." I look to my right but I see nothing. Only blackness. I feel a small hand trying to work its way into my clenched fist.

"I'll take you to meet him."

I unclench my fist and take her hand in mine. The world around me turns white. Snow stretches all the way to the horizon and appears connected to the white clouds in the sky.

"Come on, let's go!" She tugs my hand and I start walking with her. We walk for an hour in silence. The flat white ground begins to rise and I'm panting from the effort. The snow becomes deeper the higher we go and my boots get heavier. She presses on quickly as if the ascent has no effect on her. Bare trees border the snowy path. Their black branches are covered with strips of snow.

"Come on. You have to see it. Before the darkness falls."

We continue our ascent and I try to keep up with her.

We reach the top of the mountain. The peak is flat and there's a clearing measuring about forty meters across. A wooden cabin stands in the middle of the treeless area. We don't go inside. We stand at the edge of the clearing and she points down toward the open expanse at the foot of the mountain.

"Do you see it?"

I look down and I realize what she's talking about and why we had to climb to the top to see it. Far below us on the white surface are the delicately drawn lines of three concentric circles that appear to be the work of an enormous compass cutting through the snow. The radius of the outer circle measures approximately one kilometer, and the other two within it divide the largest one into equal parts. It would have been impossible to see from below.

She retrieves a dark green military compass from one of the pockets of her white fur coat and aims the sight at the center of the circle. She takes a small notebook out of her pocket and jots down a figure. Then she puts the compass back into her coat pocket and pulls out a second instrument. She turns it on and aims a red laser beam at the center of the circle far below us. She writes down another figure in her notebook.

"We'll go there tomorrow morning," she says and turns toward the cabin. "Let's go inside. It'll be very cold soon."

She opens the cabin door. We go inside and close the door behind us. It's very cold outside and the temperature must have dropped a few degrees below zero. There'll be more snow tonight for sure. It's freezing inside the cabin. A thin layer of ice covers the floor and the structure's single window is frosted over. Standing in the center of the room is a wood-burning stove with a large iron kettle resting on its surface. There's a wooden closet near the front door and two bunk beds stand on either side of the room, with the window between them.

"I'm thirsty."

I open the closet door. Stacked on one of the shelves are folded woolen blankets and white sheets. On the shelf above it are several cans of corn, a bag of rice, spices, eating utensils, and a large box of matches.

I turn around and she's standing behind me with an ax.

I jump back, but she hands me the ax. "Hurry. Before it gets dark. Before the wolves come out." She points outside. I understand and leave the cabin. It's very cold out now and I'm shivering.

I walk a short way down the path we climbed earlier and chop down a few large branches. The branches are dry and frozen and break easily and I prepare a number of piles of logs about half a meter in length that I carry back to the cabin and stack in a neat pile opposite the wooden closet. All this time she is pacing around the cabin and looking in every direction, as if she's afraid that someone will show up.

LAST INSTRUCTIONS

I pick up the last pile of logs and the ax and return to the cabin. She closes the door behind us with a large iron bolt.

I use the ax to chop one of the logs into thin strips, which I then place in the stove and light with a match. The small pieces of dry branch catch fire quickly and I stack a few thick logs on top of them and close the iron door. I take the kettle off the stovetop and go outside to fill it with snow. When I come back inside she bolts the door behind me again.

"Where do you want to sleep?" I ask her and point to the beds.

She shrugs. "I don't care."

I rest the kettle on the iron stovetop and make up the two bottom bunks with sheets and clean pillowcases, before placing a woolen blanket on each of them.

The water in the kettle boils and I make two cups of tea with sugar. We stand beside the stove drinking tea and warming ourselves. The layer of ice on the floor of the cabin begins to thaw and steam collects on the window. She uses her finger to draw a smiley face in the condensation.

I ask her name.

She doesn't respond.

"You should get some sleep," I say. "You must be very tired." She lies on her bed and I tuck the woolen blanket tightly around her.

I carefully open the door of the hot stove, add a few more logs and then close it again. I go over to my bed, get in, cover myself with a blanket, close my eyes, and allow my fatigue to lull me to sleep. Then I feel something small and warm creep under my blanket. She presses herself up against my back. I can feel her breathing.

The kettle on the stove continues to spout steam into the cabin air.

The howl of a wolf comes from outside.

December 5, 2016

Carmit woke up and stretched, taking care not to disturb Guy, who was fast asleep beside her. The dream was a new one. She got up and went to the bathroom and then to the kitchen to drink a glass of water.

She put on her favorite tracksuit, grabbed her iPhone and headset, and stuffed a key to the apartment in her pocket. The streets of London were deserted at two in the morning and she played a particularly noisy Prodigy playlist as she inhaled the cold night air and started running.

December 6, 2016

"You brought him in."

Rotem was sitting on the edge of the desk in Grandpa's office.

"Why did you do it?"

"Mint tea with sugar?" Grandpa asked, pointing at a flask on his desk.

Rotem remembered she was thirsty. "Do you have Coke?"

"No. It's not healthy."

"What you did with your psychopath was unhealthy, too. Why did you allow him to make it through? He clearly wouldn't have gotten even a foot through the door had he gone through our regular screening process. We are very good at weeding out nutcases. Okay, I'll have some of that tea."

Grandpa poured some hot tea from the flask into a thick glass and handed it to her. "Look, Rotem, I'm about to tell you a few things that can't be passed on within the Organization. I know you know him better than any of us, and I need your brain to catch him. So I'm deviating here from our regular procedures. I can count on you in this regard, right?"

"Shoot."

"This particular agent was recruited for the purposes of the Bernoulli Project, with which I'm sure you're familiar. There were twelve assassination targets and he received three of them. Now's not the time to go into why three and why specifically the three nuclear scientists out of the twelve scientists in total, but he did his job and he did it well. His objectives were eliminated. The fact that he also killed many innocent bystanders is a shame; but in the end, a nuclear warhead that was going to be used against the State of Israel remained hidden in some remote location that no one knew anything about."

"Aside from him," Rotem said.

"Do you think 10483 knows the location of the bomb?" Grandpa asked.

"Of course he does. And in the ten years he's had to plot his revenge—you can be sure that he's already positioned it where he wants it and that it will explode on the day and at the time he's determined."

"Why do you think he knows?"

"Nobody learned the location of the bomb. We know that. It was never used so it remained hidden somewhere. He met three targets, which makes his chances of hearing or seeing something much more likely. We have to go on the assumption that it's in his possession."

"It weighs anywhere between one hundred and two hundred kilograms. How could he have moved such a thing all the way from Mongolia to Tel Aviv?"

"Don't underestimate him. And don't be sure about Tel Aviv. Maybe he plans to raze the Old City of Jerusalem, or at least something big on a regional scale. You have yet to tell me something I didn't already know, by the way."

"We needed someone creative. That's obvious. But we also messed around with his brain."

Rotem's eyes widened. "You messed with his brain?"

"We implanted an expiry date. He was supposed to commit suicide on December twelfth, 2006. Exactly ten years ago. But it didn't happen."

"How did you do it?"

"By coloring relevant areas of his brain with a light-sensitive material and projecting behavioral learning patterns at the appropriate wavelengths through his eyes, while playing an audio file through a headset. The manipulation of the primary senses while the subject is unconscious is more effective than hypnosis because the subject doesn't end up functioning like an automaton."

"Fuck me," Rotem exclaimed, rising from the desk and beginning to pace around the room. "Are you fucking crazy? Who does that kind of thing? How come my division knows nothing about this?

Fuck! How come *I* don't know anything about it? How many other people have you done this to? This will blow up in our faces. It already has. What did you call it? Transformation? You're playing with fire. Who knows about this besides the inner circle? Who performed it? When did you do it to him?"

Rotem pulled a set of keys out of her pocket. "Here's a flash drive. Put the transformation file on it for me. I want to hear what you implanted in his brain. You're insane."

"It wasn't a single transformation. We performed several on him."

"Fuck!"

"Four throughout his training and also during the course of his activities abroad."

"Fuck!"

"He underwent seven transformations in all."

"Fuck!"

"I can share just the final one with you. The others remain at the level of the inner circle only."

"Fuck! You said he also underwent transformations during the course of his activities abroad. Who performed them? A mobile laboratory overseas?"

"A subcontractor. She performed three transformations for the three assassinations he carried out," Grandpa said, taking the flash drive and copying an MP3 file onto it.

"Okay, I'll listen to the file and then I want to speak to her."

"That's impossible."

"I need her to tell me about his responses to the process he underwent, and how she managed to get to him. You said the subject undergoes the treatment while unconscious, right?"

"Yes."

"So your subcontractor managed to render 10483 unconscious on three occasions? I need her."

"We do, too, but she's disappeared. She's not answering her phone and we don't know where she is. Where in London that is. London is a big place."

"What's her name?"

"Carmit Schneider."

"And there's still something else I don't get."

"What?"

"Why did you knowingly recruit a psychopath into the Organization? You haven't explained that to me yet."

"And I won't be doing so in the future either," Grandpa responded, putting an end to their conversation.

December 6, 2016

Surrounded by eucalyptus trees, the Organization's home base sits in the center of the country. The small group of gray concrete buildings with a perimeter fence guarded by soldiers could be any other Signal Corps or Adjutant Corps base, but most of it lies deep underground, and the guards in uniform are not soldiers. A few dozen meters below, there's an endless series of reinforced concrete bunkers, complete with parking levels, generators, computer rooms, more and more levels of offices, war rooms, communications centers, and living quarters. The gray concrete structures aboveground are air defense systems, for the most part, that are manned around the clock.

Rotem left Granpa's office and skipped her way toward the elevator, getting in and pressing the button to the fourteenth floor. She hurried off to her office on the so-called Mineshaft Floor, the nickname the field operatives gave the level occupied by the Organization's psychology departments, where much "digging" took place. She entered her office, locked the door from the inside, sat down in front of a computer, and inserted the encrypted flash drive on the key ring into a USB port. First she copied the instruction file she'd written yesterday onto her own computer for backup purposes, and then she put on a pair of headphones, played the MP3 file, and listened with her eyes closed. After coming to the end of the audio file, she backtracked a little and listened again to the last part of the recording.

> *You remain seated on the stone. You know what you have*
>   *to do.*
> *The grass and woods around you disappear.*
> *Your breathing quickens.*
> *You won't remember this conversation.*
> *You feel wonderful.*

You won't dream anymore.
Never again.
You'll continue sleeping now until you are no longer tired
and then you'll wake up.
This is your last dream.

"Holy fuck!" she exclaimed out loud and then realized that someone was knocking on the door.

She opened the office and Avner stepped in.

"They programmed him to commit suicide on December twelfth, 2006," she said. "After he did all that work for them. They made him kill himself in 2006."

"Do you refer to the inner circle?"

"Yes. Grandpa gave me this recording of the final transformation he underwent."

"Transformation?"

"A rewiring of the brain of some kind. Sophisticated hypnosis. Don't mention to Grandpa I told you all this."

"So it didn't really work out for them then, I guess. Fact is, he's alive and kicking."

"Perhaps he tried? Whatever it was that they did to his brain must have caused him to try. Maybe he jumped off a building or shot himself in the head or tried to hang himself or doused himself in gasoline and set fire to himself or slashed his wrists in a warm bath or did a thousand other things that didn't work. We have a lead!"

"Meaning?"

Rotem went over to the whiteboard in her office and cleaned it. She then drew a timeline with December 12, 2006, as its starting point.

"Let's say he jumped off the roof of a building," she began. "And let's say he wasn't killed. We need to check hospital records for December twelfth—for patients admitted following suicide attempts. Their records show everything. We can start in the center of the country and widen our search if we don't come up with anything around here. When we find our attempted suicide victim, we can check the duration of his stay in the hospital, the date of his discharge, if they made a photocopy of an ID card he was carrying, or anything else like that."

Rotem added a second point to the timeline, labeling it "Discharge," and at the end of the timeline she wrote: "Today—12/06/2016."

"Get it?" she asked. "We haven't looked for him until now because we were sure he'd died in his apartment ten years ago; but that's not the case. He burned a body that he carried up from the basement and placed on his bed, then he began plotting his revenge, but his plans were interrupted on December twelfth, 2006. For how long? Two weeks? Two years? Let's go check out some hospitals. They won't give us the information over the phone. We need to go there in person. We'll start with Tel HaShomer."

The door to Rotem's office swung open and Grandpa peered inside. "Avner, I need you for a few minutes."

"I'm coming. Rotem, don't leave without me."

The two men walked down the corridor, then went into one of the conference rooms and sat down.

"Avner," Grandpa said, "I need to ask you to do something that won't be easy for you, but is essential."

"If you're going to ask me to back away from this investigation, then forget it."

"You're emotionally involved. I wouldn't expect any of us to be objective under such circumstances; but it's going to hinder your decision-making and put the rest of the team at risk."

"Listen to me, and listen well," Avner said. "I'm in on this no matter what. If I was simply a new recruit, I'd listen to what you have to say; but we've both been here for long enough to know how the Organization works. The Organization is not used to working on home soil, and it's not designed to think twice before pulling the trigger. As long as everything is conducted on foreign soil against outside enemies, we don't have a problem. But when things are going to be happening here, with my wife possibly in close proximity when they close in on him, no one is going to carefully calculate the trajectories of the bullets they fire into his skull, and that's only if they choose to use firearms rather than explosives. If it was just a SWAT team, I'd feel more at ease; but let me take a wild guess and say that you have more than one team on this. How can you expect me to remain here in my office while that psychopath thinks of ways to turn my wife and Amiram into some sick piece of so-called art? Not a chance."

"Look, Avner—"

"No, I'm in on this—no discussion."

Grandpa sighed. "I'm too old for this," he said. "Okay, team up with Rotem. The two of you will look for him in addition to another team I've dispatched. We'll be getting help from all the other entities—the army, the Shin Bet, the SWAT unit. Our cover story is that we're dealing with an Islamic State terrorist. Work in conjunction with the second team. Try to think rationally despite your wife's involvement. Keep a level head."

Avner didn't respond. He stood up and left the conference room, and Grandpa remained in his chair for a few minutes before returning to his office.

December 6, 2016

Several people were sitting around the table in the conference room. The furniture in the room was old and heavy, and thick carpeting muffled the sound of voices deep in conversation. The door opened and an elderly man with white hair and bright blue eyes entered the room and sat down at the head of the table. He read from a sheet of paper in his hand:

> *Majid Shariri is living in Israel under the name of Sharon Tuvian. He resides at 7 HaNarkisim Street in Holon.*

"I received this two days ago, in an envelope that was slipped under the door to our offices here. No fingerprints or any identifying marks. The envelope also contained an updated photograph of Shariri. He looks completely different and may have undergone plastic surgery. Friends, we may be able to get our hands on the bomb."

One of the individuals at the table raised his hand. "Who could have slipped that information under our door so long after we lost contact with Shariri? Maybe it's a setup. Someone keeping tabs on us and trying to bring us down."

"Maybe. And maybe it's someone who's looking out for us."

"What's the next step, Herr Schmidt? Are we sending someone to Israel to look for Shariri?"

"They're on their way already."

"Who did you send?"

"The twins. They'll get every piece of information out of Shariri and then make him deeply regret the ten-year delay he's caused us. We could have had that bomb a long time ago. I've instructed the twins to keep him alive at all costs until he's given up the exact location of the device. Stay in Toronto. We'll meet here at four p.m. sharp every day to monitor the developments."

"Are you sure?"

"That's what the records say. Here, look—an unidentified man in his late twenties was admitted at one twenty in the afternoon on December twelfth, 2006, following a suicide attempt."

"And when was he discharged?"

"Just a moment, let me check."

The archive clerk at Tel Aviv's Ichilov Hospital browsed through a stack of scanned documents on her computer screen. It was easier than they'd expected. Following their visit to Tel Hashomer Hospital, where they found no evidence of an attempted suicide on December 12, 2006, they drove to Ichilov.

"Interesting," the archivist said, "he wasn't discharged to his home. He was transferred from here to Lowenstein Hospital a month later. It says here that he never regained consciousness. According to protocol, patients who fail to regain consciousness are transferred a month later to an appropriate institution. No one came looking for him, he wasn't carrying any identification, and the accident left his face smashed to pieces. The system lists him as a John Doe."

"Accident?"

"Yes, he jumped in front of a speeding bus on Ibn Gvirol Street. Smashed pretty much every bone in his body. He was hospitalized here for a month and was then transferred on Sunday, January fourteenth, 2007, to Lowenstein. There's a picture here of him, but it's not going to do you much good."

The image on the computer screen was of a face completely wrapped in bandages.

"Thanks, you've been very helpful."

Avner rose from his chair and Rotem followed suit. They went out to the parking lot and got into Avner's car. According to Waze, the drive to 278 Ahuza Street, Ra'anana, would take forty-eight minutes.

"I wonder how it affected him," Rotem thought out loud.

"What?"

"The accident. Incredibly traumatic and shocking for both body and mind. It must have wreaked havoc with all the transformations or reprogramming or whatever you want to call them. I wonder how it affected his personality."

"I can assure you he's still a fucking lunatic," Avner sighed. "Amiram's gone missing, too. They found his overturned Jeep at the entrance to the town where I live. I think he's abducted both of them. Efrat and Amiram. He's holding them somewhere."

"We'll find him," Rotem said. "And I get the feeling that we're not the only ones looking."

"You're right."

I sit down on the ground at a secure distance from the black rock and reach into my backpack. I retrieve some small shells, dried-out crab legs, and long black spines I snapped off the sea urchin skeletons that litter the hot orange sand. I use the shells to create a small circular formation in front of me. I take a reddish dried-out crab leg with a pincer at one end and place it alongside my shell creation, next to which I place a pile of sea urchin spines. And I wait, using the time to remove a piece of dry bread from my backpack. I place small bits of the dry bread on my tongue, close my mouth and allow my saliva to soften the bread, then I chew it slowly and swallow.

A low humming sound rises up around me. A whirlwind throws orange specks of dust into the air. The sea urchin spines shift slightly and lift off the ground. They settle on the shell formation, creating a dense spiny structure. I know what I have to do.

I take off my clothes and leave them in a neat pile next to my backpack. I walk toward a specific point on the dome of the black rock, stand in front of it and raise my arms to an angle of 45 degrees. I stand motionless and wait. The fear I felt earlier is gone.

All at once, black spines come shooting out of the holes that dot the black rock on all sides. They emerge at blinding speed and stop. They are about 5 meters in length and have pointed tips. The sharp spines shoot between my spread legs, above my head and close to my outstretched arms, missing me by just a centimeter or 2. One shoots past my forearm and scratches, but doesn't pierce my flesh.

I hear the hissing sound of compressed air and the metal rods retract slowly into the rock again. I look at the perforated bodies scattered around me. They should have known.

I walk toward the rock until I'm within touching distance. It's made up of small and smooth slabs of black quartz and I can see an indentation in the shape of a hand on its surface. I place my palm on it. The rock moves slowly to the side on a track of sorts, revealing an opening in the sand, and the initial part of a long stairway hewn into black quartz. The light that shines into the opening makes the walls inside glimmer in flashes of orange and white.

I step inside and start my descent.

02/12/2016–9 *weeks since waking*

I'm walking through the Witches' Market in La Paz. There are various charms and amulets on display at the stalls, along with small dried creatures of some kind. I ask one of witches about the creatures, and she tells me they're dehydrated alpaca fetuses. The dried fetus is buried under the foundation of a new home to bring good fortune. Like a mezuzah. A mezuzah contains a parchment scroll made from sheepskin or calfskin. It's interesting. Pieces of dead animals on doorframes and under foundations to bring good fortune and blessing. People believe prosperity stems from the death of other creatures.

I eat a sandwich that I buy from a chola. It has strips of roast pork, pickled sweet vegetables, and hot chili sauce. The local SIM card I purchased at the airport is slow but works. I search the Net for a car rental company that also offers commercial vehicles. The companies at the airport only had small cars. I find a car rental company called Imbex and rent a pickup truck, a Toyota Land Cruiser. A steel drum with a nuclear warhead inside it should fit easily into the back. I need some additional equipment in order to find it and lift it into the pickup truck. I brought a Geiger counter with me from Israel. The warhead must be buried underground somewhere.

As the car rental employee deals with the insurance paperwork, I reach for a sheet of paper and a pen from the counter and prepare a list:

1. Pitchfork
2. Shovel
3. Leather gloves
4. Powerful flashlight and batteries
5. Gasoline-powered chain saw
6. 50 meters of rope

7. 4 pulley wheels to match the thickness of the rope
8. 10 2-meter long wooden beams (thickness—10×5 centimeters)
9. Canvas tarpaulin
10. 5 colorful woolen blankets
11. Anti-radiation protective garment
12. Large tent
13. Drill set—various sizes
14. Small hacksaw
15. 40 packages of razor blades
16. Chargeable power screwdriver
17. Long screws—10 centimeters
18. Hammer
19. Long nails—10 centimeters
20. Small nails and screws of various lengths
21. 5 packages of black duct tape
22. Packet of bags used to transport cement or gravel

"Sign here, please, Mr. Mercier," the rental firm employee says to me. I sign the paperwork for the pickup and fill in my details—René Mercier, French citizen. He asks me why I need a pickup truck and I tell him that I'm meeting 2 friends and we're going to look for silver deposits in the Potosí mines. I'll need the room for all the digging tools and the silver ore we find. The man wishes me luck and takes a deposit of an additional $500. "That's so you take care not to scratch the back of the pickup too much with all your equipment," he says.

"Don't worry, we're going to get rich," I respond in a French accent.

"Make sure you don't leave your equipment in the back. Anything left not under lock and key will disappear in a flash if you don't keep your eyes on it."

"Is there a store around here where I can buy digging tools?"

"You'll find one on Avenida Mariscal Santa Cruz. There are various stores there that sell hiking gear, tools, and stuff like that. Look for shops for farmers."

I thank him and he hands me the keys to the pickup.

I need to find a dentist.

The slow SIM card finds a dentist in La Paz. Dr. Pablo Morales's clinic is on El Prado Street and I park my vehicle outside and go into the office building.

Dr. Morales specializes in emergency dental care and root canal treatments. I read on the website of the clinic where he works that they also have radiography equipment and do panoramic X-rays of the mouth cavity. That's good.

Dr. Morales asks me to sit in his dental chair. "No, thanks," I say, "my teeth are just fine."

"Mr. Mercier, why did you schedule an emergency appointment if your teeth are fine? I'm a dentist, you know."

"You have X-ray equipment here, right?"

"Yes, but only for dental X-rays. If you've broken your arm, I suggest you go to the Hospital Boliviano Holandés. That's where all the tourists go."

"Is there a lead partition in the wall of your treatment room? When you do an X-ray, do you walk out and stand behind the wall? Is that how you protect yourself from the radiation?" I point toward the wall between the treatment room and the waiting room outside.

"No. I have a lead apron that I wear when doing X-rays. I put the apron on, leave the room, and activate the machine by remote control. It's not as efficient as a lead wall but it works. I appreciate your concern for my health, Mr. Mercier, but what exactly do you want from me?"

"Here's $1,000. You can buy a lead shield for your wall. Or a new apron."

"A new apron?"

"Yes. I need your apron. Sell it to me."

"Are you serious?"

"Yes. I'm serious. I need a lead apron."

"What do you need a lead apron for?"

"I made a bet with a friend. We're going out on a trek tomorrow. In the Tuni region. 3 days of mountains, frozen lakes, and snow. Huayana Potosí will be the highest point on our route. An altitude of more than 5,000 meters. A helluva mountain. After a few beers yesterday we made a bet about something and he lost. According to the bet, the loser has to wear an item of clothing of the winner's choice for the entire 1st day of the trek. He's probably thinking I'm going to choose a funny shirt or a dress, but I'm going to bring him this apron and he'll have to climb with a lead apron that weighs 10 kilos. Not only is it heavy, but he'll look funny, too. We always make bets like these. The loser suffers."

"What was the bet about?"

"We flipped a coin. He called heads and got it wrong."

Dr. Morales started laughing. "Take the robe. I'll buy a new one. Here's a business card with my email address; send me a picture of him climbing the mountain in the apron. I'll frame it and hang it on my wall here."

"No problem." I take the heavy apron and go back down to my vehicle.

I notice that certain things amuse me. Before the accident, nothing made me laugh. I also see faces in everything now. A folded blanket, a towel on the floor, clouds. The center of my brain responsible for recognizing and analyzing facial features may have improved. I hope it hasn't improved too much. When I get back to Israel, I will get a brain MRI.

I read through the Lonely Planet guide book I bought at the airport in Israel before my flight. Uyuni is a flat town in a flat desert in a high-altitude country. The town itself doesn't have much to offer and usually serves only as a starting point for treks to the surrounding desert and the large salt lake nearby. It's a desolate place.

Dry in parts and covered with a thin film of water in others, the salt lake, Salar de Uyuni, is flat and wide. And because the lake reflects sunlight back into space like a giant mirror, it serves to calibrate satellites. The Lonely Planet strongly recommends joining a guided tour of the lake.

I'm surrounded by a lot of dust and salt but there's no sign of a nuclear warhead so far. I've been here for a week already, driving down every possible street. The streets here are wide and deserted and the roads are made of dirt, no asphalt. My pickup is already covered with a thick layer of dust. I've been to the Salar. There, I filled 10 sacks with salt and placed them in the back of the pickup truck with the rest of my equipment. If the warhead is buried in the Salar itself, it will take me several years to find it.

My Geiger counter, the RAM R-200, is resting silently on the front passenger seat. I know it's working properly because it came with a calibration unit that emits small amounts of radiation and the counter responded immediately when I held it up to the unit. I conducted the test in the basement before my trip. I didn't want to take the calibration unit with me on the flight in case it would cause one of the security devices at the airport to start beeping. I pull over to the side for a moment, remove the battery of the RAM R-200 and touch the 2 terminals to my tongue. I feel the sting of the current.

I check one more time.

And then again.

The battery is fully charged.

I put the battery back into the RAM R-200 and continue driving through the streets of the town, marking the places I've been to on a map I printed. It's easy to find your way around here. The town is crisscrossed with wide dirt roads like the bars of a prison cell.

I remember the excerpt from the Bernoulli files I read. There was a transcript of a conversation between 2 people. I reach into my pocket to retrieve the small piece of paper on which I printed the text:

- The device has arrived and is in a secure location, as we agreed.
- In the cemetery?
- Yes.
- The remainder of the sum will be transferred to you in full through the agreed accounts within a month, following an inspection of the device.
- We're pulling out of there. Does anyone apart from you know the location?
- No. I will inspect the device personally, and I'm the only one who knows the location.

Federico Lopez hadn't repeated those words for nothing.

"Bolivia Uyuni"

"Bolivia Uyuni"

"Bolivia Uyuni"

I'm sure the warhead is here. Federico Lopez tried to have it moved elsewhere, but he was engulfed by a raging fireball and he and his telephone went up in flames. I don't think he was able to convey the message. Had he managed to do so, the bomb would have been detonated somewhere at some point during the past 9 years. I'm pretty sure I'm the only one who heard it. Well, not really heard it. I read his lips. I was standing at a safe distance with a pair of binoculars and I read Federico Lopez's burning lips in the burning park on Avenida Ezequiel Bustillo.

The 1st place I checked in Uyuni was the town cemetery. There was nothing there. Not a single beep from the RAM R-200. I walked through every row of graves with the RAM R-200 and looked for a gravestone with a steel drum buried below.

Nothing.

I continue to drive around in the pickup truck until evening, then I return to the Hotel Julia where I'm staying. The desk clerk asks me if I've been to the train cemetery yet.

"A train cemetery?"

"Yes. Drive to the end of Avenida Potosí, turn left out of town, and you'll be there in a minute or so. In 1882, the British and the Bolivians completed construction of a rail network to be used for exporting minerals from the region, but the natives living in the area didn't like it and they repeatedly sabotaged the tracks until the trains eventually stopped running in 1940. Now they're all crumbling to pieces on the tracks just outside the city. It's a good place to take photographs."

"The natives were right. Those steam trains must have made a terrible racket."

"I guess so, señor," the desk clerk says with a smile.

"*Sabes que?* I think I'll go there now. The sun will be setting soon and I'll be able to get some nice pictures."

"*Seguro.*"

I follow his directions and drive to the train cemetery. I leave the pickup at the entrance to the graveyard and take only the RAM R-200 with me.

The remains of the piston-driven steam engines and rectangular train cars take on a rusty orange hue in the light of the setting sun. The RAM R-200 comes to life as I get close to one of the trains, beeping at an ever-increasing rate until I'm standing in front of one of the mineral freight cars and the device is going crazy, sounding one continuous beep. I make a mental note of the exact location of the freight car and I use a stone to mark the car with a small white X. I return to my vehicle, retrieve the shovel, and dig a small hole in the sandy earth. I remove the battery from the RAM R-200, smash it with a rock, place the broken pieces into the hole, and cover it with earth.

I drive back to the town. It'll be dark soon. I'll head out to the cemetery tomorrow morning at 4, just as the sun is rising, and before any tourists get there—although the chances of that are pretty slim. The *mochileros* like to sleep in.

It's good that my body has produced sufficient red blood cells to compensate for the lack of oxygen. I'll be able to work tomorrow without my lungs exploding. During my 1st few days in La Paz, even the slightest effort would leave me breathless. La Paz sits at an altitude of 3,650 meters and Uyuni is only about 50 meters higher. When climbing to an altitude of more than 2,500 meters, it's advisable to ascend just 100 meters per day to allow your cardiovascular system to acclimatize. I flew directly to La Paz, so I suffered headaches for the 1st few days. If you ascend too quickly to altitudes of more than 5,000–6,000 meters without acclimatization, the resulting side effects include headaches, vomiting, fatigue, loss of appetite, insomnia, dizziness, and death.

I set the alarm clock on my phone for 3:30 in the morning and plug the phone in to charge. I connect the power screwdriver to its charger for the night, too, and then go to sleep.

December 6, 2016

The control room was dark, with the keyboards and mice on the control desks illuminated only by strategically placed spotlights. The desks were arranged in a semicircle on a raised platform a few steps off the ground. They faced a semicircle of huge monitors, all black but one, which displayed several graphs in white and rows of numbers in green. The two Shin Bet operators that were on duty were busy exchanging war stories from their military service in the IDF.

"Then they said, 'Keep an eye on him,' and left me alone in the Cipher Room with the body of a terrorist wearing an IDF sweater and fatigues . . . and one of the Golani Brigade soldiers still had the nerve to turn around and say, 'And don't touch him,' before they closed the door and the room's automatic external locking system kicked in . . . I was left there all alone with the body. They didn't say when they'd be back to collect him and I had to stay there until eight in the morning. I was just a nineteen-year-old soldier. And don't touch him? Like all that was missing in my life was the chance to touch a dead body."

"What time did they bring him in?"

"Two thirty-six a.m. I made a note in the shift log. His eyes were open but blank. They looked slightly grayish, like someone had cooked them in hot water—a little like hard-boiled eggs. The green uniform he had on was stained brown with blood. I just had to call Yarden from the command center. I saved a recording of the conversation on my computer. Want to hear it?"

"Of course."

"Okay, listen. It's quite hilarious."

> *"You won't believe what they've just done to me. I'm alone here in the Cipher Room with a dead body they just brought in."*

"A dead body?"

"Yes. Some Golani soldiers tossed him into the room here with me next to the printers, and he's stone-cold dead."

"Soldiers from the same battalion as Avi the hottie?"

"Yes. But Avi's sick, poor thing, bed rest for a week. He was stung by a wasp and he's allergic. You should have seen the size of his ear. Like an elephant's."

"Aww, poor thing!"

"But did you hear what I said? There's a dead body in the room with me."

"Okay, so I won't bother the two of you then."

"Not that kind of body, you idiot—the body of a dead terrorist."

"What?!"

"Yes, that's what I'm trying to tell you; they dumped him here in the Cipher Room with me and told me not to touch him. As if I would touch him. Eww, gross!!"

"Why in the Cipher Room of all places?"

"God knows. Maybe he has a USB connection in the back of his neck and they want to get something out of him."

"Well, what do you expect? Your room is the only one that locks from the inside. They probably left him locked in there with you to prevent the entire battalion from

showing up to take pictures and post them on Facebook.
That wouldn't look good at all. Do you have a weapon?"

"There's an Uzi for whoever's on duty in the Cipher Room.
But why would I need it?"

"Maybe he's not quite dead yet?"

"Oh my God! Wait a sec, I'm going to check; don't hang up.
I'm putting you on speaker."

"That's when I went over to the emergency cabinet and retrieved the Uzi. I inserted a magazine and cocked the Uzi. Listen to some crazy bits coming now."

"What's that noise?"

"I cocked the Uzi. Just a sec, I'm going to poke him with a
squeegee stick and if he moves, I'm gonna kill him again."

"Woo hoo, G.I. Jane!"

"And did you actually touch him?"
    "I touched him with the end of the stick, which I was holding in my left hand, while I had the Uzi in my right; and because I'm left-handed and my palms were sweating so much, my finger slipped on the trigger of the Uzi and I emptied half the magazine into his body. Wait a moment and you'll hear the gunfire on the recording."

Rat-a-tat-tat-tat-tat-tat-tat-tat-tat

"What the hell is that? What happened?"

"Oops, sorry. Didn't mean that. My finger slipped."

51

"Okay, I've heard enough. That's gonna give me nightmares."

"Okay, I'll just tell you the rest then. So this is what happened. I'm busy talking to Yarden, and suddenly this hissing sound starts coming from the body, like the sound of a balloon deflating, and his hand opens and a grenade rolls out and I hear, *Click,* and the pin of the grenade flies out and I hear, *Pssssssst,* and nothing happens except for a bit of smoke coming from the grenade. And I jump behind two IBM disk cabinets and count, 'Twenty-one, twenty-two, twenty-three,' and nothing happens. Except for the fact that the door opens because I'd forgotten to lock it from the inside, and the Go-lani soldiers burst in all freaked out and start yelling at me for killing him again, and Yarden is yelling back at them over the speakers in the room, telling them that they should be ashamed of themselves, leaving a corporal all by herself with the body of a terrorist, and I tell them how lucky it was that the grenade he had in his hand didn't explode, pointing at it on the floor under their feet by the stairs. I swear I've never seen soldiers run so fast in my life. And up a flight of stairs no less."

The two operators had changed the subject of their conversation and were now engrossed in descriptions of sumptuous meals they ate while on vacation as civilians. Meital was in the middle of a detailed description of a dish of deep-fried sticks of breaded Hal-loumi cheese when the encrypted communication system came to life.

"AngelFire, commander here," they heard.

Meital leaned forward and pressed the Push-to-Talk button. "AngelFire here, over," she said.

"Commander here. I have three objectives for you. Timeline ref-erence point—yesterday morning at nine forty. For each of them I want to see all movements a week prior to the reference point and then unbroken from then until now, and onward. Keep an eye on the monitors all the time. First objective—private home, 21 Mevo Na-hagei HaPredot Street, Ganei Yehuda. Second objective—private home, 17 HaShikma Street. Mazor, at the end of the path. Third objective—apartment building, 203 Ibn Gvirol Street, Tel Aviv. Is that a Roger? Over."

"Roger, repeating, please confirm. Reference point—December fifth, 2016, nine forty in the morning. First objective—private home, 21 Mevo Nahagei HaPredot Street, Ganei Yehuda. Second objective— private home, 17 HaShikma Street. Mazor, at the end of the path. Third objective—apartment building, 203 Ibn Gvirol Street, Tel Aviv. Over."

"Roger, confirmed. I'm on my way to you with three civilians. Prepare the system. Over."

"Any need for a blackout? Over."

"No, they have the necessary security clearance. Over and out."

Meital leaned back in her chair again, "Shit," she said, "I thought it was going to be a quiet day."

Dafna started typing and the screens in front of them flickered to life. "Tell me something, isn't 203 Ibn Gvirol the building that blew up yesterday from a gas leak?"

"If they want us to look at it, there must be another reason for the explosion. Do you think it's a terror attack they want to keep quiet?"

"Strange. And the three civilians must be Mossad. They're the only ones outside the Shin Bet who know about this facility. But if it was a terror attack, they wouldn't have given us two additional objectives. And certainly not two objectives that aren't border crossings or in the territories or East Jerusalem."

"Okay, I'm sending you the coordinates for the three objectives. Open three logs and display the images on screens two, three, and four. Drag the three sequences of images to cache storage so we can run through them quickly when the guests arrive. I'll clean up the mess here a little in the meantime."

There was a buzz from the intercom some thirty minutes later and Meital pressed the button to open the front door of the building.

The commander of the AngelFire facility hurried in together with three civilians, and the four went upstairs to join Dafna and Meital in the control room.

"Okay, listen up," the commander of the facility kicked things off with a brief explanation. "I'll tell you a little about what we can offer you, and then we'll move onto the matter that concerns you. This AngelFire facility is in concept similar to facilities with the same name in the United States. Hovering above every major city are meteorological balloons. Some are really just that and are used to record temperature and wind speed and various other weather-related parameters; and then there are our balloons, which aren't meteorological at all and are equipped with extremely high-resolution cameras that transmit data. Each camera takes a picture every two seconds, each image is about half a gigabyte in size, and the image files are transmitted from the balloons to points on the ground below at high speed, thereby giving us a sequence of images for every location. All the data from the balloons flows into a central computer system linked to this control room. The daytime images are clear, the nighttime images are grainy and contingent on starlight amplification. So if the night is dark, you can't see a thing—but that's rare. We've uploaded the sequences of images of your objectives to a cache so we can run through all of them quickly. What you have here is a time machine of sorts. We save all the images, so from the time point that concerns you, we can access all the images up to some eighteen months back, which was when the system was set up, or forward up to right now minus two seconds."

One of the civilians who appeared to be the team leader turned to Meital. "Let's start with 203 Ibn Gvirol Street."

"Okay, look at screen number two," Meital said. Displayed on the screen was a frozen close-up of the building at the precise moment of the blast, with fragments of concrete caught in midair. "This is an image from yesterday at nine forty and thirty-two seconds. We have set this as our timeline reference point. We call it Line Zero."

"Run the sequence back a little."

—*Click*—

The building appeared intact again.

—*Click—click—click*—

The computer emitted a clicking sound each time the image on the screen in front of them changed, the cars on the street appeared as blurred objects.

"Can you make the images a little sharper?"

"No more than you see now, and that's after they've already been processed and manipulated as much as possible. Don't forget that the camera covers a very large area of Tel Aviv and you are seeing only a tiny part of the entire image."

The sequence of images continued to run in reverse at two-second intervals. The stream of vehicles and pedestrians on Ibn Gvirol Street moved quickly backward. Night, evening, afternoon, morning appeared on the screen in front of them. The three civilians watched with obvious fascination. "Line Zero minus one day," a robotic voice announced through the speakers. Followed by: "Line Zero minus two days," "Line Zero minus three days."

"Pause it here," the civilian spoke again. "I don't see anything special, but can you run it back as far as possible afterward to look for anything suspicious outside the building? Someone in the vicinity who's staking out the building or sneaking inside? It'll take a few hours that we don't have right now."

"No problem. We'll run through it and report to you if we see anything suspicious. Can I get your cell number?"

The civilian handed her a business card for: Rafael Cohen, certified electrician—Electrical works of all kinds. "Ignore the title," he smiled, "it's only the telephone number you want. Let's move on to Ganei Yehuda. Line Zero. Run it backward as well."

"Screen four."

—*Click—click—click*—

The image sequence appeared on screen number four. Dots that were people and rectangles that were cars moved in reverse at intervals of two seconds. "Line Zero minus one day." The nighttime images didn't show any people, only the headlights of vehicles in the area around the satellite branch where some of the activities of the past few days had taken place. "Line Zero minus two days." The sequence continued to play in reverse.

"Stop it there."

The time signature of the image on screen number four showed [12.3.2016 / Saturday / 09:55].

"Run it forward a little more slowly."

"Stop." [12.4.2016 / Sunday / 01:39] The team leader turned to his two companions. "The car parked there is Avner's and the dot that just walked into the base is Avner. The guard there gave me the entrance log for the past few days. Run it forward."

"Stop." [12.4.2016 / Sunday / 02:52] "Can you see that? Someone is approaching from the side of the faulty camera. Notice how he's making sure not to step into the field of vision of the other cameras. Here he's getting under Avner's parked car. Do you see?"

"Let's run it back a little to see where he's coming from," the other two civilians said in unison.

"Just a moment. Make a note of this point on the timeline. Let's see what else is going on here. Run it forward."

The dot under Avner's car reappears and then disappears again in the direction of Savyon Junction. Avner steps out for some fresh air and then goes back inside a few minutes later. Grandpa enters the satellite base at 04:05. He leaves at 04:45, gets into his car and drives away. A few minutes later, another car enters the parking lot and Rotem gets out and enters the satellite base. A while later, Rotem leaves, and Avner follows her shortly thereafter. The only other movements are those of the guards ending and beginning their shifts.

"Stop. Go back to the fourth of the month, two fifty-two in the morning. Let's see where 10483 goes from there."

"Okay."

The images race back quickly and stop at the moment 10483 is seen emerging from under Avner's car.

"Run it forward."

10483 appears to pause for a few moments. Due to the poor resolution of the image, it's impossible to see exactly what he is doing while standing next to the car for those few seconds. He starts to proceed on foot in the direction of Savyon Junction, turns into one of the streets of the Savyon neighborhood, gets into a van, and starts driving. He takes the road leading to Messubim Junction and then turns onto Road No. 4 and heads north.

—Click—Click—Click—

"Why are the images moving slowly now?"

"This segment isn't part of the sequence of images we uploaded to cache storage. We've moved farther away, so the system is displaying the images from the regular storage drives."

The images continue to appear one after the other, the van 10483 was driving continues to head north on Road No. 4.

"SHIT!" all those in the room exclaim more or less simultaneously as the van disappears under a thick layer of clouds.

"What do you mean he disappeared a year ago?" Rotem asked. "A patient of yours lies here for nine years in a vegetative state and then you discover one morning that he's disappeared from his bed and you don't think to investigate or report the matter to someone? Are you out of your minds?"

"Report to who exactly?" the Lowenstein Hospital doctor sitting across the desk from Avner and Rotem asked laconically. "An unidentified attempted suicide victim who's had five reconstructive surgeries and doesn't look at all like the person he was before jumping in front of a bus, with no ID on his person, and no one looking for him—who exactly were we supposed to report him to? If he's so important to you, where were you for the nine years he lay here like a mummy? But we actually did do something. We informed the police and the answer we got was that there'd be no investigation due to a lack of public interest. The police said that if he got up and left, that's his business, and if no one is looking for him, they can't do a thing. After we insisted, they sent over some investigator who questioned everyone and said that the Ra'anana police would handle it. She thanked us and said they would update us on any developments. It's really nice of you to remember now—a year after he woke up and ten years after he was admitted."

"When exactly did he disappear?"

"December fourth, 2015. Almost exactly a year ago. The nurse on duty was doing her morning rounds and he wasn't in his bed when she got there. We then discovered that he'd stolen shoes and clothes from the doctors' lockers. He must have left during the night in uniform."

"Do you have a picture of him before his escape? Ichilov had a photograph of a bandaged head, which hasn't helped us very much at all. Just don't tell me that during the nine years he lay here, you didn't bother to take even a single photograph of his face."

"Just a second, I think I can help you with that. Wait for me here for a moment."

The doctor left the room.

"That's good at least," Avner said. "He had only a year to plot his revenge."

"It's not good," Rotem replied. "He had a whole year to plan his revenge."

The doctor returned to the room with an A4 sheet of paper displaying a color image of 10483's new face. "Here, take it, I made you a copy. I hope you manage to locate all the money he stole."

"Yes, he's our only connection to the robbery of the Brinks van in '98. Almost five million shekels. If he hadn't disappeared on us ten years ago, we would have solved the case already."

They got up and left the room, thanking the doctor for his help. They were wise to arm themselves that morning with two police IDs which made it easier for them to get answers. They now had a photograph that they could run through the computers of the Organization, the Shin Bet, the Border Police, and local authorities to get a picture of where he'd been during the course of the past year.

They were getting into Avner's car when his Organization cell phone rang.

"Hello."

"Avner Moyal?"

"Yes."

"We believe your car was tampered with outside Ganei Yehuda. Can you check the underside of your vehicle?"

"Who is this?"

"Rafael. Let's just say we have a common target."

"And how do you know that something was done to my car?"

"We have our ways. Also, it seems that it was 10483 who tampered with your car, so you'd be wise to get out of the car if you're in it now, and ensure that no one is near the vehicle." The call ended.

"There's no need to hurry," Rotem said. She remained in her seat as Avner closed the door he'd just opened. "If he wanted to blow us up with whatever he fixed to the underside of this car, he would have done so already. So . . . Grandpa's sent another team after him. Just as I thought. I wonder if we would have found out had they not warned us now about something under the car."

"Grandpa told me there was a second team."

"Why didn't you tell me?"

"Old habits die hard. I'm sorry," Avner said with a smile.

Rotem faked a look of anger despite knowing after her talk with Grandpa that there was at least one more team on the trail of 10483 aside from them.

They got out of the car and Avner crawled underneath the vehicle. He emerged moments later with a package the size of a book that was wrapped in black duct tape.

"It was stuck to the underside of the car," he said.

Rotem took the package and slowly tore off the strips of duct tape. Inside was a cell phone connected to several rechargeable batteries. The phone was locked.

"He's been keeping track of us," Rotem said. "He must have Waze open, or some other GPS application with sharing. So he knows now that we know what he looks like."

"That we know what he looks like?"

"He's seen the route we've taken—Tel Hashomer, Ichilov, Lowenstein. I'm assuming he knows now that the staff here has given us a photograph of him. Don't turn off the cell phone. I don't want him to know that we've found it. Perhaps we can use that to our advantage. In any event, I'm guessing he won't be using it to get to us at this stage. He'll save us for dessert because we are the tastiest. Let's go back to the main base for now."

"Just a moment," Avner said before using his own cell phone to take a picture of the 10483 image they now had. He looked through his list of incoming calls, attached the picture to a text message, and sent it to the number of the last call he received. He wrote, "This is him. Good luck."

Seconds later he received a reply: "Thanks. May the best team win."

December 6, 2016

"I'm walking barefoot in the snow. My feet don't make a sound. Snowflakes swirl in the gentle breeze. The shrubs in the large court-yard look dark green in the moonlight, they're covered with domes of snow. I move toward the figure in front of me. It's a young girl. She's wrapped in a blue coat, the hood covers her head completely and she wears yellow boots. She's looking down at the snow. Black sunglasses cover her eyes. She looks no older than six or seven.

"My bare feet and hands don't feel the cold as I move toward the girl. I'm not wearing gloves. The snow continues to fall. I come to a stop and she looks up at me. She removes her sunglasses. *'My name is Keiko and you killed me,'* she says."

"And then you wake up?"

"Yes. I've been having the same dream almost every night."

"Are you still involved with the transformations?"

"No. I've cut all ties with them. With all my handlers. With the Organization. With the Chinese, with the Norwegians. I'm no longer doing any of that. I even threw away the cell phone I used to use to communicate with them, and I dismantled the lab and released all the mice into Hyde Park. I can't understand why this dream keeps recurring."

"Who requested the transformations on the Japanese guy?"

"On Kazuo Shimizu?"

"Was that his name?"

"Yes. The client was a large Chinese government backed corpo-ration. They paid upfront in full with a single bank transfer. I have to figure out what went on there. Elliot, I have a flash drive with me with the encrypted transformation file they sent me to perform on him. I didn't destroy it. They got me to use the same transformation file on Kazuo five times. The very same file—with no changes. Never before has a client asked me to perform the same transfor-mation on a target over and over again. Work your magic and see if you can figure out what they were trying to do. Let's meet here again tomorrow. I have to work out what went on there and who that girl is. She's the same girl who was standing beside her parents at the Geneva airport. The same young girl I sketched without even knowing I could draw. The same girl who appeared in my dreams after I'd completed the transformation on Kazuo Shimizu."

"Can't you access the audio file? What's the problem? They were supposed to send you the password so that you could play it into Kazuo's head, right?"

"No. There's no password. They sent me the encrypted file along with an iPad app that unlocked the encryption during playback and then locked it again afterward. Following the final transformation, the system deleted the sound file. But I copied the original file to a flash drive before the final playback, so I still have that copy. I tried to play around with it but have no idea how to open it."

"I'll try to work on it this evening."

I continue my way down the quartz stairs and hear the rock above me slide back into place. It blocks the sunlight and I'm enveloped in complete darkness. I continue down the stairs. My right hand brushes over the passageway's rock face to my right, and my left hand is stretched out in front of me to prevent me from bumping into anything. I stumble and almost fall when the stairs end and the ground below my feet flattens out. I don't have my phone with me and I'm not wearing a watch, but I estimate that I've been descending for about 52 minutes, assuming I covered the 3,120 steps at a rate of 60 per minute.

I make my way down a long quartz tunnel and see a faint dot of light in the distance. I think, There's light at the end of the tunnel, *and I'm amused. I continue until I emerge from the tunnel into a large park. My knees hurt and my legs are shaking. A cold sun shines over the park's grassy expanse, and the leaves on the trees, in various shades of green, yellow, red, and brown, flutter in the cold wind. Some of them fall to the ground to join the colorful carpets of leaves under the trees.*

The park is filled with families and young couples. Children are playing on the green grass, adults are sitting around picnic tables and drinking coffee from flasks, and the smell of hot dogs drifts through the air. There is a small restaurant located at the juncture of several pathways. The grass, tree, and pathways stretch out before me in every direction.

Suddenly, all the families, couples, and individuals who are wandering around the park stop what they're doing and turn their heads in a certain direction. They remain frozen like that for a few seconds, and then, all at once, they continue going about their business.

I walk along one of the pathways that winds among the trees and cross several streams by means of small wooden bridges. The sun shines through the branches of the tall trees. The people around me don't appear to be interested in one another, but every few minutes, they freeze and turn their heads toward that same point. I follow the path I'm on toward the point they keep looking at.

I step out from among the trees into an open grassy expanse. There aren't any trees here, and no benches or pathways. The area is also void of people. I walk toward the center of the open field. The grass is moist and my shoes get covered with a layer of dew that wets my socks. The wind turns icy and the bright white light that shines from the sun does little to ease the sudden intense chill in the park.

I continue to make my way to the center of the big field of grass. I keep going until I reach a circular paved surface. Peeping here and there between the paving stones are small tufts of grass, and the paving stones are covered by reddish green moss. A stone fountain stands in the middle of the circle. Its 3 tiers are chiseled in the shape of 3 blooming flowers. The fountain is surrounded by a circle of smooth stones, and an inner circle of 5 benches made from wood.

The fountain is dry. There's no water in it. I see there is text engraved into one of the smooth stones. It says:

> *If you ask me whence this story comes, I will tell you it comes from a storm of wind and iron, from orange-flaming arrows of fiery glass and the ashes of the dead.*

I sit down on one of the benches and rest for a few minutes.

The stone fountain comes alive. A gentle stream of water gushes from the fountainhead and pours down into the floral-shaped tiers below, filling them one after the other until the bottom one is full to the brim. I peer into the large floral-shaped structure. An ethereal image looks back at me from the water. A young boy lies in bed, and someone, his mother perhaps, is sitting on the carpet by his side. She's leaning over to look at something and all I can see is her back. I can't make out the identity of the boy. The image is blurred and fuzzy, and it fades and disappears in a puff of smoke. The fountain goes dry and the 3 floral-shaped tiers are drained of water at once, remaining bone-dry again. I touch the stone. It's very cold.

I get up at 3 in the morning, before my phone has a chance to wake me, and I turn off the alarm. The hotel lobby is deserted and I go out to my pickup. The lumber in the back of the pickup is in disarray and one of the lengths of wood is lying on the ground a few meters to the side of the vehicle. The cargo bay is dotted with blood, and there's a blood trail leading from the pickup truck down the street. I unlock the vehicle, remove a pair of thick leather gloves from the glove compartment and put them on. I retidy the pile of lumber and retrieve and replace the piece that's lying on the side of the road, taking care not to cut up the gloves on the razor blades I've embedded in the wood. Someone tried to steal them during the night, or tried to get to the tools underneath, and now he must have a good few rows of sutures.

I start the engine and drive to the train cemetery. This is the 1st time I've ever kept gloves in the glove compartment. It amuses me.

I drive alongside the trains and shine a flashlight on the cars until I find the one marked with the white X. I park my vehicle next to the car and turn off the lights. The light of the moon will suffice for now, the sun will be up soon. I put on the gloves again and unload the lumber. I saw 2 beams to 10 pieces, 40 centimeters each, then I use 4 beams together with the pieces I sawed using a hammer and nails and build a 4-meter ladder. The banging of the hammer breaks the silence around me.

I rest the ladder against the side of the train car and climb up. Looking in, I see that the car is filled with salt or some other mineral. I taste a few grains. Yes, it's salt. There's something black sticking up out of the center of the salt bath. When the car was full to the brim with salt, the object would have been completely hidden; but over the years, the high-altitude desert's cold winds have clearly scattered some of the open freight car's load, and the treasure buried there has been exposed. I climb in and push my way through the salt toward the black object, which turns out to be the rim of a black barrel. I dig a little into the salt around it. The barrel is in good condition. It doesn't have any holes and the salt hasn't caused excessive corrosion. The dry air of the high-altitude desert probably played a part, too. I check out the sides of the freight car. They're thick and strong. I won't be able to cut through the bottom to allow the salt to spill out. I'm going to have to lift the barrel out of the salt from above. I have lots of work to do. It's already 3:40.

I retrieve the roll of rope from my pickup and cut off a 6-meter piece, I tie one end to one of the lengths of wood. With the other end of the rope in my hand, I climb the ladder again, dragging the length of lumber behind me. I do the same another 6 times, throwing all 7 pieces of wood into the salt inside the freight car. And then I bring up the rest of the equipment. I leave the tent in the pickup. When I bought it, I thought I'd be digging into the earth and I was going to use it to cover the hole I made, but now I'm going to be digging up salt in a freight car. I join 2 lengths of wood to form a V, and then do the same with another pair. I plunge the 2 V-shapes into the salt on either side of the barrel and connect their respective apex points using 2 beams that I fix together to form a single thicker one. The structure I've created has 4 legs that support the double beam above the barrel. I've reinforced everything with dozens of screws. I saw the last remaining length of lumber into several pieces to form a counterweight to go with the pulley wheels I purchased. I take a break for a few minutes to allow my body to rest and I drink some water from the bottle I brought with me. I put a few grains of salt from the freight car into my mouth. They don't taste the same as cooking salt.

I cut 3 pieces of rope, dig around the barrel, and create 2 loops of rope tied to it. I connect the 2 loops with the 3rd piece of rope and all this is connected to the pulley stand I built and to the beam hanging over the barrel. I pull the rope and the barrel rises. Without the pulleys I could not move it. It must weigh at least 150 kilos. And then, with the barrel suspended in the air above the side of the freight car, I use my one foot to push it past the edge, before releasing the rope and lowering it slowly to the ground at the foot of the car.

I leave the pieces of equipment I know I'll no longer need buried in the salt, throw the wooden pulley system I constructed down to the ground, and collect the rest of my gear and carry it down the ladder. Using the chain saw I then cut the ladder into several pieces. I use the pulley system to lift the barrel into the pickup truck's open cargo bay, before dismantling the wooden structure and packing the lengths of lumber into the back of the vehicle. I secure the barrel to the cargo bay with some rope. It's already 6:30 and the desert around me is glowing in the early morning light. I take some pictures of train engines at sunrise, return to my hotel, and pay my bill.

"Did you get some nice photographs?" the desk clerk asks.

"Very nice," I reply. "The old locomotives look fantastic at dawn. Thanks for the tip. And here's a tip for you, too." I take out a 50-boliviano note and give it to him.

I return to my vehicle. I put on the radiation protective apron that I bought from the dentist and begin driving back to La Paz. The apron will protect me from most of the radiation emanating from the barrel. My exposure time will be lengthy. I won't be able to leave the barrel out of sight for even a moment, lest it be stolen. At night I'll sleep in a tent alongside the pickup truck. I can get food supplies in villages along the way. I have a 2-day drive back to La Paz, and then a journey of another 30 days or so to Tijuana in Mexico. From there I'll cross the border into the United States somewhere near San Diego.

02/21/2016—Evening, 10 weeks and 2 days since waking

A full day of driving takes me to the town of Oruro, where I buy some vegetables, a bag of rice, a loaf of bread, and a few spices. My pickup is parked outside the small store and I don't let it out of my sight. While I'm at the store, I refill 2 large bottles with water, dropping iodine purification pills into each. I drive for another half an hour in the direction of La Paz, then make a right off the main thoroughfare onto a dirt road, which I follow for about 10 kilometers into the wilderness.

I prepare dinner with the groceries I bought. While the rice is cooking in a pot with some hot spice I picked up at the store, I erect the tent and lay out my sleeping bag. I eat the meal I've made, drink some of the iodine-tasting water, and go to sleep.

I wake the following morning at dawn, put on the lead apron and check on the barrel in the pickup's cargo bay. No one is going to bother me here and I have time. I drill a number of small holes into the side of the barrel near the top; then I use larger and larger bits to gradually create several holes of approximately 3 centimeters in diameter each. I make a point of not drilling too deep into the barrel. I shine my flashlight into the barrel through each of the holes to see what's going on inside. I can see that the barrel is made up of 2 parts. Fitted to the bottom section is a metal covering with a 5-centimeter gap between it and the outer lid of the barrel. There are 3 hand grenades with their pins removed in the space between the 2 sections. The grenades have been fixed to the inner covering such that their safety levers are pressed up against barrel's outer lid, which, in turn, is holding them in place and preventing the grenades from exploding despite the fact that the pins are out. Removing the barrel's outer lid would release the 3 safety levers; and 3 seconds later, the 3 grenades would explode. By the time the person removing the outer lid had realized what was happening, he or she would be blown to bits and the warhead, would be destroyed in a regular blast and not a nuclear explosion since a nuclear explosion has to be triggered internally by the complex detonation mechanism within the warhead. That would be a real waste.

I drill more holes in the barrel, farther down the sides, to see if there are any other booby traps, but find none—only layers of plastic sheeting and grease in which various items have been stored. There are 15 holes in the barrel by the time the rechargeable drill's battery dies. I wander around my vehicle and tent and collect 3 thin twigs from a dry shrub nearby. I use duct tape to fit a thin nail to the one end of each twig. I hold the flashlight in my mouth to leave my hands free to grip the twigs with the nails, and I peer through the holes in the upper section of the barrel. I carefully insert a thin nail into each of the grenades to replace their missing pins, making sure that all 3 nails fit firmly in place.

I open the outer lid of the barrel and remove the grenades from the surface of the inner metal covering one by one. I leave the grenades equipped with their makeshift pins, breaking off the twigs and wrapping several strips of duct tape around the top of each device to prevent the nails from moving. Just to be sure, I fix each safety lever to the side of the grenade with several strips of tape, too. I remove the barrel's inner lid to see what's inside.

Wrapped in several layers of greased plastic sheeting I see the nuclear warhead. There's no mistaking it. I leave it closed up in the plastic.

There are several other smaller plastic-wrapped bundles alongside the warhead. I open them. The 1st contains 4 thick instruction booklets in Russian. I browse through a few pages and am able to partially understand the text thanks to the Russian I learned back in Israel before setting out. I'll use the road trip to Tijuana to continue with my Russian studies at night so I can properly understand the operating instructions for the warhead.

The 2nd package contains a Russian-made Makarov pistol, 2 empty magazines, 2 boxes of 9mm rounds (50 rounds per box), a compass, and binoculars. I dismantle the pistol and examine it. It's clean and well-oiled. I open one of the boxes of rounds, put my gloves on, and fill the 2 magazines. One I insert into the pistol, tapping it gently upward to lock it into place. Loading the bullets into the magazines with the gloves on is cumbersome and slow, but it's vital not to leave any fingerprints on the cartridges. Spent cartridges are an excellent source of fingerprints. The gun can be easily wiped clean later on. I return the gun, the 2nd magazine and the boxes of bullets to their plastic wrapping, along with the 3 grenades, and put the bundle back into the barrel.

The 3rd package includes an old Nokia cell phone and 2 batteries. I don't try to activate the phone and return it to the barrel. The 4th package contains various maps of Bolivia and 30 bundles of 100-euro banknotes, with 100 notes in each bundle. I fold up the maps and return them and the bundles of cash to the barrel. I empty one of the sacks of salt into the upper section of the barrel where the grenades used to be, replace the outer lid and use strips of the black duct tape to seal the holes I made in the sides of the barrel.

I fold up the tent, pack my belongings into my backpack, get into the pickup truck and head off in the direction of La Paz. It takes me 4 hours to get there. I drive around the city trying to locate a suitable vehicle for my trip to Mexico.

I don't find one right away. My search continues for a few days.

Every evening, I drive out of the city, make myself dinner, and sleep in the tent beside my pickup.

I press ahead with my Russian and Spanish studies before going to sleep.

For example: "Officer, I'd be happy to pay my fine to you in person," in Spanish is: *"Oficial, estaría feliz de pagar mi multa a usted en persona."*

And the phrase, "The ideal altitude for a nuclear explosion is 2.253 km," in Russian is: *"Идеально высота ядерного взрыва 2.253 км."*

December 6, 2016

"We have a photograph of him," Rafael says, tinkering with his cell phone and returning the device to the front pocket of his pants. "I've sent it to you. He doesn't look anything at all like the one we received from the Organization."

The other two team members look at their mobile devices and memorize the new image.

"Let's have a look now at Avner's residence on Moshav Mazor," Rafael addresses Meital. "Line zero. Run it backward."

They observe the movements around Avner's home in reverse— Avner returning home from the Organization, looking for Efrat and heading out again; a second vehicle approaching in reverse and a figure carrying a second figure out, laying the figure on the ground; then the figure on the ground getting up and entering the home and the second vehicle moving away.

"That's 10483 abducting Efrat. Make a note of the time; we'll go back there shortly. Keep running it in reverse."

—*Click—click—click—click*—Avner heading to the Organization, another car pulling up at Avner's house, the same car diving away.

"Stop." [12.3.2016 / Saturday / 23:06]

"Run it forward a little slower."

The car heads down the dirt road and stops outside Avner's house. Someone gets out, meets a second figure who emerges from the home and the two go inside. "That's Amiram coming to give the notebook to Avner. Run it forward a little faster until he comes out again and then follow the car."

"No problem."

—*Click—click—click—click*—Amiram's car heads toward the exit from the town, and then disappears suddenly from the screen.

"What the hell?"

"Just a moment. Dafna, come here for a second and give me more contrast."

—*Click* back—a car appears.

—*Click* forward—it's gone again.

"Look here by the side of the road," Dafna says, using a cross-shaped cursor to indicate a black mark on the screen. "The mark wasn't here two seconds ago," she continues. "The vehicle you're looking at flew off into a ditch at the side of the road and overturned. That's why the color of the object has changed from the white of the roof to the black of the underside of the car."

"But there was nothing on the road!"

"I'm running it forward," Meital says, resuming control over the system.

They see someone walking toward two dots on the side of road and then moving on a little farther. Fortunately, the trees on the side of the road are cypresses, without long branches that would have hidden everything. The figure approaches the overturned car, crawls inside, emerges again, and then doesn't budge for about fifteen minutes. Someone else then gets out of the overturned car and the two individuals remain there together for a few minutes. Then one walks back toward the town, while the other remains lying in the ditch alongside the overturned vehicle.

"Did he kill Amiram?" one of the team members asks.

"I don't think so. Run it forward faster and follow him."

The figure walks a few hundred yards into the town, turns onto one of the pathways leading off the main street and disappears under a clump of trees. A minute later, a van emerges from under the trees and stops on the road alongside the overturned car, the prone figure is dragged into the vehicle, which then drives away.

[12.3.2016 / Saturday / 23:55]—*Click—click—click—click*—10483's vehicle leaves the town passes Be'erot Yitzhak, turns left at the interchange onto Route 471, and eventually turns right at Bar-Ilan Junction onto Road No. 4, heading north.

"Fuck, I don't believe it!"

The vehicle disappears again under a thick cover of clouds.

"Is there any way to see where he exits after the clouds?"

"No. The cars on the road at night all look very much alike. If the sequence of images at two-second intervals is broken, we don't stand a chance."

"Run it forward to the point at which he abducts Efrat. The images are a lot clearer there since it's morning."

[12.4.2016 / Sunday / 10:25]—*Click—click—click—click*—10483 drags Efrat into his car, the car heads out of the town; it passes Amiram's overturned vehicle, which in the daylight can be clearly seen from above but not from the road itself, and then immediately disappears again under a cover of rain clouds.

"Shit!" Rafael exclaims as he sits down on one of the vacant armchairs. "I hate the winter. Okay, listen up. We know that he lives in the Sharon region or the North. On both occasions that we managed to follow him for some of the way, he was heading north on Road 4. A town in the Sharon region, around Kfar Saba or Ra'anana, is probably our best bet, unless he moved farther north. We know for sure that he's holding Efrat and Amiram and we have an updated photograph of him. Come back to the main base and we'll cross-check his image with everything that moves."

Before leaving the Shin Bet facility, the three civilians voiced their gratitude to the AngelFire commander and the two operators. "Thanks, girls. And don't forget to review the image sequences for the movements around the building on Ibn Gvirol Street—at least eighteen months back. Try to see if this same car was in the vicinity of Moshav Mazor and Ganei Yehuda, and if there was anyone inside keeping an eye on the two locations. Check if he messed around with one of the Ganei Yehuda cameras a few days ago. Whenever you see him, try to follow him and see where he came from, and where he was going."

"No problem."

The three-man civilian team leaves the room escorted by the

AngelFire commander, and the heavy door closes behind them with a dull metallic thud.

"Interesting huh? I'm making coffee. Want one?"

"Of course!"

"A baguette. God, if only I had a nice crispy baguette with pesto and thin slices of tomato and mozzarella cheese, with a little olive oil . . . I'm starving."

"And a large burger with onion rings on the side."

Both girls sighed in unison.

December 6, 2016

Elliot took the Underground from Hammersmith to Acton Town. After leaving the station and circling the building to make sure no one was following him, he went into a small café adjacent to a dry cleaning store, ordered a cup of Earl Grey tea and scones, took a seat on a stool facing the street, and opened his laptop. Before accessing one of the Darknet's commercial sites, he first made sure he'd leave no signs on his computer after completing his work.

19:31	ZeuS1212: Hey Botnet herders!
19:31	ZeuS1212: Need a~50K Botnet for 6h tonight
19:33	ComeToPapa666: Bitcoin mining?
19:33	ZeuS1212: Nope. Decryption
19:33	ComeToPapa666: 55K herd, $35 an hour
19:34	ZeuS1212: Deal
19:34	ComeToPapa666: Pay in advance (Bitcoin)
19:34	ComeToPapa666: Once transferred you get control for 6h

Within less than five minutes, 55,000 PCs were at his disposal for six hours, at a cost of $210. Elliot again thanked the torrent gods for the people who upload cracked software, TV series, and movies and unwittingly leave themselves open to networks that take advantage of their computing resources and the content stored in them. He uploaded a cracking program with centralized admin to the Botnet network. Five minutes later, he uploaded the encrypted file to the system and put the cracking instructions into motion. Fifty-five thousand computers began working on the task.

Elliot removed the flash drive and closed the laptop. "Shitty weather, isn't it?" the waiter said, placing a cup of steaming hot tea, a plate with two scones, and two small bowls with butter and jam on the table. "Yes," Elliot responded, "it's been drizzling incessantly for four straight days now."

Elliot drank his tea and ate the scones. He left the payment along with a tip on the table, exited the café, and returned to the nearby Underground station. He spent the next few hours running errands and shopping, then took the Underground again, to a different area of London, went into a pub, ordered a pint of Guinness, and reopened the laptop. Although just three hours had gone by, he received a <COMPLETE> message when he logged into the Botnet that was running the crack. He downloaded the cracked file onto his flash drive and erased the cracking software from the Botnet.

```
22:38     ZeuS1212: All yours, keep the change ;)
22:38     ComeToPapa666: THX
```

Elliot took a sip of his beer and inserted a pair of earphones into his ears. He listened to the cracked audio file until he finished his beer and the recording came to an end. He wondered if he should tell Carmit that he hadn't been able to crack the encryption. It was going to shock her for sure.

He returned the laptop and flash drive to his bag, paid his bill, and rode the Underground back home again. He'd give her the recording tomorrow. She needed to hear it.

December 7, 2016

- Did you bring the handcuffs and the rope?
- You have trust issues, Ricardo; you need to learn to rely on people.
- Did you bring the handcuffs and the rope?
- Yes, of course I did. When is the son of a bitch supposed to arrive?
- In ten minutes. I got a text message. The fucker is on his way.
- The son of a bitch has nice sofas. He has good taste when it comes to design. Refined taste.
- They're just white leather sofas.
- No, they're not just sofas. The stitching is precise. Someone made them with love. The leather is soft and velvety. Well processed. From a young cow. The son of a bitch has good taste. It's not every day you come across someone with good taste. It could be yak leather.
- What kind of leather?
- From a yak.
- How do you know what yak leather looks like? You live in fucking Manhattan. You weren't around the last time a herd of yaks or buffalo or any other animal aside from a duck or a puppy on a leash passed through there.
- I've seen a yak. Two months ago. In Nepal. It looks like a cow, but with a smoother hide and curved horns, long ones. But the one I saw was brown. Not white.
- You were in Nepal? What were you doing there in Nepal— mushrooms?
- I was there on assignment. I didn't have time for nonsense.
- For Herr Schmidt?
- Yes, for Herr Schmidt. I brought back something from Nepal for him. Something in a box.

77

- Yak leather?

- It was a small box. I don't think it contained yak leather. The box may have been big enough for a small piece, but I don't think that Herr Schmidt would have sent me all the way to Nepal to bring him a small box with a piece of yak leather inside. Listen to this, Ricardo, I saw a yak when I was in Nepal and that yak changed the way I perceive the world. That's what that yak did.

- What did it do?

- Listen. I'm sitting in a restaurant in Kathmandu. Herr Schmidt's box is on my lap and I'm eating.

- Yak meat?

- No. I'm eating a dish of chicken and noodles with red chili peppers—so fucking hot that it melts the toilet you shit it out on the next day. I see a big brown yak walking slowly down the street some two meters away. It gets to a tap, opens it with its tongue, and drinks a few gallons of water straight from the tap.

- That's one smart yak!

- It's one fucking smart yak. Listen, when it's finished drinking, it closes the tap again with its tongue. Can you believe it? It closed the tap.

- That's one motherfucking smart yak!

- And I'm telling you, Ricardo, if a fucking yak closes a tap after drinking from it, then it says something about us, too.

- Are you sure you didn't drop some mushrooms there?

- It means that we have to respect the planet and stop wasting its resources. And we should learn to appreciate beauty. Like this sofa we are sitting on right now.

- Fuck this fucking sofa and fuck this fucking country. I'm telling you, when we get back from here, I'm quitting.

- What wrong with Israel?

- The steaks here are shit. And wherever you go, people look at you like you're a criminal. The person who stamped my passport when I arrived interrogated me for an hour as if I were a criminal;

every mall I go into I'm checked with a metal detector as if I'm a criminal; every time I go into a restaurant, the security guard at the door looks at me as if I'm a criminal.

- Perhaps it's because you're a criminal.

- I'm a businessman.

- In any event, if we finish our work here quickly, we'll be on a plane back to New York.

- We'll stay here for as long as it takes. Until Tuvian or Shariri or whatever his name is gives us the location of Herr Schmidt's bomb.

- I'm simply saying, for argument's sake, that we shouldn't drag it out for too long.

- Now listen to me carefully. We're not going to kill him until he's finished talking and has told us everything he knows. No matter how annoying he gets. No matter how ugly he is. And even if he spills some blood on these beautiful sofas made from the hide of a young yak, you're not going to smash his head in with a crowbar and you're not going to strangle him or electrocute him. Herr Schmidt has asked me to make it perfectly clear to you that this guy has to tell us everything he knows before he is sent to meet his maker.

- What if he pisses me off?

- Restrain yourself. We need what's in his head, not his head itself. I'll deal with that when the time comes. You just make sure that he doesn't constitute a danger, and count to a hundred when you feel like gripping his head between your hands and smashing it into the floor tiles. And when you get to one hundred, take a deep breath, unclench your fists, and drop your hands to your sides, and stop looking at the rope with one eye and the ceiling with the other. We're not going to hang him. Do I have your word, Lorenzo?

- Deal. As long as he doesn't dirty this sofa.

- I hear footsteps on the stairs. Turn off the light. Did you bring the handcuffs and the rope?

- Yes.

December 7, 2016

You're on a bus in downtown Osaka.

You're on your way to an important meeting.

The bus comes to a standstill in a traffic jam.

You see a girl standing in the middle of the bus.

She smiles at you and presses a switch she's holding in her hand.

The girl blows up along with the entire bus, and metal ball bearings penetrate your right cheek and your chest.

The ball bearings that flew through your right cheek get lodged in the backrest behind you. The ones that entered your chest stop in your heart.

You feel terrified. Your body is covered in a cold sweat. Your breathing is rapid and shallow. Fear engulfs you. You know what you need to do so that it doesn't happen again.

You feel your life slipping away.

You die.

Keiko

You're a soldier in the Battle of Iwo Jima in February 1945.

You're lying in a trench.

The ground is muddy and your uniform is stained.

You're hungry.

Your commander shouts: "Charge!" And you emerge from the trench and charge forward.

A bayonet rises up in front of you from a trench you didn't notice and pierces through your shirt.

A girl is holding the rifle.

You're impaled on the bayonet and can't move.

The girl watches you die.

You feel terrified. Your body is covered in a cold sweat. Your breathing is rapid and shallow. Fear engulfs you. You know what you need to do so that it doesn't happen again.

After you stop breathing, she removes the bayonet and cleans your blood off on her pants.

Keiko

You're asleep in your bedroom.

The whole building starts to sway.

The ceiling collapses and you're buried underneath it.

You crawl out from under the rubble.

You stop crawling when you see a pair of small sneakers in front of you.

Standing in them is a girl.

She's holding a hammer and looking at you.

The child takes—

Elliot stops the recording. Carmit removes her earphones and they sip their coffees for a moment without saying a word.

Carmit is the first to speak. "It's a two-hour recording," she says. "I don't have the video file, but I'm assuming they bombarded his eyes for two hours with images of a girl killing him. And they performed this transformation on him five times. They made him suffer PTSD from this child."

"Not just any child. His daughter."

"Why?"

"Did you bother to find out what happened to Kazuo Shimizu after the transformations?"

"Not really. I read that he committed suicide."

"I did some research on the subject last night. They covered up some of the story; but several hours before he killed himself, he strangled his daughter."

"What?"

"The Chinese corporation that hired you wanted him out of the picture and wanted it to look like a suicide. They also wanted it to shame his family in such a way that they wouldn't want anything to do with what Kazuo Shimizu had built and would sell the Shimizu chemical conglomerate immediately after his death. Kazuo was a strong man; they knew it would be difficult to manipulate him into harming himself, so they caused him to suffer PTSD from his daughter. He saw her in his subconscious as someone who would kill him one day, and all that needed to happen to spark him into action was for him to return home in the evening after drinking too much sake, and for the transformation to kick in while he wasn't at his best. That's how it probably happened. He killed her and when he sobered up and realized what he'd done, he shot himself. Your dreams are echoes of the transformations you performed on him."

"I killed him. I killed her, too. When I started all of this, I didn't think my career would include the murder of innocent people."

"What's done is done. You've put it behind you. Don't get all depressed on me now."

"Depressed? No, not depressed. I'm pissed off big-time. I know that the Organization also used me to kill lots of innocent people. I don't know what their objectives were in doing so, but I do know what the results were."

"What do you mean?"

"Look," Carmit said, taking a note out of her pocket, "these are the three dates on which I performed transformations on one of the Organization's agents. Back then, I warned Grandpa that they were screwing with his mind. When I flew to Geneva—a building collapsed with all its occupants inside. When I flew to Argentina—a park caught on fire and toasted everyone who was there. When I flew to Canada, there was that story about the guy who broadcasted a hypnosis recording over the radio and killed eleven thousand people. You must have heard about these three incidents. I connected the dots only after the hypnosis incident. I realized that each of the three occurred after I'd performed a transformation on that agent of theirs. He must have been involved in all these incidents."

"Just a moment, are you telling me that the Organization got you to perform transformations on the same agent on three occasions and in three different countries? How did you know he was one of their agents?"

"He was a compete nutcase. He kept a journal in which he recorded everything that happened to him, and I read through it while he was unconscious. In it he talked about his childhood and how he was recruited into the Organization. He was a lunatic even before they messed with his head. I read the journal when I was performing the transformation on him in Argentina. It was the second transformation, after he'd already brought down the building in Geneva, but I didn't know it then. I didn't have time to read the entire journal, only the part where he wrote about his childhood and his recruitment into the Organization. The transformation ended and I had to get out of the room. If I'd read more, I guess I would have gotten to the part about the building in Geneva—maybe I would have stopped the treatment there and then. They went way too far."

Carmit placed her coffee cup on the table. The barista at the Starbucks in Hammersmith called out the name of a customer who had ordered a triple latte. "The Organization is responsible for those disasters. I don't know why, but I'm going to find out. First I'm going to deal with the Chinese so I can stop Keiko from appearing in my dreams. I think I'll go to China."

"I don't think you should do that. Forget everything and go back to your family. Put it all behind you."

"I can't."

I turn and walk away from the fountain. I sit down on the bench again and look at the flat stones that have been pieced together to form the floor around the fountain. The face of the same boy who appeared earlier in the waters of the fountain emerges now from one of them. His face is made of stone, as if it's been pressed into the rock to form a 3-dimensional mold. He opens his eyes and gazes at me with his 2 stony white eyeballs. His stone mouth opens but no sound comes out. The stone face replicates itself. 2 boys stare at me and suddenly rise atop stone bodies that emerge from the rock, which appears to become plasticine or modeling clay of some kind. The 2 stone children turn to me. They take a few steps and stand in front of me. I'm sitting on the bench so my eyes are level with their empty orbs. One raises a finger to his lips. The 2nd points toward a silvery metal pyramid some 20 meters away. Funny how I hadn't seen it before. Then all at once, the 2 stone children crumble and fall to the ground in a pile of dust. A gust of wind carries them away. I get up and walk toward the metal pyramid. It stands 20 meters high and its 4 triangular sides are made of silvery mirrors. I move closer and look into one of the mirrors. I see the man I once was, the man I am now, and the man I will become. Something is happening inside the pyramid. I try to peer inside. The pyramid shatters and comes crashing down, taking the old me with it. The new me is watching the scene unfold and smiling.

Standing next to me is a woman in jeans, a black T-shirt, and sneakers. A cold wind blows through the park. I feel the icy chill on my face like you do when you open a freezer door. A thin layer of ice covers the paving stones around the sidewalk and the surrounding grass takes on a thin layer of frost and goes from green to white in a widening circle.

"It was customary at one time to make a death mask," she says without turning to me. We are both looking at the remains of what used to be the pyramid and the body of the old me is lying in front of it, a thin layer of ice forming over it, too.

"If you were a poet, philosopher, composer, or some other important persona in the 18th or 19th century," she says, "you'd be fitted with a death mask. Following the departure of the priest, the death mask craftsman would show up with strips of fabric and plaster. After mixing the plaster in a vessel of water and soaking the strips of fabric in the solution, he would gently lay the strips over your dead face, fixing them firmly to your mouth and closed eyelids and using them to cover your cheeks, which by then would have already turned the color of plaster. Once the strips dried, he would remove the plaster mold of your face and fill it with wax or clay. Napoleon had a death mask. Beethoven and Chopin, too."

She runs a hand through her hair.

"They also used them to document a violent death or suicide. In France, people who were found dead in the city were put into glass cabinets and displayed to the public on the banks of the Seine. A few of the onlookers would be people looking for a missing relative, but most would show up simply to satisfy their morbid curiosity. The murmurings of the crowd would sometimes be broken by a stifled cry from someone who recognized a loved one. They'd make death masks for some of those bodies, too, for documentation purposes."

The circle of frost continues to spread all around us.

"L'Inconnue de la Seine also drowned in the river. She got her death mask by chance, from someone who couldn't ignore her beauty as she lay in a glass cabinet on the bank of the Seine. He ordered and paid for the work of the death mask craftsman. She was young. 16 or 17 perhaps. The mask was the final courtesy extended to her before she was buried without a name. She was believed to have committed suicide, but there were other rumors, too."

The old me is now covered by a thick layer of ice.

"She became known as L'Inconnue de la Seine, *the unknown woman of the Seine. Replicas of her death mask were produced over and over*

again. Molds were made from the replicas and more replicas were made from the new molds. Her face, alongside Napoleon's, stood proudly on display in many a French home, and the story about the beautiful young girl continued to spread, changing from time to time—the mistress of a banker who killed herself, a young girl who fell overboard from a ship on her wedding day, the victim of a horrible murder. Her face is everywhere today. The face of the Rescue Annie doll, which is used for CPR training, is a replica of L'Inconnue de la Seine. *"*

She goes silent for a moment.

"Staring up into the face of everyone who undergoes CPR training these days is the face of L'Inconnue de la Seine. *Her mouth is slightly open. She was designed in that way by Asmund Laerdal so that air can be blown into her. But in the original death mask, her mouth is closed—with that same hint of a smile she displayed as she lay in her glass cabinet on the bank of the Seine on that sunny winter's day. Every one of the 300 million people who have been trained in CPR with a Rescue Annie doll and every one of the 17,800 people who are currently undergoing CPR training courses in various countries around the world right now as we speak is working with a Rescue Annie doll and they cannot see that smile—the smile that says: 'You couldn't do it.' "*

The woman turns her head and looks at me, "This place is the death mask of the unknown man you used to be."

She turns and walks away.

A cold wind is blowing.

Gina and Mark are an Australian couple. They've been traveling around South America for 8 months and have managed to get through Venezuela, Chile, Argentina, and Bolivia, and now plan to move on to Peru. They're driving around the continent in a large RV that they shipped from Brisbane, Australia, to Santiago, Chile. They flew to Santiago, met up with their RV, and kicked off their travels from there. I buy it from them with the 300,000 euros from the barrel. Initially, they didn't want to part with the RV. Gina said they had so many beautiful memories from their time driving around in it, so I doubled my offer from 150,000 to 300,000 euros.

"With 300,000 euros," I said, "you can continue traveling for a very long time, and buy a newer and nicer RV."

The increased amount did the trick; and after 2 days of faxes and emails to the Australian Licensing Department, the vehicle ownership was transferred to the name of Oscar Salstrom, a Swedish citizen—me.

A much smaller sum was enough to persuade several locals to help me to carry a particularly heavy barrel from my rented vehicle to my newly acquired RV. When they asked me what was in the barrel, I told them I had filled it and several sacks with salt from the Salar and that I was going to sell it all in Sweden as a medicinal antiaging product for the skin and make lots of money. I also gave them most of the lumber I no longer needed. I kept 4 lengths of wood that I tied to the roof of the RV. Gina joined me in the RV for the drive to the car rental agency and she used the time to fill me in on how to maintain the vehicle's various systems and how to hook it up to the power supply and sewage facilities in the trailer parks, and Mark followed us in the rented pickup. I returned the rental vehicle, paid a fine of $150 for a few scratches and dents on the back of the pickup's open cargo bay, and said farewell to Gina and Mark, who then hired a car for themselves. Before saying good-bye to one another, we all enjoyed a wonderfully tasty cup of coffee from a flask offered by the rental agency employee.

I'm now using my Swedish passport—one of several I still have from the time when I worked for the Organization in Europe. I kept them in the basement. I've replaced René Mercier the Frenchman with Oscar Salstrom the Swede after checking online and revealing that a Swedish passport will allow me entry into Peru, Colombia, Panama, Costa Rica, Nicaragua, El Salvador, Guatemala, Mexico, and the United States without having to acquire a visa for those countries. The only problem I may have will involve arranging the RV permits to go from one country to the next, but I'll make the necessary arrangements beforehand so as to speed up the process.

I say farewell to the Australians and visit a number of stores and a gas station to collect the items on my shopping list:

1. 10 20-liter jerrycans
2. 200 liters of fuel
3. Strong fishing line
4. Sufficient food for a week until my next purchase
5. Shampoo, soap, conditioner
6. 2 cartons of whiskey
7. Cartons of Marlboro (50 packs)
8. 2 large truck jacks
9. 3 1-inch steel irrigation pipes, each 2 meters in length
10. 1 packet of 1-inch metal nuts
11. 1 power drill
12. 1 standard electrical switch
13. 1 set of drill bits of various sizes
14. Nuts and bolts of various sizes
15. 1 length of strong metal cable
16. A length of thin metal cable
17. 1 puncture repair kit

18. 1 box of contact adhesive
19. Another box of duct tape
20. 1 1 × 1 meter sheet of metal

To check:

Condition of spare tire

I visit several hardware stores and a gas station. It's harder here to find all the items I need. In Europe or North America, I would have been done with my shopping list within 2 hours. Here it takes me 2 full days to get to the end of my list. I waste a lot of time finding the cartons of cigarettes. None of the stores carry much stock.

I leave La Paz and head down Route 1 in the direction of the border with Peru. I turn off the main highway near the town of Guaqui and drive north until I get to an isolated beach on the shores of Lake Titicaca. I park in a spot that can't be seen from the nearby trails and get to work on the mobile home for a few days.

I place large rocks behind and in front of the RV's 4 wheels to prevent it from moving and use my shovel to dig a large hole under the vehicle. The hole is a meter and half deep and its opening extends slightly beyond the sides of the RV so I can climb in and out with ease. It takes me 2 days to dig the hole.

I empty the RV's sewage with the designated flexible conduit pipe, rolling the pipe out to its maximum length and using it to drain the waste from the tank. Once the tank is completely drained, I disconnect the pipe, roll it up again, and dip it into the mound of waste I've created on the ground. With the tube now filthy and smelly, I return it to its place in a compartment near the floor at the back of the trailer. I recall the work I did for the Organization at the Iranian Embassy in the Netherlands. The sewage there smelled a lot worse. I remember crawling through the sewage pipes along Duinweg Street.

I climb back into the hole and dismantle the RV's empty sewage tank. I bring it out of the hole and measure it. The warhead isn't very big and will fit inside, but it's very heavy and the screws and 2 metal strips that hold the sewage tank in place won't be able to bear the weight of the nuclear device.

I cut a rectangular opening into the upper part of the sewage tank and place the piece of the tank that I've sawn away off to one side. Using the steel pipes, the rope, and the pulley wheels, I construct an improvised set of tracks along which I slide the barrel down the steps of the RV. I then carefully roll the barrel into the hole I've dug under the RV and leave it there for now.

I'm hot and I take off the protective apron I purchased from the dentist. I'll wear it when I'm on the road and that will suffice.

I climb down into the pit again and drill 2 parallel rows of 5 holes each into the underside of the RV, above the spot where the sewage tank sits. Into each pair of holes I insert a length of metal cable to create 5 loops. When the 5 cables are in place, I roll the barrel a little closer and retrieve the 2 jacks, placing them on the ground under the loops I've created. I then saw away the side of the barrel and roll the plastic-wrapped warhead onto the square sheet of metal I position on the 2 jacks. I secure the 5 loops around the warhead and slowly raise the jacks, 2 to 3 centimeters at a time, stopping to tighten the loops before continuing. By the time I'm done, the warhead is tightly secured to the underside of the RV.

The rectangular hole I've cut into the sewage tank allows me to fix it back into place over the warhead. I secure the tank and reseal the opening using the piece I sawed away.

I place several small and somewhat purplish Bolivian potatoes into a pot of water and begin cooking them on the RV's stove. When they are done, I'll make some mash with the butter I purchased. There's a picture of an alpaca on the butter's wrapping.

I learn by reading through the warhead's instruction manual that its fuse can be programmed. Its activation mechanism has 2 setting options—arming and detonation on impact, or arming and detonation some distance above the ground, the device fitted at its tip has a barometric pressure gauge. This is very good.

I use the RV's toilet to check for leaks in the sewage tank. The warhead in the tank is wrapped in several layers of plastic and grease and will soon be covered in a layer of shit, too. The Australians gave me special tablets to drop every day into the toilet bowl in order to melt the contents of the sewage tank and thus make it easier to empty its contents with the pipe. I don't use them so as not to damage the protective layer of plastic around the warhead.

I sleep every night outside the mobile home in a sleeping bag in a tent, dressed in the dentist's lead apron. The apron protects me from the radiation. I make sure I add iodine tablets to the water I drink. The iodine destroys any germs and bacteria in the water and also prevents radiation damage. Radioactive iodine-131 can be harmful. I need to look into the subject of iodine and radioactivity.

- Remember to read up on it when I'm somewhere with cellular coverage again

In my current location, the RV's radio picks up nothing more than a single Bolivian AM station that plays songs that comprise primarily of wails of various kinds.

I plug my iPhone into a charger that's connected to the RV's cigarette lighter. Gina and Mark either left it for me as a gift inside the glove compartment or simply forgot it there.

I press ahead today with my work on the RV. I open the package containing the 3 hand grenades and remove the strips of duct tape such that the nails alone are serving as their safety mechanism. I dismantle the RV's plastic ceiling panel and fix the grenades to the vehicle's roof. I run a length of thin metal cable across the ceiling and wrap it around each of the nails 3 times, knotting everything into place with several pieces of fishing line. I then dismantle one of the RV's inner panels and run the end of the thin metal cable down the side of the vehicle before tying it to a metal ring I've removed from a key ring that was in the RV. I replace the ceiling cover and the side panel. If I pull down hard on the ring peeking out from under the side panel alongside the driver's seat, I'll have 3 seconds to get myself out of the vehicle.

I connect the switch I bought to the fuel pump's electrical cable, in a hard-to-find spot under the RV's engine well, and I turn off the power. I'll deactivate the fuel pump whenever I park the RV; and if someone tries to steal the vehicle, they won't get farther than a few dozen meters before the fuel feeding the spark plugs runs dry.

I gather some dry branches and place them in a heap in the barrel I sawed in half the previous day. I set them alight and throw the package with the cell phone, its 2 batteries, and the collection of maps of Bolivia into the fire. I have one PDF map on my cell phone and don't need any others.

I hide the pistol, the extra magazine, and the box of bullets in the RV, behind the microwave oven. I'll have to ditch them in Mexico, before crossing the border into San Diego.

03/08/2016—Night, 12 weeks and 4 days since waking

I park at the side of a dirt road near the town of Tulcán in Ecuador. The border crossings from Bolivia into Peru and from Peru into Ecuador went by smoothly, with the gift of a few cartons of cigarettes and a bottle of whiskey for the border guards. For most of the way through Peru, I follow the roads that run along the coastline, and in 4 days I cover a distance of 2,754 kilometers to the border crossing near Huaquillas. From there I travel north into Ecuador for a farther 823 kilometers to where I am now; and tomorrow I'll cross the border into Colombia.

I do my food shopping in small towns, and I sleep every night in open areas at least 20 kilometers from the nearest community. I'm not troubled much at all along the way. Now and then hikers appear and marvel at the RV. I greet them and wish them luck on their travels. Tonight I get a visitor of a different kind. While lying in my tent and reading through the Russian-language instruction manual and translating the words I've yet to learn with the help of Google Translate on my iPhone, I hear the door to the RV slam shut, the engine fire up, and the vehicle drive away before the engine coughs, splutters, and dies. Someone is trying to steal my trailer. He may have been sent by the Organization.

I count prime numbers in my head until someone rips through the side of the tent to my left with the sudden slash of a knife. He slips quickly inside and sits on my sleeping bag and leans over me. "Get the RV going again right now if you want to live," he says. He's holding a knife in his right hand, which is raised above me. I wonder if he knows about my warhead or if he simply wants to steal the RV. I'll get him to tell me that tomorrow.

I tell him that I don't think I'll be cooperating with him and that he should put the knife down and get off me because it's uncomfortable. I raise my one arm toward the roof of the tent to reach for the hammer from my toolbox that's hanging there. His eyes follow my hand and he sees the hammer. He slams the knife into my chest. He looks surprised. The look in his eyes reminds me of the expression on the face of the black-coated, blue-hatted man who followed me in the Netherlands the moment I pushed him onto the Metro tracks. I manage to get my hand on the hammer and bring it down onto his head. Not too hard. I still need to talk to him tomorrow morning.

It's good that I wear the lead apron at night. It protects me not only from the radiation. I crawl out of my sleeping bag, leave the tent, and get things ready for tomorrow's talk. I take 2 strips of duct tape and repair the tear his knife made in the side of the tent. 1 strip on the inside and 1 strip on the outside. I spread contact adhesive over and around the 2 strips to reinforce the joint. I don't keep the pistol in the tent because local police sometimes show up at night to conduct standard drug raids. The hammer is enough. It's good that I started dreaming again when I was hospitalized for 9 years. I have heard a doctor tell a nurse that my muscles are in relatively good shape because I move in my sleep. It took me some time to move my muscles on demand, something the man who tried to kill me can't do right now. I get back into my sleeping bag and go to sleep.

I'm woken in the morning by the sound of shouting and cursing in Spanish. I stretch and leave the tent and walk over to the RV, which is parked about 100 meters or so away. I turn on the fuel pump and turn the RV's ignition switch. It takes a minute for the fuel pipe to fill again and for the engine to come back to life. I park the RV close to the tent again and turn off the engine. The shouting continues.

I go into the RV, brush my teeth, and make a cup of coffee. I go outside and sit on a rock in front of the man I caught the night before. He is buried in the ground with only his head sticking out of the earth and resting against a rock. I put it there so he'd be comfortable and wouldn't have to strain his neck muscles when he woke up. His body lies buried at a slight angle in the trench I dug during the night. The trench is about half a meter deep at his feet and about

20 centimeters deep at his head. Aside from his head, he is completely covered with earth. His hands and feet are bound securely with rope and a heap of rocks is holding him down just for good measure.

"Is your neck stiff or has the rock helped?" I ask.

"Get me out of here now. I have friends and they're on their way here. If you want to live, you'd better release me."

I take a sip of coffee and remain silent. I look at the man. I look at the open expanse all around us. I see a large eagle-like bird in the sky. I look at the man again and take another sip of coffee.

"Who sent you?"

"My friends. They're on their way."

"Your friends from the Organization?"

"Yes, from the Organization. We control anything and everything that moves around here—the traffic of goods, the smuggling of diamonds, and very soon they will all come looking for me. We are the most powerful organization here."

"Did Amiram send you?"

The man goes silent. I finish my coffee and start to collect dry branches and twigs that I arrange in a pile next to the tent. I then divide the pile into 3 smaller ones—thin twigs, slightly thicker branches, and branches with dry leaves on them. I start to stack the thicker branches in the form of a pyramid. The head of the man who tried to steal my RV is in the center of the structure.

"Get me out of here!"

When I'm done with the thicker branches, I move to the twigs and use them to form a 2nd layer around the base of the pyramid. I cover the structure with a canopy of dry leaves. I then go back to the RV to retrieve a lighter from the kitchen. I return to the pile of branches and set fire to the dry twigs in a few places.

"Who sent you?"

"You're insane!"

The twigs are crackling and a cloud of white smoke rises into the blue sky from the orange flames.

"Who sent you?"

"You're insane!"

"Insane!"

"Insane!"

The man who tried to kill me is very loud. I return to the RV, turning my head to call out to him, *"Que le vay a bien,"* before stepping inside to have my breakfast. Yesterday, I bought a bag of croissants at the bakery in the town of Latacunga and froze them in the refrigerator's icebox. I defrost a few of them now in the microwave and eat them with some strawberry jam I still have left over from Peru. The shouting from outside ceases and I finish eating and clean up the kitchen. I go outside and look at the charred head of the man who wanted to kill me, surrounded now by the last remaining smoking embers.

I once used to kill in the framework of my work or simply for the sake of art. I realize now that my liquidation of the thief puts me in a particularly good mood. I take 2 small sticks, tie them together in the shape of a cross, and place the cross in the pile of stones over the man's body. To the tip of the cross I attach a piece of paper on which I've written:

> Died as a result of an acute
> Allergic reaction to fire

I break into a rendition of "Light My Fire" by The Doors, crawl under the RV to check that everything is securely fastened and hasn't come loose during the long drive, return to the vehicle, put on the lead apron, and start driving toward the Colombian border. By the time the local police come across the body I've left behind I'll already be a few countries away from here.

December 7, 2016

The multimedia room six floors below ground at the Organization's home base was more crowded than usual. Avner and Rotem arrived first and began the search, and three others joined them an hour or so later.

"It looks like we're after the same target," one said, noticing the image of 10483 on one of the screens.

"Rafael?"

"Nice to meet you, Avner—I assume?"

"Yes, and this is Rotem, the head of the Personality and Psychopathology Research Department."

"Have you come up with anything yet?"

"Yes. Regarding Amiram first—there was a deep impression clean across the front grill of his overturned Land Rover. 10483 flipped the vehicle into the ditch with the help of a metal cable he tied between two trees on either side of the road. A field investigation revealed markings on the trees. There were no signs of any injury to Amiram. The same goes for Efrat—no signs of injury or harm besides a few drops of blood. As for 10483 himself, we're running a search based on the most recent image of him from the date he regained consciousness through to the present. Few places hold onto video footage dating back even a year, but we know that the Israel Airports Authority stores their footage indefinitely, so we started with Ben Gurion Airport. We fed his image into the IAA's system and it took no more than a few seconds to get a hit."

Avner directed the trio's attention to one of the monitors, moved the cursor to a point on the screen, and clicked PLAY.

"Here, on the ninth of February, at five thirty-five in the morning, he boarded an Iberian airlines flight, IB 3321, to Madrid. The flight departed at six. Here, the camera shows the departure gate, and there you can see the monitor with the destination—Madrid."

"What passport did he fly with?"

"We don't know yet. We could ask Iberia for the passenger list, but I'd rather keep this in-house for now. We'll keep looking through all the footage and wait to catch a glimpse of him scanning his boarding pass through one of the airport's QR readers, then we can cross-check that through the system and find out. I'm just about to get the IAA's security chief on the line. Take a look meanwhile at the footage from his return: Can you see him coming out of the bridge and into the arrivals terminal? The flight that arrived through that gate was Lufthansa LH686 from Frankfurt. March twenty-ninth. He flew to Madrid, returned via Frankfurt, and used two different airlines. The question is: What was he doing for two months in Europe—or elsewhere perhaps, if he flew on from there? The fact that he used two different airlines seems to indicate that he wasn't exactly sure where he'd return from, or that Europe was simply a connection, or that he's trying to cover his tracks. We could easily check with the Spanish or German airport security authorities, but we don't want to involve other countries yet. We don't want his image to fall into the hands of some organization that will connect the dots."

"And do you know what passport he used to reenter Israel?"

"No, not yet. Here, too, we'll cross-check the timing and see if he came back in on the same passport."

"Okay, let's divide up the work and run through other video sources that may have captured his image. Government ministries, seaports, the borders with Egypt and Jordan. Maybe we'll come across something else."

They spread out among the various workstations. Rotem went up to her office for a few minutes and promised to return shortly. Rafael reached for the receiver of one of the room's telephones and dialed a number.

"Hadar here. How may I help you?"

"Hi, Hadar, it's Rafael. Do you have anything for us?"

"I'm afraid not. I've been trying to get in touch with you. You've dropped down on our list of priorities. We can't work on it now."

"What do you mean? Where's Meital? Put her on the line."

"Sorry. Turn on your TV or a radio. Haven't you heard about the terror attack?"

"No, we're in a location with no cellular access."

"There's been a terror attack in Jerusalem. Two terrorists. One blew himself up inside a bus and the other ran into the crowd of rescue workers and blew himself up ten minutes later. A huge fucking mess. Right now everyone's focused solely on that."

"When can you get back to us?"

"I can't say for sure. Based on similar incidents in the past, it could take up to two weeks."

"Two weeks??"

"Could be. I see you're calling from a red line so I can give you a few details, but I can't tell you much. You realize of course that we now have to study and run checks on every individual who got onto the bus from the time it left the Central Bus Station on its first round early this morning and through to the moment of the blast. And that means tracking every single passenger who got on or off the bus, going back in time several months with respect to every single individual, finding the terrorist and seeing who he met with, who the other members of the cell are, who parked outside whose home, who their handler is, where he hangs out, the banks they used to receive finances, who made the explosive belts, where he got the material from—and the same goes for the second piece of shit who blew himself up among the ambulance crews."

"The man we are looking for is extremely dangerous, too. He blew up an entire building in Tel Aviv."

"I know. Zero fatalities. The count so far in Jerusalem today is twenty-three."

"Fuck!"

"Exactly, and that number will rise. You know how it goes. The Shin Bet's Operations Division Chief is the only one who can shuffle our priorities now, and believe me he's not going to do so."

"Okay. Can you let me know the moment you're free to continue the work for us?"

"Of course."

Rafael replaced the receiver. The others in the multimedia room looked at him. "We don't have Eyes in the Sky now," he said. "Their immediate tasks now involve gathering essential information concerning a terror attack that just took place in Jerusalem, and that's going to neutralize our search with the aid of aerial footage for about a week or two. We'll have to collect data from regular cameras and alternative means. Come on, we have to find out what he's been up to over the past year."

"Eyes in the Sky?" Avner queried, looking up from his screen.

"A Shin Bet facility. Cameras that are fitted to meteorological balloons and shoot images from the sky every two seconds."

They continued to run searches through various systems in an effort to find a match for the image they had—but without any further success. Avner finally reached Ben Gurion Airport's chief security officer; Rotem had returned from her floor with a thick book bearing the title *10483,* and was flipping quickly through its pages.

One of the members of Rafael's team sighed. "The guy's fucking invisible," he said. "He doesn't appear in any footage apart from the video from the airport. He probably walks around all the time with something that keeps his face hidden from the cameras, or simply turns his head to the side. He hasn't been picked up by any of our facial-recognition programs."

Rotem looked up from the book she was reading for a second. "In certain lines of business, it pays to be paranoid," she commented before looking down again.

The door to the multimedia room buzzed and someone from the Operations Division walked in. "You need to see this," he said, inserting a flash drive into one of the computers and projecting the data onto one of the larger screens on the wall. "This is what we managed to retrieve from one of the head-mounted cameras that survived the blast. We got nothing at all from the memory cards of the other cameras. They were completely destroyed."

After a few seconds of static and snow, the sound of heavy breathing could be heard and the video screen on the wall displayed the descent from the floor of the closet into the basement. Beams from the five head-mounted flashlights of the team members who went in wearing gas masks flickered through the dark expanse.

"Look. That's the cage he constructed. It's empty now."

Rotem stood up and moved closer to the screen. The team member whose camera footage they were viewing noticed something on the floor of the cage and was bending down to see what was there. He was cleaning the floor with a small brush.

"Stop it right there for a moment."

The frozen image on the screen displayed the text:

12/29/2005
The fucker got me
My name is ■■■■ ■■■■■■■
I won't get out of here alive
Notify my family
03 - ■■■■■■■.

"It must have been left there by the person imprisoned in the cage. The one whose teeth he later worked on and then torched upstairs in the apartment. Forget him for now; he's of no interest to us. He was just someone 10483 killed. There's no point in trying to identify him now. Keep going."

Rotem's nose was almost pressed to the screen.

"You're in the way."

She moved back a little and the video continued. They all watched the team member use a small digital camera to take a few pictures of the text on the floor.

"Did you find that camera?" Avner asked, pointing at the screen.

"Yes, in a million pieces. Like everything else. All we have is what you're seeing right now."

The team member on the screen finished documenting the text

on the floor and left the cage. He looked around the basement and his camera momentarily caught the beam from the head-mounted flashlight of a second team member who was focusing on a large dinner table and then turned to record cabinets filled with equipment and some kind of electrical panel that probably served to operate the systems in the basement.

"Go back!" Rotem exclaimed. "Replay the second that shows the table frame by frame. Try to make the images as sharp as possible."

The images appeared one after the other in a slideshow fashion—the dusty utensils on the table, the body of a woman draped in a dusty robe with a yellowed IV tube fixed to her skin at one end of the table, the body of a man also hooked up to an IV tube at the other end of the table.

"Stop! Back again for a moment."

The images jumped in reverse.

"See it? The IV tubes are connected to a large tank there in the back. He kept them alive and tied to the chairs for a very long time! He's one sick bastard. Avner, this is what he described on that page he left for you on the table after grabbing Efrat."

Rotem paced the room. "Fucking sadist," she muttered. "The scene's been configured to resemble that painting, whatsitsname, *The Last Supper*."

Avner leaned forward in his chair and stared at the frozen image on the screen.

"He kept them tied to the chairs like that for two months."

Avner didn't dare think about what might be happening to Efrat at that very moment. He tried to focus on the task of finding 10483. Three days had passed since Efrat's abduction, and they still didn't know where he was holding her or if she was even alive. Maybe he decided not to waste time by holding Efrat and Amiram somewhere? Maybe Amiram tried to resist and he shot them both? Maybe Efrat tried to escape and he killed her? The thoughts gnawed at him. Maybe a quick death is better than prolonged torture?

Rotem returned to the desk she was sitting at earlier and quickly scribbled a few notes on one of the pages of the book she'd left there. "We have to get him," she said to no one in particular.

The video continued for another minute with the only sound the team members' heavy breathing. Then a metallic buzzing noise, the camera turns upward to catch something moving along the ceiling, a dash for the ladder back upstairs, and then more static and snow without sound.

They all sat there speechless for a full minute until the visitor who'd come with the video broke the silence. "That's it," he said. "That's all there is. I'll leave this copy here for you. I've sent the only other copy to the inner circle. I'm out of here."

Rotem got up again. "You can see that he triggered the blast by remote control," she said. "It wasn't a booby trap, like something they stepped on or a motion sensor. He had a camera on them all the time they were there, and he moved it deliberately just before deciding to press the button."

"Why?"

"So they'd know they were about to die. I'm guessing he recorded it and now takes pleasure in watching the team scrambling for the ladder to get the hell out of there. Death porn."

I wake up with a sense of foreboding.

I poke my head out from under the woolen blanket, look around, and remember that I'm in a cabin on the mountain.

I hear soft footsteps outside in the snow, that soft crunching sound you hear when shoes or boots sink into deep fresh snow. I open my eyes and look around and remember that I'm sleeping with her in the cabin on the mountain. The rays of the rising sun are already coming through the foggy window and I gaze at the four square panes of glass fixed to the wooden cross.

His face suddenly appears for a split second behind the glass.

A tremor runs through me and I immediately sit up in bed, my eyes searching for the ax. It's resting alongside the pile of logs near the door and I move quickly to retrieve it before he has time to come crashing through the cabin door.

The girl is still asleep in the bed. Her name was on the tip of my tongue, but it's gone again. It eludes me all the time. I have the ax in one hand, and I use the other to cover her with the blanket completely so that he won't see her if he manages to get past me.

It's quiet outside.

I release the latch and open the door. Sunlight fills the cabin.

There's no one out there.

I go out and walk around the cabin. He isn't there. I can see tracks in the snow, but they're wolf paw prints not human feet.

The clouds have dispersed; the sky is a clear shade of blue and a bright and cold sun is rising. The snow reflects the light and blinds me.

I look down and see that the circles in the snow have disappeared. The snow that fell during the night has covered them completely. I hear something behind me and turn around to see her standing in the doorway of the cabin in her socks.

"There were wolves during the night," she says.

"Yes, I saw their tracks around the cabin. The circles in the snow down there have vanished completely."

"It's okay. I recorded their position and the distance to their center in my notebook. Let's make breakfast."

"What would you like to eat?"

"Anything's fine."

I look through the contents of the cupboard again, take out a pot, fill it with snow and place it on the stovetop. The fire in the oven burned out during the night and I refill it with logs and set them ablaze. I fry some corn from a tin in a pan while the water boils, and then add some rice, oil, and salt to the pot. When the rice is ready, I throw in the fried corn and dish up a bowl for each of us.

We sit on the bed and eat in silence. When we're done, I clean the dishes off in the snow outside and put them back in their place in the cupboard. I also fold the sheets and blankets and return them to their shelf. Despite the snow on the ground, the sun is warm now and we're wearing tank tops, long pants, and boots.

She hands me a tube of SPF 50 sunscreen she pulls out of her bag. "Put some on here, too," she says, pointing at the nostril area of my nose, under my chin, and my armpits. "The snow reflects the rays and you'll get sunburned from below."

She takes two pairs of sunglasses out of her bag and hands one to me. "Look after your eyes. Don't take off the glasses. The reflection from the snow is blinding."

We tie our jackets and long-sleeve shirts to our bags and begin our descent. From time to time, she checks our course with her compass and shines her laser beam back at the top of the mountain to see how much distance we've covered.

After walking for two hours, she stops and checks our position and the distance once more.

"We're close. We need to be careful."

She retrieves a packet of marbles from her bag and throws one onto the snow a fair distance ahead of us. Nothing happens. We go in the same manner. She continues to throw a single marble in the direction we are heading, and we keep moving forward—until the last marble she throws hits the ground and dozens of pointed black spines spring through the snow to form a spiny dome of sorts before slowly disappearing again below the surface a minute later.

"It's here."

She signals for me to stay where I am and walks around the circle of spines. Every time they disappear below the surface, she remains at a safe distance and throws another marble, causing them to spring out again. She continues to do so until she's walked around the spines several times.

She comes back to me and gestures for me to bend down. I drop to my knees in the snow in front of her. We're the same height now. She brings her face close to mine and I think for a moment that she wants to kiss me; but she touches her forehead to mine and we remain like that for a few seconds. She then backs away a little and smiles for the first time. "It'll be okay," she says. "You can do it. Put on a long shirt and a jacket. You may be cold there."

I untie the items that are attached to my bag and put them on. I put the bag on my back again and tighten the straps.

She leads me by the hand to a certain point. "Raise your arms to the side," she says. "A little higher. That's it. Just like that. Now start walking slowly forward. Ignore the spines that are going to spring up right next to you. When the spines retract, walk ahead at their pace until you run into something buried in the snow. Clean the snow away and you will see that it's a black rock of sorts with the impression of a hand on it. Place your hand on it and the passageway will open."

"You're not coming with me?"

"I can't. I don't belong there."

"See you," I say and start to move forward.

"Bye."

The sharpened black metal rods shoot up all around me but they don't touch me. They start to slide back down and I move ahead at the same pace. I bump into something, bend down, and clear away the snow. A smooth black rock. And on it the impression of a hand. I place my hand on the rock and it slides away to reveal a long staircase. I turn around and wave good-bye to the girl whose name I don't recall. She waves back, turns, and walks away. I walk down a few steps, the rock slides back into place, and I'm enveloped in total darkness. I take a small flashlight out of my bag, switch it on, and begin to descend.

December 7, 2016

Carmit got out of bed and joined Guy, who was already in the kitchen.

"Coffee?"

"Yes, please. I need to wake up."

"You were talking in your sleep."

"Really?"

"Mumbling something unintelligible, but I caught the word, 'wolves.'"

"I had a strange dream. Have you seen my bag? The small one. The one I use as a carry-on."

"In the laundry closet. Upstairs. For your trip the day after tomorrow?"

"Yes. China for two weeks and then I'm hoping for an extended break."

She thought it best to refrain from saying a word about Israel. She didn't want to worry him. They sat in the kitchen and chatted and she drifted into the parallel universe in which she functioned and lived—the universe in which the end-of-the-year ceremony for Taylor's judo class and Emily's math grade and the shipment of books that were due to be delivered to the store that day were the significant issues on her agenda.

I approach a large parking lot. The wheels of my RV leave tracks along the dusty road, raising orange-red clouds of dust in their wake. It's quiet here early in the morning and there are no other vehicles around. I pass the sign that reads:

> Welcome to Niagara Falls. Attention! The site's management disclaims all responsibility for any injury or harm—physical, respiratory, or other—suffered as a result of your visit to the falls. You enter the site at your own risk. Entry for pregnant women and individuals with asthma or other respiratory disorders is strictly prohibited. We encourage you not to leave valuables in your vehicles. The site's management disclaims all responsibility for thefts from vehicles in the parking lot. We wish you a pleasant visit.

The lot is empty for the most part, and I park the RV in the section near the entrance to the site. I walk in the direction of the falls. My boots kick up dust. I pass a group of children covered in a gray film of dust. They are jumping around and laughing in an area where the dust has collected into a thick layer of powder.

The noise increases the closer I get to the falls and I reach the point where you can lean over the safety railing and look out. Sand comes pouring down from above and crashes loudly into the sand lake at the bottom, continuing downstream from there in the form of a yellowish-orange river of sand. I watch as a blackened tree trunk is swept along and comes crashing down the falls, only to be dragged farther downstream in the current of the sand river. The spray of dust rises skyward in the form of large clouds, before slowly drifting back down to the ground and covering everything in the vicinity. A maintenance vehicle fitted with a scoop passes by and collects a layer of dust that it then dumps back into the flowing sand. I walk a little farther ahead through the powder until I get to a point where I can touch the sand river. I dip my hand in and the sand flows over it. It's very cold.

03/11/2016—*Morning, 13 weeks since waking*

I wake early in the morning, fold up my sleeping bag and tent, and head north in the RV along Highway 25 in Colombia. I drive without stopping to fill up with gas, using the fuel in the jerrycans that I filled ahead of time instead. After passing through Bogotá, I head north-west in the direction of Medellín, from where I plan to cross the border into Panama, and then go from there to Costa Rica, Nicaragua, Honduras, Guatemala, and Mexico. I've already covered 40 percent of the journey to San Diego. I listen to a radio interview with a local candidate in the municipal elections and eat some strange green fruit that I bought from someone on the side of the road. They look like pears but taste like a mixture of a mango and a guava.

The road I'm following is very quiet. Mine is the only vehicle on it right now. I spot a patrol car blocking the road up ahead, and the 2 policemen standing next to it signal me to pull over. I move onto the shoulder and stop. One of the policemen tells me to remain with him outside the vehicle. While he checks my passport, my international driver's license, and the vehicle's papers, his partner goes into the RV and emerges a few minutes later with 2 boxes. One contains several bottles of whiskey and the other is half-filled with packs of Marlboro. I'm already running low on whiskey and cigarettes after sharing my stock with policemen, customs officials, border authorities, and vehicle testers at the Bolivian, Peruvian, and Colombian border crossings. And sometimes the whiskey and cigarettes weren't enough and I had to hand out several $100 bills to speed things up.

"We're confiscating these."

"Why?"

"These are commercial quantities of alcohol and cigarettes and you don't have a trading permit."

"Perhaps I do. You didn't ask."

One of the policemen stands next to me. "Would you like to spend some time in a Colombian prison or continue traveling?" he asks.

The clasp on his hip holster is open and his weapon isn't secured in its pouch. If I reach out and grab it, I can shoot them both in the head before they realize why Oscar Salstrom, a supposedly peace-loving Swedish citizen, is now resorting to violence and the use of firearms. I can also tell them that hidden inside the vehicle is another box, and we can all go in together to find it. On the way in, I'll pull down on the metal ring that's attached to the grenades and then back away. By the time they turn around and follow me out, the grenades will explode. I reject both courses of action. My mission is of paramount concern. I'm not there to educate Colombian police officers.

"Keep up the excellent work. Let's hear it for the Colombian Police," I respond.

One of them steps into the RV for a 2nd look around. The noise coming from inside the vehicle seems to indicate that he's riffling through the drawers and cupboards and tipping out their contents. He emerges again without my money or passports or gun. It's a good thing he didn't find them.

The policemen decide to make do with what they've got and they walk back to their patrol car and drive away. I tidy the mess in the RV and continue heading toward the border with Panama. I'll take a break a little later to use the bathroom, have a coffee, and get something to eat. I'm very hungry The green fruit did little to satisfy me.

The maintenance section of the Russian-language instruction manual stipulates that the warhead's power supply must be replaced every 18 months. There's also a diagram that walks you through the process. The battery—long and rectangular, with a capacity of 12 volts—is not a standard model. I'll have to disassemble the battery and replace it with an American 110V AC to 12V DC power adapter. It shouldn't be too complicated but will require leaving the warhead somewhat in pieces and connected to an external power cord. A regular 12V battery won't fit inside.

- Remember to buy a power adapter in the U.S.
- Stock up on Marlboro + whiskey this evening

I reread the introduction that appears in the warhead's instruction manual and review the list of models that preceded the model in my possession, then I search the Internet for information on Russia's latest warheads. After drawing up a table that includes several models, I use a marker to highlight the capabilities of my warhead. It's relatively old and there are models today that are far more efficient and powerful.

The initials RDS, *РДС* in Cyrillic script, stand for *Реактивный Двигатель Специальный,* or Special Jet Engine, and the Russians used this term as a codename for their nuclear bombs in an effort to confuse the Americans—without any real success. The instruction manual I have includes information on the older models, but the Internet offers very little information on the newer ones, aside from the types of missiles the particular warhead can be fitted to and their respective ranges.

Type	Weight	Filling	Yield	Produced	Direct Impact	Comments
Little Boy	4.4 Ton	Uranium-235	15 Kiloton	1945	66,000 Dead	Used at Hiroshima. (Base unit, USA)
RDS-1	4.6 Ton	Plutonium	22 Kiloton	1949	1.7 Rate = ~111,000 Dead	Первая молния
RDS-4	1.2 Ton	Plutonium-239	42 Kiloton	1953	3.3 Rate = ~218,000 Dead	Татьяна
RDS-37	???	Uranium-238 core, Lithium-6	1,600 Kiloton	1955	123 Rate = ~8,123,000 Dead	Two-stage bomb
RDS-9I	135 Kilo	Plutonium-239	28 Kiloton	1958	2.15 Rate = ~142,000 Dead	**My warhead**
8F675 (Mod2)	7 Ton	???	20,000 Kiloton	1966	1,537 Rate = ~101,537,500 Dead	R-36M2 / SS-18 Satan
W54	23 Kilo	???	10 to 600 Ton	1961	0.046 Rate = ~3,000 Dead	Suitcase nuclear device (USA)

A hydrogen bomb is modeled on the Teller-Ulam design, which, in essence, is a combination of nuclear fission and fusion in a single warhead. A powerful fission bomb is used to ignite fusion reactions around a plutonium core, thereby causing the buildup of a large quantity of X-ray photons inside the warheads' tightly sealed casing, which is filled with polystyrene. The polystyrene turns into plasma, the plasma compresses the 2ndary material, Lithium-6 usually, and the plutonium trigger within begins a process of nuclear fusion, causing a chain reaction, and the fusion of the Lithium-6 becomes tritium that bonds with deuterium to form Helium-4, a single neutron and energy of 17.59 electron volts. Matter that turns into energy. It's interesting to see how a material with similar characteristics to cooking salt can cause a blast hundreds of times more powerful than a single-stage atomic bomb.

My warhead is a transition model between the old ones and tactical nuclear weapons for medium-range missiles. It doesn't weigh tons like the initial American- and Russian-made bombs, but neither is it elegant like the United States' more recent tactical artillery shells or their suitcase nuclear devices that were manufactured in the early 1960s.

It isn't as powerful as a hydrogen bomb either.

It'll still satisfy my needs.

03/19/2016—*Morning, 14 weeks and 1 day since waking*

I pull off the road west of Tijuana and park the RV on the shores of Presea El Carrizo, a high-lying lake surrounded by mountains. I'll be crossing the border into the United States this evening and I need to ready the vehicle for the drive. I remove the ceiling panel and dismantle the grenades, securing them again with strips of duct tape before placing them in a plastic bag. I throw in the pistol, the extra magazine, and the bullets and toss it all into the lake. After crossing the border into Mexico, I retrieved the pistol from behind the microwave oven and slept with it every night, laying out my sleeping bag in a spot from which I could keep watch over both the tent and the RV. The tent served as bait in the event of an attempt by someone to attack me or steal the RV like that guy with the severe fire allergy. Already on my 2nd night in Mexico, a group of 3 young men fired a few rounds into the tent and tried to steal the vehicle. I shot all 3 of them while they were standing beside the RV and trying to figure out how to restart the vehicle after it cut out on them a few seconds after their 1st attempt, and then I ate the tasty cornbread that I found in one of their bags with the spicy red salsa I had in the RV's refrigerator. Mexican food is delicious.

I throw the lead apron into the lake, too, and it sinks below the surface in no time at all. I can't risk being questioned at the border. I make a neat pile out of all the equipment I purchased and have been storing in the RV and on its roof. I fill the RV's gas tank to the brim with fuel from the jerrycans and then pour the remainder on the pile of equipment and set it on fire. The RV looks neglected and dirty and I give it a good scrub down with water from the lake and dishwashing detergent. It looks as good as new by the time I'm done. I clean the inside, too, getting rid of all food and drink aside from a single bottle of water that I leave in the refrigerator. Everything else goes into the bonfire, including the leftover whiskey and cigarettes. They won't do me any good at the U.S. border.

The only things I don't burn are the Russian-language instruction manuals for the warhead. I wrap them in several plastic bags and bury them in the ground on the shore of the reservoir, close to where I was standing when I threw the lead apron into the water. I hang on to the operation manual only.

Among the passports I have is an American one. I thought initially that I'd use it to enter the United States, but I don't know if they've run any checks on it over the past 9 years and it may be invalid by now. Furthermore, my English isn't American English, and that, too, could arouse suspicion at the border—not to mention the hassle of the paperwork that would be required to transfer the vehicle into the name of the individual listed in the American passport. I'll stick with the Swedish passport and use it to cross the border.

I fold up the tent and sleeping bag and pack them away in the RV. I then take a shower and put on clean clothes, turn on the fuel pump switch, get into the vehicle, and drive to the border crossing.

On reaching the border, I head for the multilane crossing point and make my way to the zone for foreign passport holders. I drive to a station where they examine my passport. A border guard asks me to place the 4 fingers of my right hand on the fingerprint reader. And then my right thumb. And then to do the same with my left hand. And then to look into the camera. "How long do you plan to stay in the United States?" he asks.

"3 or 4 months, sir," I respond. "I'm making my way through the Americas, from my starting point in Bolivia and all the way up into northern Canada."

"Do you have sufficient funds to be in the United States for 4 months?"

"Yes, sir. I have $7,500 in cash and that should be plenty because I sleep in the RV and don't have to pay for hotels. I'm an outdoor kinda traveler, not a shopping mall one. My plans over the coming days include a drive through the Colorado River Reserve toward the Grand Canyon. And then I'll continue north from there."

"Your passport is worn out. I suggest you renew it."

"Yes, sir. I'll get a new passport when I return to Sweden in a few months' time. This one really has been through the mill."

"You have no plans to leave your vehicle in the United States on a permanent basis, correct?"

"That's correct, sir. I'll be selling it in Canada at the end of my trip."

"Move on to the vehicle inspection station," he says, pointing in the relevant direction.

My RV undergoes a comprehensive inspection. They go over it from top to bottom, opening every storage compartment and using a sniffer dog to scan the interior for signs of drugs. The border guard grimaces when he opens the compartment on the side of the RV where the sewage extraction pipe is stored, and he quickly shuts it again. A 2nd officer examines the vehicle's registration papers. "I have to replace that sewage pipe," I say. "It ruptured somewhere in Bolivia and I haven't been able to find a suitable replacement anywhere. I can finally deal with it now that I'm here."

The border guard doesn't respond. He enters some data into his terminal and hands back the registration papers and my passport. "You're clear to go, Mr. Salstrom," he says.

"Thank you, sir."

I get back into the RV and begin the long drive ahead to McLean, Virginia. I'm currently on the West Coast and need to get to the East. To do it in one shot, without stopping, would take 38 hours. I'm planning on a week of driving, with stops and rest along the way.

I pull over at a rest stop along the I-8 East at noon. I fill up the RV and go to a Starbucks for a chicken and smoked bacon sandwich. While eating my meal with a large glass of orange juice, I compile a list:

1. 2 white porcelain vases
2. Plastic flowers
3. Box cutter

4. Band-Aids
5. Duct tape
6. Hammer
7. Nails
8. Wood saw
9. Hacksaw
10. Screws
11. Chargeable power screwdriver
12. 2 strong wooden boards measuring 2×1 meters
13. 8 wooden beams—2 meters in length each
14. 6 metal rods—2 meters in length each
15. Silicone sealant
16. Roll of heavy duty nylon sheeting
17. Rubber gloves
18. Box of matches
19. 2 large jacks
20. Garbage disposal bags
21. 6 metal pulley wheels
22. Roll of metal strip
23. Food for breakfasts and dinners in the RV
24. Powerful vacuum cleaner with an operating switch that can be left in a fixed ON position
25. 110V AC to 24V DC power converter
26. Electrical adapter that can be screwed into a lightbulb socket and fitted with an electric outlet
27. Home UPS system
28. Android phone with a $500 prepaid SIM card
29. Phone charger
30. Smart-house electrical system with one smart socket
31. Multi-outlet
32. Wire cutter
33. Electrical cable (2 meters)
34. Stepladder
35. Flashlight and batteries

36. Extension cord
37. Black marker
38. Lock (internal cylinder) for a door (confirm type when
    I have the key to the storage unit)

I spend the night in a trailer park again. The bumper sticker on the RV parked next to me reads: WE'RE BURNING THROUGH OUR CHILDREN'S INHERITANCE, and an elderly couple is sitting outside the vehicle. They're eating dinner and invite me to join them. They ask me questions about Sweden and I make up stories about my native land. When they ask where I'm going, I tell them I'm on a very important mission and would have to kill them if I were to say anything more.

The 3 of us laugh.

December 7, 2016

The buzz and a series of clicks informed Amiram and Efrat of the arrival of their daily meal. They'd been imprisoned in complete darkness for three days now. The metal bowl in their cage filled with dog kibble, and two bottles of mineral water dropped down. The food dispenser that was fixed to one of the cage's sides kicked into motion at the same time every day—they picked up on this during the first two days, when their cell phone batteries were still up and running. Once the batteries ran out, they had no light and no way of telling the time, or knowing whether it was day or night. Efrat didn't think she'd be able to hold out under such conditions for very long, in darkness, with the audio recording that played over and over again every five minutes on an endless loop.

> *You betrayed me, Amiram.*
> *Your husband betrayed me, Efrat.*
> *This is just the beginning.*
> *You're going to be here for a very long time.*
> *Remember, the cage is your home, keep it clean.*

"It's driving me crazy," Amiram sighed. They were sitting side by side with their backs against the bars. He hadn't told Efrat about the contents of the notebook. He didn't want to subject her to the same sense of despair that had befallen him. All he told her was that the man who had imprisoned them there was a rogue agent who wanted to exact revenge on the Organization through them, and that they needed to hold out until the Organization tracked him down and came to their rescue.

"Perhaps we can try to send a message out from here?" Efrat said as she fumbled around in the dark and picked up one of the empty water bottles on the floor. "If we can cut through this bottle and tear off a piece, maybe we can scratch a message onto the plastic and throw the piece into the toilet, and maybe it'll find its way to some-one who will read it?"

"We don't know where we are. We don't really have anything to write or anything to write with. And what are the chances of some-one poking around in the sewage and picking up a filthy piece of plastic? We have no choice. We have to wait. If he wanted to kill us, he wouldn't be giving us water and food in here. He'll show up at some point, and perhaps we'll be able to convince him to release us somehow."

He didn't really believe what he said.

December 9, 2016

- I don't think it's causing him much pain at all.

- I think you're right.

Lorenzo and Ricardo looked at Sharon Tuvian lying at their feet. His hands and feet were bound with zip ties that were fixed to hooks in the floor of their hotel room in Netanya. The hooks had been fixed in place the day before. Ricardo had positioned them such that whoever was tied to them would be lying in the pose that appears in that Da Vinci illustration. The other hotel guests paid no attention at all to the sound of the drilling when Ricardo screwed them into the floor—and that was a good thing. Because if by chance the fucker managed to spit out the rag in his mouth and scream, no one would really care much. And the fucker didn't scream. Didn't say a word. Either he was really, really stupid, or there was something that frightened him more than the twins standing over him. Ricardo had already extracted one of Tuvian's wisdom teeth without the use of an anesthetic. He had also relieved him of the small toe of his left foot without even a squeak from the man.

- If we chop off a few more toes, do you think you'll still be able to stand up straight?

- He's not going to answer. Perhaps he's mute. Do you think he's mute?

- No, I think he's just a quiet one.

- Perhaps he isn't answering because we're using the name he assumed here in Israel and not his original name? Maybe he'll answer if we call him Shariri? Doesn't that make sense?

- No, I don't think that's the issue.

- Tell me, Ricardo, I've been wanting to ask you something since the day we landed here.

- What?

- Why were you served your food before anyone else on the flight over?

- Because I ordered a vegetarian meal. I logged into the KLM website before the flight and requested a vegetarian meal.

- Yet you sat next to me yesterday and devoured a 500 gram medium-rare burger.

- One has nothing to do with the other. I order vegetarian meals on airplanes because the flight attendants serve them long before they get to you with their meal cart. That way I get to eat before everyone else, and everyone around me sees me doing so and gets pissed because they haven't been served yet. I chew noisily and swallow with gusto just to annoy them even more. Sometimes I request a kosher meal, or halal, or gluten-free. Whatever I feel like. As long as I get mine first.

- You're a sick man. Are you aware, Ricardo, that I traveled to Colombia a few months ago to sort a few things out?

- Yes, I heard you were there. You're a real man of the world wandering around like that in Nepal and Colombia. But I didn't hear anything about the reason for your trip.

- I had to kill some woman.

- So it was a business trip then?

- Yes, you could say so. I was reimbursed for my travel expenses.

- Who was she?

- Who cares? That's not what I wanted to tell you about. I wanted to tell you about the ants.

- Ants?

- Yes, there's a unique species of ant there, a very dangerous one.

- Where?

- In Colombia.

- What are they called?

- Who?

- The ants. Do they have a name? What type of ant?

- I have no idea. Just really big ants. Black ones.

- Too bad.

- Who gives a shit, Ricardo, if the fucking ants are called Black Chickloderma Ants or Booga Ants?

- It's important. Names aren't simply chosen randomly. They mean something.

- The important thing is what these ants do.

- Let's suppose you didn't have a name. What would I call you? Tall Man?

- I'd call you: Obsessive Man Who Won't Let It Go. That's what I'd call you.

- I'm simply making a case, for argument's sake, on the importance of a name. That's all. There's no need to make a big deal out of everything like a teenage girl who can't get her hair to look right before school. That's all.

- Okay, so do you want to hear about the ants?

- Yes, very much so. Those black ants—are they venomous?

- No, not at all. Yet they can still kill a man just like that—*Boom!*

- Were you tripping there on peyote or something?

- I'm telling you, Ricardo, these ants can kill a man in a minute. They have a unique method.

- What method?

- They rest quietly in a circle around their victim and keep an eye on him, patiently waiting for him to fall asleep.

- And then?

- And then all at once a thousand or so ants crawl into his mouth and nose to create a ball of ants in his throat, and he chokes to death.

- What?

- You heard me. By the time the person wakes up, he already has a black ball of ants stuck in his throat. They showed me a picture of it from an autopsy done on a local from the Florencia region, of the doctors pulling a black ball of ants out of his throat.

- But don't the ants die by doing that?

- Yes. Most of the ants in the victim's throat die, but they sacrifice themselves for the greater good, so that the others can eat. The ants can live off the body of a person or a lamb or a dog for an entire year. But they can't do the same to a horse or a cow. Their windpipes are too wide and the ants can't block them. With a person it's easier.

- I'd like to see that.

- No problem. I have a box full of these ants that I smuggled in from Colombia and I'm gonna set up a camera. When this asshole falls asleep here on the floor, we'll end up with one helluva movie. We'll be able to sell it to *National Geographic*.

Lorenzo left the hotel room and returned a minute later with a closed cardboard box in his arms. He placed the box on the floor and opened it, and hordes of black ants came crawling out. Instead of moving randomly around the room, they arranged themselves in a black circle around the figure of Shariri shackled to the floor.

- I don't believe it! Just like you said. Just look at those little bastards!

- I don't expect him to talk anyway. So at least we'll have a nice memento.

Lorenzo retrieved a tripod from his suitcase and positioned it in front of the man who was lying on the floor with a look of terror on his face. He mounted a video camera on the tripod and aimed it at Sharon Tuvian.

- I advise you not to fall asleep.

- That's it, the camera's ready. When he falls asleep and the ants move in, I'll start filming.

- Are you getting the full circle of ants in the frame? Don't cut out any of the circle. It's really beautiful.

- Yes, everything is set to go. You know what, I have about twenty hours of available recording time on the camera's memory card; let's go out for a nice plate of hummus on the promenade somewhere and the ants meanwhile can do their thing when he falls asleep. I slipped three sleeping pills into the water we gave him to drink earlier. He'll be snoring like a pig in no time. We can edit the movie afterward and sell it to *National Geographic*.

- Or maybe we should simply upload it to YouTube. And then his wife and kids can enjoy the show, too.

- Great idea. Remove the rag from his mouth so the ants can get in.

Lorenzo pulled the rag out of Sharon Tuvian's mouth, and both twins then turned to head for the door. The ants waited patiently. "I'll tell you everything you want to know," Tuvian started screaming. "Just get them the hell away from me!"

December 9, 2016

When Jing Feng opened his eyes and tried to get up from the arm-chair in his living room, he discovered that he wasn't able to. His hands and feet were bound tightly to the chair, and several loops of rope held his stomach firmly in place against the backrest. It was late at night, and Jing Feng tried to remember when and where he had fallen asleep. His mind was a foggy blur and he shook his head from side to side. He sensed movement in the living room and real-ized he wasn't alone.

"Zhè shì shuí?" he shouted.

A flashlight went on and lit up the face of a woman who was sitting on the carpet in front of him. The beam from the flashlight in the woman's hand moved away from her face and illuminated a white towel spread out on the home's wooden floor. Lying on the towel was a syringe containing a rosy liquid, an iPad connected to a set of reg-ular headphones with thin coiled cables, a pair of glasses, and an oxygen mask that was hooked up to a green metal canister, which looked like an oxygen tank, by means of a thin transparent tube. The flashlight's beam returned to the face of the woman in front of him.

"I hope I've mixed my materials well," the woman spoke. "I'd al-ready thrown away everything I used to have in my laboratory, and I was forced to visit a few different places to prepare this sauce. All my mice are gone, too, so I couldn't test the sauce first. You'll be my lab mouse now."

"Caroline?" Jing Feng recognized her voice.

She stood up, turned on the light in the living room, and then sat back down on the floor in front of the armchair with her legs crossed. He could now see the person he had only ever spoken with by phone. She was wearing long black jogging pants and a black sweatshirt with a hood, and she had black sneakers on her feet. On the floor beside the towel was a small backpack, and next to it he could see a plate of roasted cashew nuts and a glass of whiskey. "I took the liberty of visiting your kitchen," she said. "This Golden Irish is superb."

"What's going on? What are you doing here?"

"You sent me to carry out the transformations on Kazuo Shimizu."

"So what?"

"Kazuo strangled his daughter and committed suicide. Just like you, Kazuo was no saint, but his daughter had never done anything wrong. She appears in my dreams almost every night and tells me that I killed her—and she's right. I can't bring her back to life, but I can atone for what I did to her by doing what I'm about to do to you."

"The transformation was designed only to cause him to commit suicide. The file we sent you caused him to shoot himself."

"Don't waste your breath. I cracked the encryption and listened to everything." Carmit picked up the oxygen mask and approached the chair. "Don't worry. I'm not going to kill you." She placed the mask over Jing Feng's face. He shook his head to try and prevent her from doing so, but to no avail. She opened the tap on the green canister. "You'll be out soon and then I'll hook you up to my equipment. I'm going to break a record today."

Jing Feng squirmed in his chair and tried to break free from the ropes that bound him.

"What I'm about to perform on you now," Carmit said, "is one long transformation three times. We have the entire night ahead of us." Carmit picked up the syringe and stood in front of the chair. "Not the same transformation that Kazuo underwent. You'll be getting something I prepared especially for you. It's a phobia cocktail— claustrophobia, agoraphobia, arachnophobia. You'll be afraid of flying, of dogs, of heights, of dirt, of syringes, of ghosts, of clowns, of death, of solitude, of being a failure, of people, of snakes, and of goldfish."

The room spun around Jing Feng. Carmit injected him with the rosy solution and then used medical tape to stick his eyelids to his forehead so they'd remain open. She then fitted him with headphones and glasses for the transformation. To protect her own eyes, she put on a pair of sunglasses with dark orange lenses. Prodigy came booming through the earphones she inserted in her ears. She turned on her iPad and the transformation software's monitoring screens began displaying the parameters that kept track of the synchronization between the pulses of blue light that penetrated Jing Feng's brain through the windows of his eyes and the recording that was being fed into his brain through his ears. Carmit dripped a little water into Jing Feng's open eyes every few minutes to prevent them from drying out and went on eating her cashews and drinking her whiskey. When the transformations were done, she collected and folded her equipment and packed everything back into her bag. It was 4:30 in the morning and her flight was due to leave Shenzhen's Bao'an International Airport in two and a half hours. She still had to return her rental car to the agency at the airport before her flight.

Carmit untied the ropes and moved Jing Feng back to his bedroom. She put her bag on her back, jumped out the window she had climbed through earlier, and closed it behind her. She walked briskly away from the villa, leaving on the ground behind her the guard that she neutralized earlier before breaking in and keeping clear of areas illuminated by streetlights. Her rental car was where she'd left it a few blocks away. She got in and set off for the airport. She stopped on the side of the highway to throw out the syringes and the green canister with the oxygen mask still attached to it. She took off the gloves she was wearing and stuffed them into the pocket of her pants. She'd throw them away at the airport, in a trashcan in one of the toilet cubicles.

03/23/2016—*Morning, 14 weeks and 5 days since waking*

I wake up early in the morning, make myself an omelet sandwich in a bun and eat outside the RV. There's a cool breeze blowing and the trailer park is filled with the song of birds. The sun will be up soon. I get the RV ready and leave the trailer park.

The drive to McLean passes quickly. The roads and infrastructure here are good, and there are trailer parks and roadside diners everywhere. 5 days of driving gets me to a trailer park in the George Washington and Jefferson National Forests. I find a spot at the far end of the park and unload the tools, metal rods, lumber, and wooden boards I bought the day before at a large Sears store. I lay everything out on the nearby strip of tarmac, put on a pair of yellow rubber gloves, and begin dealing with the RV's shit tank. I carefully disassemble the tank and drag it out from under the vehicle. Fixed tightly in place above it is the warhead, which is now caked in a thick brown-black layer of waste. I position the 2 new jacks I purchased at Sears directly under the warhead, and I use them to support one of the wooden boards to which I've nailed planks along the sides to prevent the warhead from rolling off. I raise the jacks so that the wooden platform is right up against the warhead. I use the hacksaw to cut through the steel cables that are holding the warhead in place, leaving it loose and resting stably on the wooden board, and then I gradually lower the 2 jacks to a height that allows me to slowly maneuver the RV to the side. By the time I'm done maneuvering the RV, the warhead remains resting on the wooden platform on the 2 jacks, with the vehicle parked next to it. I use the metal rods I bought to construct a pyramid above the warhead; and with the new pulley wheels and metal strip I purchased, I lift the warhead above the wooden board, and it sways in the air and drips large brown clumps of waste onto the wooden platform underneath. I peel away one layer of the plastic sheeting and stuff the filthy wrapping into a garbage bag that I place to one side. I measure the exact dimensions of the warhead and construct a strong crate using one of the boards and the lumber I bought, reinforcing the structure with additional lengths of wood on all sides. After further strengthening my construction with several bands of metal, I place it under the swinging warhead, which I then cautiously lower inside the crate. I wash off all my equipment and leave it out to dry. I also hose down the strip of road around the RV with the pipe that serves to supply water to the vehicle. I shower and change clothes. I place the 2nd wooden board on top of the crate, nail it shut and leave it next to the RV. I open the tent, cut away its floor, and position it over the wooden crate to protect it from rain and prying eyes. I'm not worried about someone trying to steal the crate at night because it's way too heavy to be moved. I reattach the RV's waste tank and seal the holes and openings at the top with strips of duct tape. I prepare myself a dinner of mac and cheese and broccoli and go to bed early.

The following morning I hire a moving company to transport the crate from the trailer park straight to a long-term storage facility some 3 miles from the city of McLean. I tell them to send 4 guys because I have a crate that weighs 150 kilos; but when the truck arrives, only 2 sturdy Russians step out. They grip the sides of the crate and lift it onto their truck's hydraulic ramp, and then into the back of the vehicle. 2 American Russians lifting a Russian warhead. It amuses me.

I follow them in the RV and we drive to the long-term storage facility where I've reserved a 2-meter by 3-meter storage unit. When we get there, I meet with Chris Martinez, the facility's manager, and pay him upfront in cash for a year's worth of storage. I ask him if it would be okay for me to come back in a few days to leave the RV with him, too, and he says yes and takes an additional sum of money from me. I ask him if it would be okay for me to return once or twice at some point in the future to sort out the contents of the storage unit. He says of course, gives me a key to storage unit No. 24, my unit, and I open it. The 2 movers carry the crate I built inside. I thank them and give them 2 $50 bills as a tip. They smile and thank me. After they drive away and the storage facility manager returns to his office, I move all the tools and other items I bought at Sears into the unit and lock it. I'll return tomorrow to continue my work. I examine the cylinder and the locking mechanism of the storage unit's door. I'll buy a new cylinder tomorrow and replace the existing one. I get back into the RV, head down Clara Barton Parkway, and park across from Sycamore Island.

The Potomac River is flowing gently and several kayakers row past. I sit on a rock and gaze at the bare trees and running water. Leaves are scattered on the ground and a large turtle on the bank of the river lifts its head and looks around. The sun will be setting soon; and before I return to my hotel, I cast one last look at the building across the river that is home to the CIA's new headquarters.

I'm pleased to have storage unit No. 24. It's an excellent number.

Israel and the United States are similar countries but on a different scale. Both are security oriented democracies; and in both countries, members of the military and the defense establishment play leading roles in their country's decision-making processes. If I really want the Organization to suffer as much as possible, I need to kick-start the worst possible chain reaction; I need to proceed in a manner that will spark the most intense rage from among the powers that be in Washington. There's no point in detonating the warhead in New York, although the number of civilian fatalities would be much higher. Blowing up McLean, however, will produce the optimal effect. McLean is home to CIA headquarters and a large proportion of America's intelligence community lives in the area. They'll want revenge, and I will point them in the right direction. And that will force Israel to shut down the Organization.

The Pentagon is a 12-minute drive from here. Washington will definitely take a hit; but more importantly, there'll be very little left of the CIA's headquarters. A large part of the agency's headquarters sits deep underground and most of the structure is well protected by a thick layer of concrete, so I'll detonate the warhead at 11 a.m. Israel time, which is 4 a.m. Washington time. Everyone will be at home at that time, and most of the homes around here are made of wood.

I'm sitting in my storage unit and eating a bacon and cheese sandwich. In front of me is the disassembled crate, and the warhead is resting on the wooden board that served as its base. On a small wooden table I built a little earlier is the Operating Instructions manual that I didn't bury in Mexico. I kept the manual with me, I stuffed it between a pile of sports magazines in one of the RV's drawers. I loosen a few flat-headed screws and detach a circular metal plate from the side of the warhead.

I disconnect the battery, take it out, and examine it. There are no signs of corrosion. I position the stepladder and climb up to the light-bulb on the ceiling of the storage unit. With my flashlight gripped between my teeth I unscrew the hot bulb and replace it with an electrical adapter that's fitted with a lightbulb socket on the top and an electrical outlet on its side. I screw the lightbulb into the socket at the bottom of the adapter. The storage unit lights up again and I take the flashlight out of my mouth, turn it off, and put it in my pocket.

I connect an extension cord to the electrical socket and place a multi-outlet at the other end of the cord on the floor below. I plug in the UPS and then connect the UPS to the power converter. I remove the old battery connection that fits the warhead and I hook it up to the OUT side of the power converter I bought with 2 electrical wires. The UPS comes to life. The converter is working and its red LED light is on. I connect the converter to the warhead and a small green light appears on the nuclear device.

The Russian-language manual is next to me and I read through it carefully and adjust a set of switches to define a detonation height of 3.5 kilometers above the ground, although the ideal altitude is somewhat less. The warhead's barometric pressure sensors may not be particularly precise, so I give myself a safety margin. I turn on the switch that overrides the trigger mechanism that arms the warhead when launched on a missile. A small red light comes on next to the green one. The warhead is primed for action. I turn it on.

I move the bomb's power switch to the *активный* position and the green light goes off and another red one comes on in its place. Both red lights are on now, and the moment the warhead reaches an altitude of 3.5 kilometers, it will explode. I recall those movies in which people are on the hunt for secret codes to activate nuclear bombs. It's a whole lot simpler in reality.

I connect the smart-house electrical system to the UPS's 2nd outlet. To its 3rd outlet I connect the control unit for the system, and to the 4th outlet I connect the charger for the cell phone I purchased with a $500 prepaid SIM card. It will last me for a long time. I plug the vacuum cleaner into the smart electrical socket.

I build another crate around the warhead, this time making the frame from pieces of wood and using sheets of plastic to tightly seal the crate with the warhead inside. I run the warhead's power cord through a slit in the plastic, which I seal afterward. I then insert the end of the vacuum cleaner's suction hose through a 2nd hole in the plastic before sealing that with silicone, too. I move the vacuum cleaner's power switch to ON and nothing happens because the smart electrical socket is inactive.

When I choose to remotely activate the warhead, I'll access the smart-house electrical system in the storage unit via the Internet and activate the smart socket. With the power on, the vacuum cleaner will kick into action and suck out the air from the crate. Within a few seconds, the barometric pressure inside the crate will drop and the warhead will detonate.

I disconnect the suction hose from the side of the vacuum cleaner and use my phone to connect to the network I've set up with the help of my cellular device. I enter a password to access the smart-house system and turn on its electrical socket. The vacuum cleaner comes to life. The system is functioning. I turn it off remotely again with my phone and reconnect the suction hose to the vacuum cleaner.

I place the 2 porcelain vases I bought on either side of the crate with the warhead inside. I fill each one with plastic flowers and arrange them nicely. "O Lord, thou God to whom vengeance belongeth, thou God to whom vengeance belongeth, shine forth," I write in black marker on the sheet of plastic on the top of the crate. On the sheet of plastic on the side of the crate facing the door to the storage unit I write: "This is the beginning of your end." I make a cut on my wrist with the box cutter and decorate the plastic sides with drops of my blood. When I'm done, I cover the cut with a Band-Aid, scatter some dry leaves I've collected from outside around my work of art, and take a photo of it with my cell phone for the sake of posterity.

I replace the door's lock with the new one I bought, arrange my tools and the rest of my equipment along the wall of the storage unit farthest from the door, unscrew the lightbulb to prevent anyone from seeing a light on inside and trying to open the door to turn it off, step outside, and lock the door behind me. I call a cab and exit the long-term storage facility, leaving the RV parked in the complex's enclosed parking lot.

The cab arrives and I get in. The driver asks me where I need to go. "Dulles Airport in Washington," I instruct him.

On the way to the airport, I open the Lufthansa website and book a ticket from Washington to Tel Aviv via Frankfurt—LH419 from Dulles to Frankfurt and LH686 from Frankfurt to Tel Aviv. I'm still using my Swedish passport for now. I don't book separate flights, but a flight to Tel Aviv with a connection in Frankfurt. At some point I'll want the Americans to know I landed in Tel Aviv.

I add the Internet address of the smart electrical system in the warehouse to My Favorites and define the password in my iPhone's Safari browser. I check that a single click is enough to reach a point from which one more click will activate the bomb. I close the browser and the phone.

- How the hell were you able to smuggle all those deadly ants from Colombia to Israel?

- I didn't smuggle them.

- So where did you get them?

- From outside the hotel. I collected them yesterday when you went to buy the equipment.

- So they're just regular ants?

- Yep. Regular ants.

- So how did you get them to form a circle around him?

- I sprinkled grains of sugar in a circle on the floor. They simply came to feed. And that bit about the ball of ants is nothing but a figment of my imagination. There's no such thing.

- Nice! Come, grab the carpet from that side and we'll roll him up in it and tie the edges. Tell me, what was that business with his tooth and finger all about? We could have started right away with the ants and saved ourselves two hours.

- He would have sensed that something wasn't right. It would have been too easy. We had to go through a process with him. You have to follow the protocol. Without protocol, we're . . .

- Simply amateurs, yeah, yeah . . .

- Where should we dump him?

- In the Negev somewhere. We'll make a nice bonfire. By the time someone finds his remains, we'll be eating bagels in New York.

- Do you think he lied?

- No. He was too terrified. Uyuni, Bolivia. The bomb is there.

- Do you think they'll send us to Bolivia?

- Unfortunately yes.

- Shit. Another Third World country. I think we may have to forget about the bagels in New York. What do they eat in Bolivia? Tortillas?

- Maybe. We'll see when we get there.

- Have you sent the information back to Toronto?

- Yes.

- Along with the three names he gave us?

- Yes. I read them out to Herr Schmidt's personal assistant. I told her to write them down. Yasmin Li-Ang, Federico Lopez, and Bernard Strauss were the three who worked with him when he was still in Iran.

- Why didn't you inform Herr Schmidt himself?

- He was in a meeting. I didn't want to disturb him. He's a very busy man.

- Did you tell her that they looked for the bomb in Bolivia nine years ago and found nothing?

- Yep.

- What was the name of that place there?

- Uyuni.

- What kind of a name is Uyuni?

- A Bolivian name.

- And that's where the bomb is. Strange that they never removed it from there. Did you mention that to Herr Schmidt's assistant as well?

- For argument's sake, I . . .

- For God's sake, Lorenzo, forget it for now. We'll have plenty of time for arguments and discussions in Bolivia.

- We'll probably receive instructions to fly there soon. Count to ten and we'll get a call to say they've decided they need us there. I want a raise. Our contract doesn't say anything about having to work in places that don't have normal food.

- We don't have a contract.

- It's a metaphor.

- Come grab the end of this carpet and let's make our way to the service elevator, then straight to the car.

- It looks like a huge candy. I'm hungry. We should grab something on the way south.

- Where did you park? On minus two?

- Yes.

- Do you have the keys?

- It's a hotel room. It opens with a small plastic card.

- I'm talking about the car keys.

- Yes, I have them, Ricardo. You need to have a little more faith in people.

December 10, 2016

Jing Feng opened his eyes. He was lying in his bed and his head ached. His dream from the night before left him extremely troubled. There was a girl who tied him to a chair and put a gas mask over his face. There was even a bitter metallic taste in his mouth. He sat up in bed and looked at his wrists. There were rope marks on them, and a needle mark on the inside of his right arm. It wasn't a dream.

His bedroom window was closed and he felt confined. The walls seemed to be closing in on him. He went over to the window, opened it, and looked out. The shadows of the trees outside started creeping toward him. Everything looked alive and menacing. The trees' branches morphed into huge monster-like claws that inched toward his throat. The chirping of insects outside caused him to slam the window closed again. Maybe it's a snake he hears, rattling its tail? Maybe it's already inside? Maybe it got into the house while the window was open? Why did he open the window? What a terrible mistake.

Jing Feng bent down to see if there was a snake under his bed, but he found nothing except dust. Maybe he's allergic to dust? Maybe he's asthmatic? He's never been tested. Maybe he'll suffer an attack now from breathing in the dust under his bed. He could choke and die alone here in this room. He coughs loudly and clears his throat. He needs to get out of this filthy, germ-infested room. But outside is no better, maybe even a lot worse. Everything feels menacing. Everything's a threat.

Jing Feng shrinks down to the floor in one of the corners of the room, whimpering.

I make my way down the stairs. The steps feel like they go on forever. I sit down to rest every now and then, turning off my flashlight to save the batteries. I can't understand why I'm so tired. I'm usually in much better shape.

The lengthy descent comes to an abrupt stop and I stumble forward when the floor flattens out. I break my fall with my palms as my flashlight flies out of my hand and lands close to the wall of the tunnel.

I bend down to pick up the flashlight and notice an inscription in small letters. The letters are tiny. Like a very dense font on the page of a book. The inscription reads: COMMON CONSCIOUSNESS ZONE →, *with the arrow pointing toward the light in the distance, at the end of the tunnel I'm in. I notice that the inscription appears every ten centimeters along the entire length of the tunnel. You don't really notice it unless you bend down and really look. I look for more clues and inscriptions, but don't find any.*

I continue walking toward the light. The air around me gets warmer. I take off my coat and long-sleeve shirt and am left in just my tank top again. I also remove my boots and long pants and put on a pair of tight gym shorts and sneakers. My bag isn't big enough for me to stuff in all the clothes I've taken off, so I leave them in a pile at the opening of the tunnel, put the bag on my back, and start walking away.

The park is empty of people. I pass by a couple of abandoned structures that were once a restaurant and a bathroom and continue along the park's trails, crossing several small wooden bridges over dry streambeds. Swirls of dust rise up from the dry stretches of grass whenever a warm gust of wind blows over them. I know where I need to go. I don't know what's there, but I sense I'm heading in the right direction. I pass a large cemetery with fading and crumbling tombstones. Crosses made of wood and stone.

I leave the park and walk through an immense field of dry thorns until I get to a paved circular stone plaza with a dry fountain in its center. The area is surrounded by stone benches, and flat stones bearing inscriptions form a wide circle of text around the plaza. I walk around and read the text. There is one word on each stone.

We are entering a time of significant changes. Soon everything will come to an end. Soon everything will begin. A second, an hour, an eternity concentrated on the end of a pin.

I sit down on one of the benches. The stone is warm. I take my bag off my back and place it on the bench next to me. I wipe the sweat from my forehead, open the bag, and retrieve my transformation kit. I put on the glasses and headphones, fix the electrodes to my temples, and hook everything up to my iPad. I take out a syringe, tear open its sterile wrapping, draw up rosy solution from a small brown glass vial, and inject the solution into a vein on the inside of my thigh. I move my bag off the bench, lie down, and activate the transformation.

December 12, 2016

Carmit woke up and looked for the puncture mark on her thigh. The dream had been particularly real. Her lips were still dry and she was sweating.

The airplane's cabin lights were off and most of the passengers were fast asleep. She stretched, stood up, and went to the bathroom at the back of the plane. Afterward, she remained standing in the galley area and poured herself a cup of orange juice, followed by a cup of water, and then a cup of coffee. She took a large chocolate chip cookie from a tray in the galley, tore away its wrapper, and devoured it on the way back to her seat. She'd fallen asleep very quickly earlier, even before the aircraft took off from Beijing, and had missed dinner. *No great loss on an El Al flight,* she thought to herself.

She tried to remember when she was last in Israel. It was a long time ago. When she'd left the last time, her coworkers at the Organization were sure she was going back to school for another semester to complete her postgraduate degree in Germany, but she disappeared and went to live in London instead. Since then, she married and was now the mother of Emily and Taylor. So much time had passed and yet it seemed to her that she'd left Israel just yesterday.

She felt as if she was still in her dream. Her leg muscles were aching from the effort of the descent down all those stairs. She leaned forward and massaged her feet. The passenger to her right stared at her curiously.

"I can help you with that," he said.

"With what?"

"I'm good at massages."

"Massage your wife."

"I'm divorced."

"Your mother then."

At least Keiko was leaving her in peace for the time being.

They're surely going to question her at Ben Gurion Airport. They're going to want to know why a British citizen is arriving in Israel from China. Paranoid—the lot of them. She'll tell them she's a reporter for *National Geographic* and has come to Israel for a week to do a piece, including a series of photographs, on the burial sites of biblical figures in the Galilee region. She has a return ticket to the UK for the following week and has already reserved a hotel room. She made sure that she readily recalled the name that appeared in her passport and on her credit cards, *National Geographic* business cards, and driver's license—Megan Jenkins.

03/28/2016–15 weeks and 3 days since waking

I wake up about half an hour after takeoff. I thought I'd sleep for longer. The past few days were full of activities.

Since I have more money than I actually need for my plan, I treat myself to a Business Class seat on the flight back to Israel. My expenses in the United States turned out to be less than I thought, and the same goes for the bribe money I dished out in South and Central America. There are no crying babies in Business Class, and Internet access is included in the price of the ticket. I search through the Tel Aviv Municipality's Tenders page to find the name of the supplier of the city's trashcans and prepare a list:

1. 50 round metal trashcans (of the kind the municipality places along the sidewalks for the benefit of pedestrians)
2. Half a ton of potassium nitrate (chemical fertilizer)—10 50-kilo bags
3. 250 kilograms of sugar
4. 50 liters of gray acrylic paint
5. 50 kilograms of sulfur
6. 50 bags of cement, a mixing vessel, and a large tub
7. 100 kilograms of small nails
8. Blue overalls + printed logo
9. Closed vehicle—GMC van
10. Wedding ring (sized)
11. Fine-point purple marker
12. Box cutter
13. A 100-liter stainless steel professional cooking pot
14. 100 Sanwa Airtronics receivers for model aircraft
15. 100 digital servomotors

16. 100 small 1.5V lightbulbs (regular, not LED)
17. 100 1.5V AAA batteries
18. Roll of thin electrical cable
19. Sanwa Airtronics remote controller + batteries
20. 100 1.5V D batteries—Duracell
21. Appropriate tools for removing and installing trashcans
22. Soldering iron and accessories
23. Roll of metal strip, power drill, and screws
24. Strong epoxy adhesive—50 large boxes
25. Bolt cutters
26. Black piece of cardboard and adhesive tape
27. 6 webcams
28. Laptop + large monitor
29. Communications switch and several 20-meter lengths of communications cable
30. Cell phone with Internet package
31. 4-inch pipe
32. Toilet
33. Sewage pump
34. 20 large bags of dog food and 50 boxes of 1.5-liter bottles of mineral water
35. Colored sheets of paper
36. White envelopes + postage stamps for the United States
37. Air-conditioner extraction pipe
38. Soldering iron for electronic components + 3 spools of solder
39. Components for the food machine (prepare separate list)

The captain announces that we've reached our cruising altitude and the flight attendant hands out dinner menus. I order a classic lasagna with grilled vegetables and Alfredo sauce. I watch Tarantino's *Pulp Fiction* on my laptop while I eat. I get to the scene in which Vincent Vega plunges a syringe of Adrenalin straight into the heart of Mia Wallace. The scene is pleasing to the eye, although in reality a shot of epinephrine directly to the heart would come much later in the treatment. 1st you need to perform mouth-to-mouth resuscitation and cardiac massage; moreover, a shot like that directly to the heart is a controversial procedure that was discontinued several years before the movie hit the screens. It's better to administer Narcan intravenously. It finds its way to the heart within 30 seconds, assuming the heart is still beating. Since most drug addicts destroy their veins, the Narcan can be given in the form of an injection under the tongue that goes to work within a few minutes. In most cases, the patient isn't going to sit up immediately like Mia Wallace does. If you do choose to plunge the needle directly into the patient's heart, it's best to aim for the vein through which the blood is pumped into the heart and not the heart muscle itself, so the red circle drawn on Mia Wallace's chest and the angle at which the needle is plunged are off the mark.

I finish my dinner and watch to the end of the movie. Then I drink a glass of red wine, adjust my seat so that it turns into a bed, and go to sleep.

03/29/2016–15 weeks and 4 days since waking

I land at Ben Gurion Airport and take a taxi to my basement. The car belonging to the family living in my apartment is not in its parking spot, so I open the window and go inside. I put my bag on the *Last Supper* table and ready the basement for my final departure.

Before collecting all my money, passports, and paperwork and putting everything in my bag, I 1st make sure that the basement's cellular phone is connected to its charger and that the camera is hooked up to the network and functioning properly. I then pick up the last page of my notebook that I tore out before giving the rest of notebook to the Aharoni-Shamir law firm and put it in my bag. I say farewell to my work of art in the basement and take a photo of it as a memento with my cell phone. I think it's improved with age.

I check to ensure that the fuse wire running through the walls of the basement to the blocks of plastic explosive is connected properly to the detonators. I then connect the electronic detonators to the smart electrical outlet and the Wi-Fi network I've set up in the basement. I define a shortcut for it on my mobile. I now have 2 shortcuts defined in my iPhone's Safari browser. One is labeled: 203 Ibn Gvirol Street Blast, and the other reads: McLean Blast, so I don't get them mixed up.

I'll keep tabs on Amiram on the day I put my plan into action. He'll probably lead me to Avner's home. And Avner will then head off quickly to the Organization after reading what I've written in the notebook. I'm keeping the last page for Avner's home. I'll leave it there after I abduct his wife.

I pick up my bag and, for the last time, climb up the ladder from the basement into the bedroom closet of the family now living in my apartment. Before ascending, I disconnect the basement's water and ventilation systems and turn out the light. I leave the apartment through the rear window and head off.

I make my way down Ibn Gvirol, turn left onto Jabotinsky, and walk to Kikar Hamedina. I sit down there at a café and order a double espresso. The jetlag is taking its toll on me, but I want to hold out until the evening and sleep through the night so that I don't get stuck on U.S. time. I use my time at the café to charge my laptop and look for a van for sale. I find an ad for an old GMC Savana, a 1997 model, and agree on a price of NIS 8,500 with Reuven, its owner. The photographs on the Yad2 website show large stickers reading MASHANI—CARPET CLEANERS on both sides of the van. The stickers cover the vehicle's side windows, too. Excellent. I ask Reuven if he can pick me up in 2 hours on the corner of Ibn Gvirol outside building number 203, and then we can go together to the nearest post office to transfer the title of the vehicle. No problem, he says.

Still using the café's Wi-Fi I search through Yad2's property listings for a long-term rental, a stand-alone residence, in the Sharon region. I find a suitable house, a fair distance from its nearest neighbors, on Moshav Yanuv. I call the number listed in the ad and speak to Shlomit. She tells me her husband's been relocated for work and that they're looking for a long-term tenant. I tell her I've just returned from an extended stay abroad in the service of the state and am looking for a quiet place. I ask her if it's okay for me to pay them upfront in cash for a year and a half. "Absolutely," she says, "and you'll see it's very quiet here. When can you come see the house?" I make an arrangement with her for the following morning.

I close the laptop and put it back in its case, along with the charger. I leave the café and wander around the nearby shops for a while, looking for someone who resembles me both in appearance and age. After an hour or so I see someone who fits the bill; he's walking around one of the stores with his wife and I bump into him seemingly by chance, knocking him into a clothes rack and apologizing profusely for not paying attention to where I was going. The man's eyes narrow and he growls something at me. I turn and walk away in the direction of 203 Ibn Gvirol Street with his wallet.

Reuven picks me up on the street corner and we complete the

transfer of ownership for the vehicle at the post office on Dizengoff Street. There's a post office branch at 107 Ibn Gvirol, too, but there's no parking there—and 107 doesn't divide by 3 without a remainder. I pay the fee and the car is registered under the name that appears on my ID card, which is the one I produce from the wallet of Roman Morozov that I stole about an hour earlier. The wallet also contains a number of credit cards, a driver's license, a supermarket Customer Club card, and several family photos. The clerk at the post office tells me I look thinner in person than in the photographs. "Cameras don't flatter me," I respond.

Reuven asks me if I can drop him back at his office and I do so. I ask him on the way if he has a few old carpets he no longer needs and can sell to me for a nominal price. He says yes and I buy several shabby rugs from him and put them in the back of the van. I part ways with Reuven and drive to the beach in Herzliya, where I go for a swim in the sea and then take a shower in the municipal changing rooms. I dine later at a restaurant on the beach, surfing the Web while I eat and looking into Roman Morozov. His Facebook page tells me where he works and what he enjoys doing. It's useful information. I park later that night on one of the streets near the beach and carefully modify the ID card. I separate the pieces of plastic with the box cutter and replace Roman Morozov's photograph with one of me, using the fine-tipped purple marker afterward to complete the Interior Ministry seal over my image. I stick the card together again when I'm done and go to sleep in the back of my van.

"Listen up, friends. It's more than nine years down the line and we have some new information."

The group was seated around the same heavy table in Toronto. It was snowing outside and white flakes swirled in the wind on the other side of the window. Central heat warmed the offices and conference room.

"Our emissaries in Israel found Shariri there."

"And did he know about the bomb? Were the twins able to get the information out of him?"

"They got him to give up the names of three of the members of one of the squads that was looking for the bomb. Three scientists who were working with the Iranians for financial gain or ideological reasons, or both. We have yet to run background checks on each of them."

"Let's bring them here!" one of the individuals around the table blurted out.

"Too late. All three are dead. Yasmin Li-Ang was killed in her home in Switzerland, Federico Lopez was killed while running through the park in Bariloche, and Bernard Strauss was killed in his apartment here in Canada."

"Who killed them?"

"I don't know. The Americans maybe. Or the Russians. Or maybe the Israelis. There's no shortage of entities that wanted to prevent the bomb's location from falling into the hands of anyone at all."

"And can that person in Israel provide more details? Can they press him a little harder in their interrogation?"

"They did press him a little harder during the interrogation—and now he's dead."

"WHAT?" everyone around the table exclaimed at once.

"I didn't ask them to keep him alive after he gave them the details about the bomb. He saw their faces. In any event, I think they got all they could out of him. I don't think he left anything out."

"It's slipped through our fingers again."

"Not necessarily," Herr Schmidt continued. "We know exactly when the three were killed. Let's try to find out who killed them and we'll get to those responsible. Get your networks in Switzerland, Argentina, and Canada on it, and let's see if there was a group of people that entered those countries in the weeks before each assassination and then left. Use facial-recognition only; they may have used different passports every time. If we cross-reference the images, we should be able to ascertain who took them out and then we can track them down and take it from there."

"What about the location of the bomb? Did Shariri know its location?"

"He gave up the name of a place. Bolivia, Uyuni. I've instructed the twins to go there immediately. They're already on their way, but I'm not sure they'll find anything. I'm assuming the Iranians have already gone through the place with a fine-tooth comb and found nothing. One of the scientists may have spoken and the bomb may not be there any longer. We'll wait to see what the twins come up with in Bolivia, and we'll try meanwhile to find out who killed the scientists who were working with Iran. And from there, we can track the bomb until we get our hands on it."

One of the men around the table stroked his short beard. "If Shariri was aware of the location of the bomb before the Israelis abducted him," he said, "then why shouldn't the Iranians be in possession of it already?"

"The location is very general," Herr Schmidt said, linking his fingers. "The town of Uyuni in Bolivia is a small place surrounded by a vast desert and close to a salt lake. They may have dug and searched until they simply gave up; and now, many years later, they've decided to try again."

"They've decided to try again?"

"I have a strong feeling that the VAJA are the ones who made sure that this envelope with Shariri's address ended up in our hands. Someone there may be aware of our capabilities, and could be watching us now, following our every movement and waiting for the moment we get our hands on the bomb so they can take it from us. We have to act with extreme caution. I think that one of the scientists who was killed nine years ago knew something more precise about the location of the bomb. Something they decided only one of them should know before passing it on to the Iranians. Something that would keep the location of the bomb safe if the people involved were ever caught. All Shariri knew was the name of a country and the name of a town. That's not enough, and it probably wasn't enough for the Iranians either. I think that the team that tried to stop the bomb from getting to Iran and killed all those scientists nine years ago secured additional information but chose, for some reason, not to act on it until now. Perhaps the additional information itself wasn't enough to reveal the location. In any case, we must try. The twins are there; and if there's anyone who can find out what happened to that bomb, it's those two lunatics. As soon as we have the where-abouts of the bomb, we'll smuggle it to Moscow and detonate it near the Kremlin, with regards from the United States."

The transformation ends long before I wake up on the stone bench. My head aches and my throat is dry. I retrieve a bottle of warm water from my bag and drink.

I notice that I'm no longer alone. He's standing next to the fountain. Bone-dry earlier, the fountain is now filled with water.

I'm still hooked up to the transformation equipment. As I disconnect myself, I sit up on the bench and notice that he's looking into the water. I continue to repack the equipment in my bag, sitting on the warm stone bench.

"It's cold here," he says.

His voice makes me jump. He sits on the bench next to me.

"It's very hot," I consent.

We talk, and then he stands up and leaves. "We'll meet again," he says as he walks away.

I go over to the fountain that starts working again and fills with water. I peer in and see a blurred image. A boy is lying in bed with electrodes attached to his head and glasses over his eyes. A woman is on the carpet near the bed. She's looking at a computer screen. It's hard to see what's on the screen. The image is blurred and indistinct.

The bed is big and the boy is small. I keep my eyes on the water and the image comes to life. The woman stands up, strokes the boy's forehead, and says something to him. She disconnects the electrodes and removes the glasses from the boy's face. She also removes a set of earphones from his ears. His eyes are open but he doesn't respond. She bends over him and blocks my line of sight, and when she straightens up again the boy's eyes are closed. She puts everything into a backpack and leaves. I don't see where she goes. The image remains focused on the sleeping boy and then fades a few seconds later.

I notice that I'm aware of the fact that I'm dreaming. It happens to me sometimes in a dream. I know we will meet again in a dream. He attracts and repels me at the same time, like two magnets whose attraction and repulsion fields exist in parallel. I feel it when he walks by me and moves farther away.

I feel like I'm going to throw up.

I sit down on the warm stone bench again and close my eyes for a moment, waiting for the sensation to pass.

I look up to see that he's far away now, a mere speck on the dusty horizon.

I get up and follow him.

December 13, 2016

Carmit checked the time on the screen on the back of the seat in front of her. It was good that she'd managed to fall asleep again for another three hours or so. The plane was nearing Tel Aviv and the flight crew had turned on the cabin lights and was busy with its preparations for landing. Carmit retrieved her passport from the seat pocket in front of her and put it in her own pocket.

The hotel reservation she displayed for the Border Control officials was for The Scots Hotel in Tiberias, but she wasn't really going there. Instead, she asked the taxi driver to take her to the David InterContinental Hotel in Tel Aviv. It felt weird to be speaking Hebrew again after so many years. She'd even picked up a British accent.

It felt so strange to be seeing the sights and breathing in the odors of the country. She'd left Guy and the children in London, telling them it was just another business trip. Her last perhaps. Guy made that face that seemed to say: "Yes, yes, we've heard that one before," and Emily and Taylor asked her what she was going to bring them from China. "Maybe a Samurai sword?" Taylor asked excitedly. And she explained to him that the Samurais were from Japan not China. "But I promise to bring you something nice from China," she said. Taylor insisted on a sword and Carmit explained that getting on an airplane with a sword would be a problem.

She smiled now as she recalled the conversation.

Perhaps she should simply go to the Organization's home base and knock on the door. Now that would be a big surprise. But it's too dangerous. The things she knows are a threat to the Organization. Even though they're using—or used to use—her services abroad. She was sure they'd like to get their hands on her just to make sure that her knowledge and history with the Organization never gets out. They obviously trust her; but what if someone were to exploit her

155

family in an effort to get her to divulge secrets? Would she sell out the Organization in return for the lives of her children?

Of course she would.

She needs to contact them securely. Only after ensuring that everything she knows will be made public if they don't allow her to leave.

Maybe she doesn't need them at all. Maybe she can find him on her own? That agent on whom she performed the three transformations. The agent who killed so many people in three different countries. If he's alive, she needs to speak to him; and if he's dead, she'll visit his grave.

She hoped he was still alive. She had more than enough dead people on her conscience. Now she was trying to fix whatever she could. The Organization used her to get him to do terrible things, and it's time for them to settle the bill.

The taxi reached the hotel after a long drive through the Tel Aviv traffic. "Fucking light rail," the cab driver cursed. "They all took bribes and now we're going to have to eat shit with these traffic jams for the next ten years. Country of thieves." And all of a sudden, Carmit felt at home. She smiled at the driver. "Too true, they're all thieves," she said.

She went up to her hotel room, put down her small suitcase, undressed quickly, and got into the bath. She filled it to the brim with hot water and a fragrant bubble bath and lay submerged in the tub with her eyes closed, allowing the surrounding warmth and silence to soothe her. She was alone again. Whenever she was away from her family, her dormant instincts as a field agent would come back to her. Every sound and sight sparked suspicion; everyone around her was a potential threat.

Carmit stepped out of the bath and dried herself. She tossed the towel onto the bathroom floor and walked into the bedroom and opened the curtains. Sunlight burst in and warmed her skin. The Mediterranean Sea lay stretched out before her, and she could see individuals and couples walking and jogging along the strip of beach below. It was a partly cloudy December day and the sun had just peeked through a gap in the layer of clouds above. She went over to the closet and removed two of its shelves, placing them upright on the floor of the wardrobe. She had another quick look at the closet from the outside. It looked good.

She dressed quickly, took her backpack, and left the hotel. She always felt naked without a weapon. Uneasy. A prickly sensation of sorts. She took a taxi to the Tel Aviv Port and wandered around the shops a little before stepping into a kitchenware store in the market.

"I need a knife," she said. "But a very sturdy and sharp one. With a ten-centimeter blade. Something that can easily cut through pumpkin, steaks, kohlrabi, yams, coconut. . . ."

"I got you," the store assistant interjected. "You need the very best in my arsenal. Take a look at this one." The assistant reached into a drawer behind him and pulled out a sharp knife, removing it from its protective sheath. "Be careful," he said as he handed the knife to Carmit. "It's sharp as hell."

She looked over the knife, gauged its weight in her hand, carefully ran her fingernail along the edge of the blade. Very sharp. A balanced handle-to-blade weight ratio. Carmit gripped the knife with both her thumbs pressed against the middle of the side of the blade and tried to bend it. It didn't budge. Very good.

"Are you a professional chef?"

"Not really, it's more of a hobby, but I've made it through now to the second round of auditions for *Master Chef* and I need a good knife. Do you know the show?"

"Of course I do. Good luck to you. Anything else?"

"You know what, I'll take another one just like it. So I have a spare."

"No problem."

"Do you keep superglue, too, perhaps? I guess I may as well get some now that I'm out."

"No, we don't. But go to Hangar 14 across the way there; there's a store there that sells it."

"Thanks."

Carmit went into the bathroom of the restaurant on the second floor of the market and took the knives out of their boxes, leaving only the protective plastic sheaths over the blades. She slipped them into her belt so that the blades in their plastic sheaths were in the front pockets of her jeans, with her long T-shirt covering them. With her backpack in its rightful place on her back again, she stepped outside and headed toward Hangar 14.

The sun was hiding now behind some thick clouds and a cool breeze was coming in from the sea. She could hear the clinking of wineglasses and the rattling of dishes from the open-air restaurants with their tables set out on the long stretch of deck that ran the entire length of the side of the port facing the sea. Someone was laughing. A baby was babbling. Carmit took a deep breath of sea air.

She felt great.

That prickly sensation was gone.

03/30/2016–15 weeks and 5 days since waking

"Nice to meet you—Roman."

I shake hands with Shlomit and Zvika. Shlomit smells pleasantly of perfume and Zvika gives off a faint odor of sweat. They live in a secluded house on Moshav Yanuv. The house has a large basement and there are no neighbors nearby, so no one will hear the renovations I'm planning. I tell them about my stint in Argentina on behalf of Israel Aerospace Industries. My family is still there and I'm visiting the company's offices in Israel, and I'm using the time to sort out the housing issue ahead of our return.

"After Buenos Aires, all we want is a quiet place," I tell them, showing them the photographs of the woman and children that I found in Roman Morozov's wallet. Zvika knows some Spanish from his trip to South America after the army and he's eager to practice the language a little. We speak some Spanish and he tells me he's been relocated to the United States for 3 years. I tell them that since I don't want to get involved with endless payments, I'll cover the rent for the full 3 years in 2 installments—half the money when we sign the contract and the other half in 18 months' time. I ask them how soon they can vacate the home and Shlomit says they're leaving in 3 months. I ask Zvika if he minds if I pay in dollars, which will probably suit them if they're heading to the United States. "I received a portion of my wages in cash and I converted it into dollars before coming to Israel," I explain.

Zvika is happy to get half the money upfront—and in dollars, too. I offer them an additional $10,000 if they vacate the home as soon as possible because my time in South America will be coming to an end soon and I want to arrange and tie up the housing issue during the course of my current visit. They agree to vacate the house in 2 weeks; meanwhile, they will arrange to have their possessions stored and will live temporarily with Shlomit's parents in Kfar Saba.

I sign the rental agreement that Zvika produces and pay him in cash on the spot.

For the 2 weeks I'm going to be homeless I purchase a short-term gym membership card so that I'll have somewhere to work out and shower. At night I sleep in the back of the van, and I spend my days picking up the items I still need to complete my shopping list. I buy the tools, webcams, blue overalls, roll of electrical wire, black piece of cardboard, adhesive tape, and bolt cutters at the Renanim Mall.

I order the servomotors, remote controller, and receivers from a store for model aircraft enthusiasts. I explain to the storeowner that I'm setting up a model aircraft club and expect to order additional equipment from him in the near future. I give him the address of the house where I'll be in 2 weeks' time and ask him to have everything delivered on April 14.

I go to South Tel Aviv to buy the lightbulbs and batteries at a wholesale electrical goods store, and I get the large cooking pot from a shop there that supplies kitchen equipment to restaurants. I visit a construction equipment store to purchase the small nails in 50 1-kilo packages. The vendor tells me I've cleared out his entire stock and wants to know why I need so many nails. I tell him that I'm an artist and plan to pour all the nails into a hollow cube of wood and then fill the hollow with a transparent epoxy glue—and then when I strip away the sides of the wooden cube, I'll be left with a transparent cube filled with tens of thousands of nails. "I'll call the piece, *Death in a Box*," I say to him, and the vendor looks at me and takes the cash I hand him for the nails, a soldering iron, and some other items I purchase there.

I order 50 trashcans from the municipality's supplier and give them the address of the house on Moshav Yanuv. "I need 50 trashcans just like the ones in Tel Aviv," I tell them. "I want to sell them to the communities in the Sharon region as a trial run. If it goes well, I'll be selling a lot more of them. Can you give me a special price?" I arrange for the cans to be delivered on April 14.

I purchase the sulfur in small quantities from various different chemical stores. I'm now a science teacher who's planning to conduct experiments in his class to examine chemical reactions with various materials. To avoid arousing suspicion I buy other materials aside from the sulfur.

At the supermarket I explain that I need 250 1-kilo bags of sugar for the cotton candy machine I use at birthday parties.

I don't have a story to tell when it comes to the potassium nitrate, which I steal from an agricultural warehouse in the south, on the road to Eilat. I cut through the lock at night and load 10 50-kilogram sacks into the van.

To keep the contents of the van that I'm driving around Tel Aviv and elsewhere hidden, I stick black pieces of cardboard on the inside of the vehicle's back and side windows to compensate for the semi-transparent MASHANI—CARPET CLEANERS stickers. I leave only the front windscreen free of black cardboard.

04/14/2016–17 weeks and 6 days since waking

Shlomit and Zvika's car pulls away and I wave good-bye to them. I have keys to the house now, and a series of phone calls to the various companies have left the electricity, property taxes, water, and gas accounts in my name—Roman Morozov. I ask the utility companies to send me bimonthly bills and tell them I will pay in person at the post office, politely refusing a direct debit arrangement or giving them my credit card number. "They always err in their favor," I say to Zvika when we make the arrangements. "I always check before I pay."

The items I've ordered will be arriving shortly. In addition to the model aircraft parts and the trashcans, I'm expecting deliveries of thick iron bars, sheets of metal, bags of cement, and various other building supplies. I don't have much time and I have lots to get done. I 1st go to get the van, which I parked farther down the street, so the couple wouldn't suspect anything. I move the van to the large front yard, pull up close to the front door, and transfer its contents into the home's empty living room. I carry everything inside and arrange it all in neat piles.

Shlomit and Zvika have left their old refrigerator in the house. They told me that if I didn't want it, I could give it to some charity or throw it away. I go back to the van to get the shopping I did that morning and I put everything in the fridge and the kitchen drawers. One of the shopping bags contains a small pot and a pan. I wash the pan and put it on the stove. I'll make myself an omelet and tomato sandwich in a short while.

The deliveries start to arrive one after the other. I carry the building supplies down to the basement, the trashcans go in the living room, and I leave the electronic equipment in one of the other empty rooms. I go to IKEA later in the afternoon to buy a chair, bed, and table. The store is only a few minutes away.

I install the cameras—5 on the outside of the house and 1 in the basement, which is focused on the area in which I will construct the new cage. I rest the additional cell phone I purchased in a spot that offers the best reception, before connecting it to its charger and turning it on. I use it to access the webcams, for which I also set up an internal home network. I run communication cables to the points at which the cameras are located outside, threading the cables through to the video devices through holes that I drill in the walls of the house. On the kitchen table I place a glass of water with 4 roses that I picked from the garden outside.

I install a large television screen on the wall facing the soon-to-be cage and plug it in.

I eat my lunch and then return to the basement to continue organizing all the materials and equipment I'll be using to construct the cage. In the evening I check the status of my bank account. Afterward I build a 150-piece jigsaw puzzle. I lay out all the pieces on the table and study them for an hour without touching any. I use my eyes to work out which pieces fit together, and only after putting the puzzle together in my head do I activate a stopwatch and quickly join all the pieces. It takes me 76 seconds to complete the puzzle.

December 14, 2016

Herr Schmidt sat in his office and reviewed the encrypted emails in his in-box with a look of satisfaction on his face. Two individuals had entered and left each time—before and after the assassination of the three scientists. But they hadn't arrived or left together. The man was first to arrive each time, and the woman then followed on a different flight and from a different location. A two-person team only. Highly efficient. If it was the Israelis, then they must have learned something from that fiasco of theirs when they burned a whole bunch of agents all at once, like meat at an Argentinian barbecue, just to kill a marginal Hamas figure. And if it was the Americans, then they'd have to take them a little more seriously from now on. *We'll know soon if it was the Israelis,* he said to himself.

He took a long look at the two images on his computer screen— one of 10483 before the series of operations he underwent some nine years ago, and the other of Carmit, nine years younger than today. The photographs were old but of good quality. There was no reason why he shouldn't be able to find them now, too. He needed to check first with his friends in Israel and the United States if the two had entered or left either country of late.

Herr Schmidt selected one of the speed dial buttons on his mobile and pressed it. A voice answered after three rings. "Hello, boss," it said.

"Ricardo. How are you two?"

"Waiting for instructions, boss. It's boring here."

"I'm sending you two images. These are the two agents who eliminated the Iranian cell working with Shariri. Find out if they've been there and what they were doing. Go from home to home in the town if you have to until you find something."

"Who do they work for?"

"We don't know yet. We're looking into it now."

"No problem, boss."

Herr Schmidt hung up and then called another number from the list of contacts in his mobile. "Hello?" said a woman's voice after a few rings.

"Lena, you're up. Check your mail," he said.

The call ended.

December 14, 2016

Leora Lipman was late for work. She always left home early in the morning so she'd arrive on time, but the traffic was getting heavier by the day. It was harder to get out of Tel Aviv in the mornings, and the daily bottleneck near Airport City was getting increasingly worse. It was 8:30 by the time she made it to the employees' parking area at Ben Gurion Airport, pulled into one of the last remaining vacant spots at the far end of the lot, grabbed her bag with her laptop and her cup of coffee and hurried out the car. As she was locking the vehicle, the coffee cup slid out of her hand and dropped to the ground, causing the plastic lid to fly off and drops of coffee to splash onto her favorite jeans. *What a wonderful start to the day; I wonder what the rest is going to be like,* she thought as she hopped up the stairs to the office two at a time. If she were to rub her jeans now with a clump of wet tissue, she may be able to wipe away some of the brown dots on the blue denim.

"Good that you remembered to come to work," Victor, her team leader, said as she tried to quietly slip by his cubicle unnoticed.

"The traffic was terrible."

"Get up earlier."

"I . . ."

"Check what's happening with the backups from the weekend. Go through all the logs and rerun everything that failed. Prepare the tapes for offsite storage for Med-1, because they'll be sending a car to pick them in an hour or so, and then replace them with a new set. Another two hundred new tapes have arrived and their numbers have to be entered into the system, so get onto that when you're done with Med-1; and then I need you to review the open calls for additional storage and see if we need to add more space or can delete old material. We can't keep on adding and adding. They think that disks grow on trees."

"But we arranged for Dima to deal with the storage so that I have time to work on the new server."

"Dima's sick."

Yeah, right, Leora thought to herself. She remembered seeing him tagged last night on Facebook downing tequilas with a bunch of friends at a pub. He must have woken up a wreck and decided to call in sick. Sneaky bastard. She sighed, went into her cubicle, plugged her laptop into the docking station, and turned it on, then headed to the bathroom to clean the coffee stains off her jeans. From there (with the stains now a little lighter and a lot wetter) she went to the kitchen to make herself a cup of instant coffee with milk and two sweeteners. It was a poor substitute for the cappuccino she'd spilled in the parking lot, but it was better than nothing. She just sat down at her desk in her cubicle to read through some emails before going to the computer room to deal with the backups when her cell phone rang. "Hello?" she said.

"Lena, you're up. Check your mail."

The call ended.

Leora froze momentarily in her chair, pulled herself together, re-defined her cell phone settings to log into her jane.webber.277@gmail.com mail account, and checked the contents of her in-box. A one-line email was waiting for her.

Check if either one of these came through there these past few weeks.

The mail came with two photos attached, one of a man and one of a woman. Leora plugged her mobile into her laptop, copied the two image files onto her hard drive, and logged into the airport's Security System servers. They worked with a replica of the production database that wasn't monitored or permanently logged. She uploaded the two images into the system and ran a search dating back two months.

A single hit.

She replied to the email:

December 13 (yesterday), 03:15, the woman entered Israel.

Leora deleted the Gmail account from her cell phone and restored her regular email settings. She erased the images from the laptop and her phone, cleaned up the system log, left her cubicle, and went to the computer room to deal with the backup tapes.

December 16, 2016

"Hola, señor, I'm Ricardo and this is my partner, Lorenzo. If it's not too much trouble, would you please take a look at these two photographs? They may look like an innocent couple but they're accused of the abduction and murder of dozens of children. They fled the United States and were last seen here in Uyuni. They're probably posing as innocent tourists. Have you seen them?"

"Sorry, I haven't. They weren't guests here at my hotel."

"Have you run into anything else? Someone acting strangely, something suspicious, something out of place and not the norm in town?"

"No. Nothing. It's business as usual around here—tour packages to the Salar and groups of travelers staying for a night or more. Aside from the recent accident—a head-on collision involving two Jeeps in the middle of the Salar and resulting in the death of several travelers—there's been nothing out of the ordinary around here. Go figure how two Jeeps choose to drive head-on into one another on a dry salt lake of more than ten thousand square kilometers and burst into flame simultaneously with all their passengers inside. *Esto es una locura!*"

"Thank you, sir. If you see or hear of anything unusual, please call us at this number." Ricardo took out a business card and handed it to the hotel owner. "By the way," he added, "there's a fifty-thousand-dollar reward for information leading to their capture."

Lorenzo and Ricardo left the hotel and returned to their rented car. They had already visited around twenty hotels. There weren't many left.

- The woman looks pretty hot actually.

- Herr Schmidt said they're both equally dangerous. They're responsible for the assassination of three people on three different continents. They entered and left without being caught and caused some serious damage. Clean work. Smoothly done.

- She looks like she wouldn't hurt a fly. The man looks pretty normal, too.

- The biggest nutcases usually do.

- Okay well, when we get to them and interrogate them both, we'll find out what they did with the bomb.

- Speaking of interrogations: Let's say you were caught and interrogated for the purpose of extracting information from you. How would you choose to move your eyes—up and down, or from right to left?

- What do you mean if I was caught? No one has ever caught me and no one ever will. I'm uncatchable.

- Let's just say you were caught. Theoretically. Just for argument's sake.

- So let's say *you're* caught then, for argument's sake. Not me.

- But you don't know the point I'm trying to make. I have to be the one to explain it to you. I ask you the question and you say right to left or up and down and I keep the discussion going.

- So you can answer and I'll keep the discussion going. No one lays their hands on me even in theory.

- If I answer the question, will you be able to tell me if I'm right? Let's say I say: Sideways. Would you be able to tell me if I was right?

- I could guess.

- Lorenzo, I'm pleading with you to simply imagine it. Just imagine it. Let's just assume—in theory only, and solely for the purpose of our discussion—that someone were to catch you. Not really catch you. Just for argument's sake. Let's say you were caught and they were trying to get information from you. How would you choose to move your eyes?

- Assuming, in theory, that my hands were tied?

- Okay, let's assume so.

- Then I'll tell you what I'll do. I'll move my eyes like so, like I'm squinting, and when the person who has caught me moves closer to see what's happening to me I'll whisper something to him very, very softly, and when he bends over to hear what I'm saying I'll lift up my head and bite into his throat until I snap his windpipe. That's what I'll do.

- It's impossible to talk to you. It's like banging my head against a brick wall.

- So what should I do then?

- If you were caught?

- Theoretically. How should I move my eyes?

- Up and down. You focus on the eyes of the person in front of you and then his mouth, and then the eyes again, and then back to the mouth. Just like that—constantly, small movements.

- And what good will it do?

- Humans have natural instincts. One of them is to care for their young. When a baby stares into the face of his mother or father, he focuses on their eyes and mouth, his eyes jumping back and forth between the two. Parents are wired to love their babies and there's a mechanism in their brains that causes them to love that particular eye movement. If you are ever caught, it would be better for you to move your eyes like that and not from side to side. Sideways conveys cunning and being on the hunt for something. That's no good.

- Are you trying to tell me that supposing someone catches you and beats the shit out of you and stands in front of you with a chain saw, *Nightmare on Elm Street*–style, to get you to start talking, you're going to move your eyes up and down like that and he's going to drop the chain saw and hug you and look for a pacifier to stuff into your mouth?

- I'm simply saying, for the sake of the discussion, that you increase your chances of survival by doing so.

- It'll always be fifty-fifty. Either you do or you don't. Fifty percent.

- Lorenzo, I'm going over to this white wall for a moment to have a word with it. I'm expecting a more favorable response than the one I just got from you.

- Be my guest. Give him my best regards. And ask him what's best to do if he's caught—to fart or to let one rip.

- You're a difficult man.

- Of course I am. I'm your twin brother. I got it from you. But what made you bring it up now? The eye thing.

- I was looking at Tuvian when we were interrogating him. At his eyes.

- And how was he moving them?

- Up and down. Nice and professional. You could see he'd been taught to do so. He probably underwent a course on the subject during his time in Iran.

- And did you get the urge to stroke his head when he did it?

- The notion crossed my mind, I will admit, but I repressed it.

- Tell me, do you think we should have passed on an anonymous tip to the Mossad?

- About what?

- About Tuvian. About the fact that his identity's been exposed.

- Why the sudden burst of generosity?

- Not generosity—just to piss them off. So they don't think he's simply run away and disappeared but know that someone got him to talk.

- Forget it. Let them go on searching for him for another two years as far as I'm concerned. Stop here. We haven't been to this one yet.

"Hola, señor, I'm Ricardo and this is my partner, Lorenzo. If it's not too much trouble, would you please take a look at these two photographs? These two may look like an innocent couple but they're accused of the abduction and murder of dozens of children. They fled the United States and were last seen here in Uyuni. They're probably posing as innocent tourists. Have you seen them?"

"No, I haven't had a couple like that staying here. I'd remember them if they were here. The woman is *guapa*."

"And have you run into anything else? Someone acting strangely, something suspicious, something out of place and not the norm in the town?"

"Aside from the accident at the Salar with the Jeeps there's been nothing unusual. Do you know about the accident?"

"Yes. Go figure how two Jeeps choose to drive head-on into one another on a dry salt lake of more than ten thousand square kilometers and burst into flame simultaneously with all their passengers inside. *Esto es una locura!*"

"That's exactly what everyone else around here says."

"Thank you, sir. If you see or hear of anything unusual, please call us at this number." Ricardo took out a business card and handed it to the hotel owner. "By the way," he added, "there's a fifty-thousand-dollar reward for information leading to their capture."

Ricardo and Lorenzo turned to walk out.

"Just a minute," the hotel owner stopped them. "Now that I think about it, I did have one guest who acted somewhat strangely. He was here alone. He didn't look like the man in the photograph you have, but he drove around here for a week in an open pickup that tourists don't usually rent and visited every street in town like he was looking for something. Just like that stream of Iranians that came through here some nine years ago."

"Stream of Iranians?"

"Yes. Lots of groups from Iran. Great for business. You couldn't find a single vacant room in any hotel in town, and not a single guide was left idle. It was crazy. And they were all wandering around here like they were on a great big treasure hunt. But they gradually disappeared. Since then, we may get an Iranian traveler once in a blue moon. Usually it's Germans, French, Israelis, Australians, you know, all those who love to explore all corners of the earth. Not Americans."

"So he was here for a week and then left?"

"Yes. He hardly slept. He'd wake up early in the morning and return to the hotel late every night, and he had a strange look in his eyes. On his last evening here I suggested he visit the train cemetery just outside of town. He was an avid photographer and you can take nice pictures there. Artistic ones. The following morning, after my recommendation to visit the train graveyard, he paid his bill and left. We never saw him again."

"When was he here?"

"Just a moment, let me look at my calendar. Here we go, he arrived on the fourteenth of February. His name's René Mercier, a French citizen."

"Do you have a photograph of him?"

"No."

"Security cameras?"

"We don't have such things, señor."

"Thank you, sir. We don't know yet if it was him; but if it helps with our investigation, the reward is yours. If you see him again, call me. You have my card. And here's a hundred dollars in advance for your help so far." Ricardo pulled out a $100 bill and handed it to the hotel owner, who thanked him profusely and scribbled down the directions to the train cemetery on a small piece of paper. The twins left the hotel and went back to their car.

- One hundred dollars? One hundred fucking dollars? That's a monthly wage here. What were you thinking?

- I believe in giving to the less fortunate if you can afford to, paying it forward.

- If you carry on like that, you'll be one of the less fortunate yourself.

- Don't fret, Lorenzo. I'll add it to our expense account. Herr Schmidt will cover it. And those one hundred dollars will ensure that we get a call within seconds if and when that guest ever comes back here.

- Okay. Are we off to the train cemetery now?

- A *delante*.

I continue walking through a dusty field with straight rows of crops. The circle of frost in the park hasn't spread this far and the layer of dust on the plants is so thick that it's impossible to identity the crops growing in the field. A mountain range rises skyward on the horizon and I need to get there. My shoes kick up small clouds of dust with every step I take.

I remember the syringe needles being pulled out of my arms, leaving drops of blood on my skin. The feeding tube being shoved down my throat. Knives opening up my body. Parts of me being replaced.

She's following me from a distance.

My body is moving fast. Responding quickly to the instructions from my brain. They must have fitted servomotors or titanium springs to my skeleton. My lungs inform me of the chemical composition of the dust in the air that I'm breathing. My legs offer information on the density of the earth beneath my feet. They must have done something to my body. They've upgraded me.

She continues to follow me. I could kill her if I choose to, but there's no point in doing so now.

I see a dusty concrete structure at the end of the field and walk toward it. The wooden table and chairs I find inside are old and dusty, and there's a basin with a rusty faucet. I drink brown water from the faucet. My tongue recognizes the pH level of the water; it's below 7—acidic. I take off my shirt and wash the upper part of my body. The layer of dust that has mixed with my sweat has turned into orange mud on my skin, under it I see a barcode tattooed on my chest under my collarbone.

When I get the chance I'll scan it with a barcode reader to see what it says.

I put my shirt back on, step outside, and continue walking.

She's still behind me, in the distance.

175

I wake up and go to the refrigerator to drink a glass of cold water. It's 2 in the morning. I check to make sure there's no one in the house and I go back to sleep.

I get started in the morning with the construction of the cage in the basement, welding horizontal iron bars to the upright vertical ones. When the cage is completed and closed, I run a 4-inch pipe from the corner of the cage to the corner of the basement, leaving its ends open. I pour a 30-centimeter-thick layer of concrete on the floor of the basement. When the concrete dries, the iron bars will be firmly fixed to the floor. I think Shlomit and Zvika will be very pleased to see the improvements I've made to their home.

The door of the cage hangs on 2 sturdy iron hinges and isn't fitted with a lock. When I put my guests into the cage, I'll simply weld the door to the bars. I have no intention of opening it again after they're inside.

I leave the door to the basement open and turn on a big fan to help the concrete set faster. I expect it to be completely dry and solid within 3 days.

I complete my next shopping list. I order the dog food and cartons of mineral water and drive to Home Center to purchase a toilet, then to a building supplies store to pick up a sewage pump designed for basements. This cage will be a lot more comfortable than the previous one, with a toilet and a lovely food dispenser for my guests.

04/21/2016–18 weeks and 6 days since waking

I use a metal-cutting circular saw to create a square opening at the back of the cage where I can install the food dispenser I've designed. I weld the dispenser in place and pour 2 bags of dog kibble into its food well, together with 30 neatly packed bottles of water. I set the timer so that the dispenser will function once a day and release a predetermined quantity of food and 2 bottles of mineral water. I check the machine. The dog food pours into the metal bowl in the cage, followed by 2 bottles of mineral water, which drop onto the pile and scatter bits of kibble across the floor. I adjust the angle at which the bottles fall so they don't cause any of the dog food to spill.

I install the toilet in the corner of the cage and fix it firmly to the concrete. I connect the sewage pump to the toilet's outlet pipe and then use a coiled pipe to connect the sewage pump to the home's waste-drainage system.

I pack the cartons of mineral water and bags of dog food against the wall of the basement and then drill a hole in the ceiling through which I'll insert an air-conditioning pipe to improve the air circulation in the below-ground room. If I don't do so, they will suffocate too quickly.

I remove one of the air-conditioner grills from the living room ceiling, pull out the flexible coiled air pipe, and attach the extension I purchased. I then fit the other end of the extension through the hole I've made in the living room floor.

I line all the basement walls and its ceiling with foam mattresses, which I fix in place with glue and nails.

The basement is ready.

I return to the living room to prepare the trashcans I bought.

I place one of the trashcans on the floor upside down and remove its metal leg. The trashcan comprises a large outer cylinder and a smaller inner one, with a space between the 2. The trash bag fits inside the inner cylinder. I use the circular saw to cut away the bottom

177

section of the trashcan, about 5 centimeters from the end, and examine the hollow space between the 2 metal cylinders that form the receptacle. The structure of the cylinder makes the trashcan durable and strong, and just right for my purposes. Excellent. I fill the space between the 2 cylinders with water and check to make sure nothing drips out. The outer cylinder is completely watertight. I empty out the water and leave the trashcan to dry. Meanwhile, I take the large cooking pot and place it on the stovetop's highest flame. I pour 5 kilos of sugar into the pot and allow it to melt, stirring now and then. Once the sugar has caramelized, I add 10 kilos of granular chemical fertilizer, 1 kilo of sulfur, and 2 kilos of small nails. I stir well until the mixture is uniform, turn off the flame, and pour the contents of the pot into the space between the 2 cylinders of the upside down trashcan. The mixture will solidify when it dries.

Using the soldering iron, I connect 2 of the small lights with 2 short pieces of wire and 2 AAA batteries each, joining the 2 batteries attached to each bulb by soldering the negative terminal of the one to the positive terminal of the other. I solder the negative terminal of the batteries I've joined to the piece of wire attached to the side of each lightbulb, and I connect the piece of wire fixed to the bottom of each bulb to one of the Sanwa receivers—the kind of receiver that is found in model aircrafts and receives instructions to change course by means of a transmission relayed by the aircraft's remote controller. I use another small piece of electrical wire to join the 2 receivers. Each receiver is set to a different frequency so that I'll have to perform 2 operations with the remote controller in order to relay the 2 transmissions to the 2 receivers. I use another piece of wire to connect the 2nd Sanwa receiver to the negative terminal of the batteries, and then I attach another piece of wire, around 40 centimeters long, to the receivers' antenna ports.

I take a pair of pliers and carefully break the 2 lightbulbs, leaving their filaments exposed and then embedding them carefully in the hardening solution inside the trashcan. I wrap duct tape around the transmission devices and batteries that are attached to the lightbulbs and place them on the hardening material between the trash-can's 2 metal cylinders. The device is large enough and won't sink in the solidifying solution. I drill a hole in the side of the trashcan and insert a screw from the inside out. Before tightening the screw to the end, I connect the 2 antenna wires to the thread and then close it completely. I cut off the end of the screw so that it doesn't stick out the side of the trashcan. The body of the trashcan will serve as an antenna for the transmission devices within. I throw away the ser-vomotors. I won't need them. I only bought them so that the store manager wouldn't get suspicious about me purchasing receivers only.

The propellant explosive material I've prepared isn't as powerful as its military grade counterpart; it's about 50 percent less effective. But the pressure that will be created within the metal structure of the trashcan will cause a powerful blast from the 18 kilos of propel-lant, with at least a 30-meter wide strike radius for the nails. I could try to prepare nitroglycerine or a propellant made from a mixture of zinc and sulfur, but nitroglycerin isn't a particularly stable mate-rial and it's very difficult to obtain a large quantity of zinc.

While the trashcan is still cooling, I go to the kitchen to make myself an avocado salad. I boil 2 eggs and then cut up an avocado that I mash with a fork in a bowl, adding the juice of half a lemon, sea salt, and ground black pepper. I take half a baguette out the freezer and thaw it. I remove the now hard-boiled eggs from the pot a few minutes later, peel them, and mash them with the fork into the avocado mixture. I slice open the baguette and fill it with avo-cado salad and sit down to eat. Playing on the radio is a song by Mashina about a beautiful and somewhat strange young woman who the writer of the song used to meet every night.

I follow dinner with a cup of coffee and then return to the living room to continue my work.

I add an inscription to the inside of the bottom of the trashcan: MADE BY THE ORGANIZATION'S AGENT 10483. FOR ADDITIONAL DE-TAILS, PLEASE CONTACT THE ORGANIZATION'S HOME BASE IN RAMAT SASHARON. I will add the same inscription to all the trashcans.

When the trashcan is no longer hot I reattach the bottom using epoxy adhesive, then I spread more epoxy all around the seam and reinforce the connection with a band of metal, fixing it firmly in place around the trashcan with some screws. I can't weld the bottom back on because if a drop of smoldering metal were to fall onto the explosive material between the trashcan's 2 cylinders, the outcome would severely hamper my plans.

I reattach the metal leg to the bottom of the trashcan and place it upright on the living room floor. I look at the trashcan bomb I've made. It looks perfectly normal. After the epoxy adhesive dries, I'll paint the band of metal in gray so that it looks like a part of the trashcan. When I want to detonate the trashcan, I'll have to move both levers on my model aircraft remote controller—the one that operates the wing flaps and the one that operates the tail flap. The moment I do so, the 2 receivers will trigger their transmission devices and close an electrical circuit that will provide power to the 2 lightbulbs embedded in the explosive material. Because they have no glass around them, the exposed red-hot filaments will ignite the explosive material. The pressure that builds up between the trashcan's 2 cylinders will cause a powerful blast. For optimal reception, I'll have to be no more than a few dozen meters away from the trashcan, so it would be best for me to be behind a barrier of sorts, like a wall or thick tree, when I detonate each trashcan bomb.

1 is ready. And now I have to make another 49 just the same. It'll take me 3 days if I work on 4 trashcans at the same time. In the meantime, I take a break from the physical work and read through the documents pertaining to the Bernoulli Project that I copied off the Organization's computers in March 2006, 10 years and 1 month ago. Among the documents is a list of the names of 12 people who the Organization needs to assassinate for the sake of national security. They are 12 scientists in various fields. The 3 nuclear scientists are the targets I received when I worked for the Organization before they betrayed me. I read through surveillance reports that include

their respective residential addresses, as well as a classified sum-
mary of the inner circle's decision to eliminate all of them.

I make paper chains out of the colored sheets of paper I bought
and decorate the basement in preparation for the piece of art I'll be
adding to the room in the future.

Dear Sirs,

I am writing this letter to you with a heavy heart because there will be
no way back for me the moment I send it—for me or for my handlers.
But the truth has to be told.

Following my discharge from the army as a lieutenant colonel, I was
recruited in 2001 by an entity in Israel that calls itself the Organization.
My decision to join the Organization was motivated by a desire to
protect my country and safeguard its citizens, and I truly believed that
my service was a calling and not simply a matter of my devotion to the
state, but also an opportunity to defend democracy and preserve
stability in the region. I thought I would continue to serve until my
retirement because I believed I was destined to do so. Unfortunately,
things didn't work out the way I thought they would, and after 14 years
of service I informed the Organization that I was leaving. The reasons I
gave were a desire to be with my family and the toll that all the years
in the army and the Organization had taken on my life. My wife's
parents owned an apple plantation in the north of Israel and were too
old to take care of it. Two years ago, my family made the move and
we are currently living in the North and making a living from agriculture.
The quiet and simple life we lead has allowed me to think about the
14 years I spent in the service of the Organization. Over the years, I was
instructed to carry out a number of missions that caused extensive
damage in four different countries—Switzerland, Argentina, Canada,
and the United States.

Why I was charged with planning and carrying out the aforementioned
missions remains a mystery to me to this day, but I'm aware of the
terrible damage caused in each of the countries. Today, I wouldn't carry
out even one of these missions. I can only assume that my state of mind
at the time and the brainwashing I underwent at the hands of the
Organization caused me to act as I did. There is no way for me to atone
for what I did, but I would like to make things right by exposing those

who were behind these criminal acts, because I didn't act alone and certainly not on my own initiative.

I was instructed in January 2006 to bring down a building on Rue de Delices in Geneva, Switzerland, with all its occupants inside. I did so by sealing off the upper floor, flooding it with water, and generating enough pressure to bring the building to the ground. The apartment I sealed belonged to Adriana Karson. She's still alive because I got her to leave her apartment so that I could work there undisturbed by gifting her a trip to Brazil and passing it off as a prize she won. I booked the tour package through the Geneva Holiday travel agency on St. George's Boulevard. Enclosed with this letter is a photograph of me from 10 years ago. You can locate the travel agent who handled the reservation and she will recognize me from the picture. I told her at the time that I wanted to send my friend, who had cancer, on holiday, but because she wouldn't accept such an expensive gift, I was going to disguise it as a prize. You can verify this with the travel agent.

In February 2006, I was sent to carry out a mass-casualty terror attack in Bariloche, Argentina, that involved setting fire to a park filled with people. I carried out my mission by using a fuel tanker that I hooked up to the park's sprinkler system. When I took possession of the fuel tanker, I was forced to murder its driver on Route 273, some 10 kilometers north of Bariloche. Before throwing his cell phone into the bushes on the side of the road I removed the battery. You can verify this with the Argentinian Police.

In Canada (also in February 2006), my mission involved mass hypnosis that caused a very large number of fatalities in the Montreal area. You can show my photograph to Dr. Victor Sadovsky in Montreal and he will confirm that I was the man who recorded him performing the hypnosis before it aired on CBC Radio One.

A year ago, on December 12, 2016, I was asked to blow up the CIA's headquarters in McLean, USA, with Washington, D.C., as a secondary target, by using a Soviet-made nuclear warhead that was made available to me in Bolivia and that I smuggled through the Tijuana border crossing. West of Tijuana, on the shores of Presa El Carrizo— coordinates 32°28'39.39" N and 116°41'19.10" W—you will find three Russian-language instruction manuals that contain information on how to maintain the warhead. In addition, you will find the lead apron I wore when handling and transporting the warhead in the waters of the lake near the instruction manuals. First search for the lead apron in the lake with a metal detector, then draw a beeline to the shore and you will find the instruction manuals buried some 20 meters inland alongside a dry tree.

Furthermore, you will find the remains of the Geiger counter I used to locate the warhead where the Organization kept it for me—in the train cemetery in the town of Uyuni in Bolivia. Look around there, too, for a train car marked with a white X. The warhead was being stored there for me under the salt in the freight car. Some of the pieces of equipment that I used to lift the warhead out of the freight car are still buried under the salt. You'll find them.

I'd be happy for you to share this information with the intelligence agencies in Switzerland, Argentina, and Canada. However, I will not be sending this information directly to them because I'm leaving you, the principal victims, to decide if you want to share it with others or keep it to yourselves.

Sincerely,

A former Organization agent.

04/24/2016–19 weeks and 2 days since waking

I print out 3 copies of the letter, fold the pages, and slip each copy into a white envelope. I apply the appropriate postage stamps for delivery to the United States to each envelope. On each envelope there are 2 stamps. One shows a sailboat with a lighthouse in the background, and the other boasts a picture of a green apple. I'm amused. I received 3 envelopes from the Organization and now I'm preparing 3 envelopes of my own.

On the 1st envelope I write:

> The White House
> 1600 Pennsylvania Avenue, NW
> Washington, D.C. 20500
> USA

On the 2nd envelope I write:

> Central Intelligence Agency
> Office of Public Affairs
> Washington, D.C. 20505
> USA

On the 3rd envelope I write:

> FBI Headquarters
> 935 Pennsylvania Avenue, NW
> Washington, D.C. 20535-0001
> USA

I'll send the letters toward the end of 2017, a year after I detonate the warhead. Endless questions will be raised during the course of the year, and my letter will put an end to them and point a finger at the Organization's headquarters. The secret details I've recorded in them, together with the enclosed image of me, will make it clear to everyone that the Organization was behind everything that occurred. I stain the end of my finger with the purple marker and leave a fingerprint on each of the 3 images that I place in the envelopes. I wonder what they'll decide to do when they find out. I don't expect the Americans to share the information with the other intelligence agencies and assume they will act independently, and the Organization will cease to exist. During the course of 2016, I'll plot my revenge against them here in Israel, too; and in 2017, I'll vanish without a trace. For now, I place the 3 envelopes in one of the kitchen drawers along with a note that reads: "Check before sending if the postage stamps are still good for delivery to the United States or if the postage tariff has changed. Check, too, if the addresses of the FBI and CIA have changed a year after the blast." They may decide to rebuild elsewhere with D.C. off limits due to the radiation.

I install 4 of the 50 trashcans I've prepared around my house—1 at the beginning of the grass walkway leading to the front door, 1 on the corner of the street, 1 at the far end of the backyard of the house, and 1 in the alley bordering my house to the rear. All are close enough and within range of my remote controller such that they will detonate all at once if I activate them from here at home.

I install the remaining trashcans, apart from another 4 that I put aside, in various locations around Tel Aviv. Each time I load several trashcans into the van and head out very early in the morning to avoid traffic jams and parking problems. It takes me a month to install them all. I dismantle an existing trashcan and fix one of mine to the sidewalk in its place, and then insert an empty garbage bag. I wear a shirt with the logo of the Tel Aviv Municipality and not one of the pedestrians and joggers on the street take any interest in what I'm doing, apart from one old lady who asks me why I'm replacing the trashcan. "There's a corrosion problem with these trashcans," I tell her. "They rust quickly. The manufacturer has now sent us new trashcans and we're replacing all of them. He's even covering the municipality's labor costs for the project. Look at the color of this trashcan, too—much nicer. Really good quality metal."

I make sure to exercise and take ice baths in the evenings. I eat eggs and meat, legumes and vegetables, and my hemoglobin levels are good. The doctor I see at my medical clinic is surprised by the results of my blood tests. "Well done, Roman," she says. "It's amazing how you've lowered your cholesterol." I tell her I've started exercising and am on a special diet that I read about on the Internet. I ask her for a prescription for sleeping tablets. I tell her that I've been waking up a few times during the night recently and that I'm very tired at work. She prints out a prescription for me and I take it and thank her. I purchase 2 boxes of 20 tablets each from the pharmacy.

December 17, 2016

- Look at that train car. Someone's marked it with a white X.

They'd been wandering around the train cemetery for close to an hour and a half, examining the corroded engines and cars and trying to find any sign that would lead them to the bomb. Ricardo stopped and crouched beside the car.

- Look, there are screws here on the ground.

- Let's climb up. Maybe there's something in the freight car.

With their feet planted in the salt, they began to dig inside the freight car. The sun was about to rise and travelers would soon start showing up at the site. They didn't have much time. After digging for a few minutes, they started to pull out various items—metal rods, lengths of lumber, pieces of rope, nails, and screws.

- Fuck.

- Someone else got here first.

- Yes. They must have used all this equipment to remove the bomb from the freight car. We now know three things—that the bomb was here in the car, that a small team of people took it out, and that it all went down not too long ago. Look, the lumber looks almost new, and the iron bars and nails haven't rusted.

- Why a small team?

- Someone put together a mechanism to lower the bomb out of the freight car. A big team would have been able to lower it carefully to the ground with just a few ropes. They wouldn't have needed all this equipment. I'd say there were two of them here, or three people at most.

- Herr Schmidt isn't going to be happy.

- No, he won't be happy at all.

- Do you know what he reminds me of?

- Who?

- Herr Schmidt.

- What?

- Permafrost.

- What's that?

- Permafrost is a permanently frozen layer of subsoil. Like the layer of earth below the surface at the poles, for example. It's permanently frozen. It has never thawed. He's the same. Whenever I'm around him, I can feel the cold emanating from him. That's why I need to thaw out with a beer every time I leave his offices.

- Beer is a cold thing, too.

- Compared to permafrost, beer is something very hot.

- Okay, let's head back to the hotel and we'll call him.

- Let's get the hell out of this place. Of all countries in the world, I hate Bolivia the most. They don't even have normal alcohol here.

- There's *chicha*.

- Do you know how they make *chicha*?

- At a winery?

- This is Bolivia, not the south of France. Here they get a whole bunch of old ladies to sit around, chew on corn and spit the mashed corn into a large bowl, and then it ferments for a few weeks and becomes *chicha*.

- Fuck, I drank some yesterday evening. And to top it all, we flew here for nothing. The bomb isn't here.

- Someone beat us to it.

- If only we had come here a few months earlier.

- It reminds me of a story about fate.

- What?

- There were once two babies who were born on the same day of the same year. One was named Chin Tang and the other Adrienne Matri. Chin was born in a small village near Gansu Sheng in China, and Adrienne was born in Kilchberg, near Zurich, Switzerland. Chin's parents were peasants who worked a small plot of land, and Adrienne's parents were a physics professor and a biology professor who taught at the University of Zurich. Chin was a smart and independent child and he knew that one day he would leave the country life and move to the big city, and Adrienne completed her doctorate at the age of fourteen.

- Is there a point to your story?

- Patience, Lorenzo. At the age of twenty-two, Chin secured a job with Shanghai Construction and started working as an apprentice on the construction of the giant towers that were being erected in Beijing. Adrienne, at the time, was working on the theory of developing an immunosuppressant drug that would be able to eradicate all forms of cancer by altering a component of DNA that would cause white blood cells to identify the malignant cells as invasive bacteria. At the age of twenty-six, Chin was sent by Shanghai Construction to London to work on the construction of one of the new high-rises in the area of the Thames Promenade, and Adrienne was renting an apartment in a nearby building while working on her project, jointly funded by the Imperial College London and Harvard University.

- I think I'm going to go to the pub across the road from the hotel for a round of *chicha*. It's not as bad as listening to your story.

- Wait, I'm getting to the moral. One Sunday morning, Adrienne was standing in the kitchen of her rented apartment, drinking orange juice and looking out the window at the construction site just across the way; and just then, the missing piece in the puzzle flashed through her mind—the piece that would complete the development of the drug. She knew for certain that it would work. And the next thing that went through her head was a piece of stone cladding that fell from the thirty-eighth floor of the building under construction, hit the scaffolding on the fourteenth floor, and flew straight into her face through the window pane.

- Now it's getting interesting.

- Do you get it? It was a stone tile that the tired Chin had fixed there the day before with insufficient cement, after working an eighteen-hour shift without any sleep. It was her destiny, you could say.

- And it's our destiny to chase after ghosts. Are you calling Herr Schmidt to update him?

- Yes.

Ricardo called Herr Schmidt.

"Yes, we visited the train cemetery and wandered around until we came across a freight car marked with a white X. We found screws and nails that looked fairly new lying on the ground next to it. We climbed into the car and dug into its sand cargo and found a bunch of wood and steel rods and tools buried there. No, there was no bomb. Someone got there before us and took it. Probably the same person that the man at the hotel told us about. His team must have loaded it into his pickup and driven away."

"Go back to Israel," Herr Schmidt said. "The woman in the photograph you have is one of the assassins of the three scientists and she landed in Tel Aviv four days ago. Find her and get her to divulge the location of the bomb."

Ricardo asked if they were allowed to resort to excessive physical pressure. "After you get her to reveal the location of the bomb, you can turn her into a scarecrow for all I care," Herr Schmidt responded before hanging up.

- Shit.

- What's shit? What did he say?

- Israel again. That woman in the photograph landed there yesterday. We need to find her and interview her.

- Shit.

05/08/2016–21 weeks and 2 days since waking

I drive around Bikat Ono early in the morning and look for a gas tanker on the road. After finding one with an orange and blue tank, I follow it in my carpet van while it makes its deliveries and then as it makes its way back to the gas depot in the old industrial zone of Rishon LeZion. The tanker stops there to refuel and then heads out for a 2nd round of deliveries. I remain outside the gas depot to study their security procedures. It'll be tough to break into the facility itself. It won't be as easy as it was in Argentina. Here I'll have to find another way to commandeer the tanker when it leaves the facility filled with gas.

It's strange to have a gas depot like that in Rishon's backyard, so close to residential areas. The facility consists of 2 large gas storage tanks, a parking area for the gas tankers, and 4 different fuel stations for dessert.

December 20, 2016

- You're doing it again.

- Doing what?

- Not listening to me.

- We've been talking now for an hour. How can we be talking for an hour if I'm not listening to you?

- While I'm talking, you're thinking about your response. You're more concerned with your response than with what I'm saying.

- But that's how people think, isn't it? If I'm speaking to you, I'm also thinking about what I'm going to say.

- And that's the problem we all have. No one really listens.

- So really listen to me then. What we are busy doing now is like looking for a single louse on a head covered with dreadlocks. We have a picture of the woman and that's it. How can we be expected to find her? We aren't in Uyuni now. This is a country with nine million inhabitants. Going from one hotel to the next will take us a year, and the Israelis aren't very cooperative. A suspicious bunch. They won't hesitate to start asking questions. And maybe she's even rented an apartment or is living with her parents?

- This pasta is pretty good. Didn't I tell you they have some decent restaurants here at the port?

- After Bolivia, everything tastes good.

- I was in Amsterdam last winter.

- What does that have to do with anything?

- I went to a restaurant there that was out of this world. The steaks were excellent and the potatoes melted in your mouth; but it was the dessert that blew me away.

- What was it?

- This salty stick of sorts that was coated in chocolate; and the saltiness of the stick combined with the sweetness of the chocolate was unreal.

- What was the name of the restaurant?

- I don't recall.

- I'd remember the name of a restaurant if I'd left it feeling very satisfied.

- That's the name. The restaurant is called: "I Don't Recall."

- Odd name for a restaurant.

- An excellent name. It's unforgettable.

- That's true.

- Tuvian was very quick to talk. Too quick perhaps. Maybe it was all an act to get us to go to Bolivia.

- I don't think so.

- Tell me, now that I think of it, before you went to Nepal to pick up the box with the yak hide for Herr Schmidt, you went to Quebec for two days to take care of some business for him, right?

- Yes. Someone I had to question on another matter. Unrelated to what we're busy with here now.

- And was he quick to talk? Just for the sake of argument, how did the interrogation go?

- He was uncooperative at first. He was tied to his bed and said nothing. So I went to a nearby store and bought a bottle of drain cleaner and poured a little onto his stomach to begin with and told him that he had better not sweat because when the substance gets wet and comes into contact with organic material, it eats away at it.

- And what did he do?

- He started to sweat of course from the stress, and the drain cleaner started to work and left him with a nice burn on his stomach— but still he didn't talk. He was a very stubborn man. And he wasn't scared of ants or anything like that.

- How do you know?

- There was nothing in the file on him about that.

- So maybe he was afraid of something but you simply didn't know? I'm just saying, for argument's sake.

- Maybe. For argument's sake—yes, could be.

- And he started to sweat just like that, from the stress? There are some people who don't sweat, even when they're stressed; and there are some who sweat all the time, even without being stressed.

- I had the heat in the room turned up to thirty-eight degrees Celsius.

- And how did you get him to talk eventually?

- I showed him another six bottles of the same type of drain cleaner. I told him I was going to empty one of them into his mouth and another one into his eyes, half a bottle for each eye. The other four, I said, were going down his shorts.

- And then he started talking?

- Yes. He gave up a few names of significance. I set him free afterward.

- Free of the shackles of this world?

- No. I released him. I let him go.

- Why?

- Herr Schmidt asked me to. He said he needed him for various things.

- What things?

- I didn't ask.

- For the sake of argument, I still think that Tuvian was too quick to talk.

- I don't think so.

- You know something, in the late 1940s in Idaho they rounded up beavers and released them again all across the state.

- Why would they want to do that?

- To create dams along several of the rivers and also to thin out some of the beaver population, so they wouldn't all be concentrated in a single location. The state wanted to cut costs and beavers do a good job—and free of charge. So they put the beavers in wooden crates with air holes so they could breathe, and attached a parachute to each crate, and an old propeller-driven plane flew above the rivers and released a crate every few minutes. Two flights in total, with ten beavers dropped each time.

- And did they get the job done?

- Yes. They threw all the beavers out of the plane.

- I'm talking about the beavers. Did they do their job and build the dams?

- I guess so.

- And what made you think about that just now?

- It's on my mind now because they filmed it, the flight and the parachutes and everything, and the film disappeared more than sixty years ago and no one has been able to find it until just recently. Someone found it by chance not too long ago in the garage of a house he'd purchased, in a cardboard box with a whole lot of other crap, and passed it on to the Idaho Historical Society. The chances of someone suddenly finding that fucking film that had been buried in that box for all those years must have been one in a million. That's what I'm saying.

- You didn't answer my question.

- What question?

- What made you think about it now?

- I'll tell you why it's on my mind now. It's on my mind now because the woman in the picture we received from Herr Schmidt is sitting here at this restaurant just six tables away from us. The chances of that are one in a million, too. That's what made me think of the story about the beavers.

- I think the beavers died.

- What makes you think that?

- If the crates failed to open, then they all starved to death inside their boxes. If the crate hits the ground hard, the mechanism that opens it could jam.

- But we're talking about beavers. If they got stuck in their boxes, for argument's sake, perhaps they could gnaw their way out through the wood?

- Yes, that could be true. If they can gnaw through a tree trunk with their teeth, they can surely do the same to a wooden crate. On the other hand, if they could do so, why didn't they gnaw through their crates and escape while they were still on the plane and before they were dropped out?

- Maybe they started to do so but didn't have enough time. It can't have been a particularly long flight within Idaho.

- Perhaps.

- About the young woman sitting here six tables away from us.

- What about her?

- We've been instructed by Herr Schmidt in no uncertain terms not to kill her before she tells us all she knows. If you get a sudden urge to throw her out the window or push her head into the toilet for a few minutes or put a pillow over her face and sit on it, restrain yourself.

- And what if she annoys me or pisses me off?

- Then focus on breathing deeply; meditate and think happy thoughts. Herr Schmidt said that she and the man in the second picture he sent us were the two assassins that Israel sent to Argentina, Switzerland, and Canada to take out the scientists who were working with Iran. She could be dangerous.

- If you have a scientific background.

- I beg your pardon?

- The woman—she's dangerous if you're a scientist. Do you think she knows where the bomb is?

- Herr Schmidt thinks so.

- We'll get it out of her. She'd better know where the bomb is. It'll all be over quickly if that's the case.

Ricardo reached for his beer glass and raised a toast to Lorenzo. They both took a long swig from their beers and went on eating their lunch, arguing about various issues and making sure that Carmit didn't leave the restaurant unnoticed.

December 20, 2016

"Fucking rats!"

Chris Martinez growled to himself and threw his large set of keys onto the desk in his office. He then went to the adjacent storeroom to retrieve a large clear plastic bag filled with traps and a container of rat poison.

When he opened the main door to the building a few minutes earlier and stepped inside, a gray rat bounded over his shoe and almost gave him a heart attack.

That's all he needed now, for a customer to show up to collect something from one of the storage units and to see a rat scurrying gleefully about the place. It could kill his business. He had to deal with this crap every few months. And it's all because of all those lunatics who took a storage unit and decided to keep food there, without thinking at all about what happens, for example, to a package of sausages after a few weeks left at room temperature. Ewww. Disgusting.

He recalled the storage unit he leased a few months ago to someone who filled it with old freezers and didn't bother to check that they were all empty. One of the freezers was full of meat. The entire building ended up smelling like a corpse. He called the man and barked at him that he had twenty-four hours to get there and get that shit out of the storage unit before he called the police. Ever since then, his lease contracts include a clause that strictly forbids people from keeping food in the storage units.

Chris picked up his large bundle of keys and started going from one storage unit to the next. In some of the units he laid traps with small bits of cold cuts to lure the rats, and in others he scattered rat poison that looked like tiny sawdust sausages.

He wasn't able to open unit No. 24, and his master key didn't work either. There's probably something wrong with the lock cylinder; *I must remember to take care of it,* he thought.

And then forgot all about it five minutes later.

I approach the parking lot. My shoes leave tracks in the deep snow. It's quiet here early in the morning and there are no vehicles around. I pass the sign that reads:

> *Welcome to Niagara Falls. Attention! The site's management disclaims all responsibility for any injury or harm—frostbite, lung damage, cold illness, or other—suffered as a result of your visit to the falls. You enter the site at your own risk. Entry without suitable clothing is strictly prohibited. We encourage you not to leave valuables in your vehicles. The site's management disclaims all responsibility for thefts from vehicles in the parking lot. We wish you a pleasant visit.*

The parking lot is empty and I cross it on foot and approach the entrance to the site. I pass by the unmanned booth at the gate and head toward the falls. My high-top shoes no longer leave tracks in the snow, which has become a thick layer of ice. I walk past a group of children skating gracefully across the ice that was once a parking lot for visitors to the site.

The silence deepens the closer I get to the falls, and I reach the point where you can lean over the safety railing and look out at the frozen falls. The water that turned into ice years ago remains permanently frozen in place. The area closest to the falls, the coldest spot, is completely silent. The cold seems to be coming from the frozen water itself. A large digital thermometer fixed to the falls shows –53 degrees Celsius. A maintenance vehicle fitted with a scoop passes by in the distance and shifts a layer of snow to the side onto a grayish white heap. I walk a little farther, taking care not to slip on the ice, until I get to a point where I can touch the frozen river. I run my hand over the ice. It's warm.

I see him standing downriver and touching the ice, too.

I approach him.

I touch his shoulder and he turns to face me.

We start walking down a straight pathway that seems to go on forever. The path turns from ice to snow and then into dusty white dirt. The sun glows orange like just before a sunset and its light catches the blackened fields of grain on either side of the path. Fields of black tar. We walk without a single word between us; our footsteps are soundless, too. Absolute silence.

After a few minutes, he turns his head to the right. "You know something," he says, "following Hiroshima and Nagasaki, studies were conducted in the United States on the mechanism and procedure for launching a nuclear attack. They wanted to be able to prevent the president from being able to personally order the Joint Chiefs of Staff to launch a nuclear strike without some kind of additional control measure in place. Everyone thinks that there's a red mushroom-shaped button that gets pressed to launch the missile, but that button exists only in the movies and not in real life. In reality, authority lies with the president and he can place a call on an encrypted phone line to the chairman of the Joint Chiefs of Staff, read out a code that only he knows, and thereby launch a nuclear strike on Russia or China for example."

I tell him it sounds too simple.

"Yes," he says, "and that's why the committee was set up. A committee tasked with designing a mechanism that would prevent the president from making a rash decision before reading out the code to the chairman of the Joint Chiefs of Staff."

I ask him what the committee decided.

"A group of Harvard professors sat down together and deliberated for a month before finding a solution."

I ask him what the solution was.

"The solution was to have someone with the president at all times. Twenty-four hours a day. And for him to be in possession of the code."

I tell him they didn't need a group of Harvard geniuses to come up with something like that.

"*Just a moment. The individual in question wouldn't have the code in his hand or his pocket or even in his head. The code would be inside a capsule, and the capsule will be fixed to his aorta. From the inside. To get to the code, you have to slice him open, get to his aorta, rip it away from his heart, and pull out the capsule, which is fixed there with two metal sutures.*"

I tell him that it would kill the guy.

"*Correct. And he will be at the president's side all the time. Just a few seconds away. Sometimes you have to make a decision about a nuclear strike really quickly—if the Russians attack first, let's say. And the designated individual would be by the president's side. All the time. And if they spend all that time together, he'll probably become the president's best friend, too. How could the president kill his best friend? That was the idea. To kill a single individual before issuing an order to kill millions. It sounds pretty simple, but the act of taking a knife and slicing open and killing your best friend so that you can get to the code will make you think very, very carefully about launching a strike. Butchering someone is a lot more real than simply reading out a code.*"

I tell him that I don't think it will work because they won't find someone to volunteer to have a capsule fixed to his aorta.

He unbuttons his shirt. There's a tattoo of a light blue triangle on his chest, a little to the left of his collarbone and two ribs down. "*This is where you need to insert the knife to get to my aorta. I volunteered; the capsule has already been implanted and I start work at the White House tomorrow. I'm going to be the president and the First Lady's best friend. I'll be with them on the golf course and in the White House and on their family vacations and in every godforsaken place he goes around the world. We'll be like brothers, and I'll make the decision to kill me the hardest decision he'll ever have to make in his entire life.*"

I ask him why he volunteered and he tells me it's because he doesn't approve of nuclear weapons. He tells me that in his bag he has a sharp knife that he received from his new employer, the government of the

United States, and asks me if I want to see it. I thank him and say there's no need.

"I'll be going on from here alone," he says, buttoning his shirt again. "Nuclear detonation devices are made for a purpose. Keep looking for one and you will turn to vapor when it goes off. Leave me alone."

He turns right into the field. There's nothing here but a huge field of the blackened grain. He walks into the field and is swallowed up by it. Gray clouds block out the sun and the white path turns black and blends with the black fields around it. I continue to follow him from a distance.

It's going to rain soon.

December 21, 2016

Bzzzzzzzzzz

Bzzzzzzzzzz

Bzzzzzzzzzz

Carmit's iPhone vibrated under her pillow and she woke immediately and silenced it. She looked at the iPhone screen. Three fifteen in the morning.

Someone is standing outside her hotel room. The small motion sensor that she stuck above the doorframe the day before has a Bluetooth connection to her cell phone and sends an alert to the application whenever someone passes by her door too slowly or stops outside it.

Carmit hopped out of bed in absolute silence, arranged the blankets and pillows to look like she was still cuddled under them somewhere, quickly grabbed the two knives that were on the bedside table, and slipped into the clothes closet by the door to the room, dressed still in just a T-shirt and panties.

Carmit made sure her phone was on silent and then reopened the application for the motion sensor, which came with a tiny camera. Two figures in black were fiddling in complete silence with the lock of the door to her room.

Carmit slowly removed the knives from their plastic sheaths.

The door to the room opened slowly and the two men walked in without making a sound. They closed and locked the door behind them and walked slowly toward the bed, with one of them signaling something to the other with his hand.

The two burly men who'd entered her room didn't stand a chance.

With her hands gripping the two knives, the closet doors opening from the inside, her silent cat steps across the carpet, a leap from behind, the blade of one knife slicing through the carotid artery of one, a sudden drop to her haunches, balancing on the balls of her feet, a particularly low half turn, as the other knife cut through the

203

Achilles tendons of the second in a circular scythe-like movement. The first is disabled. He collapses clutching his throat, the second drops to the carpet beside the bed. A leap onto him, a knife thrust at his throat. He's very strong. He shakes off the shock, grabs her wrist, and twists it, she screams and the knife slips from her hand, her free hand reacts quickly, plunging the second knife straight into his heart. And again. And again. And again. And again.

Carmit rolled off the man she was on and lay on the carpet next to him, catching her breath and examining her right hand. Painful, but nothing was broken.

Agitated knocking on the door made her jump to her feet again. She went back to the closet, retrieved her iPhone from the floor, and looked at the image of the hotel guest from the adjacent room standing outside her door. Carmit poked her head out of the door, hair disheveled and still breathing heavily.

"People are trying to sleep here!" said a middle-aged woman in a French accent, fixing Carmit with an angry stare.

Carmit smiled at her. "I'm terribly sorry. We didn't think we were being so loud. We'll try to keep it down."

The woman muttered something about an unruly generation, turned around, and went back to her room, and Carmit closed the door and locked it. It's a good thing she stuck only her head out. The rest of her body was covered in blood.

She turned on all the lights in the room and looked at the two men on the floor. She didn't recognize either of them. She searched through their pockets. No identification papers at all. Only a few lengths of strong nylon rope on one of them and several 200 shekel bills on the other. She took the money and put it next to her backpack. She removed her T-shirt and panties and placed them in one of the plastic bags provided by the hotel's laundry service. She put the plastic bag next to her backpack, too. She went into the bathroom, washed the knives in the sink, and then stepped into the shower, opening the tap to produce a hot stream of water. The blood washed off onto the white floor of the shower swirled in circles around the drain cover before disappearing. Soap. Shampoo. Conditioner. Soap again. Why do they put such small bottles in the bathroom? Mean bastards. She dried herself off, stepped out of the steam-filled bathroom, got dressed, packed her bag, and checked to make sure she didn't leave anything behind.

Before she left the room, she went back to the two bodies lying on the floor and examined the veins in their arms and legs. There were no needle marks.

* * *

"I'm so sorry but I've just received word from England that my father is in a very bad way. I have to check out and fly home immediately."

The desk clerk in the lobby looked at Carmit's teary eyes. "Of course," she said. "No problem. I'll charge you for just the one night."

"And could you please call a taxi to take me to the airport?"

"Certainly, I'll call one right away. You can sit here in the meantime. Would you like some cold water?"

Carmit thanked the desk clerk. She must remember to also thank Elliot and his geek friends for the sensor camera they gave her before her trip to China.

Within ten minutes the taxi was there to collect her. On the drive to Ben Gurion Airport, Carmit ran her hands over the handles of the knives in her belt. They truly are of the finest quality. She stepped out of the taxi at the airport, waited outside for a few minutes, and then hailed a second cab. "Good morning," she said to the driver. "To the Dan Hotel in Herzliya, please."

Now she'd have to change her appearance. If her straight black hair became blonde curls, no one would recognize her. "Hair makes a big impression." That was one of the phrases that stuck in her head from back in the days of the basic agents training course.

Any moment now a maid was going to walk into Room 607 at the David InterContinental and start screaming at the sight of the two bodies lying on the carpet in large pools of blood.

05/25/2016–23 weeks and 5 days since waking

Yesterday I finished installing almost all the trashcans. I wake up this morning and head out for a day of errands.

I go to a printing services company and order 3 decals of the Tel Aviv Municipality logo for my vehicle—2 large ones and a smaller one. The owner of the print shop tells me that the decals will be ready at noon and I pay him upfront in cash. I then drive to a store in Or-Yehuda that stocks tools for building contractors and purchase a generator, a large jackhammer, waste removal bags, a pickax, a shovel, and a roll of red-and-white striped barricade tap.

I call the Pazgas gas company and order 2 large gas tanks. I give them the Moshav Yanuv address and tell them that someone stole my home's 2 tanks. I arrange to have the tanks installed in the afternoon. Earlier this morning I disconnected the home's 2 tanks and put them in the basement.

I collect my order from the print shop at noon and drive to the Reding parking lot, where, at the far end of the lot, I apply the Tel Aviv Municipality decals to my carpet van. It's a municipal vehicle now, not a carpet van.

I drive around the city in my municipal vehicle and collect Tel Aviv Municipality's stand-alone steel barriers, packing them into the back of the van. Later in the afternoon I go back to the house on Moshav Yanuv to meet up with the gas technician, who installs 2 large gas tanks to replace the missing ones. Once he leaves, I disconnect the new ones again and put them in the back of the van, replacing them with the 2 original tanks that I bring up from the basement.

I take the 2 trashcan bombs I still have left and put them in the back of the van, along with a few additional tools, a carton of mineral water, and cans of corn and peas, a can opener, plates, and a set of disposable cutlery.

05/26/2016–23 weeks and 6 days since waking

I get up very early in the morning, before sunrise, and drive to Rabin Square. I mount the curb and drive the van into the square. I park my municipal van in the center of the large open expanse and form a 20-square meter perimeter around the vehicle using the Tel Aviv Municipality barriers I collected the day before and the red-and-white barricade tape, which I tie between them. I also hang up 4 posters—one on each side of the perimeter—that I ordered yesterday from the print shop.

Caution!
Work underway to repair ruptured water pipe
Commencement Date–Thursday, May 26, 2016
Completion Date–Friday, May 27, 2016
Our apologies for the temporary inconvenience
Tel Aviv Municipality–Yours and for You!

I connect the jackhammer to the generator and arrange all my tools. I begin digging a 2-meter by 2-meter hole in the square at exactly 7 in the morning. I use the jackhammer to remove the layer of paving stones, taking care not to break the stone tiles so that I can use them afterward to cover up the hole. After removing the paving stones I go to work on a layer of gravel and compressed earth, under which the ground is soft and easy to dig through. I fill the waste disposal bags with the earth I remove from the hole. At the end of the day I have a 1-meter deep pit. The work was tiring and I pack my gear into the municipal vehicle, get in, eat a dinner of corn and peas, and go to sleep on the pile of carpets at the back of the van.

I'm up and out of the van the next day at 5 in the morning. Still wearing the municipality shirt from the day before, I stretch and gaze at the facade of the City Hall building in front of me. Not one of the numerous municipality employees who passed by all day bothered to question the nature of my work here in the square yesterday.

I take the 2 trashcan bombs out of the van and lay them down inside the hole I dug. Next to them on each side I place the 2 large gas tanks that I retrieve from the vehicle. I connect a single length of electrical cable to one of the screws on the outer casing of each trashcan bomb—to serve as an antenna. I run the cables to the lip of the hole.

A passerby comes over to peer into the hole just as I'm starting to cover the gas tanks and trashcans with the earth from the bags I filled. He sees the gas tanks and trashcans and the electrical cables connected to them. He turns and takes off quickly and I hurdle the barrier I've built and bring my shovel crashing down on his head. I quickly drag him by his feet into the hole and cover him with earth along with the trashcan bombs and gas tanks. After firmly compressing the earth I add a layer of gravel, which I then cover with a 1-centimeter thick layer of concrete. I give the concrete a few hours to dry before covering it with a thin layer of sand and replacing the paving stones, closing the gaps between them with a filler material identical in color to the other tiles in the square. I allow it all to dry for a little longer and use the time to dismantle the barrier I built, pack the generator, jackhammer, and the rest of my tools back into the van and cast my eyes over the square. It looks good. If I detonate the device I've buried during the course of a large public rally in the square, the damage will be considerable. I drive back to the Reading parking lot, remove the municipality decals from the van, and throw them into the nearest trash bin. My vehicle is a carpet-cleaning van again.

From the parking lot I drive to the Organization's main base to do some reconnaissance. I have to be careful about remaining in one spot for too long, and I can't drive past in the van too often so as not to arouse suspicion. I spend a few weeks surveying the location and trying to figure out if I can get close enough to the base with a gas tanker in order to carry out one of the stages of my plan—but I don't find a weak spot. The base is protected by several security perimeters; it appears to have an internal waste disposal system, I can't find any piping leading into the facility, and the roads into the base are protected by concrete barriers to prevent vehicles from crashing into the facility. Even if I were able to break through with a gas tanker and detonate it on the roof of the base, the damage would be minimal because the facility is built entirely underground.

I abandon my plan to blow up the Organization's main base and drive north to carry out some reconnaissance around the Haifa Bay area instead. I drive through the fields bordering the area of the Oil Refineries and petrochemical plants. They appear easily accessible. If I hijack the gas tanker at the beginning of its route, I can disable the driver and keep him in the cab with me or stop by my house and put him in the basement before continuing north. I can tie the gas tanker's steering wheel in place and jam the gas pedal to the floor and send the vehicle crashing into one of the facilities, but the damage I'd cause would be limited. It would be better to find a central sewage or rainwater drainage pipe that serves the petrochemical plants into which I can empty the gas tanker's entire load. The gas will spread under all the facilities at the site and rise up through hundreds of different openings; igniting the gas will then cause an explosion across the entire site and much more damage.

The old ammonia storage tank at the site won't be able to withstand the blast and will certainly rupture, leak, and explode. In April of 2013, an ammonia storage tank exploded in Texas, some 30 kilometers from the town of Waco. The tank was holding a little under 300 tons of ammonia and the explosion left 15 people dead and 160 injured. The tank in Haifa contains 12,000 tons of ammonia and sits just a few kilometers from the surrounding communities, including the city of Haifa itself. Waco is a town without much luck. It's also the place where David Koresh torched himself and 76 of his cult followers in the wake of a 51-day FBI siege around his so-called Branch Davidians center there. I'll visit there one day. 51 divides by 3, without a remainder, to leave you with a prime number.

I spend the next few weeks visiting the Haifa Bay area and documenting the waste disposal and drainage system openings around the site, as well as the facilities of the various plants, sketching maps in my notebook. I find it strange that the waste disposal infrastructure under the site isn't protected at all. Once I'm done with the fine-tuning of the final stage of my plan, I put an end to the trips up north and focus on getting into shape and preparing equipment for my escape in the event that they manage to track me down.

December 22, 2016

Rotem ended her conversation with Grandpa and replaced the receiver of the encrypted phone. She'd informed him that they'd come up with nothing new since learning about 10483's hospitalization and subsequent escape, and that aside from his departure and return through Ben Gurion Airport he hadn't been spotted anywhere else at all. Grandpa wanted her to try to get bumped up the priority list of the Shin Bet's Eye in the Sky facility; but because the facility was focused solely on the terror attack in Jerusalem, with the prime minister dedicating all available resources to the matter, he didn't think they'd get a time slot until the investigation was over.

Avner's gaze was still fixed on the screens in front of them. "I don't even want to think about what Efrat is going through right now," he said. He and Rotem were sitting in the multimedia room, with images of different faces flashing by on the screens before their eyes. Faces in front of bank ATMs, faces at train stations, faces at Interior Ministry offices, endless faces—and not a single hit from the facial-recognition software. "It's been eighteen days since her abduction, and ten days without even the slightest piece of information concerning her whereabouts or fate."

"Or Amiram's," Rotem added. "He must be holding them somewhere. They're his bargaining chips. As long as he has them he knows we can't do all we'd like to. The Organization isn't going to blow up his house even if we locate it tomorrow, because we know that they could be inside."

Rotem was lying.

Avner knew she was lying.

Nothing was going to stop the Organization from achieving an objective, and objective 10483 was firmly in its crosshairs.

The door to the room opened and a curly head peered in.

Rotem turned her chair toward the door and saw the face of the coordinator of the Domestic Recruitment Department. "Hi Maya," she greeted her. "What's up?"

"You have to see this."

Maya stepped into the room and placed a printed sheet of paper on the desk. "Two days ago," she said, "someone filled out an online application form on the Organization's recruitment website, and in answer to the question: 'Do you have any significant plans for the near future?' he fed us this text that I've printed out here for you. In the section of the online form in which you can attach files like a resume, he uploaded two files. One an image file and the other a video. I've sent them to your mail, Avner. You have to see this."

Avner and Rotem leaned over the printed page on the desk.

Greetings,
A number of matters for your attention and response:
1. Beginning at 08:00 (8 in the morning) on Sunday, the first of January, 2017, a powerful bomb will go off in Tel Aviv every 10 minutes. The blasts will continue until 15:20 (3:20 in the afternoon) of the same day.
2. On Sunday, the first of January, 2017, at 15:30 (3:30 in the afternoon), a very powerful explosive device will be detonated in a public place in Tel Aviv.
3. On Monday, the second of January, 2017, a strategic facility in Israel will be hit by an explosion. The damage it causes will far exceed the damage caused by all the explosive devices on the first of January (the day before).

To prevent the aforesaid, you must take the following action:
1. At 20:30 (8:30 in the evening) on Saturday, the thirty-first of December, 2016, all three of Israel's major news channels (Channels 2, 10, and 1) must air the following message: "Gabriel Silverman (Serial Number 10483) was recruited into the service of his people and homeland and

he served them well. Nevertheless, we tried to assassinate him following the completion of his duties. We apologize for the distress we have caused him and hope for his forgiveness."

2. The apology must be issued on air by one of the Organization's senior officials (inner circle) who must be standing in a conference room at the Organization's main base with the backdrop of an Israeli flag and the Organization's official emblem.

3. If you choose not to air the apology on the thirty-first of December and then change your minds later when the bombs start going off, you will be able to issue the apology and thereby suspend the blasts by means of a live radio broadcast. Since I won't be in front of the TV on that day, you will have to broadcast the apology on the Reshet Bet radio station. In such an event, I will suspend the bombing campaign; but for the entire rest of the week, you will have to air the apology on all the eight o'clock evening news programs again, along with an apology to the residents of Tel Aviv for the distress they suffered as a result of your inability to meet my demands on time.

Good luck!

"Un-fucking-believable!" Avner exclaimed.

"The first of January is just a week away," Rotem said.

"We have to notify the inner circle. I'm calling Grandpa again. Call Rafael and get him to come here. Can we check the IP address of the computer he used to fill out the form?"

"Just a sec, let's look at the files he attached. Open your mail for a moment."

Avner touched the space bar on the keyboard of his laptop. He ran his finger over the fingerprint reader and entered a key phrase to log into the Orion system. He looked for Maya's email in his in-box folder and opened it. Attached to the email was a file named BARS AND ROSES.JPG. Avner opened it, and the image of Efrat and Amiram that appeared on the screen took his breath away. Both were standing in an iron cage in a basement somewhere, illuminated by a beam of light, and both were holding a single red rose in their right hand, their arms reaching through the bars of the cage. Their faces were expressionless. They looked pale. Both had lost weight. Hanging on the bars of the cage on either side of them were two white sheets that were pulled to the side like curtains.

They're alive. He hadn't killed Efrat. He can still save her. There's hope. The sense of relief that washed over Avner was soon replaced by a sense of dread. The clock was working against them. Avner tried to remain calm and focused, but he couldn't. He jumped up from his chair. "Dirty motherfucker!" he exclaimed. "He's got no intention of releasing them at all. He's going to turn them into one of his grotesque works of art in that basement, too. We have to find him."

Rotem placed her hand over Maya's. "Maya," she said, "can you get someone from Information Security to come here right away? We'll take a look at the video he sent meanwhile."

"No problem," Maya said and left the room. Avner opened the attached video file. He and Rotem watched a recording from the basement that was blown up on Ibn Gvirol Street on December 4. The last few seconds of the video showed a caption that read:

> I have a camera in my new basement, too. If you don't want another movie like the one you've just watched, you'd better carry out Instructions 1 and 2 that I outlined in response to the question: "Do you have any significant plans for the near future?" on your standard online application form.

The video ended and Rotem and Avner sat there in silence for a while. They had both known members of the team killed in the blast and watching the scene unfold this time from an angle that offered a view from above of the entire room was a harrowing experience.

Maya returned to the room accompanied by a burly young man with long hair in a ponytail. "Hi," he said, "Alex from Information Security. What can I do for you?"

"See what you can get from these files."

Alex started by examining the data of the image file. "It was taken with an iPhone with the Location Services option on. Let me see if he hasn't erased the EXIF data." After pressing several keys and clicking the mouse a few times, Alex opened a Notepad document and recorded the coordinates he found. He then opened a GIS application and entered the data. "Write down this address," he said. "Thirty-one HaHarzit Street, Savyon. It's at the end of the street. A stand-alone house. I'm checking the video file now." He uploaded the file to the network's share platform and ran it through various software programs. "No. It's completely clean. There's no data aside from the video itself."

"Tell me, do we know the IP addresses of the computers applicants use to complete our online forms?"

"Of course. It's one of several checks we run on the forms, to make sure they come from legitimate places, and we save the information with the metadata of the application. Do you have the application's serial number?"

"Yes," Maya said, and she promptly read out a long number to him. Alex entered the serial number into an admin application and added the IP address he found to the Notepad document that was still open on Avner's computer. He then logged into the Organization's Intranet and entered the IP address he had just recorded. It took just a few seconds for a street address to pop up: HaHarzit Street, Savyon.

"This form was filled out near where the photo was taken. In the same place," Alex said. "Or someone could have doctored the image file and planted the location. That's also a possibility."

Avner stood up. "We need to go there now," he said. "He may have bought or rented the house there and could be keeping them there in the basement."

"It could be a trap," Rotem responded, getting to her feet.

"We'll take two teams from Operations and approach with caution. We've got no choice. They could be down there now with their time running out. If he wants to do all he has planned for the first of January, he may want to kill them first then so they don't interfere with his plans. Call Rafael and tell him to bring his team, and I'll speak to Grandpa and ask him to give us another team from Operations."

I slide the tip of my finger across my iPhone screen and unlock the device with a 4-digit code. I look at the 2 shortcuts I've defined in the Safari browser.

203 Ibn Gvirol Street Blast
McLean Blast

I slowly move my finger toward to the McLean Blast label, touch it gently, and turn on the television, selecting CNN. Nothing out of the ordinary transpires on the news for the 1st 2 minutes or so, and the sports reporter continues to question some NBA player about his 3-point shooting average. But then the interview is interrupted and the transmission switches to the newsroom, with an anchor behind the desk. He appears to be on edge and flustered. "We have a special newsflash for you from Washington," he says. "It appears, according to reports that have just come in, that there's been a major explosion in the Washington, D.C., area. I'm about to go to our camera in Washington; but please note, we will be airing unedited and graphic footage and some of the images may be harsh and offensive."

The newsroom is replaced by a somewhat shaky shot of a huge mushroom cloud. The voice of the reporter next to the camera can be heard in the background. "We're bringing you the first live images from the scene here in Washington," she says. "You can see people running through the streets. We're broadcasting from North Bethesda, Maryland, the blast here felt like an earthquake and you can see that the streets are full of broken glass from the windows that simply shattered and crashed to the ground from buildings around us. If this is what has happened here, I don't even want to think about what is happening now in downtown Washington, D.C., about 7 or 8 miles from where we are. You can see the huge mushroom cloud that Patrick, our cameraman, is focusing on now; and although I'm no expert on the subject, of course, I have to say that

217

what I'm seeing now looks like a nuclear explosion. What you are seeing now as a black mushroom cloud was previously a giant ball of fire, like a small sun. It's still too early to say what has happened in Washington, but the devastation must be immense. Immense."

The reporter's voice trails off and makes way for a cacophony of sounds from the scene—people screaming as they run aimlessly through the streets, sirens of rescue and emergency vehicles and alarms of cars and stores in the area. The camera focuses on them for a minute and then moves back to the black mushroom cloud that hovers over Washington like an enormous jellyfish. The broadcast jumps back to the studio and catches the anchor straightening his shirt; and then it switches again, this time to camera footage from a helicopter of the same mushroom cloud and the burning city below it.

08/11/2016–34 weeks and 6 days since waking

I wake at 1:30 in the morning and look at my iPhone that's charging on the bedside table. I slide the tip of my finger across my iPhone screen and unlock the device with a 4-digit code. I look at the 2 shortcuts I've defined in the Safari browser without touching them. I turn on the television, to CNN, and watch a report about the arrest of an American tourist in North Korea. The reporter is interviewing his parents, who live in Champaign, Illinois.

My dream seemed very real. I lock the iPhone screen and wait patiently for the final stage in my plan against the Organization. The plan must be implemented one step at a time.

I call a military supply store and order 7 bulletproof vests that offer protection against shrapnel as well as 9mm and .44 Magnum rounds. I ask them to add ballistic plates to the pockets of the vests so as to enhance their protective capabilities against 5.56mm rounds from an M-16 and 7.62mm rounds from a Kalashnikov. The vests are made of Kevlar fiber covered with Cordura fabric. I also order 7 protective helmets against shrapnel and gunfire. The guy who takes the order from me asks what I need all the equipment for, and I explain to him that I'm making preparations for the arrival of a team of Japanese journalists. They're coming to cover various aspects of the Israeli-Palestinian conflict and will be wandering around the territories. "Do you know that they refused to provide them with insurance coverage if they didn't go about their business dressed in bulletproof vests and helmets all the time? And they certainly won't be able to hide from the insurance company. They'll be documenting themselves on camera all the time."

The store assistant laughs. He says everything will be ready in about a week and asks if I want to give him a credit card number now. I tell him I'd rather go to one of the chain's branches and pay in cash. "They're paying me in cash so I'd prefer to simply pass it on. And you can make out the invoice to Roman—Group Tours," I tell him. I arrange to pay for my order at the factory store in Petah Tikva and I go there and pay in cash and take the invoice. I check with the Orders Department to make sure that the payment has been recorded and that the equipment will be delivered on time to the Moshav Yanuv address I've provided.

Meanwhile, I purchase a professional sewing machine and very strong yarn that I leave for now in the living room of the house. I'm in much better physical shape already. I've set up a gym in one of the rooms of the house and I train for at least 2 hours every day.

Since I have so much time on my hands, and a good jackhammer, I dig a tunnel from the basement of the house to the grove of trees across the street. I reinforce the tunnel with lengths of lumber that I fix together to form T-shapes and then place along the length of the structure at 2-meter intervals to support a corrugated steel ceiling, like Hamas does in its tunnels. I calculate my daily excavation rate and expect to complete the tunnel in 2 months' time. When I'm done, I'll keep my carpet van parked across the street close to the opening of the tunnel, and then, when they get to me one day, I'll slip out through the tunnel, make my way to the van, and flee. When the tunnel is complete, I'll cover the end across the street with a piece of corrugated steel and then a thin layer of earth on top so that the opening can't be seen from the outside.

The work in the tunnel creates a lot of dust and I wear a protective mask on my face. I scatter the excavated earth around the house and in the nearby fields, carrying it out through the basement. In conjunction with my excavation work, I also plant parsley, mint, and citrus tree seedlings in the garden. The parsley grows slowly, but the mint plants are quick to flourish.

08/17/2016–35 weeks and 5 days since waking

The doorbell rings and I suspend my digging and ascend from the basement. I wash my face and neck and go outside. My order of bulletproof vests and helmets has arrived and I sign for them and take the packages. "I've been working in the garden," I tell the delivery guy. "That's why I'm covered in dirt. Would you like something to drink?" The delivery guy thanks me and walks back to his vehicle. He has more deliveries to complete and is pressed for time. "Everyone's buying bulletproof vests these days because of all the stabbing attacks," he says.

I open the packages in the living room, pull out the vests, ballistic plates, and helmets, and get to work. In order to be able to work with both hands free, I dress the backrest of a chair in a long black sweatshirt and place one of the bulletproof vests over the sweatshirt. I sew the 2 items together with a needle and thread. It's a lengthy process that takes several hours. When I'm done, I take the rest of the vests, dismantle them, and use some of their pieces to fortify the sweatshirt's long sleeves, too. I do the same with a pair of black jeans. I use pieces from the vests to fortify the denim fabric from top to bottom, sewing everything together by hand. I use the sewing machine I bought only to secure the edges of the pieces of Kevlar before I sew them by hand to the sweatshirt and jeans. I take the pair of trekking boots that I also purchased from the military supplies store and fortify them, too. When I'm done, I'm left with an armored suit that I will use if the Organization figures out my location. The chances of them doing so are very slim, but I need to be prepared for any and every eventuality. I hang the suit on a hook I've fixed to the living room wall, with the helmet suspended above it. It looks like a robot. I take my iPhone out of my pocket and take a picture of it as a memento.

I thread a strong belt through the loops of the jeans to hold them up. The jeans weigh about 4 kilos and I decide to sew them to the sweatshirt to create a one-piece suit that can be put on in a hurry and won't fall off me. I detach the vest from the front of the sweatshirt, cut a slit down the front of the black fabric, and sew on Velcro pads that I've removed from the other vests, thus allowing me to dress and close the suit quickly. My protective suit is heavy. It weighs close to 15 kilograms after I've inserted the ballistic plates into the pockets of the vest; but it will do its job well.

Night has fallen. I go into the garden, pick a few mint leaves, and make myself a cup of hot tea. Then I shower, eat a dinner consisting of a chicken breast and broccoli, and go to sleep.

December 22, 2016

Grandpa came to the end of the letter that 10483 had sent to the inner circle via his fictitious application—and the conference room fell silent. The large stretch of lawn, under the gray light outside, was visible through the room's glass walls. Heavy gray clouds hung in the sky, but the rain had yet to come.

"Do you think he'll go through with it?"

"Unfortunately, yes. We've learned thus far that he was in a coma for nine years before disappearing from Lowenstein Hospital about a year ago. We also know that he spent a little less than two months abroad. From the ninth of February to the twenty-ninth of March. We have an updated photograph of him from the hospital and he was caught on camera at Ben Gurion traveling to Spain and returning from Frankfurt. Since then, he's had eight and a half months to prepare, and we all know what he's capable of."

A gray-haired woman rested her intertwined hands on the table. "Clearly we aren't going to go to the news with this psychotic text," she said.

"Clearly," Grandpa said, and continued. "If we don't get to him before he kicks off his New Year's party, we'll simply have to wait for the first of January and keep all our eyes, and those of Unit 8200, trained inward rather than outward, and join forces with those of the Shin Bet to see how he detonates the explosive devices and from where, and to wait for him to make a mistake that gives us a chance to get to him. We won't have much time."

"Do we have any idea what he was doing while abroad?"

"No."

The mood in the room was gloomy, and one of the men sitting at the table spoke up: "He can cause us tremendous damage," he said. "Seeking assistance from the Shin Bet and army exposes us. We can't let anyone else in on this. Using a cover story and pointing a finger at Islamic State, Tel Aviv can be placed under a curfew the moment he detonates the first bomb. That should minimize the number of casualties. But he also talks about a strike against a strategic facility the following day. He could be referring to the Electric Corporation's Orot Rabin power station near Hadera, or the reactor in Dimona, or the Weizmann Institute, or something like that. We'll have to up the alert status ahead of the first of January to give everyone time to prepare. We can say that our source in Islamic State has informed us of plans to carry out such an attack in Israel, and thereby give the army, the Tel Aviv Municipality, the reactor, Ben Gurion Airport, and every other strategic installation time to get organized. I don't think he will try to take a shot at the army. It would be too difficult. We have to get our hands on him before he manages to put his plan into practice."

Grandpa continued. "We have yet to come up with a single lead," he said. "He hasn't been caught on camera anywhere and he appears to have assumed an identity we are unaware of. He hasn't touched the credit cards he still has from his time in the Organization. He's using a bank account we don't know about. Cash only probably.

"I'll be demanding immediate access to the Shin Bet's AngelFire facility. 10483 poses a greater threat than the issues they're working on now. We may not have been able to demand priority before this, but we certainly can now. With the same cover story about an Islamic State threat. I'll be contacting the prime minister's bureau to arrange the priority issue immediately after this meeting."

"I suggest we come to a decision now in this forum to put an end to the business of the transformations," said the gray-haired woman. "We are playing here with things whose long-term consequences and effects we know nothing about. It began with the mess of your Grasshopper Project and has only worsened now. Let me remind everyone here that two years ago I barely managed to quash an idea raised here in this forum to perform a transformation on the prime minister's wife."

"Grasshopper Project?" one of the members of the inner circle asked with a puzzled look on his face.

Grandpa took a sip of his coffee. "If you'd like to discuss a little bit of history, then yes, the initial transformations were performed on grasshoppers."

"Grasshoppers?"

"Yes. Because the first experiments were conducted on flies, we moved forward in relatively small steps. While studying the technology, we came up with the idea of performing a dual transformation on the grasshoppers. One transformation was designed to cause them to identify the smell of plastic as the smell of a gourmet meal such as corn leaves or wheat, and the second transformation involved altering their built-in guidance system from electromagnetic to radioactive. This was before we began incorporating sound and video into the transformation process."

"What?"

"It's very simple. We didn't want them to plot their flight courses based on their inherent guidance system, which takes the structure of the electromagnetic field around the Earth into consideration. Instead, we wanted them to be drawn to radioactive radiation, gamma radiation."

"What for?"

"So we could send them off to Iran. So they'd be drawn to the nuclear reactors there and land in droves— I'm talking about several swarms we were planning to raise, with millions of grasshoppers in each one—and start to gnaw away at all the plastic insulation around the electrical wires and circuits at the reactors, thus leading to an endless number of electrical shorts and system failures followed by reactor meltdowns at all the facilities."

"How?"

"When the power systems go down, the cooling systems stop drawing water to cool down the reactor's core. Just like in Fukushima. Everything explodes. It would knock them back twenty years in terms of their nuclear aspirations."

"I have to say that that has to be one of the most outlandish ideas I've ever heard. Why didn't you go through with it in the end?"

"We did. We had already started to set up the grasshopper breeding facility in one of the bunkers on Mount Hermon, but the transformations weren't able to generate the precise level of attraction to radiation that we required. Every time we released several thousand for a trial run, those fucking grasshoppers flew off in the opposite direction, to the south, even though we released them on Mount Hermon with the idea that they would be drawn north through Syria. We were forced to deploy crop-spraying aircraft to exterminate the swarm—and even then, several dozen grasshoppers managed to get to Dimona and do some damage there."

"Dimona?"

"Yes. The radiation from the reactor in Dimona proved to be more of a draw than the radiation from the Iranian facilities. Apparently the radiation coming from the Dimona reactor is so strong that it hampered everything we were trying to do. We had more success with people than with grasshoppers."

"It's good that you did a trial run," said the woman with the gray hair. "I don't even want to think what would have happened if all those swarms had landed on the Dimona reactor. I propose that we come to a decision now concerning a ban on all future use of transformations and the shutting down of the department responsible for the matter. Who's in favor?"

Everyone around the table aside from Grandpa raised their hands.

"Motion passed."

The rest of the inner circle members nodded their heads in agreement. Grandpa stood up. "I'll keep you posted on our progress in the investigation."

"Just a moment, one last question before we end this meeting," one of the participants said. "How did you prime him for mass killings? What mechanisms did you trigger?"

"We used his hunger mechanism. The only way for him to feel satiated was for him to carry out mass killings. Failure to do so would leave him hungry all the time."

We're sitting on the sand and looking at the sea. The lights of the city create a yellow-orange-white aura behind us. The beach itself is dark and a cool breeze is blowing in from the sea. The sky is cloudless and dotted with countless tiny stars and a large white full moon. It's the middle of the month.

"You know," he says, "after the accident with the bus, I was lying on a stretcher in the ambulance. It was driving fast but I could see everything in slow motion. Someone was sitting next to me and holding my hand and shouting to the driver: 'No pulse now for two minutes.' We are all born with two hundred forty million heartbeats and the countdown begins immediately. Tick. Tick. Tick. Tick. Tick. Until your time is up. It's an internal clock that counts the moments of your life from beginning to end."

"That's assuming you live to be eighty-four."

"The ambulance siren sounded as if it was coming from far away. The driver raced over a speed bump, jolting everything inside the ambulance, including the stretcher with my broken body. It hurt. The ambulance made a sharp right turn and a sharp left immediately thereafter and then stopped abruptly. The rear doors opened and I was wheeled down white corridors with fluorescent lights on the ceiling. I heard someone shout: 'Quickly, to the operating room.' And we went down another corridor that ended in a set of white doors with round glass windows set in them. The doors opened and they wheeled me in on the stretcher. Everything was hazy. I heard them count: 'One, two, three.' And hands gripped me and moved me over to the operating table. I was surrounded by doctors."

"Were you conscious?"

"Yes. I heard a woman's voice say: 'He's unconscious, applying desflurane mask.' 'Respiration rate normalizing, oxygen saturation above ninety.' 'He's under. All yours.' "

"And did you remain awake?"

"Yes. I could feel the doctors performing surgery on me. The anesthetic left my muscles paralyzed and I couldn't move. I couldn't see much other than blurry images of people standing over me, but I could feel everything—the doctor who was setting the bones of my legs in place, the one who was reconstructing my face, the power drill that was fixing steel plates to the bones of my legs. I experienced degrees of agony I had never felt before, despite the fact that I have a wealth of experience when it comes to pain. If I could have moved a muscle, I would have grabbed one of the scalpels resting on the metal tray near my head and slashed the faces of all those doctors who were butchering me without checking if I was properly anesthetized. The doctor dealing with my eyes was reciting a children's song while he worked on me, and then he started chatting with the nurse next to him."

"What did they talk about?"

"He asked her if she was familiar with the definition of anxiety. She said: 'An intense fear of something specific perhaps?' And then he said to her: '$A = Th \times Ti$.' "

"Which means?"

"Anxiety is the product of thought multiplied by time."

"And did you remain awake throughout the surgery?"

"No. Shortly afterward I was sucked into a black tunnel, like a movie stunt double with a wire attached to his back who's tugged backward quickly to simulate being blown backward by a bomb blast. The lights of the operating theater that were shining orange red through my closed eyelids withdrew rapidly and disappeared, and I suddenly found myself in a pitch-black space, a timeless dimension."

I lean my head against his shoulder and look up at the sky. The moon disappears. I lift my head.

"Did you see that?" I ask.

"What?"

"The moon was up there a second ago and now it's gone."

"It must be hidden behind a cloud."

"But I saw it happen. It was too quick. I saw the moon disappear like a streetlight suddenly going out." I push my bare feet into the sand. It's warmer below the surface from the sun it absorbed before night fell a short while ago. I wiggle my toes in the sand and feel its warmth slipping between them.

"There wasn't a single cloud in the sky; and if there was one, we wouldn't be seeing all the stars right now. If there was a cloud, it would be hiding them, too."

"You pay too much attention to detail. Stop being so concerned about what's happening around us instead of sitting here on the sand and making out with me."

His eyes are on me now and not on the stars. We kiss.

"Do you know what it means?" I ask.

"What?"

"If the moon vanished like that in a flash, it means we don't have much time."

"What do you mean?"

"The moon is responsible for the ocean tides. Its gravitational pull affects them. When it hangs above the center of an ocean, the waters rise up toward it like a huge hill of sorts."

"I should have paid more attention during physics class. Does this mean there'll be no more tides?"

"Correct."

He runs his hand through my hair.

"That's a shame," he says, "because change is a good thing. It's nice

when it's low tide and you can walk arm-in-arm along the seashore looking for shells."

"We won't be able to do that any longer."

"That's a shame."

He gets up and brushes the sand off his pants. He still can't comprehend the significance of what just happened.

"Come," he says, "we still have time to grab something to eat before the restaurants fill with people and noise."

"We don't have time."

"Sure we do. We can make it. It's still really early now."

I look at him.

"Why are you so sad all of a sudden?" he asks.

"We don't have time because if the moon has disappeared and is no longer drawing up the hill of water from the center of the ocean, then it's approaching."

"What's approaching?"

"A tsunami. Bigger than anything we've ever seen before. And there's no point in trying to make a run for it. The water will surely reach as far as the hills of Jerusalem."

December 22, 2016

Carmit woke early, remnants of the images in her dream still fading. She got up and stretched. Heavy gray clouds hung over the Herzliya shoreline and she gazed at them through the window of her hotel room. The reflection in the glass appeared unfamiliar and Carmit was startled for a moment when she saw the mop of blonde curls looking back at her. She wasn't used to her new look. She exhaled onto the cold glass to form a circle of condensation and drew a smiley on it with her finger.

It's cold outside. She should dress warmly and buy an umbrella, too. She left hers in London. She must have forgotten somehow that Israel, the land of eternal sun, also has a winter in December. She closed the curtains and went out into the hallway. A quick look left and right, nothing suspicious. A look up. The tiny motion sensor she'd dismantled from above the door to her room at the InterContinental in Tel Aviv and fixed to the doorframe here was still there. She got into the elevator and went down to the dining room on the lobby floor.

Soon she'd go to the Organization's main base. She had yet to decide exactly when and exactly who she was going to speak to, but she decided that it was something she had to do. She'd put a few safeguards in place beforehand, just to make sure they don't get any ideas in their heads, like trying to make her disappear, for example.

When it came to breakfasts at Israeli hotels, the size and variety on offer always surprised her. Even when she'd lived here, she never understood why someone would want to eat so much so soon after getting up. She served herself a hard-boiled egg and a small portion of Greek salad and went over to one of the small tables at the far end of the dining room. She'd just sat down when a waiter approached and asked if she'd like some tea or coffee. "Earl Grey, please," Carmit replied and took out her laptop in the meantime. She connected to the hotel's Wi-Fi network, logged into her Gmail account, and composed several emails with particularly incriminating material that she scheduled to be sent automatically from her account to a number of intelligence agencies in a week's time. If the Organization decided to hold her somewhere, she'd have a bargaining chip.

She closed the laptop, returned it to her backpack, finished her tea, and got up. She went out to the parking lot, got into the car she'd rented the day before, and started the engine. The car's temperature gauge showed 11 degrees Celsius outside. Carmit turned on the heat, ran her hands over the two knives in her belt, and drove off in the direction of the base.

She stopped for a moment a few dozen meters from the entrance to the base, her gaze fixed on the big steel gate and the guard post next to it. But before she could muster up the final drops of courage she needed to enter the place that was once her second home, the gate opened and three cars, tires screeching, came flying out one after the other. Carmit spotted a familiar face in one of them. She knew Avner from her training period at the Organization, when she was still a rookie. Without giving it much thought, she waited for the cars to pass her and then did a U-turn and started following them from a safe distance.

The three-car convoy sped along Route 5, turned onto Route 4, and exited at the Bar-Ilan Junction. She followed them to the entrance to Savyon, and then from there to HaHarzit Street. As soon as she saw the cul-de-sac sign at the beginning of the street, she parked her car and allowed the convoy to continue on. She got out of her car, locked it, and continued on foot down the street.

When she caught sight of the three vehicles parked outside the secluded home at the very end of the street, she slowed down and stopped, gazing from afar at the scene unfolding ahead of her and doing stretching exercises as if she had just come to the end of a long walk. She watched as the cars' occupants left their vehicles and surrounded the house at the end of the street. Nobody opened the door for them from the inside, and one of them climbed through one of windows and opened the door for the rest. Two remained outside and everyone else went in. They all emerged again some fifteen minutes later. A group of men remained standing outside the entrance to the house and someone appeared to be briefing them, and another two individuals had moved away from the house a little and were talking on their cell phones. From where she was standing she could tell almost for sure that one of them was Avner, and that the other was a young woman. They were walking slowly in Carmit's direction and she finished stretching, turned away so they wouldn't get too close to her, and pressed herself flat to the ground after the shockwave from two big explosions threw her to the sidewalk.

Carmit jumped quickly to her feet. Luckily she'd managed to break her fall with her hands and not her face. Her palms were grazed, she had minor cuts on her skin, and a ringing in her ears. Apart from that, absolute silence. She turned to look in the direction of the vehicles and the people who had been standing outside the home. They were strewn across the ground.

She hurried toward them, bypassing Avner and the woman lying next to him and going first of all to those who were closer to the house. They were all dead. Severe blast injuries and countless fragments of shrapnel had given them no chance. She left them and went over to the young woman sprawled unconscious on the road and put her ear to her mouth. After confirming that the woman was still breathing, Carmit gently checked her over with her hands. Nothing appeared to be too badly broken, but she may have suffered internal organ damage and there were several bits of shrapnel lodged in her back. She had been standing with her back to the house. The bombs that went off must have been packed with a large quantity of metal fragments. A red stain was spreading rapidly over one of the young woman's legs. Carmit took one of the knives out of her belt and quickly cut through the entire length of fabric, exposing a thigh wound from which blood was pouring out in spurts. Carmit removed her backpack and placed it on the ground next to her. She took out the laptop charger, disconnected its power cord, wound the cord around the young woman's thigh twice, close to her groin, and then knotted it. She tightened the improvised tourniquet until the blood stopped flowing from the wound, stood up, and went over to Avner, who was lying unconscious on the road some two meters away. He, too, had suffered blast and shrapnel injuries. More severe, it seemed, than those of the woman she had just treated. A deep tear in his forearm was causing him to lose blood rapidly, too. Carmit reached for her laptop charger again, this time using the cable that ran from the charger to the laptop itself—and she wound the cord around Avner's forearm, close to the elbow, tightening it until the blood stopped. She left the charger connected to the other end of the cable and stood up. By now two people had emerged from neighboring homes. Both looked like foreign workers employed to do maintenance work at the villas nearby. It would still take a few more minutes for the security forces to show up. Carmit ran into the house at the end of the street and had a quick look around. There was no sign of anything out of the ordinary. She picked up the phone and dialed 101.

"Magen David Adom."

"Come quickly! A terror attack with fatalities at the end of HaHarzit Street in Savyon."

"Who are you? I nee—"

Carmit hung up the phone and noticed that her backpack was still open. She'd forgotten to close it after taking out the laptop charger. She closed the bag and noticed two holes in the fabric at the back. Carmit opened the bag again to check the state of its contents. Two steel nails were deeply embedded in her copy of Scarlett Thomas's *The End of Mr. Y.* Mr. Y had saved her spine. "Thank you, Ariel Manto," she said to the book, kissing its scarred back cover.

Carmit closed her backpack and raced back to her car. She got in, started the engine, pulled out of the street, and headed for the exit from Savyon, where she stopped at the side of the road and waited. The first vehicles to fly past were two fire trucks with sirens blaring and lights flashing red. "Not much work for you," Carmit said to herself. The fire trucks were soon followed by several ambulances and police vehicles of various kinds. Carmit remained in her car and sipped from a small bottle of mineral water she'd left on the front passenger seat. A few minutes later, two wailing ambulances flashed past on their way out of Savyon. She stuck to them and followed them for a few minutes to the Tel Hashomer Hospital. She watched the ambulances offload the wounded before turning around and driving away.

December 24, 2016

The drops fell slowly one after the other in the drip chamber of the IV connected to Rotem's arm. She was lying in a hospital bed under the influence of a sedative of some kind. She'd regained consciousness for a few minutes after being admitted, and the doctors decided to knock her out again after she tried to get out of her bed and flee the place in her hospital gown. She was lying motionless now, and her visitor was sitting on a chair in front of her and looking through a newspaper. He leaned forward and said something to her but she didn't respond. When he leaned back again, he felt two metal points pressing lightly against his sides, slightly above his waist.

"Don't do anything foolish if you're fond of your kidneys," Carmit said. "Dialysis is a shitty thing and there's a long waiting list for transplants."

"I've been waiting for you," Grandpa responded. "You've picked up a nice British accent, it suits you. You can put the knives away. I have no intention of doing you any harm. In fact, I could use some help."

Carmit put the knives back in her belt and stepped out from behind the curtain. "I'm surprised you didn't arrange to have a security detail here. I looked. But maybe that's because I dispatched the two guys you sent to my hotel room. Did you really think they'd get to me?"

Grandpa looked into Carmit's brown eyes. "I swear I have no idea what you're talking about," he said. "And you really do have to get rid of those curls. Not you at all."

"Two gentlemen tried to kill me in my room at the InterContinental. You must have heard about it on the news."

"That was you?"

"Yes."

"I should have guessed," Grandpa said with a smile. "No, they weren't there at my behest. You know we like to play cat and mouse, but I'd never harm you. I have bigger problems right now."

"I know. But you've brought them upon yourselves. That bomb blast in Savyon."

"It's way worse. You don't even know the half of it," Grandpa sighed.

"It's your fault. And mine, too. You used me to transform him. To drive him to seek maximum collateral damage. And I helped you do so. I wasn't aware of what I was doing. But how does it go? Ignorance of the law excuses no man. I've been sentenced to live with what I've done."

"Don't tell me, Carmit, that you've developed a conscience all of a sudden."

"Not all of a sudden. It was a gradual process, following the birth of my children. I'd already made up my mind to sever ties for good, but a series of dreams convinced me that I need to fix a few things before I managed to get a decent night's sleep like a normal human being. That's why I'm here. I'm doing some fixing. I've come to help that agent on which you performed all those transformations."

"Help him? Are you fucked in the head?"

"My head is just fine. It's his head that's fucked up. You fucked it up. You—"

"Just a moment. That agent was our mistake. We realize that now after reading his notes and seeing—"

"Do you have the notebook?"

"You know about the notebook? How do you know about it?"

"I read parts of it when I performed the transformation on him in Bariloche. I only got through the beginning."

"And you didn't tell me about it at the time?"

"I didn't feel like it. How did you get it?"

"He sent it to us. He wanted us to read everything. I have it all here with me, a scanned PDF file, and I have no problem sending it to you. In fact, I want you to read it. And I want to show you a movie."

Grandpa retrieved his laptop from its case and opened it. Finger-print, password, key phrase, and he opened the video file that showed the agents going into the basement and the events that followed. "Do you see what he did?" he said. "He kept two of our agents alive in that basement for months, hooked up to IVs so they'd die slowly and in agony. That was ten years ago. And he sent the notebook to us now knowing that we'd read it and send people to find the basement; and he sat somewhere with a remote control device and a camera and simply waited for us to go in so he could blow up the entire building on Ibn Gvirol with our people inside. That was twenty days ago. And then he sent us to Savyon to find a nonexistent basement in a house whose owner is currently living abroad so that he could blow us up again—and that, I'm afraid to say, is still only the be-ginning."

"You caused him to do those things."

"No. It's him. He's damaged. We exploited his fundamental character traits for our own needs, with the reinforcement of the transformations—and we got it wrong. He does more harm than good. Much more harm than good. He saved us in the past from a nuclear threat, but my concern is that this same threat will come back to haunt us through him, and he is far more efficient and dan-gerous that those we feared in the first place. The final transforma-tion that you performed on him included an expiration date. We implanted a date on which he was supposed to commit suicide. Re-grettably, it worked only partially. Ten years ago, he jumped in front of an oncoming bus, but he didn't die. Apparently he's a lot better at killing others than he is at killing himself. Unfortunately, an ambu-lance that was passing by rushed him to the ER at Ichilov Hospital and they managed to save him there. We learned all of this just re-cently. You have to understand something, he's still the exact same person—even after the run-in with the speeding bus on Ibn Gvirol and nine years in a coma. It wasn't you who turned him into what he is; I can assure you that his brain contains no remnants of the transformations you performed on him. We can't take credit for who he is. And now he's abducted Avner's wife and Amiram, too. He's sent us a letter outlining his plans to detonate various explosive devices in various locations around Tel Aviv if we don't broadcast outrageous apologies through all the news media outlets. Here, read this." Grandpa opened the application form on his laptop and passed it to Carmit. She took the laptop and read the document.

"And what's he been doing for the past ten years? Why did he decide to take action now?"

"Like I said, he was unconscious for nine years. At Lowenstein Hospital. We weren't looking for him all that time because he killed someone, placed the body in his house, and torched it along with the entire structure. We were sure he was dead. We thought back then that we'd seen the last of him. He needs to be taken out."

"If you want my help, I'm going to need more details."

"The three assignments he received—around the time of the transformations you performed on him—involved the assassination of three members of an Iranian cell that was in the process of purchasing a nuclear bomb from Kazakhstan. He killed all three and caused extensive collateral damage."

"You can say that again," Carmit interjected.

". . . and I believe he managed to get his hands on the bomb."

"What?"

"I think he managed to get one of his victims to give up the location of the bomb and has smuggled it into Israel. That's the worst-case scenario, and we need to act accordingly and assume he's going to detonate the bomb here."

"He's not going to detonate it here. That's what he went to the United States for. And I don't buy it." Carmit and Grandpa turned their heads to look at the bed. Rotem had her eyes open and repeated her words: "I don't buy it."

"Don't buy what?" Grandpa asked.

"That you performed the transformations on him just to assassinate three scientists. You had another agenda, too."

Grandpa remained silent.

"And the bomb isn't here," Rotem added. "It's in the United States."

"What?"

"I've been thinking about this now while you've been talking," Rotem continued. "He flew from Israel to Spain and returned from Frankfurt. I think somewhere along the way he collected the bomb and transported it to the United States to detonate it there. We're looking at Europe but Europe isn't the issue. We're seeing only the beginning and end points of his trip."

"But why the United States?"

"Because it will cause us more damage there than if he were to detonate it here or anywhere else. He's disturbed but not stupid. If he detonates it here, the entire world will be behind us. It'll result in a very large number of casualties in the short term; but in the long run, as crazy as it sounds, it will strengthen the State of Israel. If he detonates it in the United States and implicates us, it will spell the end of Israel. If Mommy and Daddy America get whacked with a nuclear bomb by their troublesome kid in the Middle East, they'll send him to boarding school."

"How the hell would he smuggle a nuclear bomb into the United States?"

"Leave it to him."

The room fell silent. Grandpa stroked his beard and contemplated.

"We have to kill him," Carmit said.

Rotem sat up in bed and stretched. "What happened to the other people who were with me when the bombs went off?" she asked. "Is Avner okay?"

"Aside from Avner, they were all killed. The two of you were standing slightly farther away from the center of the blasts. There were two devices."

"Fuck. Rafael and his team, too?"

"Yes."

"How's Avner doing?"

"He's out of commission. He'll be here for a good few weeks still.

Several nails had some fun with his liver, lungs, and one of his kidneys. His condition isn't life threatening, but he has to remain hospitalized. Fortunately, you got off more lightly."

Rotem closed her eyes and went quiet for a moment. "Okay, bring me some clothes. I need to get out of here," she said.

Grandpa pointed at a bag next to her bed.

Rotem pulled off the strip of surgical tape that was holding the IV needle in place. She pulled the needle out, took a ball of cotton from a plastic drawer next to the bed, and stuck it to the puncture mark with a fresh strip of surgical tape. She turned her back to Grandpa and Carmit and removed the hospital gown she was wearing. "Did he ruin my fairy?" she asked.

"I'm going to have to say yes," Carmit responded, looking at Rotem's back. The fairy tattoo was dotted with shrapnel scars and small sutured cuts.

"He has to be killed. What about the Eyes in the Sky? Are they working on it for us?"

"Yes. We're top priority now."

"Did you say that two men showed up at your hotel?" Rotem remembered to ask Carmit.

"Yes. At some time after three in the morning. Not very nice guys."

"They weren't ours," Grandpa took the trouble to mention again.

"Someone else is looking for the bomb, too," Rotem said before jumping to her feet, throwing off her hospital gown, and putting on the clothes that were in the bag next to the bed. "I wonder how they found you. Does anyone else know you're here?"

"Just one other person, who I trust a thousand percent."

"Yet they knew about you and knew that you're here in Israel, and maybe they want to get to the bomb through you. You may be under surveillance right now. They believe you're connected to 10483."

"Why?"

"Wherever he's gone, you've gone, too; it's pretty simple," Rotem said with a smile as she paced around the room. She thought for a moment and then added: "I assume the guys who showed up at your hotel weren't carrying IDs of any kind. Did you speak to them? Did you pick up on an accent perhaps?"

"They didn't get any time to talk," Carmit said, closing the laptop and returning it to Grandpa.

Grandpa stood and placed his hand on Carmit's shoulder. "Thank you for what you did there in Savyon," he said. "We found your fingerprints on the laptop charger you left there."

"What did she do in Savyon?" Rotem asked and looked at Grandpa.

"She applied tourniquets to you and Avner after the blast. One could say you're both still here now thanks to her."

Rotem skipped toward Carmit and hugged her.

10/22/2016–45 weeks and 1 day since waking

I'm standing outside the dental clinic in Yehud. There's no security here on the weekend and I open the back window of one of the offices on the ground floor and jump in. I close the window behind me. I go to the lobby and disable the alarm, and then into the employees' kitchenette to pour myself some water in a plastic cup. I wait for the alarm company to send someone to check on the building from the outside and examine my beard in the mirror in the meantime. I've been growing it now for several months. The alarm company's security guard doesn't see me in the kitchenette. After he leaves, I find a mask that's used to administer laughing gas and a canister of the substance. The gas, a combination of nitrous oxide and oxygen, sedates the patient and ups his pain threshold. Nitrous oxide is also used as rocket fuel or in motor racing. Since it's richer in oxygen than regular air, the injection of nitrous oxide into an engine means that more oxygen is available during combustion. And because you have more oxygen, you can also inject more fuel, allowing the engine to produce more power.

I connect the mask to the canister, lie down in the dental chair, look at the time on my iPhone, and inhale deeply with the mask over my mouth. 5 minutes later I wake up in the chair feeling somewhat dizzy. I put the tank and canister in my backpack and leave the building through the same window I used earlier.

I go to Tel Hashomer Hospital and wander around the wards until I find a deserted dressing room in the Internal Medicine Department. I go in and put on a set of green scrubs. I wander around the various departments and go into the ER. It's very crowded, with dozens of people waiting for emergency care, and it's easy for me to walk into the nurses' room and search the drug cabinet for something marked Propofol or Diprivan. I find the Diprivan and take 3 vials, along with several sterile syringes that I get from the equipment cabinet.

I go the bathroom in the ER and take off the orderly scrubs and dress in my own clothes again. I put the scrubs in my backpack. I may need them again in the future. I drive back home and begin working on my carpet van. I park the van just outside the front door and unload all the equipment I've bought from various stores and suppliers.

1. Steel plates
2. Blowtorch, electrodes, and a protective eye mask
3. Electrical cable and 12V lightbulbs
4. Power drill and screws
5. Transparent epoxy adhesive
6. Plate of armored glass
7. Metal rings
8. Wooden cabinets
9. Tubs of epoxy coating for parking garages

I remove the wheels of the vehicle one by one. Each time, I raise one wheel off the ground with the jack, remove it, and then lower the vehicle again onto a log I've cut to the appropriate height. 10 minutes later the van is perched on the logs, with the 4 wheels off to the side. I deflate the tires, lay them flat on the ground, and drill a 2-centimeter wide hole in each of them. Using a funnel I fill the tires with the epoxy coating for the floors of parking garages and allow the material to dry and harden. When it solidifies, it will make the tires puncture-proof. The ride will be bumpier because the shock absorbers won't be as effective, but I don't drive fast.

I open the back doors of the van and weld the steel plates to the sides of the vehicle. The plates block the windows, which I've already covered with pieces of black cardboard. I use rope and pulley wheels to lift and position the steel plates. It reminds me of the work I did in Bolivia. I weld steel plates to the inside of the vehicle's front doors, too, up to the height of the windows. I use the clear epoxy adhesive to stick the plate of armored glass to the inside of the van's windshield. The plate of glass doesn't cover the entire windshield and there are small gaps on the sides, but it will do. 90 percent of the windshield is protected. I apply 2 squares of armored glass on the inside of the front windows in the same manner. The armored windows are thicker now and I won't be able to open them, but that's okay. I apply a layer of the epoxy adhesive to secure the armored glass to the window frames around them so that the armored plates aren't dependent solely on the regular glass and don't fall when it shatters.

I weld steel plates to the back of the driver's seat and on the inside of the 2 doors of the vehicle's cargo bay. I fix narrow wooden cabinets to the steel plates now covering the sides of the cargo bay and fill the drawers with the equipment I need to move ahead with my plan. I make sure that everything fits and locks in place before removing the equipment again and returning it to the house.

I install a series of bright lights along the roof of the cargo bay and connect them to the van's battery, with a manual ON/OFF switch. I weld 4 metal rings to the floor of the cargo bay. 2 at the back and 2 in the front. When I'm done, I cover the floor again with old carpets.

10/29/2016–46 weeks and 1 day since waking

After leaving the wheels to dry and harden for a few days, I put them back on and go for a test drive in my carpet van. It responds more sluggishly than usual because of the heavy armor plating and full tires, but the overall ride is satisfactory.

I return to the basement and install an infrared camera that's directed at the cage and can be accessed via the Internet, with a password, so that at any given moment I can use my iPhone to view what's happening in the cage. Connecting the camera to the wireless network I've set up in the basement is simple and takes no time at all. It was a lot harder 10 years ago to set up a video camera on a wireless network.

At a sex store in Tel Aviv I buy 4 pairs of metal handcuffs like those used by the police. Their packaging says that the handcuffs come with 2 keys each and are not toys. They can be opened with a key only and are recommended for people who want to experience an authentic sense of helplessness. The shop assistant also offers me scented massage oil and a set of black leather bondage straps. I pass and buy the handcuffs only.

I'm warmly welcomed when I return to the tools and building supplies store. I'm a regular customer by now and the sales assistant behind the till calls out: "Hi, Roman. What's up?" I tell her I've secured a contract to renovate a villa in Herzliya and pay in cash for a 50-meter length of galvanized 10-millimeter-thick steel cable. The cable has a maximum weight-bearing capacity of 6.8 tons and will fit my purposes. The consultant at the store asks me how my work is going for the customer who requested an armor-plated room with bulletproof windows. I tell him that I've completed the work and that the customer is very satisfied. "I won't be doing another project like that for him," I say. "Those steel plates weigh a ton and the guy intimidated me a little. Seemed to be a mobster of sorts."

I go back to the military supplies store and buy a particularly durable backpack I'll use to carry the steel cable after I measure out the precise length I need and cut it accordingly.

I buy blue overalls and a pair of brown pants and a matching brown shirt similar to those worn by UPS workers. I take the items to a fabric print shop and have the same MASHANI—CARPET CLEANERS logo that I have on the van printed onto the overalls, and the UPS logo printed onto the brown uniform. The saleswoman is curious and asks me what I need the clothes for, and I tell her that my wife and I have been invited to a costume party on Friday night. I'll be there in the overalls with a small rug in my hand, and my wife will be wearing the UPS uniform and carrying a small parcel. The saleswoman thinks it would be great idea to add 2 peaked caps to the costumes. I agree and purchase 2—1 brown and 1 blue.

When I get home, I fold the UPS uniform and place it on a shelf in the closet. On top of the pile of clothes I place a parcel comprising a shoebox half-filled with earth and wrapped in brown paper, a writing pad, a pen, and sheets of paper with the UPS logo and places to sign that I've printed out. I fold the blue overalls and place them on a different shelf.

December 24, 2016

At 11:45 at night the shift at the AngelFire facility changed. The team that had spent the past two and half weeks analyzing the terror attack in Jerusalem had wrapped up its work, and the two operators on the Core shift, joined specially for this latest task by eight Shin Bet investigators, finished uploading the data to the systems and distributing it among the relevant parties—the terrorists' point of origin, the identities of the people they were seen within the months leading up to the attack, who crossed the border from Jordan to make contact with them. Everything had been figured out and documented, and the squads in the field would get to work that night—the Duvdevan elite special-ops forces, undercover counterterrorism units, SWAT teams, and the Border Police.

Meital and Dafna stepped in to replace the exhausted team that vacated the facility. They liked working together and always tried to arrange joint shifts. The girls that had been there before them looked so spent that Dafna opted not to say anything about the state in which they had left the facility. Pizza boxes and empty soda cans were scattered all over the place, empty water bottles, photocopies of maps, candy wrappers, and half-empty bags of snack food.

"What a bloody mess!" Meital remarked after the departing shift had left. "Let's tidy up this dump a little."

They took a roll of large garbage bags from the kitchenette cupboard, filled four of them with trash, and left them in the kitchenette. The cleaner would take them out in the morning with the rest of the trash.

They both enjoyed the night shift. Fewer uninvited guests and bothersome phone calls, and they could focus on their work. The project this time was an interesting one. They'd asked the girls who were there before them to load the cache with the locations they needed to work on, and everything was ready for them to start when the communications system came to life.

"AngelFire, commander here, over."

Meital took the Push-To-Talk. "AngelFire here, over," she said.

"Commander here with an update for you: Drop everything else and give top priority to the three sites, one of which is Ibn Gvirol. The matter we started on with those civilians a short while ago. Is that a Roger? Over."

"Roger, we are just about to begin with it now, over."

"Good. Don't liaise with the individual you were working with previously. He isn't available. I'll be giving you a different contact. Over."

"Roger. A different contact. Over."

"Commander here, over and out."

Meital replaced the PTT. Both she and Dafna were standing on the raised platform with the computer screens and keyboard controls. Dafna swung and shook her arms to loosen her muscles, like she did before beginning a gym workout. Meital did the same.

"Outer doors locked?"

"Locked."

"Inner doors locked?"

"Locked."

"Switching to Kinect."

The lights in the auditorium dimmed at once. And in their place, the entire ceiling of the large room took on a soft, light blue hue. Spotlights on the ceiling cast an orange glow over the raised control station. Dafna raised her arms to her sides, parallel to the floor, the palms of her hands turned downward. She stood like that for a few seconds before swiveling her wrists suddenly and directing her palms upward at the ceiling. A few small green LED dots lit up at the corners of the walls around them. Dafna slowly raised her arms upward toward the ceiling. All the facility's walls around them began sliding up to reveal an almost-full circle of twenty screens, which linked up with the four that were visible previously and constituted just a small segment of a complete circle of screens all around the room.

"Should we kick things off with Florence and the Machine, 'Shake It Out'?"

"Excellent choice."

The song started playing in the background and Dafna set the system in motion with a few deft hand movements. The control screen filled with counters to keep track of the percentage of material uploaded; the coordinates of the three locations were fed into the system; and three of the screens displayed the last image taken of the three places two seconds earlier. Two private homes and a building in ruins. Hands forward, palms pointing forward. Right hand retracts, the left remains outstretched. The counters run quickly in reverse. Right hand stops. In sync with the music, the surrounding speakers loudly announce: "Line Zero, December fourth, 2016, nine forty."

"I throw out and you keep track?"

"Go for it."

The three screens displaying the three locations begin moving back in time at an ever-increasing rate. The individual clicks accompanying the switching images become a long string of rattles and then a buzz, Florence is singing in the background, and the system calls out the times. The demolished building is whole again. Far back in time on the building, on Ganei Yehuda, and Avner's home, too, a suspicious movement a few days before the fourth of December in Ganei Yehuda, a deft hand movement and Dafna reproduces the screen she's monitoring; the display appears on one of the other screens around them and Meital takes charge of it, starting to run the images forward and in reverse, documenting the routes of pedestrians in green and vehicles in yellow on the huge digital aerial photograph on the screen. Forward. Back. A mark. Back. Forward. Another mark.

Shake it out

Shake it out

The two girls dance in sync to the chorus and laugh. Someone enters the ground-floor apartment of the soon-to-destroyed building through a window. A second replicated screen. Meital takes charge of that one, too. The images on her two screens run forward and backward and she plots routes on both at the same time. A third screen, from Avner's house this time, and then another from the building on Ibn Gvirol, and another screen, and another. That's why there are no male operators at the facility. Girls can multitask. Another screen. And another.

Shake it out

Shake it out

All the screens around them are running forward and in reverse. Florence and the Machine booming through the speakers, and Dafna and Meital are engrossed in their mapping dance.

"I adore her voice! Look at screen fifteen. He's doing something in Rabin Square. It looks like he's digging a big hole. Put a timeline tag on it." Full revolution on the spot, a jump, hands in the air. "Screen nine, look how much time he spends hanging around their main base. He spends at least a month surveying the place." Half a turn to the right, hands to the side. "He drives here for hours behind something that looks like a large truck."

"Throw me to eleven."

"Coming right at you. Bring up all we have from the Ra'anana area, too."

Shake it out

Shake it out

Routes plotted in green and yellow, timeline tags in red, targets numbered within blue circles on the backdrop of the two-second-interval images. The static images turn into a story, a motion picture, twists and turns and splits that move off in various directions and then come together again. Song follows song, and one dance follows another. Meital and Dafna dance 10483 to his demise.

11/20/2016–49 weeks and 2 days since waking

I open my laptop and look for the addresses of Avner and Amiram in the personnel file I took from the Organization some 10 years ago. I hope they haven't moved in recent years, particularly not Amiram. My plans will be disrupted if the courier from the Aharoni-Shamir law firm doesn't find Amiram and moves on to the next address on the list.

Amiram will go straight to Avner's house 15 minutes after the delivery of the notebook. That's how long it will take him to realize what he's received, dress quickly, put on shoes, and leave.

I leave the house at 4:30 in the morning and drive to Amiram's house to stake it out. Amiram still lives at the same address. I see him leave the house at 7 in the morning, get into his Land Rover, and drive away. I head out and buy a few items I need—a jerry-can, rubber sheeting, a sealant, and several other things. I fill the jerrycan with gasoline at the gas station and buy a tuna sandwich and a bottle of mineral water. I return home in the afternoon and install lighting in the tunnel I've constructed from the basement to the outside.

I check through the material I took from the Organization for the location of the satellite branch nearest to Avner's house. I assume that after reading through the notebook for an hour or 2, he will make his way quickly to the branch closest to him in order to gain access to a computer and make a few encrypted phone calls. The nearest branch is in Ganei Yehuda. I drive there dressed in a sweatshirt and sports pants, park the carpet van on HaMitnahalim Street, and jog around the area. The branch is disguised as a regular villa and is surrounded by cameras. If I disable the one pointing east, I can create a blind spot through which I'll be able to get into the parking lot and deal with Avner's vehicle.

I visit the area of the satellite base in Ganei Yehuda and jog around there for a few more days, at different times, to figure out the guard rotation schedule and monitor the routine activity at the branch. It's pretty sleepy.

I open YouTube and type "turn DVD laser" in the search box and get a long list of video clips that explain how to disassemble an old DVD, remove the signal reduction component, and boost the intensity of the laser beam. One of the clips shows how to insert the mechanism into a Maglite flashlight and I buy the list of equipment that I need to do so at an electronics store and prepare the flashlight at home. I test it and aim the beam at a candle that I place on the other side of the room. The wick lights up. It's very simple to turn an old DVD into a powerful laser. I read online through the specifications for Amiram's Land Rover so I can figure out at what height to stretch my steel cable across the road in order to achieve the best result.

I drive again to the satellite branch in Ganei Yehuda. I park my carpet van down the street a few dozen meters from the camera, attach the flashlight to a camera tripod to keep it steady, aim the beam until the red dot is fixed on the camera lens, and leave it in that position for 5 minutes. 1st they'll send a technician to try to repair it, but he won't be able to. He'll order a new camera and then replace the old one. I have a few days.

I go the following morning to stake out Avner's house. He, too, is still living in the same place, on Moshav Mazor. I examine the tall cypress trees that line the road into the community and measure the distance between them with fishing line. 28 meters of steel cable will do the job and when I get home later I'll cut the cable so that I don't have to carry around the entire 50 meters. The cable is very heavy. I'll attach fixtures to the 2 ends of the cable to allow me to wind and tie the cable around the trees in a hurry.

I buy a 2nd LG G3 prepaid cell phone and large D-type batteries. The LG's internal battery is a Li-Ion 3000 mAh with an output of 3.7V. I connect 3 D batteries to one another. This gives me 4.5V. I prepare 2 more trios of batteries in the same way and connect the 3 trios in parallel. The output remains 4.5V but it will take them a lot longer to run out. The phone will function for about 2 weeks straight. I remove the original battery from the phone and solder the plus and minus terminals at the back of the open device to the large battery I've created and wrap everything together with black duct tape. I set up 2 fictitious Facebook accounts, install Waze on the phone, define the 2 Facebook accounts in the social network settings of the app, check that the 2 phones are partnered, and turn the new one off.

12/03/2016–1 year less 1 day since waking

It's 9 in the evening and I'm sitting in the cargo bay of my carpet van near Amiram's house and using my iPhone to view video of the house from the outside that's coming from a GoPro camera fitted to the vehicle. I pour myself some coffee from a thermos I prepared and drink it. The courier is supposed to arrive at 10:20. The Aharoni-Shamir law firm had been instructed to deliver the package at precisely that time. I told them it was essential for the package to arrive on the right day and at the specified time. I see the courier arrive and walk into Amiram's with the package containing the notebook I wrote 10 years ago. My day of revenge has arrived. 113 minutes suffice, and Amiram rushes out the house, gets into his Land Rover, and speeds away. I head for Avner's house, making no effort to follow Amiram's vehicle. I have enough time to get there and I don't want him to suspect that someone may be on his tail.

I reach the entrance to Moshav Mazor, park my van along a small side road, and use the time that Amiram spends in Avner's house to tie the steel cable to one of the roadside trees. I run the cable across the road to the other side and leave it resting on the ground, with the loose end next to me in a ditch on the side of the road. I'm surrounded by darkness. Heavy clouds cover the sky and the moon peeks through now and then, briefly illuminating the road and black trees around me.

Toward 11:30 I hear the Land Rover's engine in the distance. I get up, pull the steel cable taut at the appropriate height, and tie the loose end to the tree next to me. I get back into the ditch at the side of the road and wait. The Land Rover speeds past me and immediately thereafter I hear the sound of screeching metal and shattering glass as the vehicle flips, flies into the ditch a few dozen meters away, and comes to a stop on its roof, engine still running, lights on, with upturned wheels spinning in the air. I walk over and peer inside. Amiram is unconscious. I go back to the road, untie the steel cable, roll it up, and return it to my backpack. I place the backpack on the ground next to the upturned Land Rover and then turn off the engine and lights and remove the ring of keys from the ignition. Amiram is hanging upside down in front of me and I remove the pistol from the holster on his belt. I also take his wallet and phone. I examine the ID in the wallet to verify that it's Amiram. Yes. It's him. Very good.

I check again.

One last time.

I stroke my beard.

I remove the battery from Amiram's phone and place his phone, the battery, and his wallet in my backpack. Then I sit down in front of the open door of the Land Rover with Amiram's gun in my hand and wait for him to wake up. In the meantime, I reach into the backpack to retrieve 2 pairs of handcuffs, a small bottle of mineral water, and a box of sleeping pills. I crush 8 pills into the bottle and shake it well.

It's 1:19 in the morning. The crickets and insects around me are making loud music. A vehicle speeds past on the road above me. It must be Avner hurrying to the Organization's satellite branch after reading the notebook. I thought he'd appear sooner. He's driving fast and doesn't notice the Land Rover in the ditch. The moon is hiding behind the clouds and Avner is surely troubled and in a rush.

Groans come from the vehicle in front of me. Amiram is moving in the seat and coming to. He releases his safety belt and falls on his head. It amuses me.

Amiram crawls out of his vehicle and freezes when he sees me sitting in front of him with his own gun pointed at him.

"What's going on here?" he asks. I tell him I've come to collect him. I throw the 2 pairs of handcuffs to him and tell him to put them on—one pair on his wrists and the other pair around his ankles. I throw the bottle of water to him and tell him to drink it after putting the cuffs on.

Then I sit quietly in front of him and wait an hour for him to fall asleep. I leave him sleeping alongside the Land Rover and go get my carpet van, which I parked on the road just above. I carry Amiram into the van, lay him down in the cargo bay, and tie the handcuffs around his wrists and ankles to the 4 metal rings welded to the floor of the vehicle.

Avner was driving fast. He must have arrived at the Ganei Yehuda satellite branch by now. I drive to my rental home, remove the sleeping Amiram from the van, and place him in the cage in the basement. I leave him shackled for now in case he wakes up. I lock the door of the cage with a steel chain and heavy padlock, go upstairs, and close the door to the basement behind me. The house is secluded and no one will hear Amiram's screams thanks to the mattresses covering the basement's walls. I've also left the TV in the living room on, on Channel 2.

I drive to Ganei Yehuda and park 2 blocks from the Organization's satellite branch. I'm dressed in black, and my tools and the tracking device I've made from the cell phone and batteries are in my backpack. I approach the villa's parking lot from the direction of the camera I disabled and spot Avner's white Mazda parked next to another car that I recognize as the guard's. Avner is standing outside. I wait for him to go back inside and then approach his car. I crawl under the Mazda, drill 4 small holes with the power drill, and attach the tracking device to the underside of the vehicle using 2 strong steel wires that I fix in place with screws through the holes I've made. I put my tools back into the backpack, making sure I haven't left anything lying on the ground, and leave the parking lot through the same area the disabled camera isn't covering.

It's almost 4 in the morning by now and I go back to Avner's house. I park along one of the streets in the community, eat an omelet and tomato baguette sandwich I've brought with me from home, set my alarm for 7 in the morning, drink a bottle of mineral water, and go to sleep in the back of the van.

I wake up at 7. I open the laptop, connect to the Wi-Fi network of one of the surrounding homes that isn't password protected, and access the camera I have in the old basement on Ibn Gvirol Street. The room is dark and I don't see any movement. They'll probably get there soon, thanks to my explanation in the notebook they received about the existence and location of the basement. I use the time on my hands to change into the UPS courier uniform and check to make sure that the contents of all the drawers are neatly in place.

Another check.

One last time.

I eat a few cinnamon-flavored Nature Valley energy bars for breakfast and drink another bottle of mineral water. I'll go back to my rental a little later and make myself coffee and take a shower.

At 9:15 I see some movement on the laptop screen. Someone is climbing down the ladder into the basement. I begin recording the video feed from the camera and watch an entire team descend and start to map the location. They look over my works of art, step into the empty iron cage in which I've erased part of the amateurish inscription made on the floor by one of my subjects, and examine the walls. They're wearing gas masks and I'm unable to identify the people there. Perhaps Avner himself has gone down into the basement with the team. I let them have their fun in the basement for 25 minutes and then use the laptop's mouse to move the camera. They all freeze and then throw their equipment to the ground and make a dash for the ladder. I'm amused. I pick up my cell phone, unlock it, and lightly touch one of the 2 shortcuts I've set up in the Safari browser—

203 Ibn Gvirol Street Blast

I close the laptop and leave it in the van, take the parcel I've prepared, a UPS delivery form, the canister of nitrous oxide and the mask, a syringe and a vial of Diprivan, and walk toward Avner's house. It's raining. My uniform and the brown parcel I'm carrying get wet. I leave the equipment on the ground next to the house and hold on to just the parcel and the UPS form. I ring the doorbell and

Avner's wife opens the door. She signs the form I've prepared and the shoebox half-filled with earth stays with her. I tell her it's an important parcel and that she needs to call Avner to tell him to come and collect it. She looks at me, doesn't say a word, and goes back inside. I walk away down the driveway; and the moment I'm out the line of sight of the kitchen window, I double back quickly around the house and take up position against the wall to the right of the front door. Avner's wife is on the phone; she hangs up and the front door opens. She rushes out and I hit her on the head with the nitrous oxide canister I'm holding. The 1st blow fails to stun her sufficiently and she lifts her arms to protect her head and tries to look at me. Another blow and she drops to the ground. I attach the mask to the canister and place the mask over her face. She closes her eyes. I insert the syringe into the vial of Diprivan, draw up some of the solution, and inject it into a vein in Efrat's arm. That's the name she signed on the form I gave her.

I leave Efrat on the floor at the front door, go to get my van, and park the vehicle near the entrance to the house. I load Efrat into the van, lay her down on the floor, tie her hands and feet to the metal rings, retrieve the last page that I tore out of my previous notebook from one of the cabinet drawers, slip the page under my shirt so it doesn't get wet in the rain, close the doors to the back of the van, and go back into Avner's house. I place the page on the kitchen table alongside a full glass of orange juice that Efrat had poured for herself but didn't get time to drink. The page outlines some of the last things I did 10 years ago, and ends by saying that I will get to them and their families and exact my revenge on everyone. I'm putting my plan into action.

I open the refrigerator in Avner's kitchen, drink the rest of the bottle of orange juice, and toss the empty bottle into the trashcan under the sink. Fixed to the refrigerator is a whiteboard displaying the message Avner left for Efrat about going to the Organization's satellite branch during the night. I add a small smiley face under the message with the erasable marker that's hanging from the whiteboard on a colored piece of string. I use the bathroom and then leave the house, get into my van, and drive away. When I get to my rental, I put the sleeping Efrat in the cage along with the sleeping Amiram and remove the cuffs around his wrists and ankles. Before doing so, I inject him with some of the Diprivan. I go up to the living room and come back down with the blowtorch and weld shut the cage door and its hinges. No one will be entering or leaving the cage in the near future.

I turn on the food machine and adjust the settings so that it will begin dispensing meals 3 hours from now, and once a day thereafter at the same time. I turn off the lights in the basement and return to the living room, go outside, tidy the van, park it in its regular spot, and return to the house.

I sit in the living room, open the laptop, and watch the recording of the team in the Ibn Gvirol basement running for the ladder. It's still raining and I make a cup of coffee in the kitchen. I was hungry earlier and had planned to cook dinner, but the feeling passed and I make do with coffee.

I take a shower and go to bed.

"I regret to say that again we got very close to the bomb and again it slipped out of our hands at the last minute."

The mood in the warm boardroom in Toronto was gloomy. Outside, the snowflakes were once again caught up in a dance in the swirling winds, and Herr Schmidt's group sat inside in silence.

"I don't believe it. What happened?"

"We've lost contact with the twins."

"Maybe they're busy tracking down the bomb and aren't accessible?"

"They've conducted dozens of missions for us around the world and this is a first. Ricardo has always made contact on time. We haven't heard from them in three days and that can mean only one thing."

"Are we going to send more people to Israel to replace them?"

"Yes. Even though our chances of finding anything have dropped significantly. We still have the images of the two. The woman landed in Israel recently. She's probably looking for the bomb, too, and she has an advantage over us now. Ricardo reported finding her in Israel and said they were going to interrogate her, and that was the last message I received from him."

"They found her?"

"Yes. She happened to sit down at a restaurant they were at."

"What are the odds of that? She must have been part of a team that was keeping an eye on the twins. They were toying with us. Maybe she was the one who took them out?"

Herr Schmidt smiled. "If the twins were killed by anyone, it must have been an entire unit of the Mossad or some other intelligence agency, and they must have worked very hard to do so." He looked at the image of Carmit that was on his desk alongside that of 10483. "This young woman doesn't look like an entire Mossad hit squad."

"But what are the odds of them just happening to walk into the very same restaurant? Perhaps she found them and sat down, then waited for them to notice and follow her? Maybe the letter we received about Shariri was a trap?"

Herr Schmidt sighed. "In any event," he said, "I'll send a larger team of people this time, even though I don't think they'll be more effective than the twins. But we have to try."

"Yes, we do. Perhaps we should send the Barber?"

"He's unstable. It could backfire on us."

"I don't really think we have a choice."

Herr Schmidt sighed. He hadn't slept much over the past few days. "Okay, I'll get in touch with him."

12/05/2016–1 day after putting the plan into motion

I turn on the light in the basement and go down the stairs carrying a bouquet of roses and white sheets. The basement here has been constructed as part of the house and I don't have to climb down a ladder from inside the bedroom closet. Efrat and Amiram shield their eyes from the sudden light that blinds them. I turn off the recording that's been playing on a loop in the basement, take a folding chair from against the wall, open it, place it in front of the cage, and sit down facing them.

I observe them for a few minutes until they grow accustomed to the light.

"Have you ever tried to shut your eyes tight and apply pressure to them?" I say to them "If you haven't, you should. Close your eyes and apply pressure to them with the tips of your fingers. Like so. Not too hard. On the verge of pain. Now leave your fingertips on your eyelids with the same pressure and wait. Initially you'll see dots of light that move from the center to the sides like small stars. Don't ease the pressure. The image will change gradually and in the middle you'll see a light blue circle of sorts that expands and switches color in its center to blue-black and then red. When you release your fingers and your eyes, that same circle will remain hovering in front of you for perhaps a minute or 2 until it disappears altogether. You can amuse yourself with this while you're here in the cage. It will alleviate the boredom. It works in total darkness, too."

They stare at me but don't say a word.

"Now you're going to stand up in front of me," I continue. "I'll give each of you a single rose. You're going to hold it in your right hand and we're going to take a pretty picture. But 1st tie these sheets nicely to the bars like so to give the image an interesting background."

I throw the sheets to Amiram but he doesn't move. They're staging some kind of a strike against me. I ask them if they're enjoying the food. I tell them that I put a lot of time and thought into designing

263

their food dispenser, but if they don't appreciate my efforts I will switch it off and come back to see them in a few days.

Amiram stands up and hangs the sheets on the bars of the cage like I show him. He and Efrat each hold a single rose in their right hand and I photograph them with my iPhone's camera. I then tell them to give the roses and sheets back to me. Efrat hands me the roses and Amiram unties the sheet curtains and returns them to me. I tell them to wait for me for a moment and not to go anywhere and go back upstairs with the sheets and roses. I go to the kitchen, make a large pot of popcorn, and transfer the popcorn into 2 big disposable bowls. I go back down to the basement with the 2 bowls of popcorn and my laptop, connect the laptop to the large screen on the wall in front of the cage, place one bowl of popcorn close to the cage so they can eat, too, and sit down on the folding chair with the other, facing the screen and not the cage this time.

"We'll watch a movie together now," I tell them and screen the clip I made with the camera in the previous basement—my creations at the *Last Supper* table, the team descending, the team members wandering around the basement in gas masks and examining the cage and my works of art, the team running for the ladder.

We watch the film several times. It's important to pay attention to the details.

"Do you know that there are thousands of different species living inside each of your bodies," I tell them when we come to the end of our last look at the video clip. "Bacteria, germs, viruses. When you're born you're sterile, but from then on and until your death you accumulate more and more different species that live inside you. Particularly in your intestines. In fact, you're giant colonies of microorganisms. If we were to collect everything living in each of you and make it into a single round ball, that ball would weigh a little more than a kilogram."

I take the laptop, close the screen, fold the chair and leave it resting against the wall, go upstairs, turn off the light in the basement, and shut the door.

I'm an 11-year-old boy. I'm rushing to class through the large courtyard in the middle of the school. The bell rang 2 minutes ago and I hope the teacher's late and I can make it to class quickly. I run through puddles in my gym shoes and the water seeps in and wets my socks. I'm looking down at the puddles on the asphalt of the big courtyard in an effort to skip over them and don't notice the girl moving toward me. I crash into her and she drops the books she was holding. They fall onto the asphalt and get wet. I bend to pick up the books. When I stand up straight again I look at the girl. She has a black braid in her hair and is wearing a blue school shirt. The girl suddenly reaches into her bag with her right hand, pulls out a knife and stabs me in the chest several times. Shick. Shick. Shick. Shick. Shick. I drop down on all fours and try not to topple over. The girl puts the wet books into her bag. I collapse on the ground. The girl stands over me and holds the knife in her outstretched hand. She twists the blade right and left in the air and allows the rain to wash it off until it's clean. The blood flowing from me mixes with rivulets of rain. The girl puts the wet knife back into her bag and continues walking in the opposite direction.

I'm an 11-year-old boy. I'm rushing to class through the large court-yard in the middle of the school. The bell rang 2 minutes ago and I hope the teacher's late and I can make it to class quickly. I run through puddles in my gym shoes and the water seeps in and wets my socks. Something causes me to look up from the puddles under my feet and I jump to the side to avoid crashing into a girl who's walking toward me. She continues to walk in the opposite direction. I get the feeling that I've seen her before and shivers run down my spine. She walks on and I continue running to class. The teacher hasn't arrived yet and I sit down quickly in my chair, panting.

I'm an 11-year-old girl. I'm walking in the rain toward the school offices to report to the secretary after the geography teacher kicked me *out of class a minute after the lesson started. She didn't even allow me to put my books back into my bag. That boy from my year is running toward me without looking where he's going. If he bumps into me, I'm going to kill him.*

12/06/2016–2 days after putting the plan into motion

I get up early in the morning and make myself scrambled eggs and a salad with an avocado that I pick from the avocado tree in the garden behind the house. It's avocado season and the tree is full. After breakfast I drive to Savyon, get off the main street, and drive along the quieter narrow roads in search of a secluded house that appears unoccupied. After searching for 2 hours I come across a secluded house at the end of HaHarzit Street. The gardens around the house have grown wild and it looks like the owner doesn't live there. I take the last 2 remaining trashcan bombs out of the carpet van and install them on the sidewalk—one very close to the entrance to the house and the other a little farther down the street. I take a picture of the house with my iPhone, return to the van, retrieve my laptop, search for an available Wi-Fi network, find an open one named ROSA, and verify that I can connect to it and surf the Internet.

I drive back to my rental and turn on the laptop. I open my photo library and move the cursor over the image of the house I photographed on HaHarzit Street. Right click, Properties, Details, scroll down a little, and copy the GPS coordinates.

I download and install EXIF Editor and use it to alter the GPS coordinates of the picture I took of Amiram and Efrat in the basement, and check to make sure that the data has been saved properly. I close and reopen the picture of them in the basement and see that the file opens properly.

Again.

One more time.

I erase all the metadata from the video file of the team in the old basement and save it to a separate folder together with the image file I changed.

If Amiram was in the basement alone, I'd turn him into a piece of art in the style of Leonardo da Vinci's *Vitruvian Man,* but I have 2 people in the cage and I need to choose a work that suits a duo. I end up going for the picture that Salvador Dalí painted on the roof of his museum in Spain. It will be relatively difficult to set up the art installation and hang them from the ceiling of the cage in the correct position. To create a perfect picture I'll have to widen their feet, too, but it will be worth the effort.

I check Waze to find out where Avner's car is. He's in Ra'anana. At Lowenstein Hospital. The car is stationary. I have to assume that Avner managed to figure out that I was there and has gone to the hospital to question the staff. I didn't think he'd pick up my scent that quickly. I need to press ahead with my plan and kick things off this month. I also have to assume that the Organization now has an updated photograph of me. I did well to refrain from hanging around in places with cameras or to avert my gaze when there were cameras around. I guess that my beard, too, buys me a little time before any camera has a chance to tell them where I am or where I've been.

December 24, 2016

Marcus Delaney felt ill at ease. The somber man in front of him in a strange hat—like that worn by clergymen in Rome—was wearing a thick black coat and standing at the counter of his small gas station store. Not the kind of person you'd expect to meet in a small town in North Dakota. Marcus had just finished tidying the shelf behind him and when he turned around to face the counter again the man was already there. Marcus got the feeling that he'd been standing there and looking at him for a few minutes already.

"Do you ever feel the need to dig into the earth with the end of your shoe?"

"Excuse me?"

"You're excused. When you're standing on soil do you ever stab the end of your shoe into the earth, with little kicking movements?"

"No."

The man in the hat fixed Marcus with a stare and shook his head slowly.

"Actually yes. Now that I think about it I do sometimes kick aimlessly at the ground with the end of my shoe."

"De careful not to overdo it."

"What would you like, sir?"

"I allowed it to take control of me. I wasn't careful. I didn't pay attention. I used to stab at the earth with the end of my shoe whenever I found myself walking over exposed soil. It didn't end well. It started with worn-out shoes that I needed to replace often, but I then started to walk home through playgrounds so I could dig in the children's sandbox there. I started with my feet and then moved on to digging holes with my hands. My nails hardened, I began losing my sight and my sense of smell got sharper. Whenever someone passed nearby I could smell what they had eaten that day and the day before, and if it was a hard-boiled egg or tuna with onion, then a week back, too." The man with the strange hat took a cigarette out of a box in his coat pocket and lit it with a Zippo, put the lighter and box back into his coat pocket, and took a long puff on a cigarette.

"You're not allowed to smoke in here."

"I started sleeping under my bed on earth I scattered there from the potted plants in my house. My wife didn't know what was happening. She took me to a psychologist, thought it was some kind of a midlife crisis, but it didn't help, and then the other changes started, too. My nails grew and a sleek black coat of fur grew over my body. My ears disappeared almost completely, and at night I'd vanish from the house and return to sleep under the bed in the morning, leaving holes behind me in all the gardens of the surrounding homes. I turned into a mole."

"Sir, would you like to buy something or pay for gas?"

"Do you see a line here? Is there a line of people standing behind me and waiting for me to finish up?"

"No."

"It's because only the two of us are here. And we're having a conversation. You're impolite. When someone speaks to you, you should listen. Impolite people have a short lifespan. Would you like to have a short lifespan?"

"I'm listening."

"I left Texas two weeks ago. The ground there is hot and living there in the burrows I dug isn't pleasant. And the burrows often collapse due to the type of soil there. Here in the north the ground is cold and hard. It's harder to dig into but the burrows remain intact and the worms in the soil here are different. Tastier. Juicier."

"Sir, you don't look like a mole."

The man swiftly drew a pistol from his coat and aimed it at Marcus. "Do you have any issues with my appearance?"

The blood drained from Marcus's face. He looked into the eyes of the man wearing the clergyman hat and for a moment the man's eyes appeared smaller than normal and somewhat reminiscent of a mole's. He wanted to say so but he couldn't utter the words.

The man's phone rang with the ringtone of a sad flute. He kept his pistol aimed straight at Marcus's face and used his free hand to retrieve the phone from his coat pocket and answer the call. Marcus couldn't hear the person at the other end of the line, only the man standing in front of him. "Hello, yes, it's me. Yes, I'm free for the next two weeks. Where? Israel? Do you know anything at all about the types of soil there? No, I mean if they're good for digging. Never mind, I'll find out when I get there. One hundred thousand dollars. Yes. Fifty now and fifty on completion. Two? A man and a woman? Send the photos to my cell phone."

The Barber hung up and put the phone back into his coat pocket. He looked at Marcus, who was on the verge of passing out, and after a long pause returned the pistol to his coat. "It was interesting talking to you. Don't judge people by their looks. What's inside is what matters."

"Certainly, sir! I mean I certainly won't judge, sir."

"Here's a fifty-dollar bill. I'll take two bottles of apple-flavored Snapple from the refrigerator here and gas with the rest. I'm parked next to the pump. Open it for me."

"Yes, sir."

December 25, 2016

"We know where he's living. You should come here and see everything on the screens and decide what you want to do. He's done a whole lot of strange things that you need to see."

"We'll be with you shortly," Grandpa said, hanging up and turning back to the group in the briefing room, where Carmit and Rotem were sitting with a large team of field agents. "Talk about timing," he said to them. "The operators at the AngelFire facility say they've found him and have seen several of the things he's been doing. Let's all go there now and see what we're up against. We have to get our hands on him as soon as possible; it's essential. We don't have much time left before the first of January."

"AngelFire? Who came up with that name?" Rotem remarked, closing her laptop and putting it in her bag.

"The Americans."

* * *

"Hi there," Meital said. "I'm Meital and this is Dafna. What happened to the team we were working with before?" She and Dafna made sure the doors to the facility were locked and then began working on the system's settings.

"Hurt in the line of duty. We're taking over. What have you found?"

"Okay, I'm turning out the lights and activating all the screens. I just want to remind everyone here that no one must breathe a word about this facility to anyone else. Even in-house. We'll start running through everything quickly and you can stop me if you have any questions. If anyone feels a little dizzy, just close your eyes and sit down for a while on one of these armchairs. Ready?"

Meital didn't wait for a response and activated the room.

"Switching to Kinect."

The room dimmed, leaving only the glow from the sky blue lighting

272

on the ceiling. Arms to the side, palms facing downward, palms turned upward, Meital caused the green LED lights to blink on and the walls slid up to reveal the circle of screens.

"We went back an entire year," Meital began. "There's nothing beyond that. You have to understand the limitations of the system. Clouds get in the way, and at night we can only track a vehicle if it's pretty much alone on the road. If a vehicle drives into a tunnel and is in there with numerous other cars around it, we aren't able to pinpoint the specific vehicle when it emerges again. We can track people only if they aren't in a crowd. And don't forget we haven't had much luck in the Shfela region over the past two weeks—cloud cover and rain almost continually. One would think we were living in Scotland. Unbelievable."

Dafna was sitting on the raised platform at one of the computer stations, entering commands into the various systems, and Meital filled all the screens around the room with a set of images with routes marked on them in different colors. Hands to the sides, a half twist of the wrists—and all the content began moving between the screens, creating the illusion that the room itself was spinning.

Stop.

"We'll show you what we have on him from December 2015 through to today. Keep your eyes on the screen right in front of us. To avoid messing with your heads, I'm running everything forward to the present and not from the present backward in time. Look here. This is the building on Ibn Gvirol before the blast. We ran back on it until we found the first time he's seen leaving through a window in the morning. The thirteenth of January. From here we tracked him riding around on a bicycle to various places, going into malls, returning to the building, nothing special. He continues in the same manner until the ninth of February and then disappears on us, from all locations, until March twenty-ninth."

"That's the period he spent abroad."

"Makes sense—we didn't see him anywhere at all. Not in Ganei Yehuda, not at the building on Ibn Gvirol, and not around the house

273

on Moshav Mazor. We haven't been able to figure out what he's been doing over the last few days either. We keep losing him under the cloud cover. Your previous team saw it for themselves when they were here last time. But we kept running back on the three locations you gave us and we found him for you. Eyes on screen two."

The team from the Organization tensed. Everyone leaned forward a little for a better view. The screen displayed an aerial image of the entire central region of the country with a green dot on it.

"Take note, the dot here is the house in Ganei Yehuda. The date is the twenty-first of November—a little more than a month ago."

Right hand slowly forward. Left remains outstretched. The dot becomes a green line that extends gradually and then comes to a halt. A second line starts to emerge from the dot and runs adjacent to the existing one. It stops, too, and another line begins and stops, and then another emerges from the dot and continues this time past the previous ones and farther toward the north. The cameras zoom out and the line continues to grow in quick jumps—*click— click—click*.

"We looked for irregular traffic patterns and movements around the house in Ganei Yehuda and there was a week in which a commercial vehicle of some kind parked several times along the surrounding streets and someone got out and wandered about. He made sure not to enter the street on which that house of yours is located, so at this stage you won't find an image of the vehicle itself from the cameras you must have there. He surveyed the location for about a week and then stopped. The broken lines that you see here are from the times the vehicle disappeared on us under the clouds. On the one occasion when there were no clouds, you can see the long line that leads us straight to his house. Eyes on screen three."

The green line remained frozen on screen two, and screen three displayed an image, zoomed in to the maximum, of 10483's current residence, with both a green and a red dot.

"The green one is the endpoint of his route from Ganei Yehuda. He parks there and then heads to the house on foot, a two-minute walk—look at the dot moving here." *Click—click—click*—a small dot leaves the vehicle and enters the house on Moshav Yanuv.

"This is the house he's living in and that's the address. But before you send in the cavalry, let us go through this with you for another half an hour. I'm going to jump back a lot and begin running forward and backward. Ignore the times, you'll only get confused, just keep an eye on the lines that form. His house is the reference point now and we're going to show you another set of routes."

Lines started to appear on all the screens around them—extending, being cut short, quickly reappearing in color again, until all the movements stopped and all the screens showed routes in various shades.

"He's been a very busy man this past year. Look at screen nine. It shows almost an entire month in which he drove around Tel Aviv, parked in various locations, and fiddled with something along the street—it looks like he's doing something with the trashcans on the sidewalk but you'll have to check that from up close."

"Show us one for a moment zoomed to the maximum," Rotem said, leaning forward and gazing intently at the screen.

Click—click—click—click—"Stop. Look. I'm almost sure that that small dot is one of those metal trashcans you find along the sidewalk, and that he's replacing it with one he's carried there with him. Can you see? He dismantles one and replaces it with another from his vehicle. That's why we weren't able to figure out the nature of the devices used in Savyon. The two trashcans near the house were the bombs. We received a report that he had hidden the bombs in trashcans, but I think that each trashcan itself is an explosive device."

"Look at screen fourteen. He spends the entire day following a gas tanker all the way to the depot in Rishon, and then drives back." Meital ran the images in reverse and then forward again, mapping out a route of twisting and turning lines. "That was May twenty-fourth," she said.

Grandpa leaned back against the desk behind him. "Reminiscent of what he did in Argentina," he said. "The same MO. What's this here on screen sixteen?"

"He wandered around here for close to a month and a half. Rumor has it that this is the location of your main base." Meital smiled. Dafna looked up from the system's control screens. "Beginning on May twenty-fifth, he hung around here for almost a month and a half, pulling over for hours sometimes relatively far away. He must have been surveying the scene from inside the vehicle with binoculars because he rarely got out."

"Can your images give us a make on the vehicle?"

"No. We can see its roof only. Based on its size, it must be a van of some kind, but we haven't done any cross-referencing with other sources aside from our own cameras. If you have more time, we can start to cross-reference his routes with speed cameras, cameras at traffic lights, banks, and more, but it'll probably take a day or two to get a good picture."

"Do so after we leave and send us what you find. Okay?"

"No problem, just leave me an email address. But bear in mind that it could take even longer. Have a look now at screen eight. It's getting even worse. Look what's he doing in Rabin Square."

"Holy fuck!" Rotem exclaimed. "Stop it a moment. Go back. Just a sec. Now forward. Wait. Back until he first arrives there. Good. Now forward to the end. Stop. What the fuck? They allowed him to simply dig a huge pit in front of City Hall in the middle of Rabin Square and nobody said a bloody thing. Do you have feed here from the cameras in the square?"

"Sorry. Like I said earlier, we're limited to our material only. You'll have to coordinate with our boss and go to another facility for ground-camera footage."

"He killed someone there." Carmit, who had been quiet until then, pointed at screen eight. "If you run it again, you'll see another dot approaching him and then turning into a short line and disappearing into the pit. He killed someone and buried him there in the pit."

Click—click—click. The images, jumping ahead in time at two-second intervals, showed someone being dragged quickly across the ground and disappearing into the hole in the square.

"Okay, that's clearly what he meant by 'a very powerful explosive device will be detonated in a public place' in his letter of demands. We can neutralize it now," Rotem said, turning to Meital and Dafna and adding: "And let me remind you, too, not a word to anyone about whatever's been said here. Is that clear? Meital?"

"Clear."

"Dafna?"

"Clear."

"Tell me," Rotem then said, "would you mind if I were to operate the room for a few minutes?"

Meital looked at Dafna. Dafna looked at Rotem. "It's not exactly standard procedure and it will take you a while to learn the interface. I can show you how to work with the mouse and switch between the screens. Maybe that . . ."

"I'll manage," Rotem said, skipping over to where Meital was standing. "Help me out if I get stuck, okay? Should we do a small test run?"

"Okay, start with your hands like this and . . ."

"It's okay. I've been watching you a little and have seen how you control the screens."

"Okay," Meital said, stepping aside and sitting down next to Dafna.

Rotem held her arms out to the side and then spread her hands and moved them both to the right at the same time. The displays on all the screens started spinning clockwise, creating the illusion that the room itself was moving in the opposite direction.

"I think we should . . ." Dafna tried to help.

"It's okay. Don't worry," Rotem responded. Each and every one of the twenty-four screens was now a part of her. A continuation of her brain and eyes. It was amazing. She started to run each of the screens backward and forward, conveying instructions to the screen in front of her with the knowledge she would see it again a few seconds later because everything was spinning constantly. Forward. Forward. Back. Forward. Stop. Forward. The members of the team in the room lost their sense of balance and sat down on the floor one by one. Carmit closed her eyes. Grandpa sat down on a chair and kept his eyes fixed on one of the small computer screens at the control station in an effort to fight off the nausea that gripped him.

Rotem was over the moon. The facility was like an extension of her brain. What a wonderful and intuitive human-machine interface. She turned her hands over and twirled them in opposing directions, and the entire display flipped onto its head and then upright again, created the illusion that the room had performed a somersault. One of the ops-team members turned a little green and closed his eyes.

She mapped twenty-four different routes simultaneously each time, closing one circuit every time 10483 left the house and then returned, and every time a vehicle pulled up at the house or stopped nearby. And then another twenty-four circuits. And then another twenty-four.

Hands to the side and then waved to the right. The room spun faster to the left. Everything was revolving and flying around at breakneck speed, and the lines were splitting and joining rapidly, with Rotem conveying instructions to the system with both hands simultaneously, and each hand conveying a separate series of instructions to the control interface. An ongoing series of dates boomed from the system's speakers. Meital stared wide-eyed at Dafna, and Dafna stared back at her with an expression that said: "What I'm seeing here isn't really happening." They were the only ones aside from Rotem who still had their eyes open.

Rotem was turning on the spot herself by then, in the opposite direction of the spinning screens, marking the final circuits and weeding out the less interesting ones; and then she raised both her arms at once and everything stopped. She came to a halt, too, and closed her eyes, her mind running through the data she had seen on the screen thus far and sorting it out.

Rotem stood there with her eyes still shut. "In formation—structure yields knowledge," she said, keeping her eyes closed. "Information. Break that word into two and put a hyphen in the middle and you get the true meaning of information. In-Formation. Data is valuable when it is structured in an orderly fashion. Look here at screen five now. He makes a series of trips to Haifa, to the Bay area. Beginning June fifteenth, and for almost a month thereafter. He drives around the entire area here." The screen displayed a network of lines, stretched out like a spider's web, around the petrochemical plants in the Haifa Bay area. "This is the strategic facility he was talking about. I wonder how he plans to carry out his strike there. To all those who thought that his letter was simply hot air and idle threats, we have the answer for them right here. I followed everything that left and arrived at his house aside from him. Look at screens seventeen to twenty-three—he ordered construction materials from various places. Screens five to eleven—electronic equipment from various other places. Screen four—a delivery of several boxes from a military supplies store. What does he need from a military supplies store? He has also done some excavation in the basement of the house, screen twenty-four—you can see the ground outside the house changing color over time. He's pouring earth of a different color outside, earth that he's probably removing from under the house. He may have fortified the house he's living in. I'd be very surprised in fact if he hasn't done so. By the way, he's at home right now. Look at screen twelve; it's a current feed, footage from his house two seconds ago."

Rotem went silent, opened her eyes, and looked at the rest of the team.

"Please tell me you're a real person and not a robot," Dafna said. "I'm going to get a knife for you now and have you play that finger game for me like that android, Bishop, in *Aliens*. That was out of this world. How did you do that? You crammed two weeks of work into fifteen minutes. You're not real. I have to call the facility's commander and you have to show him what you just did. Want to work for us on a regular basis?"

"Despite the fact that I'm totally in love with your facility, I'm going to politely decline. Do you have the name of whoever designed it? I'd love to have a chat with him. Or get into bed with him for a few hours."

"We'll get it for you," Meital said, trying not to laugh but failing somewhat.

"Excellent!" Grandpa said, slowly getting to his feet. He was still a little dizzy and off balance and was careful not to make any sudden movements. "At least we know where he is now and can apprehend him?"

"Are you crazy?" Rotem exclaimed, hopping down from the raised control station and pacing quickly back and forth across the floor below. "If we go there now, he could detonate his explosive devices. We have no way of knowing if the bombs have been primed to go off by means of a cellular signal. If we have an edge over him now, why waste it? We have to work slowly and dismantle everything he's put together in Tel Aviv and Haifa before we pay him a visit at home. Grandpa, think . . ."

"That's not going to happen. We're picking him up today from home. We'll dismantle everything he's prepared afterward. First things first, I want him in our hands. And don't forget that Avner's wife and Amiram are imprisoned there in that house you see on screen twelve, and God knows what will happen to them if we don't act immediately."

"There are one or more things that he's prepared that we haven't seen," Rotem responded. "And that's what's troubling me more than anything else we've seen here. Not that I agree with you about having to get to him right away. I think you're mistaken."

"What haven't we seen?"

"What he did outside the range of our cameras. What he did for almost two months abroad."

Besides one member of the team who remained at the facility, the rest of the group stood up to leave. They thanked the facility's operators and Rotem skipped over and hugged Meital and Dafna. The door to the facility opened with an electronic buzzing sound, and on the way out they stopped for a while to allow one of the team members who was still feeling nauseous to go to the bathroom and throw up.

Their two cars started to make their way back to the main base. Grandpa wanted them to get organized there, coordinate the raid on the house on Moshav Yanuv with the SWAT team, the Shin Bet, and IDF's Home Front Command. The team member who remained at the facility sat with his eyes fixed permanently on screen twelve.

Grandpa placed a call to the Operations Room at the main base from the road.

"Put me through to the head of the Operations Division."

After waiting on the line for thirty seconds, Grandpa continued his conversation with the division chief. "I want you to call the Shin Bet's headquarters and ask them to cordon off Rabin Square and send people to all the traffic junctions around the petrochemical plants in the Haifa Bay area. I want all the entrances to the plants closed to traffic. I also want them to start going through Tel Aviv and dismantling all the trashcans on the sidewalks in the Sarona area. They need to coordinate things with Home Front Command and the Israel Police with respect to who's going to take the lead, but I don't want them fighting over territory like little kids. We're dealing here with a matter of national security with disastrous potential. Repeat the words, 'mega attack,' a few times when you talk to them. And mention Islamic State, too; they love that combination."

Rotem signaled Grandpa and he passed the phone to her.

"Hey, Mario, it's Rotem. Is this call being recorded? Good. Tell them the trashcans are on Eliezer Kaplan Street outside the Defense Ministry compound, on the corner of Arania and HaArba'a, along HaArba'a in front of the restaurants all the way to Sprinzak, on the corner of Kaplan and Ibn Gvirol, around the Charles Bronfman Auditorium and HaBima Theatre, on the corner of Ahad Ha'Am and Borochov, on the corner of Rothschild and Shenkin, on David Elazar toward Kaplan, on Begin toward Azrieli, on the HaShalom Interchange bridge—on the bridge itself and leading north away from it, and at the HaShalom train station. That's all I saw, but there's a good chance we missed some. Start with those. They need to dismantle every one and transport them all to a secluded location because some are bombs. To be on the safe side, when they're done with those, they should dismantle all the trashcans in Tel Aviv."

Grandpa took the phone back from Rotem, concluded the call, and read a text message he received from the team member they had left at the AngelFire facility: "He's still at home. I'll update you if there's any movement."

"You remembered all that by heart?" Carmit asked, staring at Rotem as if she were an alien.

"My mind works like that. Visually. I look at maps, diagrams, text, and a bunch of other things and see them as a mixture of colors and emotions. It's hard to explain."

"I have a knife on me. When we get to the base, I'm going to get you to do Bishop's trick like that girl at the facility mentioned. I want to check if there's blood in your veins, or silicone."

"Speaking of knives," Grandpa interjected, "if you want to remain with us on the hunt, we need to get you properly armed with a pistol when we get to the base."

"I'm tagging along for sure. But without a gun. Guns give you an exaggerated sense of security. I've seen more armed people get killed than unarmed ones. I prefer not to carry one. My senses are sharper without one."

December 12, 2016 (13 days ago)

- Remember that guy that Herr Schmidt sends to take care of tough cases?

- He sends us to take care of tough cases.

- Then the guy he sends to take care of very-hard-on-the-verge-of-completely-lost cases. The Barber.

- The one who smells soil and digs holes in the ground?

- Exactly.

- He's one crazy motherfucker. Just thinking about him gives me the chills.

- Do you know why he is called "the Barber"?

- What?

- How the Barber got his nickname. He wasn't called the Barber when he was born.

- I think his parents gave him this name. He must have come out from between his mother's legs wearing that weird priest's hat on his head and that black coat he wears all the time. I tell you, this person's brain is scratched on an extreme level.

- You may be right about the hat and coat. I wasn't there in the delivery room so I can't contradict you but for the sake of discussion there is a possibility that it was like that.

- So why is he called "the Barber"?

- When he was about seventeen or eighteen his young sister came back from gymnastics, went straight up to her room, and he heard her crying; so he entered her room, sat on the bed beside her, and asked what had happened but she didn't want to tell him anything at first because she was afraid of what he might do. His family knew he was crazy. Even his sister who was six or seven at that time was afraid that he would react badly.

- And did he react badly?

- It depends who you ask. I think he reacted very well. He persuaded his sister to tell him what had happened and she told him

283

that after class all the other girls had gone home and the gym teacher had asked her to stay for a few more minutes to practice her split and while she did it he felt her, telling her that her leotard was a bit small and she needed to replace it, and he is checking what size she needs to tell her mommy to buy, and he has put his hands in places where a gym teacher's fingers should not be on a young girl's body.

- Son of a bitch.

- Son of a fucking bitch. That's also what the Barber thought then, when he was not yet called "the Barber." He stroked his sister's head and told her that everything is going to be okay and he's going to have a small chat with the gym teacher and explain to him that he behaved badly and did something that he shouldn't have done. He smiled at his sister and told her she was a great kid and it was not her fault and that the gym teacher would understand it and apologize to her and then he left the room.

- And went to visit the gym teacher?

- Yes.

- And the gym teacher apologized?

- Not at first. When the Barber left his sister's room he was still smiling at her with reassuring eyes until he looked away and started down the stairs. Then his eyes suddenly emptied and he got that hollow ghost face of his. You know. The one that makes you lose your appetite even if you are hungry.

- Yeah, you do not want to meet him when he's like that.

- He arrived at the gym and the gym teacher was there, alone, arranging the mattresses and closing the lights and when he wanted to come out the Barber stood there at the door and asked him politely to explain why he had to shove his hands in all kinds of places to measure the size of a leotard.

- And?

- The gym teacher pushed him back and told him that if he ever accused him again of such things or even set foot in the gym he would make him go to jail. "I have friends in the police" he said.

"And you can tell your mom to fuck off and never send your sister here again and you can explain to her that it's because of your big mouth."

- And did the Barber react badly?

- Here, too, it depends who you ask. In my opinion, again, I think he responded very well.

- What did he do?

- He turned back like he was going away but then did a quick spin and slammed his elbow straight into that place where the nose of the gym teacher meets his forehead and the gym teacher fell to the ground like a sack of tomatoes and lost consciousness.

- A sack of potatoes.

- Tomatoes.

- For the sake of discussion, a sack of potatoes is usually said. That's what is customary to say. It is a globally adopted standard.

- What does it matter what's in the sack?

- I'm just saying that this is the expression one would usually use.

- Okay then, he fell to the ground like a sack of potatoes and his nose started spattering blood like a sprinkler.

- So maybe it is a sack of tomatoes after all, the color is more appropriate.

- Lorenzo, I swear to God that if you start with me again I'm stopping this story and focusing only on my plate until we finish eating.

- Okay, so what happened next?

- When the gym teacher woke up he was tied to those wooden ladders you have on the walls of gymnasiums in the position of Christ crucified. And naked.

- The Barber picked him up and tied him there without any help?

- He just looks thin but under that black coat of his there's muscle. He undressed him, picked him up like a rag doll, and tied him to the ladders, hands spread out and legs apart.

- Jesus's legs were straight.

- What?

- You said he tied him in the position of Christ crucified, for the sake of discussion, I say, Jesus's legs were in a straight line on the crucifix. More or less. Not apart.
- It's impossible to have a conversation with you.

Ricardo stopped talking and turned his attention to the dinner table. He cut a piece of his steak and chewed it slowly. Then he followed the steak with a long gulp of beer and went back to cutting the next bite. Another beer. Another bite. More beer. Fries. Beer. Steak. Beer. Fries.
- So?
- So what?
- So what happened when the gym teacher woke up tied to the ladder?
- I tell you, Lorenzo, this is one of the best fries I have ever eaten. The thickness and the degree of making are just right. Perfect. Not too soft and not too burned. Golden, I would say. And just the right amount of salt. Do you know who makes the best fries in the world? The Dutch. The bastards know how to make it. They fry it first in a hundred and seventy degrees and then when it's soft they fry it at two hundred and fifty degrees only for just a little more time to get it crunchy from the outside but soft on the inside. Just when you think you have seen it all you wander around in Amsterdam and you say to yourself "I'm hungry, what shall I eat? Oh, here is a fries store right here in the street close by, why won't I have some fries now, I know fries, I like fries" and you buy the fries and you taste one, and it's the best fucking fry you ever had and it makes you—
- And the gym teacher?
- Ah, do you find that story interesting?
- Very interesting, actually this is one of the better stories I have heard recently.
- Right. And you will never know how it ends.
- Why?
- Because it's fucking impossible to have a conversation with you.

Because you're always picking on the little things and shifting the conversation to side tracks instead of driving on the Turnpike with Cruise Control.

- Okay, I'll try to hold back. What happened when the gym teacher woke up tied naked to a ladder in the gymnasium?

- He saw the Barber standing in front of him with a roll of fishing line, a needle, scissors, and a Stanley Knife.

- This sounds good. Do continue.

- The Barber who was not yet called the Barber told the gym teacher who was still a gym teacher "I will turn on my phone camera and aim it to your face and you will apologize to Chrissy on video and tell her you are sorry you touched her that way and will never do anything like that ever. Not to her and not to any other girl."

- Chrissy is his sister?

- Yeah. Christine. She lives in Iowa today, I think.

- And did he apologize?

- Nope. He wouldn't say anything. He probably assumed the recording could circulate on the Net and then all the girls he had been harassing would file complaints and their families would come to haunt him in an endless series of trials for rape and sexual abuse so he kept his mouth shut and didn't say a word. Just looked at the Barber and shut up.

- I assume it would have been better for him to speak and record that apology.

- You assume correctly. The Barber looked at the naked man on the ladder for a minute and then went and closed all the windows and locked the doors of the gym, switched off most of the lights, and went back to the gym teacher. He tied many twists of fishing thread around the top of his scrotum and with one cut of the Stanley Knife he took off his balls.

- Motherfucker! That's unpleasant.

- Damn right. The gym teacher was screaming like a slaughtered pig and the Barber knocked a small training weight on the side of his head so he wouldn't disturb him while he was stitching.

- Stitching?

- Stitching the scrotum around the chin of the gym teacher with the needle and fishing line.

- So you can say he gave him a double chin.

- Yeah, a fucking double chin.

Ricardo began to laugh out loud. Lorenzo's jokes were mostly annoying but this one was a gem. Some of the diners at the nearby tables turned their heads toward the twins. "Fucking double chin! I tell ya, HA HA."

- You know, that still doesn't explain why he's called "the Barber." I would say "swordsman" or "samurai" or "butcher" or "tailor" would be more appropriate.

- Once he finished stitching he took a step back and looked, but the picture was not perfect in his opinion so he took the scissors and gave him a nicer chin haircut. Something more modern for the hair on the gym teacher's balls hanging from his chin, you know, like a French beard. Then he went to the bathroom, filled a bucket with cold water and poured it on the head of the gym teacher and woke him up and as he started screaming again from the pain down his groin and up his chin the Barber stood there holding his phone and recording a video of the whole thing.

- And did he kill him after that?

- Nope. He left him there tied up and went home and that's how they found the gym teacher the next morning. Tied to the ladders with a fashionable double-chinned French beard. Before the Barber went away he told the gym teacher that he is welcome to go to the police and press charges. He hasn't done so until today, twenty years or so after that night, even when the Barber sends him an email every Christmas with greetings and an attachment of a few seconds from the video he took back then.

- So he had no friends in the police.

- Who?

- The gym teacher. He said he had friends in the police.

- He must have lied.

- So that's how the Barber got his name?

- So they say.

- Who?

- Everyone.

- It's interesting that I haven't heard of it until now. Ricardo, are you sure you did not make it up here in the restaurant while we were eating?

- My imagination is not that wild. You can call Chrissy if you want to hear more details.

- I would rather die in torture than mess with the Barber's sister.

- You are a wise man.

12/20/2016–16 days after putting the plan into motion

I go down to the basement, turn on the light, open the folding chair, and sit down in front of the cage. I tell Amiram and Efrat that in honor of my birthday, which falls today, I've decided to give them a deck of cards to play with and a full day of light in the basement. I light a candle and leave it on the basement floor and go back upstairs without turning off the light. I begin playing a collection of children's birthday songs on a loop through the basement speakers.

I sit at the kitchen table to sort out the notes I've made to myself. I go through them and neatly copy their contents into my notebook. Later I'll decide which of them can be incorporated into my plan and which can't, but everything has to be well documented.

- Connect cable from high-voltage pylon to metal railing (disconnect earth).
- Connect trashcan bomb to large helium canister, release close to a stadium hosting a game with the wind blowing in the right direction.
- Fly a plane into the main base (check the possibility of getting work as a flight attendant for an airline that flies to Israel).
- Small circular candles under the tires of a vehicle I wish to disable (not immediate).
- Sealing a room and lighting a portable burner inside will empty the space of oxygen. (Within how many hours? Check formula.)
- Arson using a large tub of contact glue—4 holes in the sides of the tub near the bottom, seal with strips of masking tape around the tub, remove masking tape, and light to set off. Within 2 minutes or so, the flame will heat the tub and produce 4 jets of burning contact adhesive.
- Check if it's better to prepare a Molotov cocktail to torch the carpet van or to keep a jerrycan of gasoline and a box of matches in the vehicle.

- To obtain a password for a laptop or tablet, you don't have to decrypt anything. The encryption's algorithms are very complicated. It's easier to listen to the electromagnetic pattern of the keys on the keyboard and thus obtain the password.
- Walk into a cosmetic surgery clinic while someone is undergoing liposuction, neutralize the doctor, and inject a liquid explosive with a tiny detonator. Could be used to bring down an aircraft.
- Buy a police uniform.
- After neutralizing the driver of the gas tanker, drive into the main base, if accessible, under the pretense of making a gas delivery, and hook up the tanker to the bunker's sprinkler system (empty the water 1st). Using sufficient pressure, the entire building can be filled with gas, and then even the smallest electrical spark will cause the whole place to explode, with devastating effect because the facility is sealed underground. No one will get out alive.

I drive to HaHarzit Street in Savyon, remain in the car, and connect to the Wi-Fi network I located the last time I was there.

I open the laptop, go to the Organization's website and click on the "Submit Application" link. The system asks me to check the boxes alongside the character traits most applicable to myself. I select "Sociable," "Team Player," and "Level-headed & Responsible," and then provide answers to a long list of questions. Education, languages, military service, employment, particulars about trips abroad.

In the Military Service section I write that I was a Service Conditions NCO and the Chief of Staff's personal chef. Under Languages I write that I speak Aramaic, Ancient Mandarin, and the language of magical fairies.

I continue to provide amusing answers to the remainder of the lengthy questionnaire, and finally, in the Additional Details section, I outline what will happen to the Organization if they don't meet my demands. In the section for uploading files such as a resume, I attach the video from the basement and the image of Efrat and Amiram.

In the section in which I outline what will happen to them if they don't meet my demands, I include only a part of my plan in general terms. I don't offer additional details because if I tell them that the strategic facility I intend to blow up is in Haifa, they will definitely set up a security perimeter around the petrochemical plants, so I leave things in general terms. Since I've planned the strike on the petrochemical plants for the following day, it will also give them a chance to apologize to me on the Sunday evening news show.

To make sure they don't ignore the form I fill in on the website, I list my 1st name as "Greetings" and write "From Amiram and Avner's wife" in the Surname field. That will get the attention it deserves as soon as they get to my application.

My plan is quite simple. On the day I set it in motion I'll put on my protective suit and drive my armored carpet van down the streets on which I've installed my trashcan bombs. Every time I get 30 meters past one of the trashcan devices, I'll detonate it. I'll plan my route to ensure that I can detonate each trashcan bomb at 10-minute intervals. After my work in the area of the trashcans is done, I'll drive to Rabin Square and detonate my 2 trash-can-and-gas-tank-bomb from a nearby street. I'm assuming they won't apologize until I prove how serious I am and begin detonating the trashcan bombs. I'll listen to the Reshet Bet radio station on the drive so I can hear their apology.

At the end of the day, I'll drive home in the afternoon and keep an eye on the news to see if there's going to be an apology. If there isn't one, I'll go the following morning to the gas depot in Rishon and wait for the gas delivery tanker whose route I'm familiar with by now. When the gas tanker drives into one of the quiet neighborhoods, I'll hijack the vehicle and dispatch the driver. Then I'll drive the tanker to Haifa. I must remember to take the rubber sheeting, a box cutter, and several containers of sealant with me in the tanker.

When I insert the gas pipe into the sewer hole closest to the petro-chemical plants, I'll have to seal it well with the rubber sheeting and sealant to ensure that the gas spreads through the waste disposal system under the entire facility. Once I've emptied the gas tanker, I'll make an opening in the seal and throw a Molotov cocktail at the sewer hole from a suitable distance. The ensuing chain reaction will ignite the entire area. I have to remember to prepare bottles, gasoline, rags, and a lighter.

Immediately thereafter I'll get into the gas tanker and head quickly southward, before the ammonia cloud starts to spread.

I check Waze to see where Avner's car is parked. Still at the Organization's main base. It's been parked there for 3 days already. Probably because he was at the house on HaHarzit Street at the time of the blast. I need to find out where he's been hospitalized and to visit him so I can give him regards from Efrat, or place a bouquet of roses from my garden on his grave if he didn't survive the . . .

*   *   *

10483 stopped writing in his journal and looked up. One of the motion sensors outside sounded an alert. He looked at the screen displaying the feeds from the cameras and saw a group of individuals—dressed in black, their faces masked and carrying weapons—approaching the house quickly in silence. He reached for the model aircraft remote control on the table next to him, dropped flat on the floor, and pressed the activation button.

Four powerful explosions went off and a hail of steel nails around the house shattered the tranquility of the community. 10483 jumped to his feet, shook off the fragments of glass from the living room windows, and ran to grab his protective suit. He pulled the protective helmet over his head, slipped into his armored suit, closed the Velcro strips, and verified that all the items he had placed in the pockets of the bulletproof vest were in place as he rushed down to the basement.

He raced from the bottom of the stairs to the opening of the tunnel, bypassing the cage in which Amiram and Efrat were now on their feet and trying to get used to the sudden light from above. A pipe that burst in the basement as a result of the blasts was spraying them with a jet of water. 10483 gave them one last look, slipped into the opening of the tunnel, and ran through. On reaching the end of the tunnel, he pushed aside the piece of corrugated steel topped with a layer of earth that was covering the opening and emerged quickly beside his parked van. Two men in black uniforms were standing next to the vehicle; and because their attention was focused on the chaos across the road, he shot them both from behind and slipped Amiram's pistol back into the appropriate pocket in his suit. He went through their flak jackets, took 1 communications radio and a Micro-Uzi submachine gun, and transferred all the magazines they were carrying to the pockets of his own protective suit.

He jumped into his van, tossed the notebook, the Uzi, and the model aircraft controller onto the seat beside him, and sped off in the direction of Route 4 West, toward Tel Aviv. He remembered that he hadn't got around to photographing his efficient food dispenser as a memento. He only has a general picture of the basement taken from the stairs leading up to the ground level of the house. The sound of police sirens in the background caused him to refocus on his driving. And back at the scene, as a result of the shockwaves from the blasts, the tunnel leading outside from the basement succumbed to the pressure of the earth above it and collapsed.

* * *

Amiram and Efrat were standing in the cage in the basement and protecting their heads. The series of blasts had shocked them, and they were covered in bits of plaster that had fallen from the basement's ceiling. The water pipe that had ruptured as a result of the blasts was a relatively large one and probably served an entire portion of the community, not just the house in which they were being held. The basement was filling rapidly with water, which had already risen to their knees. 10483 had hurried past them into the tunnel earlier and the structure had collapsed behind him some thirty seconds later. Amiram was hoping with all his heart that 10483 hadn't made it out the other side and was now lying under a few tons of earth. The muffled sound of gunfire could be heard from outside.

"We're here," he started yelling, and Efrat joined in.

"Help! We're down here!"

It took a few more minutes before the teams outside stormed into the house, spraying the living room and kitchen with bullets.

"He isn't here!" Amiram shouted. "He escaped through a tunnel."

"Get us out of here!" Efrat screamed. The water level was rising. It was at her waist already, and also at the height of the electrical sockets in the basement. The home's ground-fault circuit interrupter stepped in to save Efrat and Amiram from electrocution. The basement went dark again.

If the tunnel was still there it may have allowed the water to drain out, but it had collapsed and the torrent of water didn't let up. The barrel of a Micro-Uzi appeared from above, followed soon by a SWAT team member, and then two others. Daylight was still coming in from the open door at the top of the stairs.

"Don't shoot!" Efrat shouted. "Get us out of here!"

"He isn't here," Amiram called out. "He went out through a tunnel. It leads that way. He dug a tunnel from down here to the outside and escaped. The tunnel collapsed but he may have made it out the other side." Amiram pointed to a pile of earth—already half-covered in water—that was once the tunnel to the outside. The two SWAT team members on the stairs switched on their head-mounted flashlights and aimed their beams at the cage, before shouting something to the teams upstairs, descending into the basement, and getting into the water, which was already at chest height. The relatively small basement filled quickly from the powerful stream of water coming from the pipe. One of the SWAT commandos approached the cage. "How does it open?" he asked.

"It's welded shut. Go get a disk saw or blowtorch. Hurry!"

"We don't have either. They're in a vehicle that should get here in a few minutes."

The water level reached the shoulders of the people in the basement. One of the commandos tried with all his might to bend the iron bars.

"Look upstairs. He has a blowtorch in the house somewhere."

"There's no time. And a blowtorch isn't going to work properly with all this water in here. We don't have time to go looking for the town's water mains. It's filling too quickly." One of the commandos swam back to the stairs and ran out. The other one looked around for something that could help him bend the bars. The bags of dog food had disintegrated and there were clumps of kibble floating in the water, which was now up to everyone's neck. Everything was swirling in the foam of the water spewing from the burst pipe.

The height of the flooded cage measured two meters. Its roof was also made of iron bars welded to those that formed its walls. Amiram and Efrat were gripping the ceiling bars and holding themselves afloat with their faces pressed to the barred ceiling above them. Two more commandos came running down the stairs carrying two wheel jacks from their vehicles and swam quickly to the ceiling of the cage. They sat on the cage ceiling, with just a meter between the bars under them and the concrete ceiling of the basement, positioned the two jacks on either side of a pair of bars, and started opening the jacks as fast as they could.

The water had reached the ceiling of the cage. Amiram and Efrat both took a deep breath and held onto the ceiling bars, floating in the water and watching the commandos working as fast as they could to widen the space between the bars. Their faces were already covered with water. Ten seconds, twenty seconds, half a minute, Amiram couldn't hold his breath any longer. He inhaled water. His hands released their grip on the bars, his body convulsed uncontrollably for a few seconds and then stopped moving. He started to sink to the bottom of the cage. The commandos had widened the bars as much as they could and they grabbed Efrat and barely managed to pull her through the space between them. The metal left deep scratches on her body. She lifted her head above the water, took a deep breath, and coughed. "Get him out quickly," she yelled.

They had just thirty centimeters of air above their heads. The water continued to rise. One of the SWAT team commandos grabbed Efrat by the arm and dragged her behind him as he swam for the stairs, and they disappeared through the open doorway at the top.

The two commandos who remained in the basement tried to squeeze through the widened bars to rescue Amiram from the bottom of the cage. It was impossible. They were too big and wouldn't fit through the bars. They had barely managed to pull out Efrat, who was a lot smaller than they were. The water reached the ceiling of the basement. Both fighters were already submerged. They turned and swam underwater toward the exit.

Amiram's body was floating in the cage. His arms were outstretched and his eyes were open.

* * *

"Get out of the car. You're going to the main base."

"I'm coming with you."

"Not a chance, Rotem. If you want to remain in the loop, get to the Ops Room and follow things from there. There's no way I'm going to let him kill you, too." Carmit pulled Rotem out the car and closed the door behind her.

"I should be there. I can help you. No one knows him better than I do."

"I'll say it again. Not a chance. He's on his way now to Tel Aviv and we both know that nothing's going to stop him from getting there. You've seen what he's set up in Tel Aviv. He's going straight to the area where he's planted his explosive devices, right?"

"Right. And from there he'll try to get to Rabin Square to detonate the large device he's buried there. I can help you to predict his next moves."

"No. Think logically. The Organization needs your brain. Rotem, you're not a field agent. If I have to knock you out to make you stay here, I will."

Rotem turned away with an angry look on her face. She knew Carmit was right, but not being at the center of things was hard for her to bear. She got into one of the few cars that was heading back to the main base and wasn't joining the chase after 10483's carpet van.

* * *

The drivers heading south on Route 4 did their best to swerve to the side and avoid being struck by the van with the MASHANI—CARPET CLEANERS stickers that was racing down the highway at 140kph with a convoy of emergency vehicles and police cars on its tail. Some managed to do so, and those that didn't were left with dents and scratches down the sides of their vehicles as the van zipped between the lanes without consideration for anyone else on the road. The wail of sirens filled the air along with the flashing

"No matter what happens on the road, you can't let him make it to Tel Aviv." Grandpa's voice echoed over the police radios in every patrol car.

The van sped through a red light at the Morasha Interchange and continued south, narrowly missing a truck that was approaching from the south and turning left toward the Glilot Junction. The police patrol car behind the van wasn't as lucky. 10483 reached into his armored vest for the police radio he'd taken from the two SWAT team members. "Heads-up," he said into the device. "He's turned right toward Glilot." The patrol cars closest to him remained on his tail, but all the other security vehicles that weren't in eye contact with the carpet van turned right toward Glilot Junction.

It took a minute before one of the officers in the vehicles racing behind the carpet van got on the radio. "Who said he turned right at Morasha? He's continuing straight in the direction of Tel Aviv."

"Who is this?" 10483 radioed through again. "You're disrupting a police frequency. That's a criminal offense." He reached the Ganot Interchange and turned right to get onto the Ayalon Highway. Most of those chasing him were looking for him on a different road in the direction of Herzliya. He continued along the Ayalon with just three police cars behind him.

"Don't let him get to Tel Aviv." The SWAT team commander's voice came through on the radio. "You're authorized to open fire on the van to stop it. Even if you're surrounded by civilian vehicles. I repeat—you're authorized to open fire."

"I see him turning left at the Glilot Junction toward Tel Aviv, from the north, near the Country Club." 10483 continued to relay misleading reports over the police radio network. The window next to him shattered after being struck by a bullet, which was fired at him from a police car that tried to pass him on the left, and was stopped by the armored glass stuck to the inside. He turned the wheel of the van to the left, forcing the police car to brake. A second police car behind him used the opportunity to pull alongside the van on the right and empty an entire magazine of 9mm bullets into the front right wheel of the vehicle in an effort to cause it to swerve to the right and careen out of control. Nothing happened. The van drove on and flew past the Kibbutz Galuyot Interchange.

"Heads-up. He's just passed the KKL Interchange heading south. He has hostages in the van. Hold your fire. I repeat: Hold your fire," 10483 radioed through as he continued north in the direction of the HaShalom Interchange.

*   *   *

It would be impossible, in all likelihood, to prepare a meal as tasteless as the one that was on the light blue plastic tray on the cabinet next to his bed. He tasted a spoonful of soup and grimaced, moved on to sample the pale-looking mashed potatoes, and then took a bite of a grayish meatball. He leaned against the backrest of the bed and covered himself with a white sheet bearing the logo of Tel Hashomer Hospital. He'd sell his soul for food cooked with some herbs and spices.

Avner tried to stretch and a sharp pain shot like a bolt of lightning through his right side. He relaxed his muscles immediately. His body's going to take a while to recover. *This body used to be a lot tougher,* he thought to himself; *I guess I really am getting old.*

No one from the Organization had come to see him today and it was driving him crazy. No one had come to update him and he didn't know if that was a good sign or not. His children had stayed there with him almost constantly, until he chased them out and back to their families. "You have your own families and jobs you need to go to, and you can stare at me all day long and it's not going to make me heal any faster. There's no need for you to lounge around here all the time. If you have to visit, you can do so in shifts, with one of you coming every evening for an hour and that's it." He was proud of his daughter and two sons and appreciated their efforts to encourage him to have faith in the Organization's ability to locate their mother, and his wife, alive. He'd already come to terms with the fact that he would probably never see her alive again.

He had more than enough time on his hands to think about her. About the decades they'd shared. The thoughts, at a certain point, became too painful, and he put them aside and focused on reading newspapers and books to pass the time.

His cell phone rang and he picked it up. He didn't recognize the number. Perhaps Rotem had decided to do him the favor of providing him with an update on the investigation. Maybe they're onto something. Perhaps a clue as to the whereabouts of the basement. "Hello?"

"Honey?" He heard Efrat's voice on the other end of the line.

Avner tensed and sat up in bed. "Efrat! Where are you? Where's he holding you?"

"Everything's okay. Your comrades rescued me. I'm here in the house where he was holding us."

"Where?"

"Moshav Yanuv. Near Ra'anana."

"Is Amiram with you?"

Efrat went silent for a moment. She couldn't find the right words. "Efrat?"

"I'm sorry. He didn't make it."

"What??"

"He died during the rescue operation. I'll tell you when I get there. They're going to take me home to shower and change clothes and

301

I'll come there in my own car soon. They told me you were admitted to Tel Hashomer."

"The Surgical Ward, fifth floor. And are you okay?"

"A few scratches. They wanted to take me to Tel Hashomer for medical and psychological examination but I refused. Told them I'm going there anyway to see you and that they should leave me alone. Don't worry. From what I've heard, I'm in much better shape than you are."

"I'm sure they exaggerated. I'm fine. Can't wait to get out of here but they won't let me out yet. Come quickly, I'm waiting for you. Is Grandpa there? Can you put him on the line?"

"No. They're all in pursuit of the nutcase."

"I thought that if you're there at the house with them, then they must have killed him."

"No. He fled in a van and everyone here disappeared after him. I'm here with someone who's going to take me home; and another vehicle or two returned to your base. All the others are in pursuit."

* * *

"Heads-up. He's on our network, relaying false reports. Everyone switch to the alternative frequency." The police forces and the SWAT team and Organization team members involved in the chase switched to a different frequency, and 10483 could no longer hear their radio communication on the device in his possession. He was nearing the HaShalom Interchange and he stuck to the right lane in preparation for turning off the Ayalon Highway. One of the unmarked cars on his tail started to pass him on the left, and the two Organization agents sitting on the right side of the vehicle opened their windows, produced two automatic weapons and sprayed the left side of the carpet van with bullets. The door on the driver's side was dotted with holes, the driver's window cracked but remained in place and didn't fall to the ground, and the MASHANI—CARPET CLEANERS logo toward the rear of the van was riddled with bullet holes. The tires absorbed the bullets and remained unimpaired.

"He's done something to that van. Nothing's happening to the tires and he's driving on despite all the holes we've made in the driver's cab."

"Stay on him. Ram him. Run him off the road! Some of the explosive devices he installed are in the area of the HaShalom Interchange. Don't let him get there."

The armored van protected 10483 almost perfectly. No bullets pierced the armor plating fitted to the driver's door and the bullets were stopped by the armored glass fixed to the driver's window. But two of the bullets did penetrate the driver's cab through the small gap between the steel plate fixed to the door and the armored window, striking 10483 in his left side. But his protective suit stopped the two bullets. He felt them strike him like two powerful punches, but they didn't pierce the protective suit. He sped on, exiting the highway, turning left toward the HaShalom Bridge, and swerving to force the Organization vehicle racing alongside him to his left into the path of an oncoming car and a head-on collision, with a loud bang and flying bits of glass. He raced ahead, reaching the middle of the bridge over the highway and spotting several police cars waiting for him on the other side, blocking the road, and behind them armed policemen with their weapons drawn. The two sidewalks on either side of the bridge were deserted.

- Zing
- Zing
- Zing
- Zing

Bullets struck the windshield of his van. The unarmored outer glass shattered, and the armored glass stuck behind the windshield with epoxy held the broken pieces in place.

10483 stopped his van in the middle of the bridge. The vehicles closed in on him. The police up ahead held their fire so as not to hit the security vehicles parked behind him. For a moment there was silence, and everything stood still, aside from the flow of traffic along the Ayalon Highway under the bridge that the police had yet to block. Police forces with their weapons drawn began advancing slowly and cautiously toward the carpet van, closing in on him from in front and behind. 10483 remained in the van and turned on the radio to Reshet Bet. The station was broadcasting ongoing reports about an incident involving a driver on a rampage through the streets of Tel Aviv who the police were describing as extremely dangerous, probably an Islamic State terrorist, armed, carrying out a shooting attack. *The Middle East really is a dangerous region,* he thought to himself, before releasing his seatbelt, crouching down to the floor of the vehicle and reaching for the model aircraft controller that had fallen off the front passenger seat during the course of the chase and was lying now on the floor of the vehicle. He grabbed it and moved the two control levers while still crouched on the floor of the van. A rapid series of explosions shook the HaShalom Interchange and sent a spray of nails flying into everything in the vicinity of the bridge and within a hundred-meter radius. The bottom sections of the two glass walls on the eastern side of the triangular and square Azrieli Towers, shattered up to a height of around twenty floors, and crashed to the ground in a downpour of glass. 10483 got back into the driver's seat of his battered and bullet-riddled carpet van, returned the Micro-Uzi and model aircraft controller to the seat next to him, and continued driving forward across the bridge. He rammed into two empty police cars in his path and drove over the bodies of the police officers sprawled on the asphalt behind the vehicles, turning left onto Begin Road. When he again heard approaching sirens and the sound of bullets striking the back of his carpet van, he came to a stop some fifty meters before the turning right onto HaArba'a Street, crouched down again inside the vehicle and worked the controller. Another series of powerful explosions shook the street. Cars in the vicinity caught fire, pedestrians who happened to be in the area fell victim to the flying shrapnel, and then everything went quiet again. The carpet van's engine died. 10483 tried quickly to start it up again several times, but without success. He fired a few shots with the Micro-Uzi into the two jerrycans of gasoline in the back of the vehicle and they burst into flame. He crouched down again on the floor of the van in front of the passenger seat, retrieved the notebook he'd been writing in since regaining consciousness at Lowenstein Hospital, and threw it into the fire. Grabbing the Micro-Uzi and model aircraft controller from the van, he turned around, fired a few rounds in the direction of the police officers behind him, and headed off on foot. A police helicopter was hovering above him and a second wave of Special Forces had crossed the HaShalom Bridge, littered now with wrecked vehicles and bodies, and was heading down Begin Road and past the ball of fire that was once 10483's van.

* * *

Mario, the head of the Organization's Operations Division, yelled into the phone. "I know it's drastic, but we have no choice if we want to avoid hundreds of fatalities."

"We've never done anything like it before," the head of the Home Front Command's Operations Division barked in response. "No one sounds air-raid sirens in Tel Aviv because of a terror attack."

"It's a rolling attack—ongoing. Pay close attention. We're dealing with an Islamic State terrorist who has spent an entire year preparing an infrastructure attack in Tel Aviv, and now he's set it in motion. If you don't have real-time intelligence, then simply turn on Channel 2 on the TV and you'll see that the HaShalom Bridge and Begin Road look like the backdrop for *Mad Max* or a scene from *Terminator*. We need to get all civilians into bomb shelters and stop all traffic in the area of the HaShalom train station, Azrieli, the Defense Ministry compound, Rabin Square from the north and also from the square to the west, all the way to Rothschild and Shenkin. You guys don't know him. We do. We know who we're dealing with; and I'm telling you now, the dozens who've been killed and injured thus far are only the beginning if we don't get everyone off the streets. It's my head on the line. This call is being recorded and I'm talking full responsibility. The Organization takes full responsibility.

305

The only thing that's going to empty the streets of Tel Aviv right now is an air-raid siren."

The conversation ended and Mario replaced the receiver. "Good thinking," he said to Rotem. "You just saved a whole lot of lives."

Rotem looked at the control screens in the Operations Room. "Too bad you can't say the same about those chasing him," she said. The screens around them were displaying live feeds from the cameras of the teams in the field. Some showed long-range shots of the clouds of smoke from the bombs and burning cars. Those closer to the action, the cameras mounted on casualties, remained fixed on a single image, some at an odd angle such that most of the screen was filled with a close-up of the road or a piece of sky.

The wail of air-raid sirens sounded in the skies of Tel Aviv. And the city's residents—well-versed in real-time Code Red alerts from the last war with Hamas during Operation Protective Edge—disappeared off the streets. Pedestrians went into designated protective spaces in surrounding buildings, vehicles stopped on the roads and drivers abandoned them, with some fleeing to public shelters if there were any nearby, and others lying flat on the ground on the side of the road with their arms shielding their heads. They were all waiting to hear the telltale booms from the Iron Dome's interceptors and the rockets from Gaza, and mistakenly thought that the explosions were indeed the booms from the interceptions. The ominous ascending-and-descending tone of the siren, which usually didn't last longer than a minute, didn't stop this time.

* * *

Carmit got back into the front passenger seat of the car and shook off the glass fragments from her shirt. The front window on the driver's side of the car she was in was gone and the head of the driver next to her was slumped forward. She looked at him and saw a wound in the center of his forehead. She put two fingers on his carotid artery. No pulse. Carmit got out of the car, walked around to the driver's side, opened the door, and dragged the dead driver out. She looked at the car. Both its front tires were punctured and the left side of the vehicle was dotted with small holes. It was a good thing that she ducked in time when she saw 10483's van come to a halt in the middle of the bridge. She yelled "Duck!" to everyone in the vehicle. But they didn't listen or didn't react in time. The two policemen who were sitting in the back were dead, too. She left them there, got into the car, and started it up. The car moved slowly with its two punctured front tires, but she didn't need speed. She only wanted to maintain eye contact with him. She watched him ram two police cars with his van, continue straight along the bridge, and then turn left onto Begin Road. She made a point of remaining at least 50 meters behind him. With their sirens wailing, two military vehicles passed her and rapidly approached the carpet van up ahead. She watched as Military Police forces aimed M-16 assault rifles out the windows of their racing vehicles and opened fire on 10483's van. It stopped. Carmit immediately crouched beneath the steering wheel and pressed her hands tightly to her ears. The blasts around her were extremely powerful, and the car she was in shook. She felt a sharp pain in her left arm. One of the flying nails had penetrated the driver's door and caused a deep laceration below her shoulder. Blood was trickling down her arm. She opened the glove compartment of the vehicle and found a first-aid kit with a roll of an ACE bandage, which she used to close the wound with a few quick loops around her arm. It was more like blocking a leak in a garden hose, but she didn't have time to dress the wound properly. 10483 had emerged from his van and was continuing on foot, and she left her vehicle and followed him from a distance. He wasn't running or in a particular hurry. He simply walked leisurely along Begin Road and then turned right onto HaArba'a Street. She realized he was waiting for his pursuers to get close to him, and she kept her distance. If she had a radio, she would have warned everyone, but she didn't have time to look for one before leaving the vehicle, and now her attention was entirely focused on 10483, who was strolling down HaArba'a Street ahead of her.

* * *

10483 headed down HaArba'a Street. The street was deserted and someone called to him to come hide in one of the restaurants, but he didn't respond and walked on. That was a nice move they pulled on him with the air-raid siren. But they're still going to try to take him down, and they'll have to move in close to do so. A bullet from a sniper's rifle struck him in the back and rocked him a little, but the protective suit he had on stopped it from penetrating his body. "Come in here and lie down on the floor. We don't have a bomb shelter," someone called to him from a restaurant on the left side of the street. He went in, lay down on the floor, and activated his model aircraft controller once more. The shockwave hit him like a blow from a heavyweight boxer. One of the trashcans was fairly close by, and the blast blew in the restaurant's glass storefront, spraying the people who were hiding inside with shards of glass and bits of shrapnel. Against the backdrop of screams and cries for help, 10483 left the restaurant and continued down HaArba'a Street, at a faster pace now, before turning right into the Sarona area. The suit he was wearing and the helmet on his head were impeding his progress somewhat, but they were essential and he didn't remove them. He ran his hands over the various pockets in his protective suit to make sure everything was in place. Still on the move, he took out his cell phone and checked the status of the battery—88 percent. He opened the browser page with the two shortcuts, one of which he had already used, left the browser open, and locked the cell phone. The back of his hands displayed lacerations caused by the fragments of glass. He looked at them. Perhaps he should have prepared a pair of gloves, too. Peering between the low-rise structures around the Sarona Market he spotted a group of soldiers running toward him from the direction of the Defense Ministry compound. Two rounds struck him in the chest. He pulled out the Micro-Uzi, sprayed a volley of rounds in their direction, released the empty magazine and allowed it to fall to the floor, inserted a full one, and walked on ahead, continuing to fire as he moved forward. He had Amiram's pistol in his other hand and was using it, too, against the approaching troops, who were shooting back at him. Additional police forces and soldiers closed in. He dropped flat to the ground once more, took the controller out of its pouch and activated it, again spraying the entire area with nails. He then stood up again, slipped the pistol into its holster, and continued walking in the direction of the Azrieli Center. Two black crows landed on the grass nearby and proceeded to engage in a raucous squabble over something that looked like a piece of red plastic. He observed them for a moment and walked on.

* * *

The security guard at the entrance to the Azrieli Mall left an orphaned chair outside and also fled into the shopping center. The wail of the air-raid sirens continued uninterrupted; and the incessant booms, which had started nearby, shattered the glass walls of the towers, and had then moved farther away, were now starting to sound closer and closer again. *Strange that the Iron Dome system is missing the rockets from Gaza,* he thought. And he couldn't understand how their accuracy had improved so much. The mall was full of people—some who'd rushed in from the street after the initial blast and were still inside due to the ongoing air-raid siren, some who were shopping before it all started, and some were soldiers from the nearby Defense Ministry compound who had popped into the mall for something to eat and hadn't made it back to the base before everything kicked off. Everyone was trying to move as far inside the mall as possible, into the shelters and protective areas, and as far as they could get from the structure's glass walls. 10483 approached the entrance to the Azrieli Center in quick strides.

* * *

"Get hold of the bunker." Rotem was sitting next to Mario and watching the feeds from the cameras around the HaShalom Interchange.

"I know what he has in mind. We have to get the Air Force to send a helicopter to the roof of Azrieli."

"Why?"

"From what I've observed until now, whenever he decides to detonate his devices, several explode at once, those in his immediate vicinity. It's been the same since the first time, on HaHarzit Street in Savyon, and then again at his house, and then here in the streets. He must have a remote controller with a limited range. That's why he's going up."

"He wants a wider range from the roof of Azrieli?"

"Precisely."

"But he's backing himself into a corner. If he goes up to the roof, he won't be coming down again."

"That's true. He surely knows that."

"Okay, I'm getting the bunker on the line to tell them to get the Air Force into action. And also to instruct all forces still on the ground to get the hell out of there. Whatever hasn't exploded until now is going to go off soon."

"What's the situation in Rabin Square?"

"It's been evacuated. It's clear of civilians. The air-raid siren sent everyone scattering for shelter."

"Tell them to get the police out of there, too."

* * *

10483 walked into the mall and grabbed a small bottle of mineral water from a deserted kiosk. He drank it down, placed the empty bottle on the counter, and walked toward the lobby of the circular Azrieli Tower, which was deserted. He went over to the elevators and looked around. There were three on each side of the hallway. He pressed the button to call the elevators and the doors of one opened immediately. He stepped in and pressed the button to the highest floor. He recalled the elevator on Rue de Delices that took him up to the floor on which Adriana Karson lived before filling her apartment with water and bringing down the building on his first target.

The first envelope out of three. That was the seventh floor. This building has forty-nine floors, which is seven squared. That's interesting.

While riding up in the elevator, he took his cell phone out of its pouch, checked something on the Internet, quickly typed an email and sent it, and put the phone back in its place. After getting to the top, he stepped out of the elevator, opened the door to the stairwell, and walked up to the door leading to the roof. The door was locked. He went back down to the bottom of the flight of stairs to avoid any ricochets, pulled out the Micro-Uzi, replaced the spent magazine with a full one, and emptied it into the lock of the door at the top of the stairs. He went back up and kicked the door, which opened onto the roof. He inserted a new magazine and went to the door of the nearby elevator room and shaft. It was locked. He backed away a few meters and fired at the locking mechanism of the door, kicked it in, went inside, and emptied another magazine into the fuse box, disabling the building's six elevators in a dance of electrical sparks.

* * *

The elevator stopped suddenly on the thirty-seventh floor, dropped a few centimeters and came to a rest with a bang, the emergency brakes locking onto the steel tracks of the elevator shaft. The lights went out. Carmit turned on the flashlight on her cell phone and shone it around the elevator. She pressed several buttons without getting any response and then placed her phone on the floor to shine the flashlight's beam onto the elevator's ceiling. She jumped up and grabbed a piece of the ceiling's decorative covering, pulling it down along with a bundle of electrical wires connected to spotlights and fans. Fitted into the exposed ceiling of the elevator was an emergency escape hatch with two metal handles on either side of it. Carmit gripped and hung onto them with both hands, raised her legs, and pushed her feet up against the escape hatch, which opened outward and fell with a bang onto the roof of the elevator. She let go of the handles and dropped to the floor of the elevator to

311

pick up her phone, which she then gripped between her teeth. Hands gripping the metal handles again, with a backward roll, she was on the roof of the elevator, grateful to herself for the long runs in Hyde Park that had kept her in shape. She looked over the elevator shaft. The door to the thirty-eighth floor was about a meter above her and she climbed up to it and looked for the safety mechanism that allow the outer doors to open. After groping around for two minutes or so, she found the small metal lever that released the door's locking mechanism when pressed. She opened the outer metal doors of the floor.

* * *

He left the elevator room and walked over to the edge of the roof of the circular tower. The range of his model aircraft controller from here covered all the trashcans he'd yet to detonate, as well as the explosive device buried in Rabin Square. The undulating tone of the air-raid siren rang out all around him. He took the model aircraft controller out of the pouch in his suit and activated it.

A series of blasts could be heard from below, and clouds of black smoke rose from locations where there were still unexploded trashcans. The biggest black cloud, accompanied by a large fireball, rose from Rabin Square to the northwest, and he watched as the fireball ascended and turned into a column of black smoke. He threw the controller aside and checked his phone battery—87 percent. He then walked back toward the entrance to the roof and slowly climbed up the steel ladder leading to the roof of the elevator room.

* * *

Carmit turned off the flashlight on her phone and put it back into her pocket. She went to the stairs and climbed up until she reached the door onto the roof. A series of explosions from the streets below echoed through the stairwell. The door was open, its locking mechanism riddled with bullets. She walked out quietly and looked around.

The roof in front of her appeared deserted and she emerged from the stairwell and stood still momentarily under Tel Aviv's cloudy skies. Then she took a few steps forward, looking around in all directions. A noise from above caused her to spring quickly to the side, and 10483, who'd tried to jump on top of her with all the weight of his protective suit, missed her by just a few inches. She swiveled quickly, jumped back, and stood facing him.

"I know you," he said.

"That's right."

"You're Kelly Grasso. I met you at a hotel in Montreal. You work at . . ."

"Cymedix," Carmit completed the sentence.

"You're an Organization employee."

"Not exactly. A subcontractor. I mean, I was. I no longer work for them. I quit." Carmit glanced sideways and focused for a second on the open door of the elevator room. Someone would probably be coming up the stairs soon. Her face remained fixed on 10483.

"You were following me back then in Montreal," he said. "I remember sitting across from you at the hotel restaurant. I remember your face."

"Yes. I was also around when you carried out the other two assassinations. I messed with your brain."

"What do you mean?" 10483 pressed the magazine release button on the Micro-Uzi, allowing the empty clip to drop to the floor with a clang. He felt for another magazine in the pockets of the vest of his protective suit. He was out. He'd gone through all of them. He released the firing pin with the barrel pointed at Carmit and nothing happened. The Micro-Uzi's chamber was empty. He tossed the submachine gun aside. His movements were slow. He wasn't rushed.

"I was sent by the Organization to the same three locations where you were at the time to do your work on those three scientists. Your three objectives. On each occasion, I disabled you during the night and in essence reprogrammed your brain. Similar to hypnosis but significantly more powerful and precise. It's known as a transformation."

"I should have suspected that something was awry. I thought the headaches I was waking up with were the result of jetlag. What did they do it for? Why did they hypnotize me?" He didn't take his eyes off her and slowly drew Amiram's pistol from the pouch it was in. The pistol's breech was pulled back and ready to slide into place at the press of a button and feed a round into the chamber the moment a new magazine was inserted. He didn't have another magazine for the gun. He released the catch holding the breech and it slid forward with the sound of a pistol being loaded. He raised the weapon slowly, aiming the barrel at Carmit's face, and squeezed the trigger.

—*Click*—

Carmit didn't flinch. She'd seen that the breech was pulled back with the magazine still inside, and she knew it was empty. 10483 threw the pistol aside.

"I don't know. I don't know what was in the encrypted transformation files they sent me, except for the final one." Carmit's right hand moved to her waist to draw one of her knives.

"What was in the last file?" 10483 reached into one of the pouches in his suit and pulled out a commando knife with a serrated blade.

"You were programmed to commit suicide on December twelfth, 2006." Carmit took a few small steps backward. He moved toward her. His movements appeared cumbersome.

"You know you don't stand a chance, right?" he said. "Your knife won't get through my protective suit."

"I know," Carmit replied, her steps taking her close to the edge of the roof.

He continued to move toward her. "It almost worked. I jumped in front of an oncoming bus that day."

"I know."

"I'm their best agent and they sent you to mess with my mind. Bunch of assholes. I arranged a nice end-of-the-year party for them and they had to go ahead and ruin that, too, with all those people they sent to my house today. Would it have hurt them to wait a while and apologize? A simple apology from them and I would have stopped everything." With the knife still in his right hand, he slipped his left into one of the pouches of his armored suit and took out his cell phone. "And now I have to bring forward my plans involving another device because of them, too. It was designed for next year but I'm changing my plans now."

"What plans?"

"I'm going to blow up the CIA headquarters now. I planned originally to send letters to the CIA, the White House, and the FBI, but we'll make do with the message I sent a few minutes ago to *The New York Times* while riding the elevator up to the roof. Their email address is: letters@nytimes.com. By the way, it's funny to give an email account such an archaic name."

"What letters? What message?" The knife was still in her right hand, her eyes focused on his.

"Letters with explicit and confidential details about all my activities abroad. They won't really be of much interest to the Americans because nothing took place on their soil, and their policy in recent years has been: 'Events outside our borders is of no concern to us.' But blowing up the CIA's headquarters and everything else in the vicinity will definitely be of concern to them. I've also sent *The New York Times* precise details about the nuclear warhead I'm about to detonate." He unlocked his iPhone. "The letters I'd planned to send are in a drawer in the kitchen of my house, the one you mounted an assault on today. Your friends from the Organization will be able to read the full text later. You won't."

"You don't have to do this. What about the lives of everyone living around there? You've hurt enough people already. You've proved your point. You don't need to be remembered as the man who blew up Washington."

"When you chop down trees, splinters fly. The Organization must cease to exist and there's no other way of achieving this objective. I won't be leaving this roof alive. I know that. I'm not a fool. Blowing up CIA headquarters will be my final act. But soon I will undoubtedly become the most famous intelligence agent in history. I attached an image to the email to make it easier for them to publish the story."

"They're not on my list of favorites either. The Organization. And I'm not proud of what I did to you. I'm sorry. But let's go downstairs. They won't kill you if you turn yourself in."

10483 smiled. Once. He never smiled. "What's your name?" he asked. "What's your real name?"

"Carmit."

"We're alike, Carmit. I live your life and you live mine. The Montreal hotel isn't the only place I've seen you. I've met you on many occasions. You must have run into me, too. Under different circumstances, we could be together. Too bad it's never going to happen. We're sitting together on the beach and a tsunami is approaching."

Carmit looked at him intently. "No. It isn't going to happen," she responded. *How does he know about my dream? Could the transformations have connected them in such a way?* Her thoughts were interrupted as he continued to speak.

"Look, Carmit, Kelly Grasso, or whatever your name is. We're both going to draw our last breaths on this roof. I'm going to kill you and all those security forces racing up the forty-nine flights of stairs to the roof right now are going to kill me. It's okay. I'm ready to go. But McLean has to go, too. It's an essential part of the plan."

"How does McLean fit in to your plan?" She tightened the fingers of her right hand around the handle of the knife.

"The mail I sent ties the Organization to the blast. The Americans will put two and two together and the rest will follow. The Organization will cease to exist."

He walked quickly toward her. She jumped aside and with a swift movement of her right hand thrust the knife into the seam on the right-hand side of his protective suit in the area of his neck. The blade of the knife broke and she jumped backward. He continued moving rapidly toward her. She pulled her second knife out of the left side of her belt and threw it at his face. He ducked his head forward quickly and the point of the blade struck his helmet and bounced off to the side. He kept moving toward her, removing his helmet and wiping the sweat from his forehead and eyes. He was on her, his fist gripping the knife and bringing it down toward her chest. She swiveled quickly, kicking out and sending the knife flying from his hand. He managed to get to her again and close both his hands around her throat, his face almost touching hers, his breathing heavy from the effort. Carmit felt the air in her lungs running out. She tilted her head back as far as she could and then slammed it forward into his forehead with all her might.

A bright flash of light.

The rays of the setting sun struck the two huge silvery rectangular sails of the Ocean Ranger, painting them in arcs of shimmering purple-orange light. She swayed slightly on the thin transparent strand of energy, eager by now to set out on her way, trying to oppose the magnetic field holding her in place. The gangplanks to the Ocean Ranger have been folded back already and the cargo is in her hold.

Fog.

You're six years old. Focused on coloring in a page. Your lips are firmly pressed together and the tip of your tongue is peeking out between them. You're doing your best to stay inside the lines and I walk past and move your hand. A red line of crayon crosses your page. You lift your head and look at me. You aren't angry.

Fog.

You're a soldier, standing at the hitchhiking station at the Golani Junction, and I stop to give you a ride. I ask you where you need to go and you look at me and smile. You tell me that you don't care where I drop you off as long as we're heading south. Your hair is in a short ponytail held by a black rubber band and you untie it and run both your hands through your hair in a single motion from your forehead to the back of your neck.

Fog.

We're both sixteen. We're swinging on the sofa swing on the porch outside your parents' house. It's just the two of us. The air is filled with the fragrance of jasmine. It's summer. Coming from inside the house is a soft jazz number by Jeannie McCreedy. There's no one in the house. I run my hand through your hair and the smell of conditioner blends with the fragrance of jasmine in the air. We kiss.

Fog.

We're lying in my bed. I slowly run my finger from the back of your neck down to your tailbone and feel you tremble. You turn to me and caress me. You say: "What makes us who we are, our lives, is our sequence of memories. What would happen if that was taken away from us? What would remain?"

Fog.

We're walking together along the cold *hot* sand *ice river and looking at the changing landscape in every direction. The bare trees around us fill with green leaves that turn yellow-red and fall to the ground, grow anew, and fall again. The* cold *hot air is full of leaves swirling in the* freezing *scorching wind. You* you *tell* tell *me that we can stay here forever.*

Fog.

The Ocean Ranger breaks away from the field and begins to move away. From pier 52, her thousands of windows look like small shimmering dots, but I see you even without seeing you. I know you're standing at the window in one of the cabins and looking out right now.

I know your hands are pressed against it, creating a ring of condensation around your fingers on the cold glass. I know you take your hands off the window and watch the picture of the outline of your hands slowly disappear from the glass.

I know I will never see you again.

I know I will never see you again.

Never.

A bright flash of light.

Both of them were out cold for a minute, lying alongside one another on the roof. They opened their eyes at the exact same second. 10483 looked around him and turned toward the knife that was lying on the floor next to him, gripped it, and swung it at Carmit's face. She turned her head quickly to the left. The knife cut her above her right ear and the tip of the blade hit the floor. She sprung to her feet, taking advantage of the fact that he was a lot less agile than she was in his heavy armored suit. She ran a few steps toward the knife that was lying on the roof a few meters from them, and the second she bent down to pick up the knife something hit her in the head and knocked her back to the ground. She tried to get up but couldn't. Her head was spinning and some high-pitched feedback was in her ears and mixed with the sound of the air-raid siren that continued to wail through the air. She remained on all fours, staring with blurry eyes at the small pool of blood forming on the surface of the roof below her from the drops trickling from the cut his knife had left in her head.

10483 looked at his foe swaying on all fours and bleeding. Good that he saw the empty Micro-Uzi on the surface of the roof next to him when she ran for her knife. He picked it up, threw it at her as hard as he could, and struck her in the head. "A gun without bullets can also be useful sometimes," he said to himself out loud and smiled. The rifle knocked her off her feet but didn't kill her. He'd finish dealing with her before every Tom, Dick, and Harry got to the roof and killed him, too, but first there was something important he needed to do to continue his plan. He turned his back to the center of the roof and looked out, standing about two meters from the edge and observing the clouds of smoke rising from the scenes of the blasts down below. He took the iPhone out its pouch, unlocked and opened his shortcuts page. He immediately pressed the MCLEAN BLAST link, verified that the action was completed, and after seeing a green circle marked ACTIVATED appear on the screen, he allowed the telephone to drop from his hand onto the surface of the roof.

At a distance of 10,000 kilometers from the roof of the circular Azrieli Tower, in McLean, Virginia, not far from Washington, D.C., in storage unit No. 24, the vacuum cleaner kicked into action.

10483 spread his arms out to the side, looking for a short while at the reality he had created in the city below his feet and thinking about the reality he had just created in faraway Washington. He started to laugh when the song, "The Final Countdown," popped into his head. It's a shame he hadn't thought about it before activating the warhead; he could have detonated the device just as the chorus started. Okay, enough horsing around, there's one last thing he still needs to do while he has the time. And that's to kill the nuisance swaying behind him and bleeding onto the roof. He turned to face the center of the circular roof again and was immediately confronted by Carmit's face and a powerful kick from her leg that knocked him backward toward the edge of the top of the tower. Had he not been dressed in the heavy protective suit, he may have been able to avoid the kick. He stumbled backward, trying to maintain his balance.

"Die already!" Carmit yelled.

The knife she threw this time struck him in the neck, right above the collar of the bulletproof vest. He grabbed the handle of the knife in both hands, stumbled backward, and fell off the roof of the building, from the dizzy height of the forty-ninth floor. The circular Azrieli Tower is 187 meters high. That means the fall would take 6.832 seconds. He'd hit the ground at a speed of 164kph. 10483 released his grip on the knife handle and spread his arms out to the sides again, his eyes still looking up at the cloudy sky above him and watching the floors of the building flash past at an ever-increasing rate, until the building and the world disappear and he's enveloped in blackness. Carmit approached the edge of the roof and looked down. From the height of the forty-nine floors she could see him sprawled on the floor of the plaza outside the building, far below her, motionless.

A deafening noise and a powerful gust of wind caused her to jump backward. An Israel Air Force Apache helicopter appeared just beyond the edge of the building a few meters from her, and the force from its rotor felt like physical blows. Its Vulcan rotary cannon fired a split-second burst of 20mm rounds in her direction, creating a rapid line of small explosions on the roof of the building, just centimeters from her feet. Carmit zigzagged in leaps and bounds as fast as she could toward the concrete cube that was the elevator room and the opening to the building's stairwell, raced through the door and jumped down the entire flight of stairs in a single leap. Just as she landed, using the palms of her hands against the stairwell wall to brake her momentum, the structure above her was riddled with a hail of Vulcan rounds that penetrated the concrete wall—but she was safe by then. When it came down to it, they were trying to kill her, too. She wasn't surprised. She knew it was only a matter of time. They needed her and she needed them, but that equation no longer held true, and she had become a threat again. The data in her head, her knowledge, was a danger to the Organization. She would have done the same if she were in Grandpa's shoes.

10483's shattered body was sprawled on the ground in the plaza between the Azrieli buildings, his arms stretched out to the side. The helicopter, which was done with turning the elevator room on the roof into a heap of concrete rubble and dust, swooped down in a steep dive and hovered over him. After observing him for a few seconds, the pilot turned sharply to the left and flew off through the space between the towers in the direction of the Ayalon Highway.

Carmit struggled to her feet. All her energy was sapped. She shook off the small bits of concrete that had rained down on her from above, allowed herself a few seconds to catch her breath, and then started bouncing quickly down the stairs. The chaos at the bottom would be at its peak and it was her only chance to disappear. On the fortieth floor, she ran into a SWAT team and soldiers who were on their way up to the roof. "Someone's shooting up there in the restaurant!" she yelled to them.

"Are you okay?" One of the soldiers looked at Carmit. The right side of her head was covered in blood sprinkled with a layer of cement dust, and the upper right portion of her shirt was stained with blood, too. No. She's not okay. She felt as if she'd just killed a part of herself. She felt the knife she'd thrown strike her, felt the fall. The impact with the ground. Her heart was racing out of control. If those feelings weren't secondhand, she'd be dead, too.

"I was cut in the head by a piece of glass while lying on the floor of the restaurant."

"Get downstairs quickly. It's dangerous here."

"Okay."

She continued to leap down the stairs at a quick pace. The high-pitched tone in her head wasn't as intense now, and her heart had slowed and was returning to its normal rhythm. She stopped to rest for a while on the second floor of the mall downstairs and grabbed a bottle of cold water from a deserted McDonald's. The series of explosions from the roof of the building and the unrelenting siren outside had left everyone in the shelters and secure areas of the mall, and there was no one else around. Carmit drank down all the water in the bottle in long gulps, removed her bloodstained shirt, threw it on the floor, and went into the restaurant's kitchen. She gave her head and face a good wash with the dishwashing hose in the kitchen, grimacing in pain as the detergent came in contact with the laceration above her right ear. She gritted her teeth and washed the deep gash well with the soap. *Twenty stitches,* she thought to herself. The back of her head, which had taken a blow from the submachine gun 10483 threw at her, was swollen and sore, but at least there was only a small cut there that wasn't bleeding much. After leaving McDonald's, she went down to the first floor of the mall, walked into a Super-Pharm drugstore, opened a package of cotton swabs, drenched them in half a bottle of iodine, cleaned her cuts again, and dressed the wound above her right ear and her left arm with a pad of gauze and several adhesive bandages. It'll hold for now. On the way out the drugstore, she sprayed herself with a little perfume from one of the shelves and then went into the nearby Castro clothes store where she put on a black T-shirt and replaced her dusty and bloodstained jeans with a pair of new ones.

She looked at herself in the mirror. "Not bad at all," she said to the mirror, noticing that she reverted to English without any Israelis around, and also that she needed a hat to conceal the large dressing over her disinfected wound. She grabbed a colorful woolen hat off one of the shelves and also put on a new jacket on the way out. She ignored the loud protests of the antitheft sensor that started beeping when she walked through the open doors of the empty store and then made her way to the Mega Sport store where she replaced her dirty shoes and socks with a clean pair of socks and a pair of black Nikes.

She wouldn't be able to get the cut seen to here in Israel. After questioning the Apache helicopter pilot, who would tell them she was hurt, the Organization would definitely be staking hospital emergency rooms. She'd get it seen to at a private clinic back in London.

Before flying back she had to pay one more visit to the house 10483 was living in up until just a few hours ago. She'd take one of the cars outside that had been abandoned by drivers who fled and sought shelter, and she'd drive to Moshav Yanuv. The only people there now would be a handful of Organization security guards, and with the temporary tag that they gave her to gain access to the main base that she transferred to the pocket of her new jeans along with her wallet, she'd be able to have a look around.

As she stepped out of the mall and onto the street, the undulating air-raid siren tapered off and went silent.

She didn't have much time.

* * *

"Hmmm . . . as dead as can be."

The moment he saw the live television broadcast from the center of Tel Aviv, he suspected it had something to do with that couple Herr Schmidt had asked him to find. He went quickly to the scene, followed the developments, and saw 10483 fall from the roof and the helicopter hover over him and then fly away.

The Barber took off his hat, held it against his chest for a few seconds in a gesture of respect, placed the hat on the chest of the body for a few seconds, then put it back on his head.

He saw him fall off the roof and was the first person to get to him, with the siren still wailing and everyone hiding like mice. Like moles in their burrows underground. He hadn't eaten anything in quite some time. The thought of earth gave him an appetite.

He looked at the knife still stuck in the body's neck.

"Hmmmm . . . dying twice can't be very pleasant."

He removed a small kit from a pocket in his long coat and lifted fingerprints off the handle of the knife. He looked at the perfect print. "Excellent," he said, placing the strip of plastic into a small paper envelope. This place would be crowded with people any minute now. He didn't have much time.

He opened the protective suit in which the body was dressed and quickly rifled through the clothing. No wallet or documents. No bone that isn't broken either. Well, fifty floors or so. He looked up again toward the roof from which the body had fallen without a parachute.

"Hmmmm . . . I think I'm done here."

All he needed to do now was to wait for her. She was the one who had chased after him and she was the one who had sent him tumbling off the roof with a knife in his throat. He liked her. He'd wait down here for her and then follow her to her house. He was intrigued by her now, on a personal and not just a professional level. He could kill her the moment she came down from the roof of the building, after first getting her to tell him everything Herr Schmidt wanted to know, but that wouldn't be very interesting. He wanted to get to her bed while she was sleeping at night, unsuspectingly. It wouldn't be as exciting as it would be if he were to kill her now. It wouldn't be poetic. It would be plain rude. He adjusted the hat on his head and waited at a point from which he could observe the entrances to the building.

EPILOGUE

I fell from above
  There's no way out of here
  It's impossible to climb smooth walls
  My stomach hurts
  Hunger is eating me up inside
  Must find it
  Must eat it
  That smell is driving me crazy
  That smell and that flavor are a place inside my head
  Can't stop
  Chewing on that airy, soft, thin, transparent material
  It's so dark
  My coat is no longer sleek and shiny
  It's falling out
  And my hunger can't be satisfied
  Won't let up
  Everything here is wrong
  Must get out of here
  Must find something else
  To eat
  Must get out
  Out
  Out

December 26, 2016

Detective Jason Cooper scratched his head. Twenty-two years as a police officer in Washington yet he had never seen anything like this. The light in the storage unit itself was off, with only the hallway lighting casting a soft glow into the open storage space and revealing its contents. Hanging from the ceiling in place of a light-bulb was an electrical cable that ran down from the empty lightbulb socket and hooked up to several pieces of electronic equipment and appliances, one of which was a particularly noisy vacuum cleaner that was running uninterrupted.

In a wooden frame wrapped in plastic lay something that looked like an open missile warhead with two small red lights aglow inside.

The vacuum cleaner was attached to the plastic over the wooden frame and was trying to suck the air out of the space in which the warhead was lying without much success due to several large holes in the plastic wrapping.

"Should I turn off the power? We thought it best not to touch anything until now."

"No. You did well not to touch anything. Don't cut the power."

The vacuum cleaner persisted and Detective Cooper turned on his flashlight and examined the contents of the storage unit. On either side of the perforated plastic over the frame was a vase containing plastic flowers that were covered in a thin film of dust. Scribbled in black marker on the outermost layers of plastic on the top of the frame and the side facing the door of the unit were words in the strange letters of a foreign language. The remaining layers of plastic wrapping were stained with something that looked like drops of dry blood.

Something here is very fucked up.

"I was doing my regular rounds this morning among the rows of storage units, you know, to check that everything's okay and that there aren't any water leaks or something like that, and that's when

328

I heard the noise coming from this one. We don't allow people to play around with the power supply. Each storage unit has just the single light, but the person who rented this one removed the bulb, left the light on, and hooked up other equipment to the power supply. It probably started running yesterday. It must have been connected to a timer or activated remotely. When I heard the noise coming from inside I tried to open the unit with my master key, only to discover that the person renting the unit must have changed the lock without permission. It's a violation of our policy. The contract states explicitly that for fire-safety purposes, no locks are to be changed. I bored through the cylinder and broke open the door, and immediately called the police on seeing all this."

"Who rented the unit?" Detective Cooper continued to shine his flashlight into every nook and cranny of the unit.

"Oscar Salstrom. A Swedish citizen. I have a photocopy of his passport here. He paid for the unit upfront. His RV is parked outside here, too. He left it here for long-term storage and paid for a year upfront."

"Do you have any idea where he is? An address or phone number he left with you?"

"It's very odd. He was around for a day or two to organize the contents of the unit and then disappeared a little more than eight months ago. Sometime around March if I remember correctly. He left a business card here with his details; but when we called a short while ago, someone by the name of Nellie Salstrom answered. And when we asked for Oscar, she started yelling at us. Apparently, the Oscar Salstrom on the business card he gave us was an American citizen who lived in Thompson, Iowa, and died from a stroke two months ago. He was seventy-six years old, so he definitely wasn't the man who was here at the storage facility. The guy who was here looked to be in his late thirties, going on forty, and I guess he must have simply used the other man's name."

"Don't touch a thing. I'm going out to my patrol car for a moment."

Detective Cooper left the storage facility and got into the driver's seat of his MPDC patrol car. He reached for the radio. "Twenty-six here. Responding to a 10-89 call, potential bomb threat, at a long-term storage facility in McLean. I get the feeling that something terrible was supposed to happen here but something went wrong. Send everyone you possibly can from the Bomb Disposal Squad."

December 26, 2016

"Does this fucking rain have no intention of stopping?"

The members of the inner circle had convened for breakfast in their conference room. Raindrops trickled down the large glass wall that formed a barrier between the warm comfort of the large conference room and the gloomy gray skies and wet stretches of lawn outside.

Grandpa was standing next to the buffet table and making himself a cup of coffee. "Forensics on his devices is complete. Laptop and cell phone. And we found three letters he wrote in a drawer in the house. It doesn't look good but we may be able to minimize the damage. I'll elaborate: There was nothing on his laptop. Apparently he wasn't using it to store any material other than the files he sent to us. As for his cell phone—that he left on the roof of the Azrieli building and didn't have time to deal with, or simply didn't care any longer because he didn't even try to throw it off the roof. We went through the phone. There were two shortcuts defined in the browser— one labeled McLean Blast and the other 203 Ibn Gvirol Street Blast. And we all know what happened on Ibn Gvirol. The Ibn Gvirol link must have led to a smart electrical system that activated a detonator connected to a series of military grade blocks of plastic explosives in the basement, and the link to the second system pertains to the blast in Washington that failed to materialize for some reason. He did use the phone to activate the system designed to detonate the warhead in McLean, but it didn't happen."

One of the participants put his fork down on the table again. "McLean's what I think it is, right?" he said. "CIA headquarters?"

"Yes. Exactly. A suburb of Washington, D.C. We haven't touched the activation mechanism again, of course . . . but we tracked the address of the site it's linked to and the IP address of the smart electrical control system and they confirm what we found in the phone. A Washington-area IP address."

"Did you manage to get into whatever's sitting on that address?"

"No. It's password protected and we didn't want to play around with it. He has a background in computers and probably incorporated defenses to trigger the warhead or erase the system from the Internet completely if someone tries to mess with it remotely. We need to keep the URL active to be able to find it."

"And you're sure he managed to get his hands on the warhead, smuggle it into the United States, and leave it in the CIA's backyard?"

"We had to assume the worst-case scenario and apparently it is indeed the case. The three letters he wrote prove so. The letters were in a drawer in the kitchen. It's actually the same letter in triplicate that he planned to send at some stage to the White House, the CIA, and the FBI. Listen to this. 'Dear Sirs, I am writing this letter to you with a heavy heart because there will be no way back for me the moment I send it—for me or for my handlers. But the truth has to be told. . . . ' "

Grandpa read out the contents of the letter, and the room fell silent when he was done.

"We have to send a team there. Now!"

"Without doubt. And we will. They'll have to scan the area of the IP address until they come within range of the Wi-Fi network it's on, assuming he didn't have time to order and set up a fixed infrastructure. McLean isn't a very big place and I expect the IP address can be found within a few days if we deploy several teams working in conjunction and equipped with suitable tools."

One of the members of the inner circle sipped from the white mug in her hand. "And what about his cell phone?" she asked. "I hope you've destroyed it."

"Yes. It's been destroyed. I, too, wouldn't want us to have the trigger for a nuclear bomb somewhere in Washington resting in the palm of our hand."

"I think we've had more luck than brains on this one," said the woman with the white mug. "Had he decided to detonate the warhead in Washington and send those letters first, and only then carry out his attack here in Israel, it would have spelled the end for the Organization."

"I believe you're right," Grandpa responded before taking another sip of his coffee. "When our teams find where he's hidden the warhead, we'll have to find a way to elegantly remove it from U.S. soil. Under no circumstances can a word of any of this ever be allowed to get out, and no one in the Organization aside from us is to know about it."

The woman at the table sipped from her white mug again. "Did you find another notebook in the house? Another journal like the first one?"

"No. Nothing in the house that can shed more light on what we know already. If he kept another journal, he got rid of it before we got to him."

"And our subcontractor? Where is she? She can't be allowed to wander around freely with everything she has in her head. We can't afford the risk of her knowledge being compromised."

"She's disappeared."

"What?"

"Disappeared. We have no idea where she is or if she's left the country. All air and sea ports and land crossings have her photograph and fingerprints, but she's a professional. She may have already managed to get out and head back to England, but not on a direct flight for sure; and we have no idea where she lives there. The Organization-issue cell phone I gave her at the main base was found on the roof of the Azrieli Tower. And if she has a device of her own here, we aren't familiar with it. We have no way of knowing where she is right now."

December 25, 2016

Ben Gurion International Airport was relatively quiet that Sunday afternoon. Tourists arriving and departing, pilgrims and business executives returning to Israel and hurrying out to grab a taxi to get back to their families.

Two nuns dressed in black habits with white collars were sitting in the food court and eating identical dishes of noodles and vegetables. They were engrossed in conversation when the man dressed in black sat down next to them. His head boasted a *capello romano* and a thick black coat hung over his arm.

"Hello, Sisters," he said. "A pleasant afternoon, isn't it?"

"Hello," they both responded, looking at him and trying to ascertain the nature of the man who sat down next them—if he was just being friendly or if he was one of those troublesome individuals they sometimes encountered.

"I noticed you're both eating mushrooms. Are you aware that you're eating pieces of the most intelligent brain on Earth?"

They both looked at the man, who placed his folded coat on his knees.

"It's a field that interests me, Sisters. I smell them when I'm digging tunnels under the ground and looking for food. The fungus itself is a huge organism that can live for thousands of years. It spreads under the surface in the form of a weblike structure that can cover an area of several square kilometers. It's a huge brain under the ground. What we see aboveground is only a small finger that the fungus extends in order to reproduce. I try not to damage them, even if it means having to burrow deeper into the earth. You're eating an animal now that is far more intelligent than a dolphin or chimpanzee. Or humans, too, for that matter."

"You dig tunnels under the earth?"

"Yes, Sisters. It's my destiny in life. Everyone has a destiny. It's the earthworm's destiny to aerate the soil, my destiny is to dig tunnels in the carth, and your destiny is to serve the benevolent God who created that wonderful organism known as a fungus."

The nuns pushed their plates to the middle of the table.

"Thank you, Sisters." He bowed to them and stood up. The woman he was following had finished eating and was heading to Concourse C on the way to her departure gate. He'd been following her since Tel Aviv. When he realized she was heading to the airport, he booked a flight to New York with his cell phone and was already in possession of an electronic boarding pass by the time he walked into the terminal. He stood behind her at the check-in counter and got a look at the destination printed on her ticket. Using a second passport under a different name, he then booked another ticket for himself, to the same destination that appeared on hers, walked away from the check-in counter, went through the security check again, for her destination this time, and caught up with her once more in the food court, where she was eating a slice of apple cake and drinking coffee. She was easy to spot with that colorful woolen hat on her head. He'd follow her onto the aircraft soon and remain on her tail from there on.

Night

The sky tonight is black as coal, starless, and a ghostly white glow from the full moon peeks through a hole in the clouds, illuminating the snowflakes falling to the ground. The air is still and quiet. Not a breath of wind. The glow from the moon lights up the thick layer of white snow covering the ground, and the river looks like an enormous black snake slithering through its white surroundings. She walks quietly through the snow, leaving in her wake a long trail of footprints that stretch from all the way back over the hills behind her and to the river she's walking toward. She reaches the bank of the river and stops. The bodies floating in the water come to a halt and amass into a single heap at points where the river twists and turns and other debris piles up. Behind the hills where she's come from, Hiroshima is ablaze in an orange glow that paints the surrounding hills in the colors of an endless sunset. She doesn't want to look back at the burning city but feels she is not alone. She turns around and sees them both close by. Standing two meters behind her. The angel folds its wings backward and its skin shines and appears to reflect the light from the moon. Just like the snow. The angel's hand is holding onto the hand of a young girl in a white dress, and both are almost swallowed up by the white snow all around them, with only the girl's black eyes and the angel's bright blue orbs distinctly visible on the white backdrop. The snowflakes around them continue to fall in straight lines and disappear silently into the layer of snow on the ground.

"Keiko?"

"Yes."

"私は今夢を見ていますか?"

"Yes, you're dreaming now."

"I'm sorry." She drops to her knees, clutching the palms of her hands together and bowing until her forehead almost touches the soft snow. A small hand lightly touches her shoulder. She straightens up in silence, still on her knees. Tears are streaming down her cheeks. "I'm so sorry."

"I know." Small hands caress her face and the black eyes look deep into her soul. "I forgive you."

"That doesn't make sense. How could you ever forgive me?"

"I forgive you. This is the last time you will see me. You know what you have to do. A huge wave is approaching. It'll be here soon. The time for playing God is over."

The angel and the girl turn around, head off hand-in-hand and are swallowed up by the falling snow. She feels the black hole that opened up in her heart a long time ago begin to close and disappear. She can breathe easier. She knows what she has to do. She stands and starts walking toward the bridge that stretches over the river.

December 26, 2016

"You need to get here now, sir." Special Agent Thomas Greene was speaking to the director of the FBI's Counterterrorism Division. "Drop whatever you're doing. I apologize for the urgency but I can't discuss the matter over the phone." The conversation ended and Thomas Greene stared again at the nuclear warhead in front of him.

He stepped slowly and examined every corner of the storage unit. Resting on the wooden table on the one side of the unit, next to a neat stack of tools, was a thick A4-size manual bound in a see-through cover. He leaned forward without touching anything and peered closely at the manual. It looked like Russian. He took out his secure cell phone, photographed the title on the cover page, and sent the image to the Operations Room at the Counterterrorism Division. "Find a translator and get back to me."

> RDS-9I 38KT
> Инструкция по сборке
> (торпеда / баллистическая ракета малой дальности)
> Инструкция по применению и Применение

Special Agent Thomas Greene was still busy documenting the rest of the contents of the unit when the director of the Counterterrorism Division arrived on the scene some forty minutes after their call and stepped quickly into the storage space. "Damn traffic jams for half the way," the director said. "What's that smell?"

"A dead rat, sir. Here behind this table. It gnawed a hole here through the wooden ceiling and fell into the storage unit. Probably died of starvation after gnawing on the plastic."

"Ask the owner to bring a garbage bag and get it out of here. It's impossible to breathe in here."

"Or a small mahogany casket perhaps, sir, with a small Stars and Stripes draped over it. A whole lot of people may owe their lives to

338

this rat, and perhaps it deserves a burial with full military honors and a three-volley salute."

Special Agent Thomas Greene briefed the director of the Counterterrorism Division on all he had learned thus far and showed him the screen of his cell phone:

> RDS-9I 38KT
> Assembly Instructions
> (Torpedo / Short-range Ballistic Missile)
> Arming and Operating Instructions

"It's a translation from Russian of the title of that thick manual there on the table."

"Oh my fucking God! It's a nuclear warhead!"

"Apparently so, sir."

"And this vacuum cleaner? Here presumably to activate that thing from a remote location? To cause a drop in barometric pressure to simulate altitude?"

"I don't know, sir, but I think the holes in the plastic made by the former rat here, God rest its soul, sabotaged the operation of the device. I called you first, sir, along with our Bomb Disposal Squad, so that you can take charge of the incident before other administration officials try to intervene. I canceled the request for assistance made to the local FBI office by the police detective who was first called to the scene. I don't want us to have too many people with something to say. Right now we only have two. The policeman and the storage facility manager, and I've made it clear to both of them that if a word of any of this gets out we'll know who to look for."

"Good thinking, Special Agent . . . ?"

"Greene, sir."

Loud sirens rang outside and a minute later three bomb squad members entered the storage unit and stood dumbfounded in front of the nuclear warhead. One of them looked up after taking a long close look at the contents of the box wrapped in the torn plastic. "We need the army here. Someone who specializes in warheads. And CIA personnel from the Russian department. Technicians who speak Russian and can read through that manual eight times so they know exactly what they're doing. If I touch the wrong thing here, Washington will go up in smoke. Perhaps we should evacuate the area?"

The director of the Counterterrorism Division shook his head. "That would cause a nationwide state of panic that would take years to recover from. We need to handle this quietly." He looked at Thomas Greene. "Have you started looking into the madman responsible for this?" He gazed at the vases with the plastic flowers, the strange writing, the dry drops of blood. A fucking voodoo ritual with an atomic bomb. Un-fucking-real.

"Yes. I sent the name of the person who rented this unit to headquarters, along with a copy of his passport. The manager of the facility gave me his particulars. The lessee's name is Oscar Salstrom and he's a Swedish citizen. Maybe someone who's carrying this out on behalf of Islamic State? That writing looks like Arabic. Border Patrol officials checked the passport and sent me details. Oscar Salstrom entered the country on the nineteenth of March through the Tijuana overland border crossing. I was told by Border Patrol officials that he entered in an RV, and the manager of this facility also told me that he left an RV here in long-term storage. It's parked here outside. Do you think he managed somehow to smuggle in the bomb in the RV? How did they miss it?"

"Is he still in the country?"

"No. I was informed by Border Patrol that he left here on March twenty-eighth. He was here for just nine days, sir."

"Where did he fly to from here?"

"To Tel Aviv, with a connection in Frankfurt, sir."

"Tel Aviv? That's odd. Get someone here who knows Hebrew so they can read what's written on the plastic. It could be Hebrew if this Oscar Salstrom flew there. Let's go outside for a moment and check out the RV. Ask the manager of the facility to get the keys, and if he doesn't have them, then tools to break in."

"Yes, sir. Later I'll compare the fingerprints from the unit here with the prints they took from him at the border crossing just to make sure we're definitely dealing with the same person."

"And we need to keep a close eye on this place twenty-four seven. After we clear out this storage unit, I want a bed and a fridge with food in here, and guards to be stationed inside around the clock until this Salstrom or whoever sent him comes back to figure out why their bomb didn't work or until we catch him ourselves if he doesn't come back here."

"Yes, sir. I'll take care of it."

They approached the RV and the members of the bomb disposal unit began checking to see if it was rigged.

December 25, 2016

A nurse popped her head into the room and asked him if he was done eating because a woman was there to see him.

"Yes. No problem. Send her in."

The door opened and in walked Efrat.

She was pale and had lost weight, but the glint in her eyes was still the same. "What did he do to you?" she asked as she approached Avner's bed and looked at all the instruments around him. "What did he do to *you*?" Avner asked in response, and Efrat leaned over the bed to hug him. Avner's pain disappeared for a short while as he held her close in a long embrace.

She sat down on the armchair for visitors at the side of his bed and wiped the tears from her eyes. "It could have been worse," she said. "I can see that you haven't touched your food. Are you still not allowed to eat much?"

"I'm as hungry as a bear. But the food here is inedible. I'm already having hallucinations about food. I swear I can smell a *shawarma* in a wrap right now."

Efrat smiled, reached into her bag for a tightly sealed packet, opened it, and took out two *shawarma* wraps that smelled absolutely wonderful. "I stopped at Shemesh on the way," she said. "I've got cabbage and pickles here, too, just the way you like it."

Efrat reached into her bag for another packet from which she pulled out two cans of Carlsberg. She opened them both, handed one to Avner, and kept the other for herself. They raised the cans in a toast and each took a long sip. And then Avner placed the can on the cabinet next to the bed and sunk his teeth into the *shawarma,* savoring every bite. Efrat tucked into hers with gusto, too.

"I don't remember you being a big fan of *shawarma*," he said.

"After a month on dog food, things change."

"A month on dog food??"

"It's a long story. We have plenty time. Let's finish eating first."
They both sat in silence, eating their food and sipping their beers.
"I've decided to quit the Organization," he said to Efrat.
The faint sound of thunder could be heard outside.
Rain started to fall again.

December 29, 2016

Taylor was the first to get to the door, and he opened it. He never bothered to check who was knocking, no matter how many times they told him to ask first who's there and only then to open.

It took him a few seconds to understand that the curly blonde figure standing in front of him was his mom. "Mum's here!!!" he shouted gleefully. And Carmit, standing in the doorway with her bag on her back still, picked him up, squeezed him tight against her, and nuzzled into his neck, inhaling his scent.

"Muuuuuummmm!!" Emily came running out of her room, wrapped her arms around her mother's waist, and pressed her cheek to her tummy. Carmit lowered Taylor to the floor and hugged her daughter.

"What did you bring us?" Taylor asked, bouncing with joy.

"I know I missed Christmas by four days, but that's it; no more work trips for me. That was my last one." Carmit freed herself of the large backpack and placed it on the floor for Taylor to start rummaging through its contents.

"You've been away for a long time, Mum. I've missed you," Emily said, still holding on to her mother.

Guy emerged from his study, barefoot, dressed in sweatpants and a T-shirt with an image of Heisenberg from *Breaking Bad*. He walked over to Carmit and held her in a long embrace. She rested her head on his shoulder and was suddenly overcome with exhaustion.

"It's over," she whispered in Guy's ear.

"I don't believe it! Lego *Alien*!" Taylor, who was sitting on the floor surrounded by pieces of torn wrapping paper and the clothes he'd thrown frantically out of the bag, raised his arms in triumph, clutching the box of Lego.

Carmit, Guy, and Emily looked at him and burst out laughing.

* * *

Late that night, when everyone was fast asleep, Carmit got out of bed, taking care not to wake Guy, and went over to her backpack. She retrieved her cell phone from one of the pockets and made her way to Guy's study, closing the door quietly behind her. She removed the phone's memory card, slipped it into the appropriate slot in Guy's laptop and opened the Pictures folder. She marked three images and printed three copies of each. Now she had three copies of the letter 10483 wrote to the FBI, the CIA, and the White House, along with three copies of his image to go with them.

She drove to his house immediately after coming down from the roof of the Azrieli Tower and fleeing the scene. The house was under guard, but the two Organization security personnel who were smoking outside let her in when she showed them the temporary Organization tag Grandpa had given her. Everyone had left to join the chase and a search of the house had yet to start. She went into the kitchen and opened the drawers one by one. One of the drawers contained the envelopes he had prepared, and she opened one of them and took pictures with her phone of the image of 10483 and the two pages of the letter that were inside, put everything back in its place, and waved good-bye to the guards as she drove away.

Carmit went to the kitchen, put on a pair of disposable cleaning gloves, returned to Guy's study, opened one of the drawers in the desk and took out three white envelopes, postage-paid for international delivery. She retrieved the pages from the printer tray, carefully folded the copies of the letters, inserted one copy of the letter and one image into each envelope and sealed them. She Googled the street addresses for the letter's three destinations and printed out labels for each envelope:

The White House
1600 Pennsylvania Avenue, NW

Washington, D.C. 20500
USA

Central Intelligence Agency
Office of Public Affairs
Washington, D.C. 20505
USA

FBI Headquarters
935 Pennsylvania Avenue, NW
Washington, D.C. 20535-0001
USA

With the gloves still on her hands, she put on her favorite gray sweatshirt and her worn sneakers and snuck out the house, listening to the peaceful breathing of her sleeping family and clutching the three envelopes in her hand. She stopped at the corner of the street beside a red Royal Mail mailbox. "The time for playing God is over," she said and slipped the three envelopes through the slot. The disposable gloves were thrown into a nearby trashcan. She looked at it closely. "It pays sometimes to be paranoid." She remembered Rotem saying something like that once.

And sometimes it doesn't, she thought to herself, and trailed the tip of her finger along the rim of the gray circular trashcan that was covered in drops of cold water and stared down for a moment at the LOOK RIGHT → sign on the zebra crossing at her feet.

She started to run.